WE THREE

Joe Costelle

PublishAmerica
Baltimore

ISBN: 1-4241-7128-8
PUBLISHED BY PUBLISHAMERICA, LLLP
www.publishamerica.com
Baltimore

Printed in the United States of America

PART 1

1

Conner Hayes loved the good life, having dreamed about it since childhood. Now, at forty-one, it seemed he had realized his dreams—and more. After all, he had a magnificent view out the corner window of his thirty-sixth floor office, situated in a posh business high-rise in the financial district of the City by the Bay, just off Jackson Square.

Fifty minutes earlier, he had received another positive injection to his good fortune, by way of showing off the incomparable San Francisco landscape to the beautiful young woman who had been his 4:00 p.m. appointment. Hayes reveled in delight as she had been taken aback by the view out his window of the Golden Gate Bridge, Fisherman's Wharf, and infamous Alcatraz Island. San Francisco Bay was alight with golden rays of sunlight slanting in from the west, and the overall impression left no doubt as to how the mighty bridge had gotten its name.

The intercom rudely interrupted his musings. With noticeable disdain at the intrusion, Conner picked up the receiver.

"Yes, Janet?"

His secretary would not have buzzed him had the call not been important.

"A Mr. Harden Kelly is on the phone, Mr. Hayes. He insisted it was of a most urgent nature—"

About the firm…

Thomas Alagia was the senior partner at Smith, Pitt and Alagia. After twelve years with the law firm, Conner had been approached with an offer from Alagia that would change his life forever.

For several years, Conner had been commuting from New York City to work with various clients in California, primarily those in San Francisco and nearby Napa Valley. Mr. Alagia had walked into his East Coast office three years earlier to pose a question.

"How would you like to relocate to San Francisco and head up our California branch?"

Conner had no familial ties or current attachments and thus made his decision quickly.

"When do I leave, Tom?" was all he asked.

"Wait a minute, Conner. You haven't heard the full proposal yet. As an inducement to tempt you to relocate, you will be offered a full partnership with the firm and all accompanying benefits. As far as the timetable is concerned, our real estate department has already submitted an offer on a suitable piece of property in downtown San Francisco."

Conner was on his way to California within the week.

2

At thirty-eight years old, Conner had flirted with marriage only once. Mary Elizabeth Pitt, daughter of the firm's deceased partner—Jefferson Dawkins Pitt—had refused to accept her father's invitation to join the firm upon her graduation from Wellesley College, and instead chose to continue her education at the University of Louisville's School of Law in Kentucky. After passing the bar exam there, she returned home to work at a state-funded legal aid office. Miss Pitt then obtained her New York license *pro hac vice*, via a reciprocity arrangement with the state of Kentucky through the American Bar Association. She was ready to go to work on the streets of New York at the tender age of twenty-six.

Conner met Liz three years later. About twenty members of the firm were enjoying a weekend gathering at Alagia's luxurious residence in the Hamptons out on Long Island. Conversing with three coworkers, as the story went, his glance fell upon a beautiful young woman who was wearing a two-piece, sarong-style swimsuit. At that moment, she was involved in an active dialogue not twenty feet from where he was standing. Her breasts tried to escape from the wrap as she leaned into the conversation, and Conner concentrated on her every movement. Her long black hair, sensing the exposure, swept around to partially obstruct the view. She caught his eye between words and, without missing a point in the exchange with her friends, locked onto the supreme moment. Imperceptibly, her attention returned to the present company and the snapshot was all but gone.

Conner, while confident and impressive in front of a judge and jury, exhibited a rather quiet disposition at social gatherings and in matters of the heart. He preferred to observe and analyze rather than be at the center of attention. In this instance necessity precluded shyness, and without much thought he knew he had to meet this young woman.

As her friends dispersed, she laid back on the lounge to relax. Letting her eyes travel back to the young man for a quick appraisal, she donned her Ray-Bans and relaxed, not unlike the moves of a supermodel. That was all the opportunity Conner needed, shy or not. He slipped away from his conversation and was standing in front of her in no time at all. Seeing no ring on the only finger that mattered, he decided to go for it in one fell swoop.

"Hi, my name's Conner Hayes. I was wondering if you wouldn't mind if I intruded on your space for a while." He added quickly, "Please—don't break my heart and say no."

"Not at all, Mr. Hayes. I've heard Thomas mention your name before, and in glowing terms I might add." *So this was THE Conner Hayes, Thomas' young protégé*, she remarked to herself.

His face flushed because of her smile. He had never experienced such a quick reaction when meeting a woman, and a little bell went off in his mind that told him this might be The One. Her smile was meant just for him and it certainly worked, her quiet, easy manner captivating beyond words. He was clearly staring at her.

Breaking the silence she offered, "Hi, I'm Liz." She hesitated to give her last name. Seeking her own identity had become an obsession, and referring to herself as Mr. Pitt's daughter was totally unacceptable. Having affection for her father was not the problem. His gentle demeanor sometimes overshadowed his genius, and she loved him for that. She treasured his love as much as any daughter could, and she freely credited his generous attention for all her accomplishments. Besides sharing his vast knowledge of the law, he had taught her to be independent and understanding. She expected the same from every one she met. If anyone liked or disliked her, agreed or disagreed, it had to be Liz, not Mr. Pitt's daughter for whom that choice was made.

It was Sunday afternoon and Conner knew if he were ever to see Liz again, he had better take advantage of this opportunity. That meant he had to push things along, and push them now. How long had he been staring? He had no idea.

"Liz, I've been admiring you from over there," he said, gesturing in the direction of his three friends. "I knew I couldn't let this weekend slip away without meeting you."

Conner sat down next to her, dragging his chair as close to hers as he dared.

The sun had begun to set before they realized several hours had passed. Parting only long enough to dress for dinner, their conversation flowed casual as the evening progressed. Conner knew that he had never opened up to any woman like this before. This was definitely different. Liz was truly someone special. He felt lost in her beauty, her smile, the sparkle in her eyes and, most rewardingly, in her artful conversation and intelligence.

* * *

Four months later, carrying a Buccellati ring acquired in New York City's diamond district on 57th Street, he pulled up to the curb. As he parked on the street in front of her office in his company-provided Lexus, she was coming out of the building. She did not give him time to be a gentleman and circle the car to hold open the door, so instead he reached across to pop up the lock. Liz kissed him as she slid into the seat, her lips warm and tender against his mouth. Though it was just momentary contact, he felt himself becoming aroused. As she leaned toward him, he noticed the way her skirt slid up above her knees. As always, he wondered how he could be the lucky recipient of such love from the beautiful, incomparable and graceful Liz Pitt. He was certainly beyond knowing her last name—and just about everything else about her. He stored every word, every picture, and every memory. It was a relationship too good to last.

His plan was to drive over to The Water's Edge, a restaurant that overlooked the East River. After all, this was a special night. To make it even more special, all she had to do was say yes. So far, the plan was working perfectly.

The waiter interrupted his thoughts.

"I highly recommend the seafood tonight," he said, smiling and looking at each in turn to gauge their reaction. He thought he detected interest, so he proceeded with the rest of his memorized dialogue. "I also suggest starting with the West Coast oysters. Then, we have an excellent butter-roasted halibut, served over rice."

He considered himself to be an experienced judge of his customers' culinary tastes and was appropriately rewarded for his intuition.

"Sounds great."

Liz was the first to answer.

Conner voiced his agreement as well. After acknowledging their excellent choices, the waiter left as suddenly as he had appeared. Conner remarked that their waiter was not really a person at all but actually a hologram, transported on cue to take their order. *Modern technology!* Conner mumbled.

From that first laugh, the evening was everything Conner had hoped it would be. The food was as amazing in presentation as it was in taste. For dessert, the waiter presented them with a delicate French berry pudding, so light that it evaporated as soon as it touched their palates.

Now the moment had arrived, the moment of truth. He pulled the small box from his pocket. Fear nearly made him freeze up as he saw her eyes brighten with anticipation. With the overhead lights sparkling off the facets of the ring he heard someone say, "Will you marry me, Miss Pitt?"

Moisture formed in the corners of her eyes and she gave a smile that appeared to envelop her perfect face. "I love you, Mr. Hayes, and the answer is an unequivocal yes."

3

The next morning, a man walked into the legal aid office on none-too-steady legs, pulled out a .22 caliber pistol from his jacket pocket, fired two shots into the first attorney he saw, and then unloaded three more into the attorney seated at the adjacent desk.

As a guard ran up with his own gun drawn the man turned, weapon still at the ready, pointing it but firing late as the guard got off three shots at the center mass of the perpetrator, just as he had been taught in his self-defense classes. The intruder fell backward and was dead before he hit the floor.

Within five minutes, the emergency medical technicians called to the scene had treated Marie Vogt, who received bullet wounds to her left arm and shoulder. They rushed her to the hospital, where she was soon stabilized.

The other attorney was leaning back in her chair, her black hair strewn across her face and a blank stare in her once-sparkling eyes. A small red dot had appeared in the center of her forehead, where very little blood flowed from the spot. Her neck wound had bled profusely, turning her once spotless white blouse a deep red. The first bullet had hit her chair and lodged in the far wall. The second grazed the right side of her neck. The last thing Mary Elizabeth Pitt saw was a drug-crazed derelict squeezing the trigger for his third shot, his eyes wide, cloudy circles surrounding a small dark macula in the center.

How had it come to this? Billy Bennett was just one of many errant souls who walked into her office every week, clients she had so desperately tried to help. Like many who entered the legal aid office, Billy's problems were already overwhelming before he had ever contacted Elizabeth Pitt.

Conner was devastated. He made his way through the funeral service and the visitation in a deep fog.

Just two nights ago…oh, my god!

He stared at the ring the funeral director had returned to him. Her thoughts, her words, and a whirlwind of pictures swirled through his mind. What could he have done to avoid such a tragedy? She loved her work and had been totally dedicated to her clients, doing her best to serve their needs. Wealth had insulated her youth from the tenement houses, alleys and gutters of the town where she had grown up, as she had always lived on the "right side of the tracks." Now she had given something back, and that something was everything.

Liz would never have abandoned her people, as she passionately referred to her clients, and her memory would last long into the coming months from all those who knew her.

* * *

Two weeks passed without much ado—the same lunch hours, the same shows emanating from the television. Conner went to work each weekday, sticking to his daily routine to a fault. However, by mid-afternoon, a blanket of grief and weariness overcame his thoughts and drove him from the office. The routine was simple but took its toll. Harrigan's Bar and Grill, in the lobby of the Centrifuge Building two doors down the street, beckoned to him every afternoon. He always sat alone in a booth, the same booth if he could get it, sipping his Gentleman Jack over ice. The door attendant watched for him each evening around ten, making certain that a taxi was available at just the right time to ferry him home.

The first night Peter—for that was the name by which everyone knew him—spotted Conner, a sad, disheveled but well dressed young man, he gently approached him and asked, "Could I hail a cab for you, sir?"

Conner nodded and pulled a crumpled $20 bill from his suit pocket, somehow managing to slip it into Peter's hand. Night after night, this cheerless ritual repeated itself.

As far as the grief was concerned, the kind he displayed at work, Mr. Alagia had approached Conner several times, but the words necessary to absolve his grief were just not available to the senior partner. He could not figure out how to lighten Conner's emotional load.

* * *

One Tuesday night, two young attorneys from the firm showed up at Harrigan's to celebrate one of the small victories of their day's work. Albert Finch was about six feet tall, and thin. He was the kind of man who seemed to have worn glasses since birth, thick lenses and all. Desmond Johnson, on the other hand, was short and stocky. Both had been with the firm about as long as Conner and they were respected for their intelligent handling of cases without undue direction from the higher-ups.

Albert spotted Conner sitting in his usual booth. Like everyone else at the firm, he knew that Conner camped out there every afternoon, staying sometimes as late as ten o'clock in the evening. Albert had finished his first scotch and was well into his second. He and Desmond spent a great deal of leisure time barhopping, making mock wagers as to who might get lucky first. On this particular evening, neither one had been successful so far.

"Excuse me, Des. I want to speak to Hayes a minute."

Buoyed by the scotch and soda, Albert approached Conner at his booth.

"How's it going, man? Do you want to have a drink with Des and me?"

Conner barely raised his eyes.

"I'd rather be alone right now, Albert. Maybe later."

"Conner, you may want to punch me but I'm going to tell you a sad truth. You've been grieving for two weeks straight, and it's high time for you to get your life back in order."

Albert planned to go all the way with this.

"However short a time it was, you had someone who loved you, really loved you. You have moments to be treasured for a lifetime. People like Des and I may never achieve that. The most we can hope for is to eventually find someone with whom we can be happy, and maybe start a family. We can call it love, respect, or whatever.

"I'm sure I speak for Des, as well, when I tell you that either of us would give our lives for five minutes of the real thing. Your opportunity at the brass ring ended tragically, but you have had your five minutes. Do not just keep feeling sorry for yourself. Remember how wonderful it was. Count your blessings, not your miseries. Wake up and enjoy your memories for the rest of your life. Be proud of Liz, but more importantly, make her proud of you.

"You're one lucky guy to have had her at all."

Color started rising up from Conner's neck to his face. He began to stand up but somehow got control of his emotions just in time.

"I need to be alone right now, Albert."

He had spoken almost too softly.

Albert's nerve had run out anyway. When he rejoined Des, they stepped to the other side of the bar and ordered another drink.

Conner leaned back against the booth, closed his eyes and brooded over what Albert had said. He mulled over the words again and again. What would Liz have wanted? What would she expect him to do?

Ignoring the half-empty glass on the table, Conner abruptly rose and headed for the door as if he had a plan. Thanking Peter, he jumped into the back of a waiting taxi and headed home for a cold shower, an appreciation growing within him for the mutual love he had already been blessed with, even for so short a time.

4

Conner and Harden had been boyhood friends, growing up in the highlands area of Louisville, Kentucky. Conner had lived on Edgeland Avenue, with Harden one block over on Tyler Parkway. However, all these friends had to do was cut across the alley that separated their houses in the rear, and they were together in less than a minute. At the end of that alley was Tyler Park, where they spent endless hours playing baseball, football, basketball and tennis, as the seasons changed.

Both had attended the St. James parochial school through eighth grade and then on to St. Xavier High School in central Louisville for the next four years. Although he did not realize it at the time, Conner absorbed all the knowledge the instructors had to offer and excelled in what was a demanding academic curriculum. At six feet four inches tall and with a slender, athletic build, Conner also achieved some non-academic success as well, quarterbacking the football team for two years and playing small forward on the basketball team during his junior and senior years.

Harden was built like his father, two inches taller than Conner at six feet six inches, with a broad chest and bulky shoulders. He excelled at any physical activity he chose. Blessed with speed as well, he played running back and took the ball regularly from Conner via hand-offs or passing plays to score touchdowns for the St. Xavier Tigers. His greatest sense of accomplishment came, not from school activities, but rather from a martial arts class his father had introduced him to when Harden was ten years old. Chiang, Harden's teacher, recognized the potential of this determined young man within a matter of a few weeks, gifted as he was with both speed and agility. Harden received every opportunity to advance in his training, so as not to be held back by the normal progress of his slower peers. By the end of his senior year in high school, his skill level went well beyond what even Chiang could teach him.

Conner Hayes, on the other hand, took all of his accomplishments in stride. Of the 281 graduates that year, Conner stepped to the platform with highest honors and was named class valedictorian.

Realizing that his achievements had come all so easily, Conner's graduation address consisted of one minute of appreciation for the academic staff, another minute of congratulations to his fellow graduates, and then a full two minutes of emotion-filled introduction, praising the accomplishments of the misshapen young man in the wheelchair who had achieved second honors. Anthony Riley struggled with his disease, studied diligently, and became highly proficient with his computer but could not overcome Conner's natural ability to absorb information and parrot it back on a dime.

Harden Kelly graduated in the top twentieth percentile and accepted a full football scholarship to Eastern Kentucky University. He chose Eastern because it was nationally recognized for having one of the finest criminal justice and police studies programs in the nation. His father had been a detective on the Louisville Police Department until his career was ended abruptly at age forty-two on a routine drug bust on South Third Street.

The operation had gone smoothly, two arrests were made, and approximately two kilos of crack cocaine were seized and taken off the street. As things were wrapping up, out of the alley behind the building a young man, suffering from severe addict dementia, saw the small bag of cocaine in Detective Kelly's hands. With logical thinking severely compromised by his physical needs, he fired one shot at Kelly. Half-crazed eyes wide with anticipation, he grabbed for the bag only to receive two rounds in the chest from the Sig Saur drawn by Kelly's partner from the holster inside his jacket. The bullet that hit Kelly had nipped his Kevlar vest, entered through the front part of his neck, and exited the side of his head, killing him instantly.

Harden was only twenty years old at the time and in his junior year at Eastern. Suddenly he felt alone. A career, a skill, was the only way he could take care of his mother. Since he was on a football scholarship, he was still able to complete the required courses for his degree in criminology.

Conner Hayes went on to Harvard University, completing his bachelor's degree in only three years. Harvard Law School presented no stronger challenge. In consideration of his unparalleled knack for absorbing information, one of his professors—James Sykes—suggested that he enter the one-year JD program. In this curriculum, students are required to complete a minimum of twenty-two credit hours and a maximum of twenty-six credit hours in one academic year. Most students complete twenty-two to twenty-four credits. Conner's hungry mind led him to complete all twenty-six credits in a single academic year.

Meanwhile, Anthony Riley had completed business administration courses at a well-respected local college—Bellarmine University— also earning his degree. Anthony made up for his lack of social life by hacking away on his computer. His growing skills at the keyboard led him to unauthorized explorations—meaning illegal—but he managed to work his way out of situations without being caught. He looked at this world beyond the screen as unexplored territory, much as astronomers are enamored with our natural universe and all of its secrets. After graduation, his position with the National Weather Service in Washington, D.C., gave him access to and experience with some of the world's most sophisticated computer equipment. Anthony took full advantage of the opportunities to explore his world, finding even more tools and information beyond what he could ever imagine. His amazement only led him to delve deeper into the labyrinth of doors and windows, with all their hidden secrets. Over time, he became especially adept at creating untraceable dead ends to hide his travels through cyberspace. Of the three close friends,

Anthony was the one to coin the phrase 'We Three Kings', in referring to the unlikely bond shared by the young men, a bond they swore would last forever.

After completing a year of post-graduate work, Harden Kelly had so impressed two of his instructors with his physical and mental abilities that they arranged a meeting with the controller of their former Delta Force unit. Harden's mother had remarried by the time he received his bachelor's degree and completed an additional year of special forensic training, designed not as medical training but rather for detecting and analyzing evidence at crime scenes. Subsequently, Harden had received offers from law enforcement agencies around the country, including his hometown, Louisville. He thus contemplated future life choices with an open mind. It was clear—there was nothing to hold him in Kentucky.

5

To ensure privacy, John Edwards, Harden's documentation instructor at Eastern, had not revealed the location of the meeting until they arrived at their destination. As they walked through the tiny lobby of the Boone Tavern Hotel in Berea, Kentucky, Harden was a bit apprehensive of the world he was about to enter. Although he had no strong ties to the past, he felt he might be stepping through a doorway that offered no return.

They turned left at the registration desk and John spotted his associate sitting in a high-backed booth, over in a corner of the dining room. Although Edwards was by no means a small man, the controller observed the young man who walked in behind John, yet was visible on both sides and towered above him. *An impressive candidate,* the man thought to himself, *impressive, indeed....*

After completing the LLM program offered at Harvard Law, Conner was approached by a number of search firms who recruited prospective employees for both national law conglomerates and companies on the Fortune 500 list. However, the proposal that interested him most was from the Judge Adjutant General's (JAG) office. This position offered an immediate commission as a second lieutenant, and a promise of speedy advancement upon completion of eight weeks of basic training plus eight weeks of advanced training in the U.S. Army induction program.

Even though Conner thought he had maintained his physical prowess he found the training a challenge, a feeling echoed by every man who had similarly volunteered. However, he enjoyed bringing his body back to a more disciplined state. The first eight weeks, spent at Fort Leonard Wood, Missouri were highly physical, with long days as well as nighttime training exercises—impromptu at that. Conner did not realize that he was receiving very specialized training by MANSCEN, the Total Force's Maneuver Support Center. Here he developed skills necessary for military combat as well as bolstering confidence in his physical capabilities.

He spent the next period at JAG training headquarters in Rosslyn, Virginia, specializing in the nuances of military law as balanced against what he already knew about civil and criminal law. Conner so impressed his superiors that, within three weeks of his arrival, he acted as assistant council on several cases. Gaining acclaim with his knowledge of case mechanics and oral delivery before military tribunals, Conner found himself assigned to some of the most difficult and controversial cases in the country.

After two years, he had already advanced to the rank of lieutenant colonel. After three years, his superiors had little choice but to promote him to "full bird" colonel at the tender age of twenty-five.

* * *

It was in his fourth year of service—the final year of his initial term of enlistment—when Conner began to have doubts about his career choice. He was assigned the case of defending a young specialist first class who had been accused of severely beating another member of his unit. The defendant's name was Aubrey Long, a career military man in his third year of service, ambitious and aggressive in his love of God, Corps and Country—all in that order. The two men involved were highly trained combatants, easily capable of inflicting fatal wounds without the use of external weapons. At the time, their unit was preparing for an undercover incursion set to take place thirty-four days from the date of the incident.

With time running out and only three days remaining to submit, Conner and the officer charged with handling the prosecution had to prepare and present their cases before the military review board. Jeff Lewis had lost his position in the unit due to the beating he had suffered, resulting in three broken bones in his face. Now, he was forced into prosecution because the fact that he was unable to complete his mission had become known outside his unit. Aubrey Long had initially refused to talk about the incident in order to preserve the integrity of the group. However, too many people had become involved and it was impossible for the higher-ups to keep a lid on things.

However, there was more to the case than met the eye—there always was. According to Long, Lewis had made what he—Long—had interpreted as sexual overtures. Long said he strongly resisted, having apparently pushed Lewis to the ground. Embarrassed, Lewis retaliated. Long, obviously the stronger of the two, became incensed. The only reason this had landed on Conner's desk was the immediacy of the mission and the need for quick discovery, argument and resolution.

After a lengthy discussion with Lewis, addressing the pros and cons of continued processing of the complaint—of course, with opposing counsel present—Conner required only a brief meeting with his client, Aubrey Long. Now, the only thing left to do was convince Lieutenant General Disney Alvis Charleton, the acting judge adjutant on this case, that the mutually acceptable solution was to return the men to their mission with as little interruption in training as possible. The primary obstacle to this solution, however, was that General Charleton was at CLAMO, the Center for Law and Military Operations, located in Charlottesville, about two hours away by car. Conner therefore contacted General Charleton's liaison and set up a lunch meeting at the center.

Since Conner carried with him affidavits acquiescing to the settlement, the judge was able to dismiss the case without prejudice and the participants were returned to their unit. This was only the latest personnel incident, but probably the most important factor in convincing Conner that he should resign his commission after four years of service and return to the civilian arena. Conner just could not see himself putting in his thirty years by resolving cases that otherwise would become a sticky wicket to the military.

Approaching his muster-out date, Conner had selected the first contact from his old file on potential opportunities for employment, left over from his research on the subject. Smith, Pitt and Alagia was a prestigious, historic law firm in New York City. However, when he first dialed Richard Jamieson—the person in charge of new hires—to broach the subject of possible employment, he found the man to be somewhat stuffy and not especially receptive.

Jamieson only managed to say, "Please leave your name and phone number with my secretary, and we'll contact you if any openings become available."

This was not the sort of greeting he had received four years earlier, when most revered law firms around the country were vying for his services, not to mention several publicly held corporations. When Sara, Mr. Jamieson's secretary, finally came back on the line, the response was not much improved.

"May I help you, sir?"

Conner reintroduced himself and this time left his cell phone number.

"What did you say your name was?" he asked.

"Sara Phillips, sir. Mr. Jamieson will get back with you as soon as possible."

"Thank you, Sara!"

Conner was not sure if he was talking to a dead phone or not, possibly even an already dead person. *Well, so much for that,* he thought.

Conner was still living in a condominium that he had purchased three years before, out in Rosslyn. Even though his papers had come through only the previous day, much more quickly than expected, he decided to have lunch at the officers' lounge. Here he had developed a very satisfactory comfort level, being on a first-name basis with most of the civilians employed at the lounge. He selected a quiet booth in the right rear corner, where he hoped to be able to make a few more inquiries on his cell phone.

Conner had broad-based experience. The JAG Corps was a different kind of law firm. As a JAG attorney, he found himself not bogged down doing research for senior partners, but instead involved in a diverse practice that ranged from military law and criminal prosecution to international law, all very much to his liking. Conner found himself litigating cases almost as soon as he began his JAG career. In the beginning there were always experienced attorneys, both military and civilian, available to guide and assist him. As a result, Conner had begun his career gaining the kind of experience that his counterparts in civilian firms were slow to eke out of their senior partners. Conner had experience in negotiating international agreements that affect the U. S. Army worldwide, argued appeals before federal judges, and represented fellow servicemen who faced overwhelming legal problems. He had made the most of his tour of duty, requesting cases in other venues to broaden his knowledge. Conner felt confident and ready to step out into private practice.

6

Berea, Kentucky, was a small college town that boasted a few tourist shops, a well-known inn, and was a popular stop for senior citizens always on the go. Boone Tavern was not yet busy, although Harden had noticed a tour bus pulling up just as he and John entered the building. As Harden followed John through the lobby and into the dining room, he gave some thought to analyzing the older man seated in the corner. That booth was definitely their destination. Thoughts clicked off quickly—six-even, maybe a little shorter, around one-eighty, possibly more, thinning dark hair, wide face, paunchy. As the man slipped out from the booth to greet them, it was easy to see that his bearing was smooth and confident.

"Good afternoon, Harden. I have heard a lot about you. The name's Anderson—have a seat, please. I have taken the liberty of ordering lunch in order to save us time. You must be wondering what my company has to offer a promising young graduate like yourself."

The man had rattled off these sentences in rapid succession, without any letup.

Anderson quietly inserted four quarters into the booth's remote jukebox controller, punched four numbers at random, and then turned up the volume as loud as it would go. The music boomed out almost immediately.

"What I have to say is quite confidential, and I should inform you that you've already been scanned for weapons and electronic listening devices."

Harden's intense expression did not change, but he registered that information for possible later use. Anderson paused and, in passing, admired the young man's controlled reaction.

The food and drinks arrived. The club sandwiches were sliced in half and overflowed with turkey, cheese and Kentucky country ham, certainly enough for a hearty appetite. Anderson had ordered just water, something generally acceptable so as to not further delay their conversation. Anderson bit into the sandwich, chewed a few times, swallowed, and then moved on to his point.

"I'm employed by the U.S. government. My specific division is generally referred to as 'The Company.' Most of the work we do and the information we process is highly classified, and that is an understatement. You are somewhat familiar with classified material from your training at the university, right? My specific mission will involve only me and a few handpicked and highly trained new recruits.

"We're establishing a training class of young men like you, which is designed to prepare a small corps of individuals for special operations as required by our government. You have shown outstanding physical prowess and certainly satisfactory academic capability at the university. We want you enrolled in our program.

"John, here, and Allen Mattingly, a forensics expert at the university, have both endorsed you quite enthusiastically.

"We've already completed a detailed background check on you and your family, plus all prior contacts to this very hour, here at this restaurant. I was truly sorry to hear about your father. He was a very good officer with strong character traits.

"Although the inquiry we performed may bother you as an invasion of privacy, we have to be certain there will be no latent, ah...surprises that could weaken your effectiveness or compromise either our position or yours."

Anderson had been doling out information at a steady pace between quick bites of his sandwich. Harden listened intently. Some of the data caused a reaction in his gut, but he showed no outward sign of it.

"I understand."

Harden's voice was strong, and he did a good job of not saying what was really on his mind.

At this point Harden noticed a signal given by Anderson, and John casually excused himself and moved toward the front door without explanation.

With only that slight hesitation, Anderson proceeded.

"As I said earlier, this recruitment and mission are classified on a need-to-know basis, and you'd be compromised if John were in on the rest of our conversation."

He paused to let this sink in.

"You'll find that, upon completing our course, the financial compensation and benefits will fall within a range quite satisfactory to you, perhaps even more than you might imagine. The purpose of the, shall I say excessive salary scale, is to keep you, ah…happy. If you accept this challenge, this opportunity, you will be entering a program both mentally and physically exhausting in the training phase, but ultimately rewarding once you get through it. If I did not think you could handle it, I would not be here. The greatest reward, however, is service to your country.

"If you're still interested, there's nothing to sign. Your assent will be your commitment.

"I'm going to use the restroom while you think it over."

Anderson paused, gazing directly into Harden's eyes to study him even more closely. Then he was gone.

Harden pondered his decision. Maybe this was the opportunity of a lifetime, or maybe it was just bullshit. His mother was content with her new life in Louisville, that was clear enough, and the only other family person he had was his "blood" brother, Conner Hayes. Conner was in the military at Rosslyn with JAG. Another childhood friend, Anthony Riley, was still in Washington, D.C., also with the government—the National Weather Service. It was funny how things worked out. All three childhood friends from St. Xavier High School had kept in touch over the years, the 'Three Kings'. Now it seemed they all would have the same employer. Harden needed direction. Having made his decision, there was nothing to keep him from moving on with his life. When Anderson returned, Harden was ready for him.

"I'd like the job, Mr. Anderson. What happens next?"

"Tomorrow morning, collect all your belongings, store what you can't carry with you, and be at Louisville International Airport for a flight to Dulles at fourteen hundred hours. There'll be a shuttle waiting to take you to Rosslyn, where they'll be expecting you."

Harden made the flight, and it changed his life forever.

7

Conner Hayes was at another turning point in his life. He was sitting in a booth in the officer's lounge at the Rosslyn complex, all alone. Finishing up his tuna-salad-and-tomato lunch, he was ready to call the second name on his list. Contemplating his approach to this new contact, he was jolted back to reality when, just as his finger touched the first number, his cell phone started to play "taps." He managed to say, "Hello, this is Conner Hayes."

"Sir, this is Sara Phillips at Smith, Pitt and Alagia. Mr. Alagia would like to meet with you if you have the time. I'm instructed to make all necessary arrangements to make it as comfortable as possible for you to come to New York right away for this meeting, of course, at your convenience."

Sara had changed, Conner mused to himself. *Not the same stiff-necked, insensitive robot that had brushed him off earlier, but a sweet, intensely interested and efficient young woman.*

"How about tomorrow?" he asked.

Conner sensed a sigh of relief on Sara's end as she took the necessary information in order to make the proper arrangements.

"Thank you, sir. I will call you back within thirty minutes with the airline and the flight time. A car will pick you up at the airport when you arrive."

Apparently, Mr. Alagia had become aware of Conner's earlier call and requested Jamieson's retrieval of their old file on Conner Hayes. With an efficient yet timely update on the file, Thomas Alagia had decided that Conner Hayes would indeed be a recruiting prize for their firm. He would be an even more valuable catch thanks to his experience over the past four years. With instructions to get the man there, Jamieson was still a little embarrassed at being "abbreviated" with Conner's initial inquiry. He was relieved when Sara was able to make the proper arrangements.

* * *

One year turned into another, and now it was the beginning of Conner's twelfth year in New York with Smith, Pitt and Alagia, a time very rewarding for him financially. As well, Conner was able to accumulate vast experience with a diversity of clients. Now, leaning forward in his soft leather chair, the bright California sun eased down in the west as he gathered his thoughts.

"Excuse me a moment, Miss Jennings."

Ashley—she preferred to be called by her given name—was endowed with a natural beauty that having recently turned thirty-seven only matured and enhanced. With her legs crossed, her Givenchy suit started several inches above her knees and was topped with a loose collar from which her ample assets tried to free themselves. Her otherwise conservative, solid-black business ensemble seemed to hold all the parts together nicely. Expressed in Conner's terms, she added to the office.

Diverting his attention back to the business at hand, Conner punched a flashing button on his telephone console.

"Hello, Hard. How are you?"

Harden had earned this nickname a long time ago. It was natural enough, since everything he did received his full strength and ability. Conner had not seen his closest friend for the past six months, but it was as if they had spoken only an hour before. Harden started in immediately.

"We need to talk, Conner."

The quiet intensity of his voice brought Conner to attention.

Six months ago, Harden had shown up suddenly at Conner's new office, wanting to talk. After an initial bear hug from the huge man, Conner squeezed his hand long enough to let Harden know that his friendship was sincere. Harden was impressed with the view as well as the position Conner had earned with the firm. In a glance, Harden had mentally recorded a picture of the room, with all the details. He knew this had nothing to do with the assignment, but training had made this procedure automatic.

"Hard, let's reconvene at Maloney's Pub. It's right around the corner."

The first time Conner had entered Maloney's it reminded him of Harrigan's, where some years earlier he had been systematically killing himself with grief. Harden had acted like a high school kid again, laughing and talking about their past adventures with his longtime best friend. They had talked for hours, feeling good about reliving all their memories. Both decided that they were certainly good therapy for each other. Then Harden was gone, vanishing from Conner's life as suddenly as he had materialized.

Now he was back. Conner had never seen this Harden, not *this* man. Even in their youth, competitiveness had always brought out his inner intensity. This was evidently more serious than a game.

"Sure, I'd love to see you. When will you be in town?"

"I'm here now, over at Maloney's—back booth, your favorite spot. Get here as soon as you can."

His clipped sentences brought more urgency to the conversation.

"I have a client right now sitting across from me. Can you give me a half hour to courteously curtail this meeting?"

"I'll be here or else I'll call you."

Click!

Conner was left listening to a dial tone. He replaced the phone in its cradle, mulling over Hard's abbreviated phone call and at the same time deciding on an appropriate course of action to delay Miss Jennings. Rather than use the speakerphone within earshot of his client, Conner picked up the receiver and spoke quietly. He did not know how much of the conversation his client had understood, although it had not been much to hear.

"Miss Jennings, I want to do a bit of research on the takeover attempt against your company. I was wondering if we could defer this discussion until Friday morning. Can I meet you at your office about ten?"

"Not at my office. They may know you there. I'll be back here at ten, Friday morning, if that's all right with you?"

Conner stepped around his desk while assuring her that he would see her on Friday. He took her hand and was surprised by the firmness of her grip. As she rose, he was treated to an even better view than that of the San Francisco skyline. Already Conner was looking forward to Friday morning, wishing, somewhat guiltily, that his friend had not called at this moment.

8

Lewis and Long parked the Jeep a mile short of their destination. "Let's take out the perimeter first, Jeff."

Jeff Lewis and Aubrey Long had reconciled their differences quite some time ago. Working in special ops for the government over the past seven years had honed their skills, programming them for an emotionless and purely logical response to situations. They both had made it through life-threatening missions by covering for each other. Life-and-death exposure can cause very close bonds to form. Their bond, however, was the chill that grew in their hearts after so many bloody missions together.

Aubrey and Jeff slipped in behind the two men who were guarding a position a quarter mile from the meeting site. The guards wore night-vision goggles, giving them a clear view of the site and all of its approaches. Another team on the opposite ridge defended that strategic location. Experience and training had enabled Aubrey and Jeff to approach undetected. Below them, two men stood next to their Cadillac Escalade, casually smoking American cigarettes, their eyes habitually darting back and forth toward the entrance to the clearing, a hot summer breeze rolling over some wild grass.

Comfortable with the sand beneath their feet, Kafu and Al-Sufa had grown up here in Abdali. Although Kuwait had been their birthplace and home for most of their lives, the country had little to offer them as career-seeking adults. Their options included hard work in the oil fields or an adventurous but dangerous life on the edge. As young men, they made many an excursion into southern Iraq and had gradually gained the confidence of the cocaine dealers based in Umm Qasr.

A widespread business, mostly ignored by the Iraqi government, had flourished for years here in this port city. The drug was imported in bulk from South America in its nondescript form of raw coca leaves, and then cheaply processed into varying degrees of pure-white powder in makeshift plants located in the region. By anyone's standards, Kafu and Al-Sufa had accumulated a small fortune and could afford to hire the necessary security, local mercenaries willing to do anything in return for USD, otherwise known as United States dollars.

Having discovered how easy it was to make money if one was willing to assume parallel risks, Kafu and Al-Sufa were unsatisfied with the markup they had been receiving for moving this material. An American, known to them only as Mr. Jones, had made contact with Al-Sufa two months earlier. This man had access to an artificial drug—labeled TR-7—developed originally as a stimulant but now mass-produced as a purer form of cocaine. With adequate facilities the drug was so inexpensive to produce, Al-Sufa was promised double his profits for handling it exclusively. This meant that he and Kafu had to break ties with the Umm Qasr cartel. In itself, that was a dangerous risk. To free themselves to operate this new enterprise, they had to fake their own deaths in a fiery explosion. It had seemed to work. To their knowledge, no one was looking for them. The only way to leave that group was through death.

They had no idea how Mr. Jones produced such large quantities of TR-7, shipped it halfway around the world, and still sold it for thirty percent below the current market price of real cocaine. Kafu and Al-Sufa did not need to know.

Their country had adequate schooling for young men, and they had learned to speak fluent English by age fifteen. Consequently, their mathematical skills were also adequate. Beyond that, they would clear an additional half-million dollars for every five million dollars in product they delivered—a sweet deal.

In addition to their perimeter guards, a man had been stationed in the trees on either side of the clearing, keeping a close watch on Kafu and Al-Sufa as well as the approach to the site. The guards were well paid and certainly did not want anything to happen to the men responsible for that payment.

Although at risk by operating so close to their hometown of Abdali, the two men were intimately familiar with virtually everyone and everything in the vicinity. Besides, they no longer had to venture into the town itself, having hired enough associates to do whatever needed to be done. Preferring American-made products, most of their needs and wants were shipped to an anonymous address and then picked up by the men they had hired. On this night, they were both wearing American jeans and loose, long-sleeved cotton shirts.

The American dealer meeting them was to exchange five million dollars in American currency for their two truckloads of cocaine—actually TR-7—and take possession of the two trucks.

Kafu and Al-Sufa never rode in the trucks. They had learned over the years that the risks were much greater when one accompanied the product. Arriving an hour earlier, their men had checked the perimeter within a half-mile radius, leaving two guards about a hundred yards away on both sides and facing the opening to the clearing. Sporting new Nike cross-trainers, Kafu and Al-Sufa made a circuitous trek around the perimeter as well. They preferred the all-white shoes to gaudy colors. Feeling comfortable with their practiced precautions, they had no worries about wearing white at night.

9

Something was wrong. Conner had worked with Harden several times before over the years, offering legal interpretations on some of Harden's activities. That had served merely as professional advice from one friend to another. This time, however, things were different. Harden's tone had an unexplained urgency to it.

Slightly less than a half hour after the call, Conner walked into Maloney's. Nostalgia still gripped him every time he entered a bar. Suddenly, memories and pictures of Liz flashed before his eyes—all good pictures, now. Albert Finch had really upset him, but Conner had long since thanked him for his timely tirade at Harrigan's back in New York. He knew he was just feeling sorry for himself, not for Liz, but it had taken Albert's little speech to shake him out of it.

Harden was seated in a booth in back, just to the left of the bar. Conner noticed at once the two bottles of Perrier resting on the table.

This is serious, Conner thought to himself as he took the last few steps up to the table. Harden knew how to have a good time but, when he was serious, he was deadly serious. As soon as Conner sat down, Harden pushed one of the bottles of Perrier across to him. It was still cold to the touch.

"At one time you had a connection with Jeff Lewis and Aubrey Long.

That is what I need to talk to you about. After an aborted mission last week, special ops reconnaissance found the bodies of three of our men, all with multiple gunshot wounds. None of the victims had fired their weapons."

"What does this have to do with me? Were Lewis and Long involved?"

Conner was puzzled by the connection.

"There were five men, umm…shall we say…involved." Harden continued. "Two of the bodies were never found—those of Lewis and Long. They seemed to have vanished. We used every resource we had to try to locate them. There was never any claim of responsibility by any organization—no notes, nothing."

"We lost a team and haven't yet solved the mystery?"

Conner tilted the cold green bottle to his lips as Harden paused.

"Why are you telling me this? It must be classified information."

Conner was still confused.

"What's the point?" he added.

"We think that maybe these two men have resurfaced, perhaps on their own. Do you remember Captain William Robinson?"

"Sure, of course. However, I have not seen or heard from Bill since our days at JAG. The only case we worked together was when I represented Long. Lewis brought charges against him about ten years ago. Robinson represented Lewis."

Conner's memory was crystal clear. This was one of the last cases he handled in his career at JAG.

"Two days ago, Bill Robinson was struck and killed by a hit-and-run driver."

Harden was nearly whispering.

"Bill was still with JAG, only now he was known as Colonel Robinson. As a matter of course, all unnatural deaths of JAG personnel are followed up by an autopsy. A significant amount of *kurari*, a poison, was found in his blood. We still do not know how it was dispensed. Colonel Robinson was either dying or already dead when the vehicle struck him.

"Kurari is rare, mostly used by natives in the Caribbean for medicinal purposes, and long since replaced by modern-day sedatives and relaxants. It is an aqueous extract from a local vine, found in jungle regions mostly, called Strychnos toxifera. In sufficient doses, it causes immobility and respiratory arrest and is related to the more common curare, found in the jungles of South America.

"We believe the hit-and-run was to cover up his murder. The perps were obviously not aware of JAG policy on autopsies. That is the point.

10

As Aubrey Long raised his S&W Bowie knife behind one of the perimeter guards, the man spun quickly and twisted Aubrey's arm back using both hands. *This guy's good,* he thought as he dropped the knife deftly from his right hand, catching it with his left. With one fluid motion he punctured the guard's neck, severing the carotid artery. As the guard dropped to the ground, the cap fell off and long, dark hair spread across still beautiful but lifeless features.

Aubrey was appalled. He muttered to himself, *what are they doing using young women for this kind of work?* Feeling concern for the killing of women did not allay the overwhelming fact that his training and subsequent missions had made life a commodity of business, no longer a moral issue.

Meanwhile, Jeff had dispatched the other guard, putting him gently on the ground without a sound.

"We're still thirty-six minutes ahead of the meeting. Let's move to the other side and see what's there."

Jeff took the lead. Their training served them well. Making no sound, they took a circuitous route behind the meeting site. Their caution paid off.

About twenty yards to their right awaited two more guards. They were posted behind a large mound of sand, weapons resting carelessly on the edge of the mound. Both men intently watched the access route into the clearing.

Within minutes, they were lying on the still warm sand with empty eyes staring up at the heavens.

Following a few more minutes of careful surveillance Aubrey whispered to Jeff, "The only other obstacle involves the two men in the trucks. I'm guessing they're heavily armed. With their perimeter guard gone, I think we can risk picking those two off from a safe distance."

"What about Kafu and Al-Sufa? They're not going to just run away."

Jeff wanted every detail in order before going forward.

"Everyone thinks they're already dead. I think it's time it became official."

Aubrey did not view the two men as a serious challenge, as shortsighted as that attitude might have been.

With eleven minutes remaining, Jeff had made his way back to the guard post on the right. Both men had recently replaced their special ops-issued Savage 110 sniper rifles with the German-made Walther WA-2000. They both preferred the Walther because of less recoil and greater long-range accuracy.

With their watches synchronized, both men attached silencers to their weapons.

"Lucky seven," Aubrey said.

At exactly seven minutes before the assigned meeting, they fired as one. With a round through the sides of their heads, each driver fell across the seat of the truck cab. Jeff and Aubrey immediately moved their sights to Kafu and Al-Sufa.

One problem—the two Kuwaitis had disappeared. With wits sharpened by years in this dangerous business, Al-Sufa had heard the movement in the trucks as the two drivers lurched to their sides. Immediately alerting Kafu to follow him, he dropped to the ground and began to crawl through the sand to safer ground, away from the scene.

"What happened to our perimeter guards? Were they not reliable men? Did they turn on us?" Kafu whispered, as they settled in a cluster of trees about a quarter of a kilometer from their original position.

Sparing no cost, Kafu and Al-Sufa had purchased their weapons from a contact in southern France. They both had chosen French FR-F2 rifles. With these highly accurate weapons, both men had become expert shooters.

Now they peered between the trees, waiting for movement toward the trucks. With a direct line of vision to the meeting site, they had their high-power scopes trained on the area. The men had spent heavily, enjoying their luxury. This would all end if anything happened to this shipment. They had used all their cash to fund this transaction. Every dollar the Americans brought belonged to them. Their supplier had insisted on full payment in advance to deliver the TR-7 powder to these middlemen.

Suddenly, a white light blinded them. The explosions were deafening. They both recognized the weapon. Their supplier had described flash-bangs to them just recently. They represented a new weapon that was designed to immobilize the enemy for easy capture.

However, Jeff and Aubrey were not interested in easy capture.

Kafu and Al-Sufa felt nothing after the two men jumped over the mound with knives in their hands. Now both men lay asleep forever on the sand, only a short distance from their hometown of Abdali. The average lifespan of Kuwaiti nationals was about seventy-six years of age. If not for the greed of some of their enterprising young citizens, it could have been much longer.

11

Conner's mouth was dry. He sipped more of the cool, bottled water. "Bill Robinson was murdered? And you suspect that Lewis and Long are somehow involved? I still don't know how I'm tied up in all of this."

This was not the happy reunion of six months ago.

"Listen carefully, Conner. We believe these two men are trying to erase their past. They want to become untraceable to pursue their own agenda. Like it or not, you are part of that past.

"They've performed well for the organization. In fact, at the time of their disappearance they had already achieved the second highest security clearance authorized by our government.

"Just before this last mission, in southern Lebanon, someone broke into our personnel records office. The complete history on these two men was taken—plus some other files, both hardcopy and computer data. How did they break the password code? Nobody knows.

"Because of tight security to protect our operatives, all information concerning black ops is contained in these files, and only these files. In order to achieve this, the perp had to know the secret location of those files within the computer bank hierarchy. It is not just a major debacle. It is a catastrophe of Krakatoan proportions.

"He'd also require a top security clearance—CRYPTO—and a voice-registered ID recognizable by our system. Both Lewis and Long were highly regarded operatives. They each had the capability of figuring out enough code combinations, through trial and error, to access those records."

Conner was fascinated by all the spy stuff but still puzzled as to the purpose of his friend's visit. Harden continued.

"Neither one has immediate family. Both young men enlisted, as soon as they were eligible, directly from publicly operated children's homes. Lewis was from California, Long from the Midwest. The U.S. Army was an ideal place for both of them. They advanced rapidly, adapting quickly to the military way of life. In every weapons category they were satisfied with nothing less than expert. These two stood out among their peers in that way. A special ops representative arranged a private interview through their captain. Shortly thereafter, the men had transfer orders that moved them to a training facility near Rosslyn, Virginia.

"It wasn't long after this that you entered the picture, Conner."

"Are you telling me that these men consider me a threat to their secret lives?"

Conner was shocked that he had even hinted as much.

"All I'm saying, Conner, is that their past was erased gradually over the past few days. I am not even sure if they could still identify the JAG defense attorney from that incident. However, they are very intelligent and very thorough, as you well know.

"I'd like to assign a man to keep an eye on you, at least until we know more. I would do it myself but they would identify me—and that would not be smart, what with our friendship and all. This is not just for your safety. It may enable us to learn the whereabouts of these two men."

12

The night had become too quiet after taking care of Kafu and Al-Sufa. Jeff and Aubrey took none of the personal effects of their victims. To be caught with a recognizable item later could be a fatal mistake. They prided themselves on not making mistakes.

Jeff jogged back to retrieve their Jeep while Aubrey began transferring the TR-7 into one of the trucks. After removing the drivers, Aubrey surveyed the damage to each vehicle. Starting each truck in turn, he tested the gearshift. Both had been well maintained. His selection was governed by which truck had the least amount of blood in its cab.

When Jeff returned with the Jeep, he found the trucks parked back to back and the load partially transferred. He carefully stepped away from the Jeep, squatted down, and performed four perfect pushups.

Aubrey appeared out from behind a sand dune. The pushups had been a prearranged security measure to protect both men. In that position, horizontal to the ground, Lewis was a poor target and could roll back behind the Jeep at any sign of trouble. In the darkness, Aubrey could still identify his partner by the pushups.

"Let's get this thing unloaded and then get out of here."

Aubrey was following his training—limit your exposure. Do what has to be done, and then scram.

The load was transferred within minutes. Aubrey jumped behind the wheel of the loaded truck and headed back up the path to the road. Jeff followed in the Jeep. At one point before their departure, Aubrey had taken time to gather six rifles, eight handguns and eight knives from their adversaries. Being careful to avoid injury, he propped the rifles against a boulder and stomped his boot down at just the right angle to permanently damage them. They would never fire again. The knives and handguns were loaded into a shirt he had taken from one of the guards. He tied the arms together to form a carryall. This package would end up at the bottom of the Persian Gulf. Aubrey had a recurring nightmare of being killed by a weapon that he had failed to dispose of on a previous mission.

As they drove across the short stretch south of Abdali to the nearest inlet of the Persian Gulf, their eyes and ears strained for any possibly lethal contact. It was almost two a.m., and anyone out at this hour was either bad news or suffering from bladder problems.

The boat was docked exactly where Jones had promised it would be. The lone man on board was powerfully built, probably not a Kuwaiti but certainly of Middle Eastern descent. Though beginning to show fatigue from their full night of work, Jeff and Aubrey, with Fez assisting, soon had the TR-7 loaded onto the boat. In broken English, Fez assured Aubrey that they were docked in a deep channel. Aubrey gathered up the bundle that held the weapons, swung it around in a full circle, and let fly. The package hit the water about thirty feet from shore and disappeared, leaving a slowly widening impact ring in the otherwise still channel.

After removing their personal belongings from the Jeep, Jeff drove it to the top of a stone ridge that overlooked the channel while Aubrey followed in the truck. Accelerating slightly they started the vehicles down the incline, and then opened their doors and jumped clear.

Both their vehicles continued down the slope, fell twenty feet into the watery graveyard and, with a gurgling objection, disappeared below the surface.

The men jogged back to the boat, wanting to take their leave before anyone saw them or their unusual activity. Fez was ready to leave immediately. The potent motor was already humming and, once Jeff and Aubrey were on board, they surged out into the channel and headed east.

* * *

In less than an hour, Fez pulled the boat ashore at Warbah, as far north as one could go in the Persian Gulf without entering Iraqi waters. Knowing they were expected, they were nonetheless astonished to see the sleek Cadillac limousine waiting for them alongside the dock.

"It looks like a funeral car," Jeff remarked.

"It probably is. They sell them off at good prices when they're replaced by newer models."

Aubrey frowned. Neither of them appreciated the connotation.

Before reaching the limo, they heard the roar of the powerful motor. Fez wasted no time leaving with his TR-7 cargo, happy to be rid of his passengers. With them on board, he had kept a watchful eye out for danger signals.

Those two men are professionals to the bone, he told himself. Several times during the trip from the mainland, the thought of the case packed with U. S. dollars tempted him greatly. Having qualms about killing the two Americans was not the problem. He had killed before. It was the possibility of dying at the hands of men more experienced and clever than he that had crossed his mind, deterring him from any foolish moves. These men had somehow silenced the two Kuwaitis and six or seven mercenaries as well—quite a formidable task and something he could not have done on his own.

The opening he watched for never took place. As he raced away in the boat he mused to himself, *I am being well paid…and I am still alive. Better alive with something in hand than dead with nothing.*

Jeff and Aubrey threw their baggage into the back seat of the limo and, with a watchful eye on the driver, settled in after it.

The mile-long trip inland to the airstrip took less than two minutes.

Pulling up to the Learjet 55, they were impressed with the arrangements. The runway stretched out in the distance, facing north. The sand had been treated and rolled. The result was a solid surface not unlike concrete. High maintenance was required. The runway had to be rolled again after every landing. The usage fees were well justified. Not only was there high maintenance involved, operating a non-licensed airfield required costly bribes and constant security.

The only structure on site was an oversized shed. One end housed a heavy industrial pavement roller. At the other end were sleeping quarters for four. The connecting space was used for a small office, occupied by a desk, two chairs and a filing cabinet.

A rough-looking attendant in Arab attire pushed a portable stair to the open door of the jet. A young woman greeted Jeff and Aubrey.

"Good morning, gentlemen. My name is Serena. My job is to make you as comfortable as possible during your flight. Please board now."

As the two men mounted the steps, Jeff let his eyes capture every detail of their new surroundings. Inside the cabin was a wide seat that faced the door, plus a single seat alongside the door. Just to the right as they entered were four individual seats, plush and comfortable, with a wide aisle in between. Behind this was a small galley and restroom facilities.

"Our bar is fully stocked with both American and European wines and liquors, as well as an adequate assortment of beer," she said. "The only food we have is a small but choice variety of sandwiches, as well as *hors d'oeuvres.*"

Serena was busy outlining the amenities as the door closed from the outside and the plane taxied into position for takeoff.

"It is my responsibility to do whatever is necessary for you to have a satisfactory flight," she took the time again to repeat her welcome.

Aubrey had been lusting after the young woman since first setting eyes on her, back when she led them into the cabin. Other than the female guard at the clearing, it was two months since he had even seen an attractive female. Serena wore a short skirt, revealing smooth and darkly tanned thighs, and an elegant white shirt cut off just above her navel, with no collar and butterfly sleeves blossoming out from her shoulders. As her arms moved about to explain the jet's features, the shirt rode up enough to expose a little navel ring designed to look like a red beetle, with inset diamonds for spots.

"The facilities include a shower and all the necessary accouterments, if you would like to freshen up. Are you interested in a liquid refreshment at this time?"

Serena balanced perfectly as the jet ascended to the liftoff angle.

Both men took their turn in the shower. Refreshed and changed into clean clothing, they sat down to attack their sandwiches. Aubrey found his club sandwich both fresh and full of delicious slices of turkey, cheese and country ham, and made short work of it. Jeff had ordered a chicken salad sandwich. Cautiously, he raised the hearty repast to his mouth. One bite told him the mayonnaise and chicken was not only fresh, but of gourmet quality. He selected a Beringer Reserve 1995 Cabernet from the wine list.

The sandwich finished, Jeff sipped his wine with eyes closed, thinking about his share of five million dollars. They had received the best training in the world from the American CIA, and now all that work was finally paying off.

Aubrey had his eyes closed, too. However, as he sipped his Buffalo Trace Kentucky bourbon on the rocks, his thoughts were of Serena.

Seeing her move around from one place to another, he got up the nerve to make a house call when he felt her thigh brush up against his arm.

"Can I get anything else for you, sir?" she asked quietly.

He thought he was still dreaming. Right in front of his eyes, her breasts did a little dance and pushed against the flimsy material of her white blouse. As he raised his eyes further, what he thought he saw was an inviting smile on her face, and he always acted on his intuitions.

"I'll go up there with you and see what's available."

Serena turned and, with a little toss of her hair, walked slowly into the galley, knowing full well that he was watching.

Aubrey did not understand how any woman could be so coordinated. He had to grab both chair backs for steadiness as he stepped into the galley behind her.

Feigning sleep, Jeff caught every movement and heard every word.

Finally, a door closed on the other side of the galley.

Feeling safe to look now, he found they had disappeared into another room. Being no fool for feminine wiles, Jeff quickly analyzed the situation as only he could.

For her part, Serena knew they must be rich Americans. People requiring the services of this bastard airline almost always dealt in cash.

She had already eliminated Jeff, sensing immediately that he could not be seduced—at least not by a woman. Aubrey was her target, and she had chosen well. He wanted bourbon. She made sure he got 100-proof bourbon. After two healthy drinks, she made her move.

Two scenarios were in her repertoire of choice. First, if she could get him to drink a little more bourbon and, if she made sure he enjoyed himself enough—but not too much—she believed there was a possibility of extending their relationship beyond this flight. That option had priority because it offered her the best chance for a lucrative monetary reward. Second, by giving him everything he wanted immediately, she could encourage him on the spot to reward her extravagantly for her well-placed affection.

Amazed at how easy it was to have attracted his attention, she lured Aubrey into a small sleeping chamber available to staff or guests, as needed.

As she moved through the galley she thought to herself, *the other passenger is asleep. Perhaps, if I fail with this one, I might try him anyway.*

She was always thinking. In her brief experience with this flight service, Serena had been quite successful in extorting money from clients. She had been all business—always. None of the patrons of this service had interested her personally, and none of them had complained to the owners.

All she cared to do was turn her assets into cash. It was not a complicated plan but one that had to be executed flawlessly, as she had told herself many times. Serena was an opportunist, and she considered this a trunk load of opportunity.

13

Born in a poor section of Amalfi, a port town in the Campania region of southern Italy, Gabriella Magia had been beautiful from birth. Her mother supported her and her younger brother by preying on the many tourists who visited the well-known seaside resort. Her education was paid for by her mother's resourcefulness, and Gabriella took full advantage of that opportunity. Faring satisfactorily with her studies through the twelfth grade, she was able to attend Our Lady of Carmel College in Amalfi.

Gabriella was bright as well as beautiful. She had completed four semesters in business administration at the college when her mother fell ill. After becoming HIV-positive her mother had contracted aids. Gabriella was then compelled to quit her studies and take care of her mother and younger brother. With no money for drugs to fight the disease, her mother was dead within five months. She had waited much too long to apply for treatment, having desperately continued to work to provide for her children.

She was gone now, with no way to account for the number of individuals she may have infected among Amalfi's vacationers. Upon their mother's death, her younger brother was sent to St. Thomas Orphanage in the suburbs. At twenty, Gabriella was on her own to fend for herself, and the tough times called for tough decisions. The first thing she managed was to apply for a scholarship grant at Carmel College.

Her first meeting was, essentially, a disaster. With her long black hair swirling around her beautiful face and her breasts swelling out against a tight white blouse, when she entered the administrator's office he was, to put it mildly, spellbound. Not only could he not keep his eyes from roving all over her, but his hands itched to do so as well. This was the first time in her life that she had used her body to achieve what she wanted—and it worked. She was offered a provisional scholarship, the terms of which he outlined most clearly. Gabriella was well aware of her body and the effect she had on men.

Because of the stigma of the occupation she felt forced into, her mother had tried to diligently protect her daughter's innocence. Despite that diligence, Gabriella eventually came to know as much about the world as her mother did.

During this particular encounter, however, Gabriella elected not to give in. Instead, she shoved the administrator away and ran from the office with tears in her eyes. She knew she would never return. Through a longtime girlfriend, she found employment with Alitalia Airlines as a flight attendant.

For the next three years, she shared an apartment with her friend, Maria Avola. Their flight schedules kept them apart; seldom were they both at home at the same time. Gabriella matured quickly with her exposure to a world well beyond her hometown. Her wages were sufficient to allow a few luxuries, such as some nice clothes and paying for her share of the apartment.

When Alberto approached her with a job offer that would double her salary, she was strongly tempted. After confirming that her duties would be the same as a flight attendant, but on a smaller scale with the private airline, she accepted. Since then, she had traveled the world. Most of their stops took place in remote areas with makeshift landing strips and, as always, hush-hush was the word.

As one might expect, their clientele varied widely. Many of their passengers were carefully coiffured businessmen who needed access to a flight on short notice. While most appeared to be on the up-and-up, some were perhaps not so. Other clients were picked up in shorts and loafers, and a few even had blood on their clothes. No questions were to be asked. In all cases, it seemed, no one was who they said they were. Everyone used an alias, usually just a single name. For instance, Alberto had always been just that—Alberto. Over the past five years Gabriella had learned many things, and her frugal upbringing had served her well. She had accumulated a bank balance in the low six-figures and learned to use every opportunity to make it grow handsomely.

She also followed the pattern of everyone else. Instead of Gabriella, she was now Serena.

14

Jeff knew Aubrey well—too well—and had once taken a beating, a real physical pounding. He vowed it would never happen again. That promise caused him to strengthen his body by perfecting every training technique the company had to offer. Jeff and Aubrey completed that phase of their training at the top of their class. With mutual respect for each other's ability, they became inseparable on missions, eccentric friends at best. There was a saying in the business—the best friends one could have were former enemies as good at their job as you were at yours. Those were people you could count on in a pinch. Having an outstanding success rate on their missions, the two men became proficient at special operations, *black ops,* and were always in demand.

Over the past nine years, they had been recognized and rewarded as a team, personifying much more than the usual "what's in it for me" attitude. They were like bookends, each complementing the other. As unlikely a friendship as could be imagined, theirs was a bond of confidence and mutual trust, based on exposure to and the survival of the most gruesome and physically exhausting missions their employers could arrange.

They had achieved the second highest level of security clearance. Their remuneration was based not on rank, as in the regular army, but rather on the degree of difficulty for any particular assignment. Neither had a family to worry about, nor did they possess any precognition of values, whether monetary or moral. With all expenses paid while on duty, their paydays were arranged electronically and deposited in banks of their own choosing, utilizing unmarked accounts in Switzerland and the Cayman Islands. Their current deposits totaled in excess of five hundred thousands dollars each. With personal goals set at a million dollars apiece, Jeff and Aubrey often discussed business opportunities that would allow them to retire in just a few more years.

* * *

As their group had assembled back at Rosslyn for the next job, Aubrey's cell phone rang. His mind quickly assimilated who the caller might be at this particular time. He could count on three fingers the number of people who had this number—Jeff, their controller, and their personal banker, Jeremy Baker.

"Hello?"

Noncommittal was the only way to handle oneself until finding out the identity of the caller.

"I need to talk to Aubrey Long. Is that you?"

"Before we proceed here, I want to know how you got this number?"

The problem was that Aubrey did not recognize the voice. *This guy sounds like he's using a scrambler,* he thought to himself. Aubrey had considerable experience with voice synthesizers.

"My name is Mr. Jones. I need to talk to you about a matter of, shall I say, mutual interest. Please indulge me and you'll not regret making that decision."

"O.K., make it fast. It's your dime."

"Oh, not on the phone, Mr. Long. Meet me at St. Francis Catholic Church, on Bank Street, about three miles from where you are standing in Rosslyn, tomorrow morning at seven. When you enter the church, proceed halfway down the far right aisle to the confession booth. There will be no confessions in progress at that time. Enter the sinner's box, sit down, and raise the wooden slide. Providing that you have come alone, I will be in the confessor's box awaiting your signal. When you raise the slide, tap twice on the armrest with your middle finger, pause, and then tap three more times. When I am sure that you are the one in the box and unaccompanied, only then will I raise my slide and make my proposal. I can assure you it will be of interest."

Click. He had hung up.

Having been given no time for a reply, Aubrey listened to dead air for a few seconds as he digested the information.

15

Conner was still analyzing everything that Harden had thrown at him over the past several minutes. The two men he mentioned no longer existed within the agency—their records gone and no one remembered them, much less could identify them or their habits. The controller only had their military files to go on. Now, those were missing as well. The controller could identify Lewis and Long. Was he in danger? Harden probably had protectors on him as well. Conner could remember both men quite clearly. He had scanned a personality profile on each man. Those would certainly still be in the JAG files. If they had eliminated Jeff Lewis' legal representative, logic would indicate that he, Conner, was also in danger. Conner wanted to assume that was why Harden had come.

Conner Hayes would not be difficult to locate, having gained some celebrity via the news media in New York. His name was also strongly linked to heavy public relations that promoted the opening of the law firm's new San Francisco office.

"If you can think of anything we've overlooked, tell me now. One other item I haven't yet mentioned is that the JAG files were pulled in their entirety and placed in the men's jackets at Rosslyn."

Harden had just dashed the one positive thought in all of this.

"The controller did this as soon as the men were certain to pass training as special ops, which took place almost nine years ago.

"Although I wasn't able to talk to their controller in person, he managed to outline the problem to me over a secure phone line. I do not even know his name. The government is totally committed to protecting their controllers. They are highly intelligent, highly trained men with broad experience in the field. They are also trusted agents who have succeeded in reaching the next level by playing the game as it is supposed to be played. They arrive there in total anonymity. With no idea who or where he is, I cannot protect him. He knows this but has requested that I waste no time or expense in finding these men. They now appear to be considered a threat to national security."

* * *

Both Jeff and Aubrey had seen enough of death to develop an invisible wall in their minds, one that shielded them from any feelings of remorse or perpetuation of morality. Every mission brought additional exposure to life-threatening circumstances. Never allowed the opportunity to contemplate when their time might come, both men lived diverse but full lives, remaining *in the moment* at all times. Their standards were polar opposites, but their respective objectives were the same. Some day their investment accounts would carry a high enough balance to take them away from this business for good.

Jeff often said, "When my account reaches a million dollars, partner, I'm gone." Aubrey always added, "I'm with you, partner." For these two men it was always the same statement and the same response, every time.

They never used their surnames in addressing each other. Not considering themselves friends, Jeff and Aubrey were simply a team—a highly trained, superbly organized set of killers.

Back to back, they could ward off any enemy. They depended on each other like brothers. Though the animosity was long gone, there was no friendship and never could be. Confidants, inseparable partners, alter egos were some of the terms that could be used to describe their relationship, but friendship was not one of them. Friendship connotes feelings, and their feelings had been suppressed for too long and eventually obliterated by innumerable missions—with the agency ultimately to blame.

16

Aubrey arranged to have Jeff cover him as he entered St. Francis Church. Jeff had gone in first, positioning himself halfway down the center aisle in a pew on the left. Carefully projecting a humble appearance, his head slightly bent, he genuflected and made the sign of the cross. He remained perched on the kneeler momentarily, then sat down and waited, alert even to the buzzing of a fly.

As planned, Aubrey entered the church five minutes later, with his head down even as his eyes took in every detail. An elderly woman sat in the third pew from the front, off to the right. She had a fancy handkerchief pinned to her hair and was dressed in a nondescript old woman's dress. Her eyes appeared closed; she was either asleep or in deep meditation. A wheelchair leaned against the wall under the stained glass window across from her. *No threat there,* Aubrey told himself, automatically scanning the environment.

Jeff was in position exactly as they had planned. In the rear pew far to the left, a middle-aged man sat with his chin resting on his right hand, as if meditating. He possessed a strong jaw and seemed a bit out of place. His left arm remained out of sight, hidden by the dark suit he wore. The suit was charcoal in color and finely textured. Aubrey could not see his shoes. He wore what looked like a Countess Mara tie, proficiently knotted at the neck of his pinstriped shirt. Other than these people, the church was deserted.

Immediately upon entering, Aubrey had located the confessional off to the right, about three-fourths of the way down the aisle. He blessed himself with a splash of holy water and proceeded slowly forward. In order to appear as inconspicuous as possible, he had dressed in khaki trousers and an open-necked shirt, topped by a tan sport coat to cover his holstered weapon.

Stopping short of the confessional, he knelt in the fifth pew from the front of the church. After once again checking the status of the other occupants, he proceeded to the curtained entrance. He paid particular attention to the right rear of the church where the man in the dark suit sat—still in the same position, still meditating. *Of course, he belongs to the man in the booth*, Aubrey mused. *He's ex-military—maybe even military police.*

Aubrey continued to mentally assess his surroundings. Entering the confessional, he closed the curtain and sat down.

Once his eyes adjusted to the darkness, he opened the divider. Just as instructed he tapped twice with his middle finger, paused, and followed with three more taps. He heard the inside panel slide open.

"You did not come alone."

The voice startled him a little. Again, it was synthesized, sounding somewhat distorted. Before he could answer, the voice continued.

"No matter. I am Mr. Jones. Your man was detected as he entered and has now been identified. My proposal is for both of you, anyway.

"We only have a short time before we arouse suspicion. I am prepared to pay for your services—more than you can imagine, more than you could make in a lifetime.

"You will more than triple your investment account with the first job that I have to offer."

Mr. Jones had gotten Aubrey's attention. *He knows my investment account? How can that be?* Aubrey asked himself. *Not only the million-plus paycheck?* Those accounts were protected by password.

"How did you get that information?"

It was more a reaction than a question.

"I know all about both you and Mr. Lewis. Otherwise, we would not be sitting here talking. You have capabilities for which I have a need and for which I am willing to be quite generous. To take advantage of my offer, you will have to separate from your present position and erase your past so that you cannot be traced. Together, we will set up a new life for you.

"You have worked hard these past nine years and been well paid—I should say, well paid by military standards. However, the half million dollars each that you have accumulated thus far will seem like a mere pittance when compared with the opportunity I wish to share with you.

"To show both good faith and my sincerity, I offer to deposit a matching amount in your investment accounts upon your word of acceptance to my proposal. The travel and the risks will be similar to those you presently experience, but the reward shall be infinitely greater.

"Please know that I am deadly serious and will brook no compromise once you are on board. Once you accept, you cannot back out.

"Please discuss this proposal with Mr. Lewis and make a decision before the day is finished. Once your decision has been made, send an e-mail to user346210@newworld.net and type only the numerical message 1111 if the answer is affirmative. You will type 9999 if it is negative.

"This must be done by midnight tonight. After that time, the address will be useless. If your reply is affirmative, your account will double tomorrow and I will give you further instructions using your return e-mail address. Please make certain that it is secure.

"Oh, and goodbye, Mr. Long."

The inside panel closed.

17

All the tables were now taken and the patrons stood at the bar, engaged in loud conversations that ranged from politics to Major League Baseball's steroid problems. Maloney's had a fine reputation. Remaining unnoticed as part of the crowd was a primary reason Harden had selected this site for his meeting with Conner.

"What I'd like now, Conner, is for you to authorize one of my people to be employed in your office until this business is settled. Use any ruse that you wish to smooth the waters. It has to be done to protect you."

Conner's mind raced overtime, not with the quantity of information but rather with the content.

"If I say yes now, can I rescind that decision if things become too awkward to explain, or if it just doesn't work out?"

"Certainly. My man will be there at nine o'clock tomorrow morning, telling the receptionist that he has an appointment with you at that time. He will introduce himself as Charles Reynolds and say that he prefers to be called Charlie. If he does not present himself in exactly that manner, lock your office door, grab your cell phone, lock yourself inside your private bathroom, and then call me immediately. While I'm in San Francisco, use my alternate cell number, 415-555-1332."

Conner jotted down the number and then raised one eyebrow.

"I certainly appreciate your concern, Hard, but do you really think they'd carry things to that extreme?"

Conner was a little shaken but still dubious as to the seriousness of the problem even though, instinctively, he knew they would indeed carry things that far.

"Listen, Conner. You were my best friend—still are, for that matter. I am here to see that no one tries to harm you. But it is also my job. No matter the JAG attorney assigned to Long or his present location, I'd be telling him the same thing I'm telling you now, and that is, 'Conner, you need to be suspicious of every single stranger, at least until my man arrives.' Be careful tonight. I'll be in touch with you soon."

With that pronouncement, Harden was finished.

They left the bar together, hugged like the old friends they were, and then Harden was off around the corner. Conner returned to the office garage to retrieve his car, deep in thought all the way.

* * *

Serena turned as she entered the exiguous sleeping quarters, shoulders back, forcing her breasts taut against the thin white blouse in a perfect model's stance. She had removed her beetle jewelry, accenting her navel and the smooth texture of her body that lay exposed between her top and her skirt.

Already aroused, Aubrey stepped into the room and closed the door behind him, feeling like a lion at a watering hole about to devour a wildebeest. Jeff still feigned sleep, waiting for the sounds that he knew would come.

After a few fragile minutes, he heard movement in the other room. *Sounds like brawling,* Jeff thought to himself. *Serena thinks she's the exploiter here, with all her experience and everything. Clearly, she does not know what she is up against this time.* Jeff almost felt sorry for her naiveté. He had cleaned up Aubrey's messes before and cringed at the thought of doing so again. *Maybe two more jobs with him and I'll have a suitable retirement pool and be done with all this crap,* he thought.

Even as he pondered this, he wondered if he would ever be able to extricate himself from the sinkhole his life had become, seemingly with no way out.

A half hour later Aubrey stumbled out the door, grabbed two pillows off a shelf, and settled down for a nap on the double seat across from the cabin entrance. He slept with his back to the wall, another precautionary habit.

Jeff heard movement as the door slowly opened.

Studying the scene, he could not believe it was the same girl who had so graciously welcomed them aboard. Serena had combed her long hair forward in an attempt to hide some blemishes, although the welts and bruises she now had on the right side of her face were not so easily concealed. Revetted but disheveled, her clothing no longer flattered her. Jeff detected a slight limp as well.

When Aubrey finally left their room Serena was dazed but conscious, her plans for profitable intercourse shattered as she saw the lone hundred-dollar bill lying on the table. The man had been crude and powerful. She originally thought she could manipulate him but, from the way he first grabbed her inside the room, she quickly understood she had been wrong.

His eyes were menacing, his movements rampant. Only once did she attempt to lead him. A flat-handed slap to the side of her face knocked her to the bed, rendering her nearly unconscious. At that point, she had decided to be as subservient as his actions required. *Dear God, please let me live through this,* she said over and again to herself. Her eyes had closed in silent prayer.

She still had the hundred-dollar bill in her hand. As she shuffled out of the room, Serena tried to compose herself. Jeff was up and at her side, startling her back to reality. Slipping a wad of bills into her fist, he spoke quietly.

"Get out of this business, miss, while you still can."

Serena stuffed the money into her brassiere without counting it and moved to the pilot's door. To get there she had to pass the sleeping Aubrey. Her body was visibly shaking as she opened the door and disappeared into the control room with Alberto.

"Please don't say a word, Alberto," she said, collapsing into the copilot's chair and shutting her eyes.

18

Thursday morning at eight forty-five, Conner walked into his office. "Good morning, Janet. Do I have any calls?"

"I put them on your desk. There is a young gentleman to see you. He said he had a nine o'clock appointment with you, but I do not have him on my schedule. He's in the waiting room."

The waiting room of Smith, Pitt and Alagia was just off the main reception area, separated by a heavy glass door and mirrored on the inside to ensure the privacy of the attorneys who were coming and going. Furnished with soft leather lounges and three worktables, as well as coffee and a selection of cold drinks, waiting was made less frustrating to visitors.

When she told Conner the man was not on the schedule, she offered him a quizzical glance.

"How did he introduce himself? What were his exact words?"

Conner's phrasing puzzled Janet.

"Ah, I believe he said, 'My name is Charles Reynolds, but I prefer to be called Charlie,' " she responded.

"Those were his exact words?" Conner asked.

She said yes.

Conner felt as if someone had thrown ice water in his face. This brought to stark reality Harden's words from last night.

"At exactly nine, please show him into my office. My next appointment is at ten. When Mrs. Carpenter arrives, please show her in immediately."

Conner strode to his door and opened it in slow motion while he thought about everything Harden had told him the previous night. Carefully placing his suit coat on a hanger in the closet, he looked out at the bright San Francisco morning on display outside his window.

Sinking into the high-backed Corinthian leather chair, Conner leaned back and closed his eyes, just for a second. Then, with a new resolve, he returned to the present and reached for his messages.

"Nothing so important it can't wait until I resolve these first two matters at hand," he exclaimed aloud.

At that moment, Janet knocked softly before entering.

"Mr. Hayes, this is Charles Reynolds."

After she brought the man in she closed the door gently behind her.

Not at all what he had expected, the man before him wore a dark-gray suit, a white shirt, and a sky-blue tie knotted evenly. His black shoes, reflecting the fluorescent lighting, were the only indication of anything military about the young man. If not for his four years in the army, Conner may not have noticed this distinction.

Charles Reynolds appeared to be in his mid-twenties with dark hair and a slender build, about six feet tall and fairly handsome. He could have passed for any junior partner in the firm.

"Good morning, Mr. Hayes. It is a pleasure to meet you. Mr. Kelly filled me in completely."

Reynolds' grip was firm without being overbearing.

"I prefer to be called Charlie."

Conner was quick to catch the significance of the coded reference.

"Well, then, good morning—Charlie. Where do we go from here? This is all a little overwhelming to me."

"Well, sir...."

"Please, if I'm to call you Charlie, you must call me Conner."

"Well, sir—Conner—I know very little about your business. My first suggestion is that you refer to me as co-counsel on some case and let me spread a reference book or two on that table over there. This cover story should be good for a few days. Maybe, in the end, that's all we'll need."

The young man was efficient. Conner was impressed and had every right to be. As he freed two large volumes from the library on the far wall, Conner Hayes was already mentally moving toward his next appointment.

Mrs. Carpenter owned one of the Napa vineyards and had been a corporate client for many years. Conner had met with her numerous times on trips out from New York.

She was having property-rights problems and was more in need of consolation than consultation. Conner furnished both services equally well. The property-rights issue was resolved promptly, but the consoling part took the balance of the morning.

The remainder of the day proved routine except for the ever-present Mr. Reynolds. They had lunch together, ate dinner together, and even went home together. Charlie refused the guest room, preferring to sleep on the couch so he could face the front entrance of Conner's condominium.

* * *

Aubrey rose slowly, closing the slide on his side of the confessional as he did. He knew that he was supposed to exit first. Mr. Jones wanted to keep his identity secret for now. Moving the curtain aside to step out, and with an almost imperceptive signal, Aubrey's partner followed him out of the church. Jeff used his peripheral vision to determine that the other two occupants of the church had remained right where they had been all along.

Aubrey had a penchant for keeping information to himself. This time, Jeff could tell something was weighing heavily on his partner's mind. Only Aubrey knew the time constraints. They had to find a secure place to discuss this, and fast. They were leaving on a mission the next morning. Did Mr. Jones know that? He had insisted on an immediate answer.

After signaling only that they needed a secure place to talk, Aubrey and Jeff drove back to the base.

They lived in separate one-bedroom apartments at Rosslyn. Aubrey drove to his apartment, where he grabbed his laptop computer. Next, they made a stop at the supply building. Aubrey pulled up alongside the building, parking so that he remained hidden except to directly passing traffic.

Once he showed his identification and a clearance pass, everything was at his disposal. He signed out a countermeasure kit. Walking casually out the door, he turned the corner back to his car.

All he needed from the kit was the advanced transmitter detector.

Activating the instrument, he scanned the entire vehicle, even the undercarriage. No listening devices were found. Even though Aubrey had been fairly certain his car was clean, long ago he learned that making assumptions like that could get oneself killed. Returning the unit to its kit, he brought it back to the lieutenant who sat behind the counter.

"Looks like I won't need this after all. The unit already has one. Thanks for your trouble."

Aubrey watched the man sign the kit in as returned. As they drove through the gates and headed toward town, Aubrey finally broke the silence.

"The man identified himself as Mr. Jones. He wants us to leave the company and go to work for him."

He paused and waited for a reaction from Jeff. When none came, he continued.

"He says the first job he has for us will triple what we've already got in our savings accounts. Yeah."

Aubrey paused again to let what he had just said sink in.

"He seems to know all about us, including how much is in our investment accounts and where they're located. Now, here's the part that's definitely got my attention. If we agree to come work for him, he'll transfer five hundred thousand dollars into each of our accounts—and he'll do it by noon tomorrow."

Although, Jeff was emotionless on the outside, the information was clicking away inside his head.

"You mean that all we have to do is say yes, and he'll wire us this money? What kind of work is involved?"

Aubrey had asked Mr. Jones exactly that.

"He said we'd just continue to use the skills we use now on every mission, only this time for private matters. The only way we can leave our unit so abruptly is to fake a mission failure, and then disappear."

Jeff had already thought of that. They both knew the other three operatives included in their mission. They were not close friends. You never made close friends in this business.

"My vote is affirmative. We can confirm that the transfer's been made before we change the mission."

Jeff was thinking that he might not have to wait nine more years after all to retire.

"We don't have anything to lose by an affirmative response. How do we get in touch with this Mr. Jones?"

Aubrey had thought it would be more difficult to sway Jeff.

"Jones gave me an e-mail address and a coded message. That is why I picked up my laptop. I agree with you. We don't have anything to lose by saying yes."

Aubrey pulled his car into the parking lot of the Towbridge Inn, located a short distance from the center of town. Out of sight around the side of the office, he booted up his computer. Closing the top so that it gave the appearance of a briefcase, they both entered the office. There were no other patrons. It was still too early in the day. Behind the desk stood a young man wearing a green golf shirt and jeans.

"Is there anywhere I can get an Internet connection here?" asked Aubrey.

The clerk did not know how far he could push these two.

"You'll have to rent a room, sir. There are Internet connections in each of our rooms. They run seventy dollars plus tax."

Jeff pulled out two one-hundred-dollar bills.

"Is there a link in the office we can use? We'll be in and out in five minutes."

The clerk grabbed at the bills.

"You can go right in there, but please get out before someone sees you."

He pointed to the doorway behind him.

Aubrey spotted the connection in the wall, unplugged the hotel's PC, and inserted his own cable into the slot. Quickly pulling up the Internet, he selected the mail icon, then new mail. Aubrey typed in the address, user356210@newworld.net. Clicking the cursor in the message box, he typed "1111." No subject, no address, no sign off.

Aubrey logged off the Web and unplugged his laptop. Ignoring the limp cable from the in-house computer that lay strung across the floor, he closed his case and followed Jeff out the door.

"We did it! Now, if that money is in our accounts tomorrow, we'll need to be prepared."

Jeff was already planning ahead.

"If we're forced to disappear tomorrow, I don't want to lose the money I already have. I think we should open up a new offshore account today through our Swiss bank, and leave ten thousand dollars in our existing accounts to keep them active. I did some research because I was already curious about how that worked.

"The requirements are simple. We each fill out an application online. In a couple of days they'll mail us requests for notarized copies of our passport photos. The application will open the account so we can make a transfer. I propose that we open with five hundred thousand dollars each. If the money does show up tomorrow, we'll have an account where we can transfer the additional five hundred thousand. That's the easy part. We'll also need to set up a post office box no one can trace once we've disappeared. You have any ideas?"

When Aubrey had no immediate reply, Jeff continued.

"Jones is really pushing us. Maybe that's part of the test of our capabilities. But I've got an answer. Remember Hans Broecker? He was quite an operator until he went sideways against us a couple of years ago. As he was dying, he grabbed my arm and thrust a Swiss mailing address into my hands. I sent it anonymously to his daughter in Innsbruck to honor his last request.

"What that means is that we can set up both Swiss bank accounts and mailing addresses through swissmail.com. It'll only cost us five or six hundred dollars a year. If our new life materializes, the cost would be justified."

They returned to Aubrey's apartment and plugged in the laptop to continue their transactions. With this impromptu office in place, they took turns on the computer. Within an hour they both had authentic Swiss mailing addresses.

The bank applications took longer but, with their new addresses, they felt comfortable in completing the application. The Neuhaur National Bank of Switzerland accommodated them with an account number for each of them. Deposits were allowed and encouraged, although withdrawals had to await formal identification through notarized copies of their passport photos.

The next stop was to the local branch of the bank where they had set up their accounts nine years earlier. While not particularly pleased about losing two sizeable accounts, the investment officer completed the paperwork for transferring their money. Within a short time they received printed confirmation that their funds had been wired to their new accounts. So far, they were not seriously damaged monetarily. The investment officer shook their hands and thanked them for keeping their accounts open with the remaining balance.

The next day they would be on their way overseas. With the laptop in hand, either Aubrey or Jeff could check on their accounts to confirm the additional deposits. They had been assigned to co-lead this mission.

19

Friday at exactly ten sharp, Janet rapped softly on Conner's door before entering.

"Miss Jennings is here, Mr. Hayes. Shall I send her in, or are you still tied up with Mr. Reynolds?"

She nodded in the direction of the young man, who had busied himself by searching through the casebooks lying on the table. Conner realized how much it bothered Janet to be left out of his scheduling of appointments. After all, it was her responsibility.

"Mr. Reynolds is just collaborating with me on another case. We won't bother him. Please send her in."

Janet was not buying that story. She studied his face for a clue, but found nothing there.

"Very well, sir."

She closed the door behind her.

None of this escaped the watchful eyes of Charlie Reynolds.

A moment later the door opened again.

"Miss Jennings, sir."

Dressed in a long-sleeved white silk blouse, her black skirt hugging her body to just below the knees, Ashley seemed to glide across the room. Conner met her halfway with his hand outstretched.

"I appreciate your inconvenience with rescheduling this meeting, Miss Jennings, but I assure you that this time we'll take all day if necessary to assess your situation."

She had a firm, athletic grip that impressed Conner. Some of his female clients offered a limp hand as if expecting him to kiss it rather than shake it. Still gently gripping her hand, he led her to the closer of two tufted leather guest chairs adjacent to his desk.

"Have a seat, Miss Jennings, and we'll get started. The gentleman over there is my co-counsel on another case we're handling. We were doing some research together—got started around nine this morning. He promises not to disturb us. If his presence bothers you in any way, please let me know and we'll make other arrangements. His name is Charlie Reynolds, by the way."

At the introduction, Charlie raised his hand in acknowledgment.

"Very nice to meet you, Miss Jennings. I promise not to make a sound."

"Hi, Charlie."

She returned the wave and turned her attention back to her counselor.

"Conner, I told you yesterday to call me Ashley. I'm more comfortable with that. And I don't feel that Mr. Reynolds is a bother. If his presence is all right with you, I have no objection."

Conner noticed that the top button of her silk blouse was unfastened again today. As she crossed her legs, the long black skirt parted slightly to reveal slender, athletic calves.

The previous afternoon, Ashley Jennings had been confiding in him about Jennings Pharmaceuticals, the company her grandfather had founded and, at which, she currently chaired the board of directors that included five other members. The company had long since gone public and was a thriving concern in an industry with a natural growth of clientele.

Conner's attention was divided between the young man across the room and the casually undone top button of the woman's white silk blouse. Likely she had done this for ease of breathing, but there was no argument that the glimpse of décolletage was both beautiful and provocative.

Earlier inquiries had enlightened Conner as to his client's qualifications. Fourteen years earlier, Harvard University had graduated her *cum laude* with a master's degree in business administration. Yale University contributed a doctorate in business after another eighteen months.

Although it was difficult to take his mind off the obvious, this woman had even more going for her on the inside of this beautiful facade. Her smile seemed seductive, even though his instincts told him this was as natural to Ashley as the part her eyes played in the conversation.

"My father and I own controlling shares in the business. One of our companies is in the midst of a tremendous growth spurt. It's very rewarding, but each time I try to look into this unusual progress, I seem to be shunted off by the other three directors. My intuition tells me that something isn't quite right there.

"The board includes my father, who's never had any real interest in running the company. He has a great many outside interests, primarily other investments. My father is acting president of an investment club that he formed with some of his wealthy friends. They've made a number of investments in condo developments along Florida's Gulf Coast, plus some other resort areas. I understand they're doing so well that they could all retire right now, and live quite fabulously.

"Of course, these weren't average investors in the first place, but well respected businessmen, most of them running their own companies.

"I'm a board member and the chairman. My father was responsible for that. He didn't want the position and, because of our controlling stock, he simply appointed me in his place.

"The other board members were older men and certainly more experienced in operations, but they respected my father's decision.

"I started with the company as assistant to the treasurer, Sam Allison. My father insisted that I learn everything I could from this man. He respected Sam, who was a long-time confidant. Mr. Allison was old when I came into the business. His health forced him to retire at age seventy, and I was appointed to succeed him as treasurer. After five years with the company I moved up to chief financial officer, and that's where I am today.

"The third member of our board came to us from Brantley Chemical, the company that's now doing so well. Mr. Riley has been with us for about three years and is quite well respected. Actually, we lost two directors over the past two years, and Mr. Riley was quite helpful in finding their replacements.

"Mr. Meriweather had been a director as long as my dad. He was a dear old man but not really in favor of all this expansion. He passed away about two years ago from a sudden heart attack. Mr. Meriweather had a history of heart problems, but we thought he was past that.

"We replaced him with the well respected chief executive officer of a closely held corporate group called Biomedical Products. Jerry Fox is about forty years old and came highly recommended by Mr. Riley.

"Percy Harrington resigned rather suddenly last year. He was another old friend of my father's, and he'd served as director for about fifteen years. Though a very passive voter, Mr. Harrington was on the board because he was well respected in the industry. Now that I think about it, I had the impression that he resigned under duress.

"He didn't seem very happy with his decision, although the official reason he gave for resigning from the board was that his company, Harrington Global Industries, needed more of his day-to-day attention.

"Mr. Riley was instrumental in promptly finding a replacement for him as well. He persuaded Henry Atwell to serve, at least as a temporary replacement, since Mr. Harrington left so abruptly. Atwell is the current chief operating officer of Brantley Chemical, where Riley is C.E.O. With his experience, Mr. Atwell seemed an obvious choice for the board."

20

I'm glad to finally get rid of those guys."
Fez had just unloaded Jeff and Aubrey. The powerful engine surged as he pulled out into open water and headed east. Although the thought had crossed his mind to take out those two men, he lacked the nerve. Fez was not accustomed to backing down. On the docks of Kuwait City, no one dared take the big man on. Since he first started taking jobs from Mr. Jones, he was exposed to many types of dangerous men. It was not their size or their muscle that emasculated him—it was their eyes. Death was to be found there. Fez was making more money now than he had ever dreamed of. He did not wish to die.

Kuwait City was his destination as he turned south around Bubiyan. He preferred open water, where there was little traffic and he could make better time. In the channel were fishing boats and any number of official vessels with mounted guns, whose captains might stop you on a whim just to offset their boredom. Mr. Jones would be waiting in his helicopter for the return of the TR-7. Only three days earlier he had delivered this same cargo to the two men from Abdali. Fez often wondered how Mr. Jones made any money this way.

Meanwhile, Mr. Jones was seated comfortably in his helicopter, having breakfast. He always had an assistant around to care for his every need.

His thoughts now were on Jeff and Aubrey, wondering if they had been able to accomplish their task and get out of there before the five o'clock deadline.

The meeting between Kafu and Al-Sufa was originally scheduled for five a.m. But Mr. Jones had discovered an unsettling bit of information. Somehow the drug lords of Umm Qasr had found out about the location and the time of the transaction. They were still searching for Kafu and Al-Sufa, not totally convinced of their deaths. The dealers fully intended to strike just before five, capturing the Americans and their money as well as those who trespassed on their territory without cutting them in on the action—namely Kafu and Al-Sufa.

Mr. Jones changed the meeting to midnight and instructed Jeff and Aubrey to finish the job and be gone well before five, filling them in on the Umm Qasr situation. Either way, Kafu and Al-Sufa were both dead men. He had insisted that the Kuwaitis pay him immediately upon delivery of the TR-7. The Americans would never pursue an operation without first confirming that the money had been deposited in their accounts. For this operation, Mr. Jones found it necessary to wire a million dollars to each account in advance. Jeff had insisted on this stipulation when he and Aubrey were briefed on the details of the mission in their hotel room in Abdali. Mr. Jones agreed because he could use Kafu and Al-Sufa's cash to pay his team, and not have any personal outlay. If the operation succeeded, he would even regain possession of his cargo. If not, he had at least managed to steal the passwords from the American's computer. If they reneged, failed or disappeared for any reason, especially if he acted quickly, he could transfer their payment back into his account.

The Americans had carried an empty briefcase to the site of the meeting. As a ruse, they gave the impression of carrying a valuable piece of luggage.

"How did they develop the nerve to ensconce themselves into such a potentially deadly situation without the cash to make the buy if there was no other way out," he mused out loud. "They must have developed inconceivable confidence in their abilities over the years."

Mr. Jones intended to resell the recovered product to the Umm Qasr people. This time he would allow the deal to be completed, letting them worry about breaking into the lucrative American market. He would still make an additional profit on the same material.

There was a roar off in the distance.

Fez came speeding across the bay. The helicopter was easy to spot from the sea. He eased as close as he could to the open door. Fez, plus the pilot and Jones' female assistant, reloaded the cargo onto the helicopter. There was almost a smile on Mr. Jones' crooked face as the TR-7 was again in his possession.

When Fez heard Mr. Jones say, "Go!" the rotors began to turn. Fez eased his boat out of the way just as the chopper lifted out of the water. Soon it banked inland and was gone from sight. Fez was left with the boat, without papers to be sure, but possession nonetheless as payment for his services. Soon he would run down the coast to Qasr, Kuwait, where he could pick up forged documents for the boat before he dared show it off to his friends at the Kuwait City docks.

21

Alberto was bringing the jet down just before they reached the west coast of Italy, looking for the hard-surfaced, private landing field just outside Amalfi. He came in low to avoid showing up on commercial radar. When he sighted the familiar runway just beyond the olive groves, he felt like he was home again. His car was parked behind the office. More importantly, he would be rid of these crude Americans. When Alberto announced that they were approaching their destination, Jeff and Aubrey quickly changed into sport jackets and slacks for their trip into Amalfi.

Serena usually completed her job by personally bidding her guests farewell. This time, however, she did not leave the pilot's cabin until the Americans disembarked and had driven away. Only then did she catch up with Alberto for the ride back to Amalfi. Alberto was counting out hundred dollar bills as she came alongside him.

"They were rough and vulgar, Serena. But like most of our customers, they pay well for the special services we offer."

He counted off two thousand dollars and put it in her hand, pocketing the rest.

Already recovering from her encounter with Aubrey, she decided that this job paid too well to quit over an impulse. She was already beginning to feel like the beautiful young flight attendant once again.

With her long hair combed over the right side of her face, she even compared herself to an old Hollywood photograph she had seen, one where the movie star had worn her hair that way all the time.

22

The morning briefing had gone smoothly. Neither Jeff nor Aubrey recognized the controller. This one was known only as Mr. Anderson. The Delta unit consisted of two of the operatives that they had anticipated, and one with whom they had never worked.

Aubrey and Jeff were operating as Delta One and Delta Two respectively. In order to safeguard the private lives of the operatives involved, no names were ever used. Delta Three and Delta Four had worked with them earlier. Mr. Anderson told everyone that this was the first mission for Delta Five. When it was an operative's first assignment, it was company policy to give that information to the other agents so they could be wary of him until he proved himself.

"We need to extract a package from the Shebaa Farms area in southern Lebanon. The package is a white male of Lebanese descent. His identification and description is included, along with a map that marks the exact farm building where you'll find him. Everyone will be airdropped just north of an area that's patrolled by the United Nations, a sector just north of the border with Israel.

"It's vitally important that you do not engage any U.N. personnel. It will be the responsibility of Deltas One and Two to make certain that you don't stray into their patrol area. This mission must be completed within two hours.

"You'll be delivered by Lear jet, a seven-passenger aircraft that has been modified for jumps. Extraction takes place exactly two hours later by a CH-53 Stallion helicopter, and you'll return to the flight deck of a carrier out in the Mediterranean. That's all. Delta One has the orders. Departure is at 0800 hours. Good luck, gentlemen."

"We have an hour and fifteen minutes," Jeff whispered to Aubrey.

"I'll take care of the files. You cover for me."

Jeff commandeered a Jeep for the short ride to the records office.

The briefing had been short, so he was able to arrive before the office was open. He slid his I.D. card into the slot to open the outer door. The inner door was both eye- and voice-activated. Jeff positioned his forehead so that his eyes fit into the slot. When the red light came on he said, "Jeffrey Lewis." The lock clicked. Granted such high-security clearance, he had anticipated no problems.

First he breezed through the alphabetical files, pulling out the ones for Jeffrey Lewis and Aubrey Long. Moving over to the computer, he selected the same files and deleted them. He then clicked on the desktop's "recycle bin" and permanently deleted just those two files.

He was not worried about leaving fingerprints. No one would suspect him of having been there. He returned the computer screen to its inactive status and, hiding the two paper files under his shirt, he exited the building. Jeff walked quickly to the rear of the building where the Jeep was parked, jumped in, and then drove out the opposite way he had entered the area.

Aboard the modified Lear jet, Aubrey and Jeff moved to the rear of the cabin as if to discuss their plans for the mission. That was where the sky phone jack was located. Hidden from view by the seat back, Aubrey plugged in his laptop. It was 1000 hours Eastern Time. After gaining access to the Internet he noticed that his message light was blinking, but first he checked their investment accounts. The money was there. They looked into each other's eyes.

Now they were committed.

Then the message…

I trust you have now planned for your separation from your present duties. Make your way to the town of Abdali, on the Kuwait–Iraq border. Do not let yourselves be recognized as Americans. It is of utmost importance that you are there by Friday morning. I will use this same address to reach you on Friday.

Suddenly they were millionaires. The realization seemed to hit them both at the same time. Quickly, Jeff logged back into their investment accounts again. This time they transferred the entire balance over to their Swiss accounts.

Stowing the laptop with the rest of his gear, Aubrey moved into position for the jump. Jeff followed close behind. It had taken them longer than expected to transact their business. Switching screens had been much slower than anticipated. They were already flying over the Eastern Mediterranean, approaching land.

It was close to 2400 hours Beirut time when they entered Lebanese air space. The copilot had started the countdown as he watched his monitor for the coordinates. On his signal, Jeff was the first to jump, then Deltas Three, Four and Five. Aubrey jumped last.

The first thirty seconds were in free fall to land the team as close as possible to each other. As Delta Two, Jeff was responsible for the timing. When he pulled his ripcord, each member did the same in one-second intervals. All five hit and rolled in a tight pattern.

After stowing their chutes, Deltas One, Two and Three formed a loose circle around Delta Five as he radioed their exact location to the copilot who, in turn, forwarded these coordinates to the helicopter pilot waiting aboard the carrier. Aubrey then planted a detection signal on a nearby tree limb, securing it with a clip.

Each man was equipped with a sensing device to find the location of the signal, and consequently the extraction point.

Delta One took the lead. Jeff and Aubrey had worked out their plan of separation on the flight over. Aubrey was intentionally drifting too far south so as to encounter the U.N. patrol. Their drop had been accurate. Aubrey discreetly glanced at his compass and veered southward.

"Look out," Jeff called out.

He suddenly fired his weapon in the direction of a patrol of about a dozen men. The alerted unit returned fire in unison, striking Deltas Three, Four and Five. Deltas One and Two had dropped back immediately after getting the attention of the patrol unit. Delta One fired additional rounds but, this time, he did it to make sure that the rest of his unit would not survive the attack. Having recognized the U.N. uniforms, Deltas Three, Four and Five were caught entirely by surprise when the patrol opened fire.

Jeff and Aubrey hastily retreated in the direction of the Shebaa Farms, heading northeast toward a new and different life.

* * *

Only three days earlier they had started off from the Shebaa Farms in southeastern Lebanon to pass through Syria. Somewhere in Lebanon they had found a farmer who at first agreed to drive them into the neighboring country in his little truck. But after a short test drive, the poor man's eyes lit up when he saw the stack of American dollars in the stranger's hand. Aubrey purchased the vehicle for much less than he had anticipated. With a detailed road map at hand, he guided Jeff just north of the Syrian side of the Golan Heights. The only straight road through Syria crossed into central Iraq.

From there they were able to take a better road southeast toward Al-Basrah. Wearing native attire, they covered their heads whenever they passed a pedestrian or another vehicle.

"What a hot and miserable trip."

Jeff was trying to take his turn at sleeping. They were forced to drive with all their windows down; otherwise they would have suffocated. But that presented no problem mechanically, since the only window that would close was the one behind the cab. That one had to be left open to let air flow through. But as the air came in, so did a great deal of sand. As they neared Abdali, Jeff took over the driving so that Aubrey could rest. Just short of the border they saw a sign that read, Abdali 75km. The locals remember Abdali Road as the highway of death.

On February 26 and 27, 1991, American jets attacked divisions of Iraqi soldiers fleeing along this road. By striking the lead vehicles, the road was blocked and the Iraqi army was immobilized, pounded by missiles, and ultimately destroyed.

All these years later there were still tanks everywhere, plus battered trucks and a few anti-aircraft guns. Nothing was worth salvaging, as the equipment awaited a cleanup that might never come.

The road cleared as they entered Kuwait. Shortly after crossing the border they were in Abdali, looking for anything that would serve as a place to stay.

It was near midday. On the main street they came upon a restaurant of sorts, with tables set outside. They decided to stop.

After living on army rations for three days, any real food was appreciated. They drove down a side street, removed their packs, and left the old truck to die a natural death.

Two men who were either Americans or Western Europeans occupied one table. Wearing white, short-sleeved shirts, khaki trousers and dust-covered boots, they had the tanned look of people who had been here a while.

Three men seated at a nearby table, most likely Kuwaiti locals, had stopped eating and were staring at them. Jeff and Aubrey selected the nearest table, carefully placed their gear beneath it, and took seats that faced the other diners. A young man approached them.

In nearly fluent English he asked, "Can I bring you something to drink, gentlemen?"

Jeff almost smiled to hear a language he could understand without an interpreter.

"Do you have American beer and hamburgers?"

He was merely probing to get the young man's response.

"Certainly, sir. For two—coming right up."

He disappeared inside the building. When he returned with two cold Budweisers, still capped, Aubrey and Jeff were relieved.

"Is there a hotel close by, some place we can get a room for the night?"

The young man pointed his finger directly down the street.

"Two blocks—American hotel chain—Best Western—managed by my older brother. Tell him O.K. sent you so he will pay me something. My first American customer called me that when I answered, 'O.K.,' when he requested a beer. Now, I am stuck with it."

Their burgers came on wheat bread. The bread was dry but the burger tasted good. They finished quickly, paid in American dollars, and were on their way. Jeff had tipped O.K. quite well, thinking they may need him again later. They made their way to the hotel.

"Good day, gentlemen. I am Ham Siran, the manager. How long will you be staying?"

"We had lunch down the street and our waiter, called O.K., recommended this hotel. We need a room for three nights, please."

Siran smiled at the reference to his very enterprising younger brother. "No problem, sir."

As Siran presented them with the key to their room, Aubrey asked, "Do you know a reputable automobile dealer here in Abdali?"

"Officially there is no dealership. My cousin has a few American cars for sale. I can have one delivered to you here, if you wish."

Siran's family seemed to have many business ties in Abdali.

Jeff was quick to respond.

"Do you think you could find a late model Jeep, not necessarily new, but in good running condition?"

"I will see what I can do, sir."

Siran appeared unfazed by the question.

"We need it within an hour, and we'll pay for that extra service."

They grabbed their bags and climbed the stairs to Room 204.

After locking the door behind them, Aubrey plugged in his laptop and tried to reach Mr. Jones. He kept the message simple.

In Abdali

As they assembled their gear and checked over what they would need, the computer beeped. Aubrey retrieved the message.

First, you need to find an average-size briefcase and stuff it with paper. Carry it with you to the meeting. Specific directions will follow at the end of this message. Two men will be waiting at this site with two trucks loaded with my product. These men have much experience in the drug business and will take every precaution. They are called Kafu and Al-Sufa. When you arrive, they will expect you to come directly down the road to the meeting site. They will have guards with them, several at least, as well as two drivers. No doubt all will be armed. Kafu and Al-Sufa will arrive separately from the trucks, as always in their new Cadillac Escalade. I do not care how it is achieved, but I need you to bring that material to my boat, the location of which is clearly marked on the attached map. One man will be on the boat. He will help you load it and drive you to a waiting plane at Warbah. This plane will take you back to Amalfi, Italy. The material will stay on the boat, and Fez will deliver it to me. The meeting is set for tonight at midnight. As you know, I have paid you in advance. Please do not let me down.

Both Jeff and Aubrey studied the map. It was simplified and started from the main street they were already on. The meeting site looked to be about a half hour to an hour's drive away. After making notes on a pad, Aubrey deleted the message.

There was a knock on the door. Siran was there with a key.

"The Jeep is out front. I hope it is satisfactory."

After starting it up and driving around the block, Jeff checked the fuel gauge. With a thumbs-up, Aubrey paid the man, surprised again at the low cost. It appeared that American dollars went a long way out here.

Having completed their plans, Jeff and Aubrey slept for a short while.

Then, at 2200 hours, they left the hotel.

23

Conner listened patiently while Ashley furnished him with an outline of the board members. Her animated dissertation, the inflections with her lips, the fire in her eyes, all combined to hold his attention.

Although he did not know this man, Conner managed to show adequate concern when Ashley mentioned that she was worried about her father's health. He had a partial blockage in one of his coronary arteries. The surgeon wanted to do a balloon angioplasty as soon as possible. Her father had no time in his busy schedule for this, although the doctor told him it could be done on an outpatient basis.

Ashley was not only concerned for her father's health. Mr. Riley was leading a campaign to replace him on the board for this selfsame issue and was already recommending replacements. Her father had told her it all was nonsense. The shares they owned, plus any reasonable number of publicly held voting shares, would continue to ensure them a voting majority.

She was not so sure.

"It seems that the other three directors are collaborating on most issues. They could swing a lot of votes. It would kill Dad if he no longer had his company to look after. He could never retire. All of his friends are still working, at least to some extent. In reality, he's not old enough, anyway. It only presents a problem because of his health.

"Over the past month I've had my secretary set up appointments to review the books of Brantley Chemical. Three separate times the appointments were cancelled at the last minute. Twice the financial officer was called out of town on emergencies. The third time, last Friday, I was told he was off sick and was asked if we could reschedule one more time.

"Conner, I'm certainly not worried about the financial stability of Brantley Chemical. Quite to the contrary, my only concern is to find applications they're employing that would translate over to our other divisions and help them do as well. Brantley's growth has been phenomenal over the past three years. Mr. Riley joined the fledgling company as C.E.O. six years ago. He attributes their success to a new fertilizer they developed four years ago. The company calls it TR-7, and demand has been phenomenal for this product over the past three years."

Conner had been listening intently, but everything Ashley had related seemed to indicate a well-run, successful business.

"Ashley, things seem to be going well at Jennings. I don't understand your concern, other than for your father's health."

"Although I don't have any concrete evidence to support my suspicions, my intuition tells me that, first, Anthony Riley is trying to take over the board of directors and, second, that he doesn't want me looking at Brantley Chemical's books.

"Conner, when I met you yesterday I saw compassion in your eyes and honest concern for me as a client. My secretary did a background check on your firm. When I approved the choice, she then performed a similar check on you personally. That's why I chose your firm for legal advise. I brought along a copy of the board minutes for the past year, plus a *Who's Who* synopsis of each member, including myself. I want you to study everything and advise me of the possibilities of a takeover of the board of directors by this Mr. Riley."

Conner was not sure whether Ashley had noticed his reaction when she finally spoke the full name of her alleged adversary—Anthony Riley.

Now Conner was really interested.

"This Anthony Riley," he began. "Is he handicapped, by any chance?"

Her eyes again took an active part in the conversation as they came to attention.

"How did you know?"

She had avoided mentioning the wheelchair to make certain Conner stayed focused on what she considered was the main problem.

"A man named Anthony Riley has been a very close friend of mine since high school. Admittedly, I haven't spoken to him in maybe the last ten years, but I've tried to reach him. At the time he was running the National Weather Service in Washington, D.C.

"He was considered something of a computer expert and had engineered new programs that advanced weather service technology decades ahead of expectations. He's an extremely intelligent individual and, with his handicap keeping him from a normal social life, seems to put all his time and energy into whatever task is at hand. Do you know anything about your Mr. Riley's background?"

"I've done some checking on him. He came from the National Weather Service directly to Brantley, so he must be your friend, this Anthony Riley.

"He's not unfriendly at all, although difficult to understand at times. The position of national director must have paid him well. The main reason he became C.E.O. at Brantley wasn't because of his management skills, but because he owned a majority share of their common stock."

She paused to let Conner absorb the connection.

Ashley Jennings could feel she was being watched, but each time she glanced over at Charlie Reynolds, the young man seemed to be intent on his case.

"Brantley Chemical is located in Cleveland, Ohio, and was quite small back when Riley was buying up shares, with a market cap under a million dollars. When he started with Brantley seven years ago, he put himself on the shareholders' ballot as chief executive officer, running against the slate the board had proposed. His shares, plus enough proxy votes from shareholders discontent with the lack of growth, got him elected.

"He must have been well qualified for the position. Within three years the company's net worth had doubled, so no one complained about his unusual tactics.

"Immediately, he set up a secure research lab with access available to only a select few. This lab has now tripled in size and is credited with the development of the TR-7 that I mentioned earlier. The laboratory's level of security is even more stringent today. Mr. Riley says it's necessary to protect our formulas from industrial espionage. I received a personally guided tour from Mr. Riley about six months ago. The research lab has apparently been converted into a manufacturing facility as well."

The story was becoming more intriguing. Since the mention of his friend, Anthony Riley, Conner's interest level had risen, and everything he heard since held his rapt attention.

"Ashley, is it O.K. with you if we break for lunch? You've been talking nonstop for two hours, and it looks like there's a lot more to this story. I've already jotted down quite a few questions.

"There's a nice restaurant right in the next block. We can walk over there and stretch our legs, if you approve."

24

Jeff and Aubrey grabbed their bags and hastily left the airfield.

A car was waiting to take them into Amalfi. They had reservations at a midrange hotel, one crowded with tourists so as to avoid drawing attention to themselves.

After they settled into their adjoining rooms, Jeff knocked on Aubrey's door. Finding it ajar, he walked in. Aubrey was expecting him.

"We have a few loose ends to take care of, Jeff. Let me itemize what I've come up with so far. First, we need to get these passport photos copied and notarized. Next, we need to take care of one more part of our past, those two JAG attorneys who represented us a long time ago. That file is incorporated into our special ops file.

"I've been reading through it. They undoubtedly would remember us and will be questioned in an attempt to rebuild our past, which we've been so carefully trying to erase. They definitely pose an obstacle. Do you have anything else?"

Jeff had been thinking as well.

"I agree that the first thing we need to do is gain access to our accounts in Switzerland. I think we should get those copies made and notarized as quickly as possible. Living in a place prearranged by someone we don't even know seems unacceptable to me. There'll be some very capable agents looking for us—perhaps they are already. The people who are going to affix the notary on our passport copies are also prepared to set us up with additional, high-quality aliases."

Aubrey acknowledged to himself that he apparently had not put enough thought into this. His mind kept going back to the numbered Swiss account with two million-plus dollars in his name. Up until about a week ago, he had saved a half million dollars through nine years of life-endangering work. Now his account held a cool two million. He did not dwell very long on the things they'd had to do to get where they were today.

Jeff continued.

"We have several I.D.s that we've used over the years, but those aren't good any more. Even with our files in our own hands, I believe they have means to trace that information. I suggest we have this contact prepare us three complete sets including passports, driver's licenses, and social security numbers that belonged to some dead guys who would have been about our ages.

"I don't feel comfortable here. We need to take care of this today, buy a car, leave without checking out, and drive to Bern overnight. From there we can fly somewhere else, maybe South America or the Caribbean."

Aubrey sensed danger as well.

"Let's go!"

They paid cash for the small Austin Healey that had taken them from the airfield to the hotel. Offered such a premium, the driver could not pass up the deal. He even threw in a full tank of petrol.

"The first step was too easy. Easy is always a reason to worry."

Jeff was always thinking.

They had directions to the print shop located in an old part of town, well away from tourists. When they told the old man that Alberto had sent them, he ushered them quickly into the back room. Although small, the shop appeared very efficient.

The camera was set up to face the rear wall. A mark on the floor told them where to stand.

Jeff went first. A click, a flash—and finished. Then it was Aubrey's turn. The old man wasted no time. He made a few notes of their requirements, set a price of five thousand American dollars, and told them to come back in an hour. They never had to furnish their authentic identification, but the man did have a photograph of them.

Aubrey spoke up.

"We'll wait here until you're ready."

He motioned for Jeff to watch the front door. Aubrey positioned himself by the rear window, where he could see out but no one from outside could see in.

The old man completed his work in record time. The mean one, the larger man, made him nervous.

After he showed the material to the two men, they paid him and started out the door. Aubrey turned back.

"Start the car. I'll be right there."

He returned to the back room. The old man had picked up the telephone.

"Put it down—now!"

Aubrey's tone was menacing.

He covered the distance between them so quickly that the old man did not even have time to replace the phone in its cradle. In a blur, Aubrey's weapon appeared and was brought down hard on the old man's head. The proprietor fell heavily to the floor. Aubrey pulled the pin on an incendiary grenade and tossed it into the center of the room. Rushing out the front door, he jumped into the passenger seat, motioning for Jeff to go. When they were a block away, the entire shop burst into flames. While it was not a loud explosion, it nonetheless attracted immediate attention. Looking in the car's rearview mirror Jeff could see smoke pouring out of the building's windows, plus people who had crowded into the street and were observing the scene from a safe distance.

"We needed to erase our past. I didn't trust that old man's eyes. He was phoning someone as I went back there. The pictures had to be eliminated. Let's head back to the hotel to collect our things, and we'll drive straight through to Bern."

Jeff remained silent, concentrating on his driving. He was well aware that they had to leave quickly. Gathering up their belongings, they used the back entrance where the car was parked. They left the hotel and headed north.

* * *

Jeff drove inland, east of Rome, to avoid heavy traffic within the city. North of the capital he again veered westward but stayed away from the coastal towns. Having passed through the provinces of Umbria, Tuscany and finally Lombardy, Switzerland lay just ahead.

Finding themselves this close to their money, both men were anxious to reach their destination. Although American driver's licenses were valid in Switzerland, Jeff maintained the speed limits as posted. They could ill afford to attract attention and leave some sort of trail, knowing with certainty that the men assigned to find them would have had the same training they received.

Both radar and automatic cameras monitored the heavily traveled Swiss roads. A photograph could prove fatal, yet another reason to stay within the speed limit.

The region of Schweizer Mittelland was near the center of the country. Bern is its capital, with a population of 122,484 citizens that oftentimes doubled at peak tourist seasons. Their objective was the Neuhaur National Bank of Switzerland at 1600 Neuhaur Boulevard, but first they needed a hotel to clean up and change clothes.

Looking at brochures, Aubrey chose the Allegro Hotel, a four-star establishment near the center of town. Disguised as visiting American tourists, they were able to obtain connecting rooms after flashing all the dwindling cash they had left. For a one-night stay, the tuxedoed concierge hardly flinched when Jeff announced that they would be paying in cash.

"That will come to eight hundred and fifty six dollars in U.S. currency, sir, as a total for both rooms for tonight only."

Aubrey was about to react when Jeff gently touched his arm.

"That will be fine, Mr. Degault."

Jeff had noticed the nameplate and was trying to be personable. He counted out the required amount and passed it over the counter to the manager, who had discreetly counted along with Jeff. The money disappeared into a drawer beneath the desk, and, just as quickly, the keys were presented to Jeff.

"Your keys, sir."

The manager cast a barely perceptible sideways glance at Aubrey. Evidently the concierge had noticed Aubrey's reaction to the price, which was a definite breach in protocol. Both men were trained not to call attention to themselves.

"Is there a shop in the hotel where we can buy clothing and accessories?"

With one more question to divert the manager's attention away from Aubrey, Jeff was being cautious. Mr. Degault motioned toward the corridor on the left.

"Just down that hallway, sir. Have a nice stay."

As they walked away from the desk, Jeff spoke softly.

"Do we have enough cash left to buy some better clothing, or do we have to hit the bank first?"

"We have enough cash for now, but I'll make a withdrawal when we get to Neuhaur, not only for additional cash, but to make sure the authorization is completed."

They returned to the car, which was still parked in front of the hotel. Taking their own bags in hand they tipped the bellman well just the same, with instructions to have the car back in front again at two p.m., about one hour and ten minutes hence.

After depositing their belongings in their rooms, Jeff and Aubrey proceeded to the shops where they each chose nondescript suits, casual wear, pairs of casual and dress shoes, and a piece of luggage for each of them.

They returned to their rooms for a shower and to change for their meeting at the bank.

25

Harden, this is Anderson. I have a problem."

"I'm at Lejeune right now, looking at recruits. I'll call you back within ten minutes."

This was standard operating procedure. Harden needed to go to a secure phone, as he had not brought a scrambler along with him on this trip.

Camp Lejeune is located in Onslow County, on the coastal plains of North Carolina. Harden was hoping to find five men with the right potential for recruiting. It mattered not to him if they came from the Marines with prior combat experience, or were raw recruits. A few minutes alone with them, and Harden would know if they were right for the job.

The base had furnished him with a Jeep and a driver for his brief stay.

"I need a secure phone, Tony."

Having been with him most of the day, Harden had insisted that they call each other by their first names only.

"Yes, sir—I mean, Mr. Kelly—I mean, Harden."

The powerful man overwhelmed the young Marine, who was somewhat puzzled by the attention Harden had commanded from the first moment he had entered the base.

With efficiency, Tony drove them to the II Marine Expeditionary Force command element.

"There are offices in this command center with secure phones, sir. I don't have clearance to enter, so I'll remain with the vehicle. They'll check your credentials at the door. Shall I wait for you, or come back in a bit?"

"Wait. This may only take five minutes."

Harden, of course, had no idea exactly how long he would be. After providing his clearance card and identification at the front desk, Harden was shown to a small, soundproof room.

"The red phone is the secure one, sir. Please use the gray phone for any other purpose."

The guard closed the door.

Immediately dialing Anderson's number, the phone was picked up before the second ring.

"Hard, I need you and another man to go on a special mission for me right away. We have casualties. How fast can you get back to Rosslyn?"

"I can probably get a chopper. It'll take me about two hours."

"Do it. I'll be in Building Q. Just ask at the desk as you come in."

* * *

As Jeff drove their car away from the hotel, they turned west onto the expressway and headed north. Neuhaur was the second exit. The address of the bank was 1600 Neuhaur Boulevard.

"Aubrey, when we turn onto Neuhaur, see if you can read an address right away to make sure we're going in the proper direction."

They had packed all their belongings before leaving the Allegro, so no return would be necessary. Aubrey grumbled about paying out all that money for rooms and not even spending the night. Nonetheless, he knew Jeff was right. They had to move to a safer place.

"Here's a '1906,' and the next one is '1908.' The bank will be on our left after we turn around. We have to go back about three blocks."

Careful to obey traffic signals, Jeff made three left turns before making a right turn back onto Neuhaur. Apparently, the financial district of Bern lay just west of the expressway along this street. Stately buildings, dating from the 1920s and 1930s, occupied entire blocks. The Neuhaur National Bank of Switzerland was no exception. Ornate but solid and built like a fortress, the building commanded considerable respect.

The parking garage in the rear loomed over the top floors of the bank building itself. The modern parking facility looked out of place among these ancient giants. Well-engineered access soon had them standing in the lobby of the facility. The receptionist spoke fluent English.

"My name is Elizabeth, gentlemen. What service may we offer you today?"

Jeff had been silently elected their spokesman.

"We would like access to our accounts, miss. This is our first opportunity to visit your facility, and we do not yet have the name of the person assigned to handle this for us."

"If you will both complete a brief access form, showing your account numbers and signing the form the same as when you opened the accounts, I will have the appropriate account manager here promptly."

Their account numbers had been memorized, yet another skill acquired through special ops training. Elizabeth asked them to be seated as she inserted the forms, one at a time, into a slot in the computer that occupied one side of her desk. This transpired so fast that she had no time to read the names or numbers on the paper as they passed through her hands into the slot.

After they were seated, Aubrey quietly expressed his observation to Jeff.

"That must be standard procedure for privacy. Elizabeth didn't even look at the forms before feeding them into that transmitter. I like that. These banks are established mainly on their privacy guarantees."

"Gentlemen, my name is Jon Heydn. Would you follow me to my office right down this corridor?"

The smartly dressed manager led the way—first left, than right, and left again as they followed him into his office.

"All that is missing to complete your accounts are the notarized passport photographs. Do you have those with you?"

Both Jeff and Aubrey produced the properly notarized documents. Mr. Heydn slid both items into a slot similar to the one the receptionist had used. He typed instructions on the keyboard and then turned toward his customers.

"May I offer you refreshments, Mr. Lewis and Mr. Long, while we wait for your authorizations to print out? If you gentlemen plan to spend some time in our city, I highly recommend taking the short ride on Sustenpass Road, with scenery you will not find anywhere else in the world."

Mr. Heydn is fishing to see if we're tourists or on a business trip, Jeff and Aubrey each thought silently. Before they could respond, the printer spit out two sheets of paper. Heydn removed them from the tray and affixed his signature and seal to the bottom of each.

"Gentlemen, whoever presents these letters upon entering our bank will have access to the accounts indicated, without any question."

He folded the letterhead stationary twice and inserted them into Neuhaur Bank envelopes, making certain to give each to the proper client.

"I want to be certain that you understand that this letter is a key to unlocking your account. Please afford the letter the security that is warranted. Of course, your password will still give you access. Are there any other services I may offer this afternoon?"

Both Jeff and Aubrey had agreed that two hundred thousand dollars in U.S. currency would suffice. The next few days would be very expensive ones for them. Within thirty minutes, Heydn presented them with the cash in identical bundles, one hundred each of one-, five-, ten- and twenty-dollar bills. The balance was in bundles of hundred dollar bills.

The manager offered each man a plain, dark brown briefcase in which to carry his funds. No emblem or name afforded advertisement.

"Thank you for your assistance, Mr. Heydn. We'll be in touch."

Back in the car, they were on their way to the airport and the Caribbean islands.

* * *

As the helicopter set down on the tarmac just outside a row of stone-and-brick buildings, Harden exited, ducking his head as he rushed toward Building Q.

While he was still presenting his identification, Mr. Anderson appeared from one of the offices and motioned for him to come in.

They shook hands warmly as they entered the room. Harden had gained Mr. Anderson's respect over the years, like no other operative. Even after all this time, Harden knew no other name for Mr. Anderson and nothing of his private life. Trust and honor was their bond.

Anderson closed the door. The conference room included an oval-shaped oak table, covered with a smooth clear varnish that allowed the grain to shine through. Surrounded by twelve chairs, none was occupied. Harden noticed five file jackets on the table at the spot where Anderson was sitting.

"Harden, this room is soundproof and clean."

The building was swept electronically every morning to ensure privacy.

"Sit over here. I have some files to show you. On Monday, around dawn, I'd arranged for an extraction from the Shebaa Farms area in southeastern Lebanon."

Harden knew the area well. There was always cause for activity in southern Lebanon.

"The United Nations has a force of border guards all along that frontier with Israel. Were they involved?"

"Harden, let me give you the whole picture. Interrupt me if there are any questions. Two of our best ops, Jeff Lewis and Aubrey Long, were in charge. When we use one of these men, we always use both. They complement each other unerringly. They had three men along for assistance, as they would most certainly be needed.

"The package they were to extract was being held in a farmhouse in the Shebaa area. Lewis and Long had the exact coordinates. Since his captors could not have been aware of our plans, we feel this package was probably lightly guarded. We don't think his Muslim captors even know of his true identity. The man is a member of Israeli intelligence and has been undercover for more than a year, trying to identify any pockets of terrorists located near their border. The latest group that he infiltrated became suspicious and is holding him under house arrest, more or less, until someone arrives to question him. That's why we needed to extract him as quickly as possible.

"All five men were dropped exactly as arranged, and the location device was set at the pickup coordinates for exactly two hours from entry. We sent a CH-53 Stallion helicopter to pick them up.

"The site was empty. Our pilot landed and removed the locator device as instructed, waited as long as he could, and then returned to the carrier empty-handed.

"Even before the helicopter was to make the pickup, I received a call from Jenkins over in the Defense Department. The U.N. forces had an encounter in their zone just south of the Shebaa Farms area. Shots were fired at their ten-man unit that routinely patrols the area. They were outside their vehicles taking a smoke break. Some of the incoming fire hit their vehicles, although no personnel were hit. They returned fire. These men were not experienced in engagement, having been activated mostly from homeland reserve units. Their response was no doubt excessive, killing three of their attackers."

Harden knew that he needed to hear all the details from Anderson, but he could see ahead to where this narrative was going.

"These so-called attackers were our extraction team, far off course to the south of the designated area. They didn't belong anywhere near the zone being patrolled by U.N. personnel. Both Lewis and Long were too experienced for that. This was not an accidental occurrence.

"Deltas Three, Four and Five were dead at the scene with multiple wounds. Deltas One and Two managed to escape the area and have subsequently disappeared. The extraction obviously failed.

"Though it may be more dangerous now than the first attempt yesterday morning, I need you to get this man out quickly. Then I must ask you to take on the assignment of finding Lewis and Long. This separation was apparently well planned. These men have too much information, and they must be found regardless of the cost. Two rounds in each of our Delta agents were fired from close range.

"Lewis and Long are now wanted for questioning as possible murderers. They evidently have a different agenda to have used such desperate measures for their disappearance.

"Harden, here are the file jackets on all five men. You'll find that the jackets on the missing agents are new, containing only a copy of their latest operating orders for the extraction. Whatever these two men did was coldly calculated in advance, including the removal of their complete histories from our files.

"Requisition whatever equipment you need, select an agent to assist you, and be ready to leave promptly at 2100 hours tonight. You're the only one I trust to accomplish this mission, Harden. Be careful. You're like a son to me. I know I've never discussed it before, but since our first meeting up there in Kentucky, you became the son I never had. My wife died of cancer fifteen years ago, so my life has pretty much been the company. You're probably not aware of it, but I've watched you grow in our organization to become, in my opinion, our best operative. Good luck, son!"

As always, Anderson left as soon as he was finished with his briefing, leaving Harden to study the files and prepare for the mission.

26

Before exiting the Allegra Hotel for their meeting at the bank, Lewis had made reservations on a flight to Roseau on the Caribbean island of Dominica. Having already paid for the hotel, they had no intention of returning there and instead drove directly to the airport from the Neuhaur National Bank.

Flughafen Bern-Belp, the Bern airport, is located a few kilometers outside the city. Built in 1929, the airport handles some 220,000 passengers per year. This number is low because most travelers to Switzerland fly into the Zurich or Geneva airports.

Jeff approached the airline ticket counter, his eyes taking in every person in the area. They were booked nonstop to San Juan, Puerto Rico, connecting there to Roseau, Dominica. The flight to San Juan was twenty hours long and would afford them some much-needed sleep. Getting to Roseau was going to cost them about three thousand dollars apiece, but they had wanted to stay relatively close to the United States while planning their next move. Stepping up to the counter, Jeff and Aubrey had broken the terminal into sectors, again working as a team on surveillance of the area.

"We have reservations on Flight 3655 and would like to pick up our tickets, please?"

Jeff had been through enough pressure situations to maintain an outward casualness.

"The names are Alan Friedman and James Zachary."

This was the first of their new identities.

"May I see your passports, please?"

Obviously of German descent the young lady was stoutly built, with a stern but outwardly courteous demeanor. As the passports were quickly observed and stamped, she continued.

"That will be $2,785.50 for each ticket, including the connection into Roseau—in U.S. dollars, of course."

Both Jeff and Aubrey had arranged their currency so as not to be conspicuous. Quickly removing their billfolds from their jacket pockets, they each counted out the correct amount and presented payment to the young lady.

"I am sorry, gentlemen."

Both men came to attention.

"I will have to give you change in Swiss coins. I do not have any American coins in my drawer."

Nearly letting out a sigh of relief at hearing this, both men spoke in unison.

"That's fine, miss."

The attendant returned their passports along with their tickets and change. They still had plenty of time to stop for dinner at the airport restaurant before boarding.

Two hours later, as they presented their boarding passes to the gate attendant, Aubrey and Jeff let their eyes sweep over the two security personnel on either side as they entered the boarding ramp. They had mutually agreed to sleep in four-hour shifts as a precautionary measure. Aubrey was somewhat dubious of the necessity for this arrangement, but Jeff's careful nature certainly had proved worthwhile to them in the past.

* * *

Harden figured that he would be traveling to multiple locations in following the trail of operatives Jeff and Aubrey. The best way to remain inconspicuous was to play the part of a tourist. Harden had told himself that this was the main reason he had chosen Sam Chandler as his assistant on this project.

Sam Chandler had been in special ops for almost five years, working closely with Harden on two previous assignments. Although all of her friends and coworkers called her Sam, Samantha Chandler was far from masculine in appearance. Her lithe model's body and long brown hair disguised the ferocity with which she had made her way through the academics as well as physical training required to become part of this elite corps.

Even though Harden generally preferred activity to conversation, on their last mission together Samantha had intrigued him to the point where he felt very much at ease with her. Their verbal exchanges lasted long into the evening.

After saying goodnight, they would retire to their own beds. The night before they were to depart, their mission completed, Samantha opened the door to their adjoining rooms and slipped through. Harden was still standing beside the bed. Although they had never kissed, Harden felt his heart swell when he saw the beautiful apparition in his doorway. Without a word he met her as she entered, wrapping his huge arms around her. Their lips met—long, deep and passionate. As he slid the straps from her shoulders, the flimsy nightgown slid to the floor. Lifting her as tenderly as he could he whispered, "I love you," as they crossed the room.

That was nearly a month ago. Harden had not been able to see her since their arrival back in Rosslyn. Anderson tied him up with the selection of new recruits, grooming him for a controller's position. Without Harden's knowledge, Anderson was intentionally diverting him from additional contact with Sam. With the experience required to achieve the position he held, Anderson missed very little of the nuances of his protégés.

When Harden announced his choice of associate for this operation, Anderson studied his eyes long and hard. He agreed in principle that playing the part of a happy tourist couple would serve as an excellent disguise for traveling from place to place in search of Jeff and Aubrey.

Chandler had shown she could hold her own whenever weapons were required, and she was highly observant of even the tiniest of details.

Harden and Sam were ready to leave at 2100 hours. Their flight differed little from that of the original mission. Their immediate objective was to extract the package and return it to safe ground aboard the carrier.

They jumped together, locking one hand in the other's belt, free-falling for thirty seconds in an attempt to land as close together as possible. The drop zone was the same as for Delta force. After marking the site with a locator module, they headed east. With compass in hand, Harden realized that it would be nearly impossible for a trained operative to go off course as much as the previous mission had managed to do.

"It had to be intentional," he said under his breath.

Making good time, they approached the target house in the Shebaa Farms area. They observed the scene from a safe distance to get an accurate body count. As they watched, three men exited the building and jumped into a nearby Jeep, driving off to the northwest.

"Now's the time, Sam. I'll go in through the front and cover the left side. You cover the rear and the right side."

Harden was moving before he had finished speaking. With very little vegetation for cover, they had to depend on stealth and surprise for their advantage.

There was one man leaning against the front of the house, his weapon propped against the doorframe. Suddenly Harden was on him, kicking the gun aside and pushing the man through the doorway. Down a short hallway into the kitchen they went, the frightened man braced in front of Harden in the event of gunfire.

Three men sat at the table. At the same time Harden was shoving the entry guard aside and disarming the man closest to him, Sam had pushed through the rear door to grab and disarm the second man. While Sam covered the three terrorists with her weapon, Harden tied each to a chair as comfortably but as securely as possible.

"We're going to get you out of here."

Sam cut the bonds on the Israeli agent's hands and feet and helped him to a standing position. Harden was busily running a line around the table legs, binding each man together and then to the table.

Harden and Sam cleared the room of weapons and communication devices before leaving.

"Let's get out of here before that Jeep comes back."

To this point there had been neither gunfire nor bloodshed. Harden wanted to make sure it stayed that way.

The package was still in good shape. The three of them made it back to the extraction point in thirty-five minutes, with fifteen minutes to spare before the helicopter would arrive.

"Thanks! My name is Axel Grabl. Back in my unit they'd changed it to Axle Grease. I've been traveling with those men for six months, but somehow they became suspicious of me over the last two weeks, putting me more or less under house arrest just last week. The rope was there just to keep me immobilized. They still didn't know who I was. Since my position with them was that I didn't know what they were talking about, somebody from north of here was to arrive tomorrow morning. I'm certainly glad you got here today. I may not have been alive this time tomorrow."

The Stallion helicopter appeared overhead. After boarding, Harden instructed the pilot to drop them at the regional U.N. headquarters, located on the border of Lebanon and Israel, after which the extracted Israeli agent could be delivered to the carrier for debriefing.

27

Mr. Anderson had previously contacted the United Nations in New York City to coordinate Harden's arrival at the Israel–Lebanon border. After disembarking the helicopter, Harden and Sam gathered all their gear and luggage, bade farewell to Axel, and followed in behind the second lieutenant to the headquarters building.

This building was also a farmhouse. In exchange for using the facility for an indefinite period of time, the United Nations had made repairs and a large addition to the building for sleeping quarters for the men who patrolled the border. The owners were quite old and only farmed a small garden for their own use. They continued to live in their own bedroom and had full access to their original home, but not to the additions. The United Nations had made a generous offer to the couple to buy their property, but the old man insisted that they had nowhere else to go. The couple simply wanted to live out their days on their own familiar property. The commander of the unit worked out a comfortable lease arrangement instead of displacing the couple.

The commander was fluent in English and cordial with his greeting.

"We were notified that you were coming, and deeply regret the circumstances. I want to take you over to the site. On the way I will tell you our version of the incident."

A driver was waiting with a four-passenger Jeep, missing its top but fairly new. With their belongings locked securely in the office, Harden and Sam took the two rear seats. The commander turned around and hooked his left arm over his seat to update them on the situation.

"We had a patrol of ten men in the area when they came under fire. Having no previous exposure to life-threatening situations except through training, they returned fire, probably excessively.

"After the original burst of gunfire from the north, there were only a few more shots fired from that direction. None of our men was hit. The corporal in charge of the unit reported seeing five men similarly dressed and well armed. When our men made their way to the point of fire, three bullet-riddled bodies were found in the sand. The strange part was that none of their weapons had been fired. We found tracks of two more men, heading northeast."

By now the Jeep had arrived at the site of the incident.

"Where were the bodies of the Americans when you found them?"

Harden wanted to get a fix on how far off course the original expedition had been.

The area had been staked and circled with yellow tape so as not to be disturbed. Indentations and bloodstains marked the placement of the three bodies, long since removed. Harden calculated that they were about a mile south of the southernmost point of their trek toward the Shebaa Farms area. They would have had to drift directly south from their drop zone in order to be in the U.N. zone. Adding to the confusion was the question of what prompted them to open fire at the patrol in the first place. Harden already knew that these questions would only be answered once they caught up with Jeff and Aubrey. Their departure had obviously been planned well in advance of the mission.

"Our men pursued, but we cannot go beyond our authorized zone."

The commander was looking for answers as well.

"I'd like to follow this trail a little farther," Harden said. "Can you have some transport here to take us back to your office in an hour or two?"

"I will arrange that for you. Good luck with your search. I must remind you that southern Lebanon is home to many terrorists, and your journey could be an extremely dangerous one."

Thanking the commander, Harden and Sam started off to the northeast, again toward the Shebaa Farms area.

* * *

Their journey took them about a mile south of the farmhouse where the extraction had taken place.

"Sam, those guys could be looking for us by now, so keep your eyes open and your weapon ready. It's doubtful that the Jeep has returned yet, but its better to be prepared."

The first farm yielded only a terrified young Lebanese couple. The place was well kept and the fields evidently cultivated. This man had no time to till so much land and still be involved in terrorist activity. They moved on eastward.

At the second farm, only a small portion of the land was cultivated. A bearded old man opened the door, smiling and cordial, happy to have someone to talk to.

"I speak good English, gentlemen."

Sam had her hair stuffed inside her beret, with no makeup on her face. Without even being asked, he continued.

"Are you looking for the two men who came through here a few days ago? They gave me many American dollars for my old truck. They were dressed like you."

"Two questions, please. First, do you know in which direction they were headed and, second, can you describe the truck for us?"

"They asked me for a map. When I had none, they asked about the best road to Kuwait. There is only one main road. It passes just north of the Golan Heights and across Syria. Then the road continues through Iraq but drops south to the Persian Gulf.

"My old truck knows the way. When I was younger, the businessmen in Umm Qasr paid me generously for picking up and delivering packages along this road. My truck is about thirty years old, rusted through in many places, red in color, with no windows in the sides at all."

The old man liked to talk.

Thanking him with a hundred dollar bill, Harden and Sam started back west, and then south to meet up with the U.N. patrol.

"We can pick up some time on them if we fly to Kuwait and start talking to people in Abdali, right on the border with Iraq."

Harden was quite familiar with geography in the Mideast.

"We have to assume nefarious motives, in which case they'll have arranged for several new identities. Are you familiar with any establishment capable of doing this around Abdali?"

Sam was trying to put herself into that situation. There was a picture in each file, recently taken, or it would be missing like the original files.

The Jeep was ready to drive them south to U.N. headquarters. The commander was waiting.

"Did you find anything? We would like to close out this incident."

"I can assure you that the press will not become aware of anything from our end," Harden said. "Can you give us the same assurances?"

"The press has not shown any interest in this zone for a very long time now. We will try to keep it quiet, but our men are not prisoners. They will write letters and use telephones to communicate with their families."

"Lieutenant, do you have any way to get us to Haifa quickly?"

As Sam had pointed out, they could pick up several days on Jeff and Aubrey by flying directly to Kuwait.

"One of our helicopters delivers mail each afternoon to our information officer. This mail is addressed to a post office box that is coded for delivery to Haifa. There it is sorted and delivered to three different headquarters buildings along this border.

"Men travel on leave by way of this chopper. I am sure that I can arrange to have you dropped off in Haifa as well. Do you wish to leave today?"

Since neither he nor Sam had unpacked anything as yet, they were ready to go.

"That would be great. While we're waiting, do you have anything else from the site of the incident, or have you sent everything back to Rosslyn already?"

"Everything was returned with the casualties. I will alert the helicopter pilot that we have two passengers for Haifa."

The lieutenant proved to be very efficient.

"I want to make flight reservations from Haifa. Can you get me a connection to the Haifa airport?"

Time was not on their side. They needed to cut into the time differential between Jeff and Aubrey and themselves.

"Mr. Kelly, HFA will probably have connecting flights to your destination, but our helicopter lands on a helipad at the post office there. The mail is delivered to Haifa the same way from aircraft carriers stationed in the Mediterranean."

This improved the situation.

"Do you have a secure room where I can make a call to the States?"

The commander led Harden and Sam to a closet-sized room in the rear. After the door was closed, Harden picked up the phone and dialed Anderson's number. The call was answered on the second ring.

"Anderson."

This was a signal recording that indicated the call had been received and the number recorded. Harden hung up the phone.

"Now, all we have to do is wait."

Before Harden could reach for a cup of coffee, the phone rang.

28

The 747 descended slowly into the sunset that cast its fading light on the sprawling beaches of San Juan. The jet glided effortlessly onto the runway with only a slight ripple to announce that they were on solid ground again. Jeff and Aubrey would have to spend the night, since their departure to Roseau, Dominica, was not scheduled until 0900 the next day.

Collecting their luggage, Jeff and Aubrey found the exit to the taxi stand and were immediately accosted by an ambitious driver.

"Let me take your bags, gentlemen. Where would you like to go?"

"Ritz-Carlton, please."

Jeff had made the reservation on the expedia.com Web site before leaving Switzerland.

Just two miles from the airport, the Ritz-Carlton hotel is located on the Atlantic coast, facing the white sands of Isla Verde beach.

Using the assumed identities of Alan Friedman and James Zachary, both Jeff and Aubrey were graciously received and ushered to their rooms.

"As soon as I check out the room, I'm going over to the spa for a Javanese lulur treatment and see what else they have to offer. I'm tight as a drum. Remember, we have to get back to the airport in time for that early flight, 'Jim.'"

Jeff could move in and out of identities like a movie actor, but he was just reminding Aubrey to call him by his assumed name while they were here.

"I'm going to shower and then try my luck at the casino, 'Alan.'"

Aubrey had decided to play along. When the people looking for them got close enough, their rooms would not even be safe for open conversation.

"Give me a call in the morning."

Not bothering to unpack for one night, Aubrey went directly to the bathroom for a shower.

"We'll have to come back here when we have more time. This is nice," he mused.

Finished completely in marble, there was also a telephone, a separate vanity area, terrycloth robes, and even a scale for the health-conscious or -curious.

Jeff was lying on the table, face down in the padded opening, enjoying the luxurious oiling and massaging.

What a blind and vulnerable position, he thought to himself. After spending his life avoiding just such a situation, he found himself unguarded and unable to reconnoiter his surroundings—and Aubrey was nowhere around.

Soon the sweet-smelling oil and the firm but gentle movement of the hands on his back relaxed him enough to start plotting their next move.

We need to review our files, memorize what's important, and then destroy all the documents and the folders without a trace. Robinson and Hayes will have to be dealt with. Also, we need to find out the identity of Mr. Jones for future stability and trust regarding additional opportunities. There's apparently exceptional cash flow involved.

Jeff's training had led his mind to enumerate all the possibilities and then plan countermeasures commensurate with each situation.

Aubrey entered the casino cautiously, casually observing the patrons to see if anyone showed any special interest in him. Under the circumstances, he realized more than ever how much he appreciated having Jeff at his back.

No way anyone could be on us this quickly, he thought.

Easily convincing himself, Aubrey moved over to the roulette table.

"Let me have a thousand in hundreds, please."

Aubrey laid out ten hundred-dollar bills.

"Good luck, sir."

Ten black chips were in front of him in an instant. Glancing at the black wheel that showed only a single green zero, Aubrey was relieved to see that the casino was using the European wheel. This significantly improved a player's odds.

Although there were a number of bets in roulette that offered even-money odds, Aubrey had always preferred the simplest one—red or black.

Putting the first chip on black, he began to deploy his system. In the past, this self-devised process had rewarded him both in return and self-appraisal. Betting one chip at a time until one color came up three times in a row, he would double his bet on the alternate color for the next spin. Fearing others might copy his system, thus leading to its failure, he had never revealed this method to anyone, not even Jeff. After two and a half hours of drinking and betting, he collected thirty-two black chips, flipping one back across to the croupier.

His pockets bulging with an extra two thousand dollars, he returned to his room for a good night's sleep. The next morning he met Jeff at the shuttle that took them and their luggage back to the airport for the one-hour flight to Roseau.

* * *

"Anderson, it's Harden. What's your analysis?"

"We received the package and it has been delivered to its owner. Nice job! Tell Sam. Now, fill me in."

"Sam and I have traced them as far as we can. We've got information that leads us to believe they drove through Syria and Iraq to Kuwait. We can hop the mail delivery chopper from here to its base carrier in the Mediterranean tomorrow morning. Can you arrange to have a jet deliver us to our air base outside Kuwait City? We could probably pick up a couple of days on them if we make this happen sometime in the afternoon."

Harden could not hide the urgency he felt.

"The carrier is the Intrepid CV-11. They'll be expecting you and Sam, fueled and ready to go. Find those two, Harden, alive if possible. We could certainly use some debriefing on this incident."

"Thank you, sir. We'll do our best."

As usual the phone went dead before he finished. Harden had been associated with Mr. Anderson long enough to know how deeply he cared for the operatives directly under his control, but still he was caught off guard with the brusqueness of Anderson's conversation.

Opening the office door, Harden found the commander waiting for him.

"We need to take that flight back with the chopper, all the way to the carrier tomorrow morning."

The commander showed them to two rooms for the night. After a restless sleep, they both freshened up and made their way through the U.N. breakfast line in order to be ready for an early flight.

"You're in luck, Mr. Kelly. The pilot has already landed here. While he makes his delivery to our troop information officer, the unit is being refueled for the return flight. You only have a few minutes before takeoff. Gather your things, and I'll get you both over there forthwith."

Harden could barely believe their good fortune, the way things were working out in regard to time. They should pick up three or four days on Jeff and Aubrey by taking a jet straight to Kuwait.

"Sam, we'll get some kind of transportation once we land in Kuwait, so we can drive directly to Abdali. We need to find some connection on that end while the trail is still fresh."

"Let's go, gentlemen."

Sam again had on a cap, and they were both wearing the same jumpsuits convenient for military operations.

Out of the Jeep and into the chopper, they were airborne within minutes.

"I understand that I'm to deliver both of you to my home base as quickly as possible. Therefore, I'll fly directly to the Intrepid before returning to Haifa."

116

With that news, Harden and Sam settled back in their seats to plan their next move.

* * *

Jeff and Aubrey again purchased a Jeep, their vehicle of preference, upon arriving in Roseau, Dominica. The small dealership was just beyond the airport. Aubrey had spotted it while the shuttle was delivering them to the Fort Young Hotel.

They were able to claim their rooms early. Both men unpacked and met for lunch at Mango's Bar and Restaurant to discuss their plan of operation. Jeff lunched on Cajun lobster étoufée while Aubrey favored the "mountain chicken," as it was called on this small Caribbean island. These were actually frog legs, Cajun-seasoned and served over rice.

"We need to find a local who knows his way around. I feel naked without some kind of weapon," Aubrey said by way of introducing this topic.

"There's a roadside stand called Corona's near Pont Casse, a few miles from here," he continued. "We can start there and see what develops. I suggest we go this afternoon, right after lunch. We need to take care of a few things before we can relax.

"I want to wrap up the Robinson piece of history, and I have another idea for Hayes. When we find a guy with weapons for sale, he'll probably have another product of interest to us."

Finishing lunch, Jeff and Aubrey climbed into the four-wheel-drive Jeep and headed inland.

At the foot of the mountains they came upon Corona's, just one of the many roadside stands throughout the mountainous area of Dominica. They both purchased small rum drinks and played the part of tourists, browsing through the merchandise—coconut and aloe body creams, fresh grapefruit and oranges, and handcrafted jewelry made from beads and shells.

"I wonder if you gentlemen would be interested in seeing some finer jewelry?"

Tall, lanky and dark complected, the man in the rumpled white suit approached them suddenly from the side of the stand.

Having already circled around Jeff's other side to keep the stranger between them, Aubrey finished the rest of his drink, tossed the cup into a trash container, and froze the man with a glare of steel.

"You may have something of interest to us. Please lead the way."

"My name is Miguel, and my more extensive inventory is in the back."

He broke the tension of Aubrey's unblinking eyes with a wide, toothy grin. He could smell opportunity here.

About a block behind the stand was a rather large warehouse, about the size of a convenience store but without any windows. Aubrey noticed the stainless-steel-wrapped padlock at once. Without a rod to cut, this would deter any but the most diligent of thieves. Miguel slipped a key into the lock, removed it from its hasp, and opened the door. They entered a hallway that ran the length of the building, a dozen doors on each side, all locked with the same kind of padlocks.

"As you can see, gentlemen, I have a wide assortment of merchandise. Are your interests strictly in fine jewelry, or may I offer a more personal service to you, perhaps some equipment for self-protection or for hunting?"

Since they had left the crowd of tourists at the stand in front, the man could speak freely without danger of being overheard. If he had misjudged his customers, they would simply leave.

Jeff spoke this time.

"We'd each like a handgun for protection. We're looking to go deeper into the mountains and want to feel safe."

Miguel looked at the two men. They seemed an unlikely pair. The man with the intense eyes continued to watch him closely while the other man was speaking.

"I believe I can help you. That storage room is down the hall, near the far end."

Miguel led the way. He could feel their eyes on his back but did not hear them following him. Walking noiselessly was another tool of the trade in which they both excelled.

The room revealed case after case of all sorts of weapons, from .22 pistols to German-made assault rifles.

"This guy obviously has bigger customers than that handful of tourists out front," Aubrey whispered to Jeff, receiving a prompt acknowledging nod of the head.

Both Jeff and Aubrey immediately chose the Walther WA-2000, which had shown such accuracy on their mission in Kuwait. In addition to the rifle, they each selected a handgun. Jeff preferred the feel of a Glock, while Aubrey hefted a Wilson combat CQB .45 ACP and immediately liked the way it felt.

"There is one other piece of information that we need. Maybe you can help us."

Jeff was loading the Glock with a fresh clip as he spoke, letting Miguel notice the ease with which he handled the weapon.

"When we were in South America, we learned of natives who used curare poison on darts for hunting, and against their enemies. I understand that you have a similar product here called kurari, used as a tranquilizing medication. I wish to purchase a quantity of the original, preprocessed poison."

His Glock lay balanced in his hand, the barrel pointing in the vicinity of a now nervous Miguel.

"Now gentlemen, that product is tightly controlled, all the way from the plant to the factory. I cannot afford to be caught trafficking in such an illegal substance."

Miguel believed Jeff to be the milder of the two men. He changed his mind quickly as Jeff was in his face in an instant, a hand around his tie and shirtfront.

"This entire warehouse is illegal. Cut the bullshit. Either tell me where I can get this product, or sell it to me yourself."

"F-f-f-follow me."

Miguel was not as glib as his original salesmanship had indicated. Jeff eased his fist off the man's shirt and exerted a slight push as Miguel went to the back of the room. Rolling a display case of hunting rifles aside, he put one knee to the floor. After brushing aside a thin layer of dirt, he put his finger through a recessed ring and pulled a metal cover aside. Lifting a glass case from the opening, he set it on the display case.

"I have a small selection of kurari and some delivery darts. From a short distance you do not need the blowgun. A drinking straw will suffice.

Kurari is an aqueous extract from the vine Strychnos toxifera. The drug results in almost immediate immobility and respiratory arrest. If administered in its purest form, death will occur within minutes."

Miguel acquired the powder from local natives who still lived in the inland jungles. Their village was located at the foot of the mountains that made up the interior of the island.

"I want the blend that's strong enough to kill a man in seconds, plus about six darts."

"That is very expensive. I must pay dearly to get this material for my stock."

Miguel actually paid his native contact with an assortment of inexpensive pots and pans, all shiny and new. Carefully he selected a small vial and six darts from the glass container.

"This quantity will cost you two thousand dollars."

It was very nearly a question.

Jeff counted out two thousand in addition to the cost of the handguns and rifles. Meanwhile, Aubrey brought the Jeep around to the back so they would not have to carry the weapons past the front of the stand where the tourists were congregated.

Jeff put the kurari and the darts in his pocket, and the weapons were stashed under their jackets in the back seat. Then Aubrey drove them back to the Fort Young Hotel.

29

Friday morning, Harden and Sam were driving north through Kuwait in the direction of Abdali. Dressed in casual civilian attire, they both carried weapons under their light jackets. News from air base intelligence just outside Kuwait City indicated that, the previous night, two drug dealers and their entourage had been killed a short distance from Abdali. The suspects were known gang leaders from Umm Qasr, in southern Iraq, who had been looking for the two men for a long time. The names Kafu and Al-Sufa meant nothing to Harden. No product was found, nor was any cash. The method in which these men were killed is what caught the attention of U.S. intelligence in the area. If the Umm Qasr people had become aware of this exchange between Kafu and Al-Sufa and their buyer, they would have overwhelmed both parties with significant manpower and still left the scene with everyone dead.

However, it was apparent that highly trained specialists had eliminated the perimeter guard on either side. The truck drivers were shot from long range with high-powered rifles, each dying from a single shot to the head. Kafu and Al-Sufa were found some distance away, their weapons never having been fired. Both men were killed in close-range action. The stealth, the hand-to-hand combat training and the degree of marksmanship all indicated much more highly trained individuals than would normally be available to recruiters in this area.

"Sam, we'll drive into Abdali first and see if we can locate anyone who had contact with Lewis and Long. Then we can visit the site of this activity."

"Do you think the men we're looking for could be involved this quickly in some kind of drug deal?"

If so, Sam knew there could be only one conclusion.

"If this is their work as well, it indicates that the incident in Lebanon was preplanned in order to give them a breaking point from the service. I already asked Anderson to see if he can get any information on the activity of these two men for the days that immediately preceded their mission. That could give us a clue as to what precipitated the break."

Harden knew if he could uncover a reason for the separation, he would be better equipped to find the two men.

They arrived in Abdali around midday and found an open-air restaurant on the main street. As Harden pulled around the corner to park his air-conditioned Jeep Cherokee, they both reacted at once. Not a hundred feet in front of them sat an old red truck, with no windows on either side and no license plate of any kind.

"Let's see if we can have lunch here before we start wandering back over there to look at it. We're supposed to be tourists, after all. Let's find a table on this side where we can keep an eye on the truck. Maybe the waiter can tell us something."

"May I offer you something to drink, madam and gentleman?"

The waiter drifted over from the shadows even as they were sitting down.

"I am called 'O.K.,' and I am at your service."

"Do you have American beer in bottles?"

Harden was careful what he consumed in most foreign countries.

"Certainly, sir. And madam?"

"Same."

Sam took Harden's lead. She wondered to herself how long O.K. had been watching them from the shadows. As soon as the waiter had disappeared back into the darkness of the doorway, she spoke softly.

"Harden, how can we tell if that's the truck we're looking for? If we could get a closer look, we may discover something they left behind."

"I'm going over there to take a peek. We can't let this opportunity fade without taking a chance."

Harden rose casually and headed for the Jeep, allowing his peripheral vision to tell him that no one was paying any heed to his actions. Turning almost as an afterthought, his pace quickened toward the truck. As he bent his head down inside the window on the driver's side, O.K. appeared suddenly from the back of the eatery.

"Are you interested in my old truck?"

There was no "sir" this time. Although he was already suspicious, O.K. knew now that this huge man was not a tourist. Displaying such avid curiosity in this obvious piece of junk, Harden knew he had been made from the tone O.K.'s voice had taken.

"Where did you get this truck, O.K.?"

Sam was watching the exchange. Her right hand had slipped inside her jacket and rested there. She was poised, ready to jump if the occasion demanded it.

"I will sell it to you very cheap."

O.K. had no particular loyalties. Besides, the two Americans had left Abdali just last night. After the evening's excitement, he doubted he would ever see them again.

Harden pulled out a wad of American money. Slowly extracting two one-hundred-dollar bills from the roll, he put the rest back into his pocket.

"Where did you get this truck?" he repeated, this time with a quiet menace as he took a step closer toward the now-frightened waiter.

His tone had the desired affect. O.K. reached for the money as the words began to pour from his mouth.

"Around noon yesterday, two men drove into town in this truck. They pulled back here as if to find a place to dump it. Since they've gone, I have been trying to start it up, but it is dead. At the restaurant, they sat outside. Much like you two, they sat at an outside table and kept looking around. I told them my brother runs that hotel down the street."

Sam had appeared at the waiter's left side about the same time that Harden had reached into his pocket, and she heard this entire exchange.

"They registered at the hotel for three nights, but they left that same evening and have not yet returned. My brother said they had much cash and paid for the rooms in full when they registered."

"Do you know in which direction they headed?"

O.K. had the money now and was anxious to get away from this pair, obviously not tourists.

"They came from the north, the highway of death—Abdali Road. I did not see them leave."

"What is your brother's name, O.K.?"

Harden wanted to be sure he spoke to the correct man at the hotel.

"His name is Siran and he is manager of the Best Western two blocks that way. You can see the sign out front."

Returning to the table, Harden grabbed the two bottles of Bud Light by their necks. According to his calculations, the two hundred dollars he had just spent would easily cover the beer as well. They climbed into the Jeep Cherokee and drove down the street. Twisting the cap off with his huge fingers, Harden downed the cool liquid in three gulps. Sam was finishing her drink as they pulled into the Best Western's small parking lot.

30

Back in Jeff's room at the Fort Young Hotel, Aubrey was pacing the floor as Jeff outlined his plan.

"I'm going to fly back to the States as Alan Friedman and administer a dose of kurari to Robinson, one sufficient to keep him out of the way permanently. Also, I'll mail a ten-thousand-dollar cashier's check today to that attorney, Hayes, as a retainer. When his office deposits the check into their account, he'll be retained as our attorney and therefore won't be allowed to divulge anything he learns about us because of attorney-client privilege. Still, we may be able to find out what he knows about us, if anything."

"I'll stay here and try to get in touch with Mr. Jones to pursue further opportunities."

Aubrey was more of a computer hacker. Between the two of them he stood a better chance of figuring out how to contact the elusive Mr. Jones.

The following morning Jeff was on an American Airlines flight to Washington, D.C. With the powder stored in an emptied talcum container and the darts having replaced the needles in his travel sewing kit, he felt quite comfortable boarding the flight. Although nervous without a weapon at hand, Jeff knew how to use his body as a weapon, even against much larger adversaries.

"Would you care for anything to drink, sir?"

The attractive, dark-haired flight attendant reminded Jeff of Serena. Aubrey had been excessively rough on that poor girl. She must have known the risks involved in earning money in that manner. Sooner or later she would have run into someone like Aubrey. Jeff remembered previous incidents where he had to step in after the fact to buy off wounded bodies and damaged feelings. Aubrey approached sex only as physical gratification, never displaying any soft feelings of love or emotion. Jeff partly blamed himself for fostering this quality in Aubrey. The confrontation they'd had in their first year of training was the only serious disagreement in all their years together. That was the incident that resulted in the involvement of the two JAG attorneys. Too much questioning and psychological evaluation that early in their careers had resulted in the two attorneys learning much more about the private lives of Lewis and Long. They were young and talked too much. That would never happen again.

Too bad for Robinson, Jeff thought to himself. He almost regretted what he felt he had to do. Realizing the attendant was still waiting, Jeff's mind switched back to the present.

"I believe I'd like a gin and tonic, please."

First-class travel had many perks, and Jeff had already convinced himself to live life to the fullest from this point onward. The risks involved in this career change could prove to be even more life threatening than special ops.

"Certainly, sir."

He watched her hips sway as she made her way down the aisle. Since the incident with Aubrey so many years ago, Jeff had frozen his sexual desire in a cold vault, deep inside himself. Locked securely, that vault had not been opened these many years.

Nonetheless, Jeff appreciated things of beauty—the look, the feel, the taste. Often dreaming of owning precious works of art, now he could afford to start collecting. To assure himself of a continuous flow of funds, he fully intended to make his services available to Mr. Jones in the immediate future. It cost a great deal of money to live the life he envisioned and he would enjoy that life, or else die in the process.

His drink arrived just as he was lowering his tray table. As she gently placed his gin and tonic on it, Jeff casually slipped a twenty-dollar bill into her other hand.

"Thank you, miss."

"Thank you, sir. If there's anything else I can get for you, please let me know."

Her effusive smile assured Jeff that she did indeed mean anything. How easy it was to fall into the good life if one had the financial resources to do so. Sipping his drink, he closed his eyes and began to plan his future. His past goal of ten more years and a million-dollar retirement fund had quickly faded from memory. His sights were set much higher now.

Jeff was jarred back to the task at hand as the 747's wheels touched down on the tarmac. Soon he was disembarking the airplane with his attaché case firmly in hand. His return flight was set for 1900 hours the same day. Earlier he had phoned Robinson's office under the guise of an appointment, and learned from his secretary that he was having lunch at 's Grill in Rosslyn. The cab driver indicated he was quite familiar with the famous lunch stop. They would be there in about a half hour.

On the drive over, Jeff extracted a dart from the sewing kit, coated it with the amount of kurari prescribed by Miguel for the desired effect, and returned the deadly missile to the kit, careful not to touch the tip against anything.

Upon entering the restaurant, Jeff spotted his target at a table in the center of the room, sitting with another man. Stopping at the counter to order some coffee to go, he carefully shielded himself from Robinson's view. After paying the cashier, Jeff paused at the condiment counter for cream and sugar. Extracting a thin red coffee stirrer from the holder, he made it look as if he were preparing his coffee, when in actuality he had inserted the treated dart into the stirrer. With his cup in one hand and the stirrer stick in the other, Jeff waited to see if the other man might leave first.

As Robinson turned to get the attention of his waitress, he jumped up from his chair and shouted, "Lewis—Lewis. I need to talk to you!"

Having been recognized, Jeff hurried out the front door with the tiny weapon still between his fingers. His coffee remained behind on the counter. Hoping Robinson would follow him outside, Jeff quickly stepped around the edge of the building.

Robinson bounded out the front door, looking both ways through the heavy pedestrian traffic. Standing at the curb, surveying the many vehicles in the vicinity, he suddenly felt a sharp bee sting on the left side of his neck. Instinctively, his left hand reached up to brush the insect off, but instead came away with a fresh prick to his middle finger and tiny traces of blood—his blood. As he flung the splinter to the ground, his body lurched into the street. Almost immediately, a late-model Lincoln Town Car, which had pulled into traffic accelerating rapidly, hit him. The car switched lanes and disappeared in seconds through heavy traffic. His lunch companion caught up to him as he hit the pavement. Robinson was dead even before he had touched the ground.

Jeff faded away into the crowd. Two blocks away, he hailed a taxi to return to the airport.

Even better, he thought. *It'll be listed as a traffic fatality.*

Jeff analyzed the situation as his cab made its way through heavy traffic. As a precaution, he had told the driver to drop him at the Lufthansa gate. With still an hour remaining before his return flight, Jeff made his way to the shuttle at a normal airport pace, not too fast, but also not too slow. Either way might help someone remember him if later inquiries ensued. After an unexpected move on Robinson's part, the resulting series of events proved a better plan than the original.

Jeff's plan had been simple. Obtain a proper angle, shoot the dart, and leave quickly. In a crowded restaurant, someone was sure to see the man blowing through the straw when later questioned. Possibly he could even be identified. He was certain no one had noticed him approach Robinson on the crowded sidewalk. Getting within four or five feet, Jeff had cupped his hand around the straw, held it to his mouth, and let the deadly missile fly. He was close enough to see the look of surprise on Robinson's face, and then something else—his face frozen in a state of shock as he fell in front of the departing vehicle.

31

Harden approached the check-in counter at the Best Western. Since he already had information that indicated Jeff and Aubrey had been there, he decided to take another tack.

"I am looking for the manager, someone named Siran."

His voice came out deep and resonant, leaving no option for nonsense.

"I am Ham Siran, sir. How may I help you?"

It was obvious to Siran that this man was not looking for a room.

Sam had circled around the back of the hotel and was now at his side. In a quiet voice she stated their business.

"Last night you rented rooms to two American males, both around thirty years of age. Did they sign the register or otherwise give their names?"

Sam already knew they would have paid in cash and refused to sign the register.

Siran decided to cooperate. He much preferred talking to the pleasant young lady than her gruff companion.

"They did not sign in, and I did not press the issue as they paid for three nights in cash—American dollars. I also sold them a car, an old Jeep with no top.

"This seemed to satisfy them. They retired to their rooms for a while, but I saw them leave about ten that night. They were carrying everything they had when I first saw them. Normally this would be alarming. But as they had already paid for two more nights, I put my curiosity aside. After I was satisfied that they would not see me, I went to the door and looked out. They made a turn just down the street and took the road east toward Warbah, on the coast."

Harden decided to enter the conversation.

"Do you know two men called Kafu and Al-Sufa?"

Siran seemed surprised by the question. He had wondered as well about the connection between the two Americans heading east the very night that Kafu and Al-Sufa had been killed. His nervous delay in answering did not escape Harden's notice.

Sam repeated the question.

"Did you know these two men, Mr. Siran?" she spoke softly, attempting to loosen the man's tongue.

"Well, I...everyone in Abdali knew of them. They had an expensive residence built a few miles west of town. We all, of course, knew how they made their money. They were involved with some drug cartel in Umm Qasr. Those Iraqis are ruthless. Kafu and Al-Sufa must have gotten into trouble with them, because this past week some violent-looking men were in town asking about them."

Harden already had a map that showed the location of the incident. He did not see how Siran could be of any more help. Sam wrapped it up.

"Is there anything else you could tell us about the two Americans?"

"They were both of average build, not intimidating like the Iraqis. But the larger of the two men had blue eyes, cold and hard. They actually seemed to reflect the light, glistening in contrast to his dark face. Both men had a certain swagger, or confidence, like they could take care of themselves. From a distance, they looked like average Americans. But up close, rather intimidating in their own way."

Harden maintained his hard countenance, while Sam slipped the man a hundred dollar bill.

"Thanks for your help, Mr. Siran."

Surprised, but relieved, Siran finally smiled.

"Thank you, miss."

Siran discreetly stuffed the bill into the left front pocket of his trousers.

* * *

Harden drove while Sam spread the map on her lap.

"The site is off the main road, but it looks simple enough to find. Take the Warbah Road for about five miles. We should see another road heading north. It's impossible to say by the map whether this road is dirt, rock or gravel, or maybe even sand."

The cutoff was easy to find. It was the only northbound turn that could qualify as a road. The incident had taken place in a clearing about two miles beyond the turn.

As they approached the site they heard a rifle crack, and a bullet screamed off the side of their Jeep Cherokee. Harden immediately swerved the Jeep behind a clump of trees to his right and came to a sudden stop. Scrambling out of their vehicle, Sam instinctively circled right while Harden went left.

They found the clearing almost immediately, just in time to see the dust cloud from a four-wheel-drive truck that was speeding north across the Iraqi border. Carefully perusing the area, they soon determined that no threat remained. Evidently, whoever was here had just wanted to slow them down so they could escape.

"Those were definitely not the men we're chasing, otherwise we would've both been dead by now. They wouldn't have aimed for the vehicle if they intended that bullet for us."

Harden had learned all he could from Anderson's description of the two men.

Yellow tape still encircled what remained of the truck and the Escalade. Each vehicle had been stripped to an almost unrecognizable condition. Harden and Sam were mostly interested in the physical location of the vehicles at the time of the incident. Not wishing to waste the time they had saved by flying here, both agents quickly surveyed the site, including the two outposts.

"Harden, according to these sketches Anderson gave us, the men known as Kafu and Al-Sufa were found two hundred yards away, behind those dunes."

Harden was carefully examining the area, looking for some kind of indication of the departure direction.

"No storms have hit in the past two days, so the tracks should still be here. With all this ransacking, there are way too many tracks. It's hard to tell which belong to our boys."

Harden was concentrating on the area around the trucks.

"There appear to have been two trucks, with the Escalade parked between them.

"One truck was backed up to the other at one point, maybe to switch the load from one to the other. Those tracks are pretty distinct and look like they head back to the Warbah Road. I would think it logical that the Jeep our men were driving did the same. I suggest we drive toward Warbah and see if we can find the spot where those vehicles left the road again."

* * *

Without passing any towns, Harden and Sam arrived at a narrow channel of the Persian Gulf. They were faced with the choice of either driving south or entering the water. Harden pulled off the road to analyze the situation. A boat dock reached into the water just past where he was standing. He searched the area for tire tracks. There was no one around.

"Only two vehicles appear to have been here recently. They both pulled off the same place we did. Looks like one or both of them drove up to the top of that ridge overlooking the water. I'm going to take a look around. Stay here in case someone else shows up. I don't want any surprises."

Harden started up the ridge. When he arrived at the edge, overlooking the water, the situation became quite apparent. Two sets of tire tracks headed toward the water. The sand and rock, as well as patches of grass, were torn away at the edge as though scraped by the frame of the vehicles as they went over the embankment and into the channel.

Harden could see nothing as he looked over the cliff and into the moving water.

Hurrying back down the slope, his momentum almost carried him into Sam as she suddenly appeared before him. He surrounded her with his arms to catch his balance and held her tightly, if only for a moment. Before releasing her he explored her eyes, which were wide and willing.

"They left here by boat," Harden said. "We have to take a look at the dock down there."

The moment was gone, and they both began scurrying over to the wharf area.

As they reached the wooden surface, well maintained for such an out-of-the-way place, a small boat was pulling up to the dock. Looking somewhat like a makeshift ferryboat, there was a flat area with space for two or three vehicles as well as quite a few passengers.

"Are you two headed for the airfield? I can take you across to Warbah. It is about a two-hour trip in my little ship."

Not wanting to lose the opportunity, Harden moved closer to the docking vessel before turning to Sam for a conference.

"Airfield, Sam. That's how they got out of here. There must have been a boat waiting after they disposed of the vehicles."

Sam was concurring as she moved.

"Let's go, Harden."

Harden helped the captain lower the ramp onto the dock as Sam pulled the Cherokee into position. The captain never mentioned a price. After the Jeep rolled into place, the captain tightened the rope to pull the ramp back to its upright position. Soon they were on their way to Warbah, across the channel. The captain automatically assumed that they were interested in the airfield, so Harden did not want to question him about that and thereby raise suspicion.

"I make this trip about once a day," explained the captain. "It is a pleasant ride—so quiet. About once a week I am rewarded with a customer. This airfield has become a popular place to leave the country."

He was being careful not to ask any questions.

"How much do we owe you, captain?"

"Sir, whatever you think is fair is fine with me. Gas has become very expensive, though. Sometimes I have trouble coming up with enough money for the trip."

This journey was not for tourists. They had evidently stumbled onto a route used by mercenaries and others engaged in illegal activity. After Sam drove the Cherokee onto shore, Harden walked over to the captain with a thousand American dollars in his hand. Before transferring the money into the captain's hungry grasp, there was an obvious question that needed answering.

"How often does a plane land here, captain."

Having been asked this question, the captain suddenly became nervous. There was always a plane waiting for the passengers he brought here. This time there was no plane in sight.

"No schedule, sir. When I bring people, there is a plane. Is your plane running late?"

He did not expect an answer. As Harden turned loose of the money, the captain returned to his ship and disappeared into the cabin.

Once he was out of sight, Harden dialed Anderson.

"Hello, Harden. Where the hell are you?"

Anderson was in.

"Sir, we need transportation and information. Does our air base outside Kuwait City monitor air traffic in and out of Kuwait? And, if so, what about flights out of Warbah early yesterday morning?"

They were so close. Harden did not want the trail to go cold now, although Jeff and Aubrey could have flown just about anywhere.

"First, I need to know exactly where you are, Harden."

"Just landed by ferry from the mainland. We're on the north coast of Warbah. Right on the shoreline is an airstrip, long enough to accommodate small jets. There's no terminal. Other than the ferryboat captain who brought us over here, no one else is in sight. We can see the airstrip from the dock."

"Give me ten minutes. I'll get back to you. Meanwhile, keep an eye on that captain. Remember, you're on an island."

32

As he was about to board his return flight on American Airlines, Jeff noticed a flurry of activity in the distance. He had been keeping an eye on the Lufthansa terminal through the glass in the American Airlines waiting area. Three patrol cars had screamed up to the entrance, along with two unmarked cars with lights flashing on top. A dozen men emerged and ran into the terminal.

Hardly able to refrain from smiling, Jeff presented his ticket and boarded his aircraft.

Now, sipping on a fresh gin and tonic, he pushed his seat back and closed his eyes. Things always work out better if you help them along. His caution had rewarded him once again. Earlier, out in the terminal, he had mailed a letter and the retainer fee to the office of Conner Hayes in San Francisco.

His cell phone was vibrating.

Quietly, he flipped it open.

"Hello."

"It's me. Our man wants to meet you in Cleveland as soon as possible. When you arrive there, check in at the Sheraton Airport Hotel and then call me. Sounds like another nice opportunity."

Aubrey was being extremely careful not to use any names.

"This flight has a stopover at Miami International. Book me on a flight from Miami to Cleveland and I'll pick up the ticket when this flight lands there. Use the same airline and make the flight as close to this E.T.A. as possible. I'll call you from the hotel. Thanks!"

Had Aubrey called in only an hour earlier, Jeff would have still been in the terminal where he could have simply changed his flight directly to Cleveland.

* * *

Jeff gazed out the window at the clouds, deep in thought. Things were beginning to work out. He sensed no danger. No one would be looking for Alan Friedman. He must have dozed off. The flight was already descending toward Miami International.

The terminal was crowded for a Monday evening. Almost as if in uniform, hundreds of individuals passed by in their dark business suits, men and women both. Jeff paid little attention as he made his way to the American Airlines counter.

With no time to change terminals he hurried back to Gate Six, ticket in hand, for his flight to Cleveland. Jeff's adventures had never brought him to this city before. He generally found most cities easy to negotiate; some were just larger than others. Of course, his mind was always registering details and storing them for future use.

* * *

Conveniently, Jeff had a shaving kit with him, if only to disguise his latest weaponry. He would need to refresh himself before meeting with Mr. Jones. After booking a room at the Sheraton as instructed, he called Aubrey.

"I'm in Cleveland, ready to meet Mr. Jones."

"I'll contact him right away. Hang loose for about a half hour."

Only ten minutes later, Aubrey was back on the line.

"Now I know why he specified that hotel. Mr. Jones is in Room 101. He wants you to meet him right away, as he'll have to leave shortly. Good hunting!"

Jeff heard the click. Out of habit, Aubrey always held his calls to a minimum. Modern tracking devices only required seconds to trace the source of a telephone conversation.

Jeff took the stairs from the fifth floor down to the first. He did not like to trap himself in an elevator, especially going down—just another developed phobia.

As he turned down the hall toward Room 101, there was a wall of a man standing outside it.

Mr. Jones has security and I have no weapon on me because of all that flying, Jeff thought. He analyzed the situation further as he came closer. With his government credentials he was always able to carry a weapon in the past. In this new circumstance, he would need to get used to traveling naked.

The man gave Jeff a daunting look before turning his back to open the door.

"Your visitor, sir," he announced.

Jeff walked into the room. The bodyguard came in behind him, closed the door, and took a seat next to a desk that occupied one end of the room. Behind that desk sat a twisted body of a man, whose eyes glistened.

"Welcome, Mr. Lewis. Please take a seat."

The words were barely discernible. Jeff had to concentrate on every word. Selecting a chair across the desk and farthest from the massive bodyguard, Jeff crossed his legs and waited for Mr. Jones to initiate the conversation.

"You and Mr. Long did an outstanding job for our organization last week. Now I have bigger plans. I want to give you a new identity and hire you as chief operations officer of my company, so I can have immediate access to your services as needed. I have had all the appropriate documents prepared. Mandrake, will you please give Mr. Lewis the folder?"

Opening the folder on his lap he was suddenly presented with a new passport, driver's license, birth certificate and company credit card. His photograph stared out at him from the passport, along with the name Henry James Atwell. Each of the documents was made out in the name of Atwell.

Up to this point, Jeff had not spoken a word since entering the suite.

"You do not have to mention the pay. You were sufficiently compensated for your previous venture, I trust. This association will reward you equally well."

"What about Aubrey?" Jeff asked.

Although no affection existed between them, there was an accepted dependency on both their parts. Theirs had not been an ordinary relationship of coworkers. As a team, they had faced the possibility of death many times. The exposure was always there.

"I have already spoken to Mr. Long. His part of the arrangement will continue to be undercover. That need continues. We have already reached acceptable terms based, of course, on your acquiescence."

"I'll have to confirm this with Aubrey. But if this arrangement is satisfactory with him, I'm certainly willing to try it out for a while. When do we start?"

"Mr. Long will fly here tomorrow. In the interim, I want you to get satisfactorily rested. Use your new credit card to buy several suits of clothing relative to your new position, and see me in my office at Brantley Chemical at nine a.m., two days hence. I will have my secretary contact you tomorrow to help get you suitably attired and acclimated. Her name is Beverly Wilson. With us today is my very dear friend, Mandrake. He takes care of some of the physical manipulations of which I am not capable.

"As Henry Atwell, you have been employed as chief operating officer of Brantley Chemical for two years now. I have just recently arranged to have you put on the board of directors of our parent company, Jennings Pharmaceuticals."

Jeff's mind immediately registered the wheelchair leaning against the wall in that church in Virginia. Aubrey had also said that Mr. Jones employed a voice synthesizer.

33

"Ashley, I want to hear everything about this problem."
Conner held the door open to the Aqua Restaurant so that his client could enter ahead of him.

Ashley was still curious as to why Charlie had accompanied them to lunch. He was certainly not involved in her business with Conner. Yet here he was at their side, smiling and cheerful.

"Good afternoon, Mr. Hayes," greeted the maitre d'. "If you will follow me, please."

"Good afternoon, Jason. How's the family?"

Conner fell in line behind Ashley as Jason led them to their table. Charlie took up the rear.

With fine linen tablecloths and such a sophisticated setting, Ashley was quite impressed.

"Fine, sir. Thank you for asking. Your waiter will be right with you."

As Conner requested, Janet had arranged for a corner table so they could continue their discussion regarding the board of directors at Jennings Pharmaceuticals.

After they each agreed on a delicate seafood preparation as recommended by their waiter, Conner encouraged Ashley to continue her story. Noticing her eyes turning to look at Charlie, Conner felt compelled to speak.

"Ashley, anything you tell us at this table is protected by attorney-client privilege. Neither I nor any other attorney involved in this conversation can divulge what is said without your consent. Please feel comfortable to continue."

"Well, I've just about articulated my concerns. First, obviously, is the success Mr. Riley has had in aligning the board in his favor.

"Second, Jennings Pharmaceuticals has developed three new products for which we're still seeking FDA approval. Meanwhile, Brantley Chemical is our main source of revenue. The third concern is that I don't even know the details regarding the phenomenal success of Brantley. All I've seen are the records that show the unbelievable success of our TR-7 fertilizer. This product line is completely new to me. I didn't even suspect that there was such a market, or such high profit potential on so mundane a product."

"I certainly want to address your concerns, Ashley. Can we begin by arranging a meeting with Anthony Riley as soon as possible? This should be a private meeting with just the three of us, if that's agreeable to you. Do you think you could set something up for Monday?"

"Mr. Riley is a strange man, but I'll see what I can do."

Ashley sorted through her Coach leather satchel bag and pulled out her cell phone. After selecting Riley's number from speed-dial, she waited for his secretary to answer.

"Hello, Mr. Riley's phone. May I help you?"

Self-conscious of his vocal difficulties, Anthony Riley elected to never answer the telephone himself.

Ashley recognized the deep voice.

"Mandrake, this is Ashley Jennings. May I please speak to Anthony?"

A moment of silence passed.

"Good afternoon, Ashley. What can I do for you?"

This sort of affable response was quite normal for Anthony. He could be charming in his own way, despite his infirmity.

"I was wondering if we could meet Monday morning to review some shareholder reports before we publish them. It shouldn't take much time. I wanted to have your input before releasing them."

"That will be fine. Would ten o'clock be satisfactory—in my office, if that's all right with you?"

That was easier than I expected, Ashley told herself.

Then aloud she said, "That's great. I also have someone I want you to meet. See you at ten."

She hit the end button before Anthony could respond to her last statement.

"We're all set for ten Monday morning. I suggest an early afternoon flight on Sunday. If it's all right with you, I'll have my secretary make the necessary arrangements. She'll call Janet with the details this afternoon."

* * *

Anderson rang back in the prescribed amount of time.

"Harden, I can get a plane to you early tomorrow morning. See if you can find a place to spend the night, maybe on that boat you mentioned. Also, it took us a while to locate that renegade flight from yesterday. Satellite surveillance of the area indicates that a small passenger jet left and flew directly to a similar field outside Amalfi, Italy. There were so many cross patterns of registered flights that this one stood out among them.

"After identifying it, our people managed to pinpoint the bastard flight's origination and destination. I'll arrange for your flight to leave as early as possible tomorrow. Good luck to both of you."

Anderson was gone.

Just as Harden was turning back to seek out the captain, a powerful cabin cruiser roared up to the dock. A giant of a man jumped off and secured a line with the grace of an athlete. Two men then disembarked. Wearing dark suits and ties, they were definitely not tourists. The large man began unloading plastic containers of a size about two feet by four feet, and perhaps twelve inches deep. Each container had a padlocked latch and was sealed with tamper-proof tape. No markings were visible on any of the boxes. Once the man was finished unloading, there were six containers in all sitting on the dock.

Harden was then distracted in the other direction just as a small Lear jet was landing on the fabricated runway. The two dark-suited men barely gave Harden a glance as they made their way to the limousine that had also suddenly appeared.

Harden motioned to Sam. They picked up their luggage and strolled over to the limousine as well. Sam asked the captain to store their vehicle until they could make arrangement to have it picked up.

Since one of the newcomers was positioned in the front seat and the other in the middle, Harden and Sam sat in the rear, acting as natural as possible under the circumstances. The trunk had been open, so they placed their luggage there before taking their seats.

As they approached the runway, Harden noticed a large shed off to one side.

The other two men had no luggage of their own other than a standard-size briefcase for each. Sam and Harden both noticed the slight bulge under their suit jackets, barely perceptible but definitely there. They were no longer concerned with carrying their own weapons onto the plane.

It took the limousine only a minute or so to reach the plane. After retrieving their luggage, Sam and Harden found that the others had already boarded the jet. Hurrying up the portable stairs, they encountered a beautiful young lady. She appeared out of place on this desolate piece of land, dressed as she was in a short white blouse and an even shorter skirt.

"I was told there were to be only two passengers today."

The words seemed to flow invitingly from her lips, even as she protested.

Sam gave Harden a nudge.

"We were a last-minute addition. They instructed us to pay either you or the pilot when we completed the flight."

"Welcome aboard. My name is Serena and I am here to make you comfortable on your flight to Amalfi. Please take your seats. We will be leaving momentarily."

Even as she spoke, the door was pushed shut from the outside and the jet began to taxi.

Serena recognized a serendipitous financial opportunity in these additional passengers. She and Alberto were paid to pick up and deliver the people, not collect tickets.

Harden moved to the rear of the plane and called Anderson to cancel the jet that he had requested, and to have the Jeep Cherokee picked up from the island.

* * *

When the Lear jet landed in Amalfi, Harden noticed the similarity in the two landing strips, both obviously unregistered and illegal. However, he had a more important objective. After the other two men had left the plane, Harden waited for the pilot to emerge. Serena had already gone outside and was waiting for Alberto at the bottom of the stairs.

Alberto emerged from the cockpit and nearly bumped into Harden in his rush to leave. Dwarfed in height and weight, he was still wide-eyed when Harden spoke.

"Those two Americans who were on this flight yesterday—I need to know where they went."

His tone was menacing. He had very little sympathy for illegal activity. He put his huge hand on Alberto's shoulder for emphasis.

Alberto did not know which men to fear the most. He reached an extremely quick decision based on the weight of the hand that rested on his shoulder, influenced partly by the weapon revealed beneath the jacket when Harden raised his arm.

"They asked about a printer who could furnish them with passports. I gave them the address of a man who runs his own small shop in the old part of town. He is very talented and can provide whatever identification one might need. Here is his address."

Alberto scribbled on a small piece of paper that he pulled from a pad in his pocket.

"Do you know at what hotel they registered?"

Alberto had not even taken notice of Sam until she spoke to him.

"We booked reservations for them at the 'Amalfi Hilton,' which is what the locals call the old Contessa Hotel. It is a popular stop for tourists, several blocks from the beach and therefore relatively inexpensive. It will be very crowded this time of year."

"Can you have someone take us there right away?

Although phrased as a question, Alberto knew better. He preferred dealing with the striking young lady. Harden had not yet removed his hand from Alberto's shoulder. The other two Americans had already driven away, along with their curious cargo. Removing his cell phone from his jacket pocket, Alberto dialed a number from memory.

After about a minute of hushed conversation, he turned his attention back to Sam.

"A car will be here momentarily."

As he finished speaking, an old Alfa Romeo rounded the side of the structure and headed in their direction. It looked to be a 1950s model and, with a little attention and polish, could have been quite a collector's item. The driver jumped out, leaving his door wide open. He grabbed their bags and hurriedly committed them to the trunk.

"Alberto says you want Contessa Hotel. I take you."

With accented and broken English, the driver wasted no time in communicating.

Harden held the door for Sam, jumping in behind her just as the engine roared to life again. In a cloud of orange clay dust, they were on their way to Amalfi.

"Could you stop here on the way to the hotel, just for a minute?

Harden passed Alberto's note to the driver.

With a puzzled look the driver said, "Sure."

He had learned long ago that, with his limited knowledge of the English language, this word always seemed to satisfy inquisitive Americans.

The streets were narrow at best, and this particular avenue was half-blocked with debris and yellow police tape. As the driver slowed to a crawl, Harden was checking numbers on the storefronts. Simultaneously, they both reached the same conclusion.

"Not here anymore."

The driver had been around long enough to accept things as they were—no questions asked.

"Pull over for a minute. Sam, wait here. I'll be right back."

Although Sam wanted to view the site as well, she knew that Harden wished to ensure that the driver would not leave with all their belongings.

Before he reached the ruin, Harden already knew someone had used an incendiary device. Nothing else would have caused such devastating damage in such a localized area. He found a member of the local *polizia* carelessly watching over the site.

"Excuse me, sir. Was anyone injured in this explosion?"

The officer was pleased to have someone to talk to. Being left behind as a watchman was boring.

"The remains of the old man who owned this shop were found in the back room. That was the room where all his equipment was located, where he took photographs and developed them himself. He must have had this shop for more than forty years, before I was even born. There was not much left of him, but the doctor found some identifying characteristics. His teeth, I believe. We suppose his developing tank caught fire and exploded. There were no witnesses."

Harden hurried back to the waiting car.

"Get us to that hotel, fast."

He flashed a hundred dollar bill in front of the driver. Though instilling fear was much less expensive, cash always managed to achieve quicker results. Evidently it was incentive enough, since the driver pulled over in front of the old Contessa Hotel in less than five minutes.

Harden and Sam checked out every person in the lobby as they carried their luggage to the registration desk.

"We were to meet two American men here today. They are in their late thirties, of average build, one slightly larger than the other. They should have arrived yesterday. Can you tell us if they are registered here?"

Harden knew the only way one could secure answers to questions that involved other peoples' privacy. He flashed a large roll of American currency, visible only to the concierge.

"Let me check, sir."

He paused until Harden had removed two hundreds and pushed them across the counter.

"We had two such gentlemen check in yesterday, in Rooms 210 and 212. However, I believe they have left the city. Our cleaning woman informed me just this morning that all their luggage is gone, along with all their personal effects."

His hand reached into the tray behind him and came back with two keys, moving slowly, until Harden pushed one more bill in his direction.

"Please be quick. I could be in trouble for doing this. Besides, Mr. Lewis and Mr. Long could return at any minute."

"Keep an eye on our luggage. We'll be right back."

Heading toward the stairs, Harden whispered to Sam.

"They must be feeling confident to have used their own names at check-in. Take the elevator, but let's be sure we enter the room together. If you happen to encounter them, wait for me before making a move."

They arrived on the second floor simultaneously. Sam knocked on the door to 212 and called out, "Housekeeping, may I come in?"

When there was no response, she tried the same thing at Room 210.

Again, with no response, they used the room key and entered 210 together, weapons drawn. Then they did the same next door. Both rooms were deserted. Using a piece of tissue, Harden carefully picked up a dirty drinking glass from each room and slipped them into his jacket pocket.

"We're running a day behind, Sam. Now we can assume that they acquired additional identification, and we have no way of knowing their next destination. Let's catch a commercial flight back to Rosslyn and debrief with Anderson. Maybe he can confirm the prints on these two glasses and alert Interpol. That should make it more difficult for them to move around Europe."

34

Jeff, as you may have gathered by now, my name is Anthony Riley.
"It will continue to be Mr. Jones for purposes of negotiating
transactions outside of the company. Travel fatigues me much more than
it did even a year ago. That is why I selected you and Aubrey Long after
a lengthy search.

"Personally, you are a better choice for what I would call my business
liaison. Aubrey, with more of a gruff exterior, will be my outside
operations manager. Your position as chief operations officer has no
duties. It is a necessary step toward inserting you on the board of directors
of Jennings Pharmaceuticals. Everyone must believe that you have held
that position for the past two years.

"Your background can continue to be vague, as I must insist that you
do not make an appearance before the board unless I am there as well.
Your primary responsibilities are to vote the way I say, and to manage the
production and distribution of TR-7. This I will show you in due time.
Your salary will be set at two hundred thousand per year, because you
must draw a paycheck in order to reflect legitimacy. Your actual pay will
be a similar share of each sale abroad of the TR-7. The amount of your
salary will be deducted from that share.

"Is everything clear to this point?"

Jeff had been watching Riley's eyes as he absorbed every word.

"It's perfectly clear so far. When do I start work?"

"You already have. On Monday morning, Ashley Jennings is coming here to meet with me. She has something on her mind. I want you to be in my office for that meeting. She is the chief financial officer and also the daughter of Jennings Pharmaceuticals' major stockholder. I've been buying up shares by using excess funds generated through the sale of TR-7. We are at a point where we would have majority control of the parent company, were something to happen to her father. We will discuss that later this afternoon. Right now, I have other business to attend to."

Mandrake was already holding the door open for Jeff's departure. Beverly Wilson appeared outside the door and led Jeff to his new office.

"If there is anything I can get for you, sir, just punch star one on your phone."

She gently closed the door behind her as she left.

Jeff used his cell phone to dial Aubrey.

"What do you make of this, partner?"

Aubrey did not hesitate.

"As long as it pays as well as it has so far, why not ride things out for a while? The way that Mr. Jones explained it, I'll be taking his place as the front man for delivery of the product and making sure we get paid. He said you'd accompany me on those field trips unless you were needed there. I feel much more secure if we can continue working together."

"Where are you now, Aubrey? Riley said you were flying in yesterday. His secretary kept me busy most of Thursday with shopping. She picked out an appropriate selection of suits, shoes, shirts and ties for my inside position at the company. Then she took me to my new office and introduced me to a few people. By the way, I am now known as Henry Atwell."

"Mr. Jones filled me in pretty well. I guess he told you he wanted me to take over the field trips he couldn't make any longer. Temporarily, I am staying at the Sheraton out at the airport. We need to make a trip together Monday afternoon, back to Iraq. Mr. Jones says if everything goes as planned, this will add another five hundred thousand to our bank accounts."

Jeff was stunned for a second. Riley had mentioned nothing of a trip on Monday, just a meeting Monday morning.

"Do you have any details on that yet?"

"Not on the phone. I'll stop by your office this afternoon to fill you in. See you then."

Jeff closed his cell phone and sat back in his chair to think things out. Everything was happening so fast. Mr. Riley certainly had an ambitious agenda.

35

Apparently Lewis and Long have been offered a great deal of money to defect. They seem to be spending freely. We trailed them from Lebanon through Kuwait, and then over to Amalfi, Italy. They most certainly were involved in the drug deal near Abdali. Those two were quite capable of handling eight or ten adversaries, easily, as spread out as they were."

Harden had spent the past half hour giving Anderson every detail of their mission to date.

"I filled you in on Robinson," Anderson said. "Now I'd like for you two to stay on this case until we find these guys."

"Next, we should get in touch with that other attorney, Conner Hayes," Harden continued. "I'll meet with him on Wednesday. Meanwhile, Sam will go into town and see if she can find out anything further on what happened to Robinson. When those two left Amalfi, we had no idea which direction to go. At least one of them visited Rosslyn. You realize, Mr. Anderson, that you're on their list as well."

"That's part of the job, Harden. Anyway, I'm not easy to find. We couldn't locate any prints on either man to compare with those two drinking glasses you gave me. Due to the nature of our business, the files are compacted and not duplicated. Both Lewis and Long have the expertise and the clearance that allowed them to remove and destroy their files."

* * *

Conner and Charlie walked into the office and caught Janet's eye.

"I put your mail on your desk. Also, I noticed you hadn't looked at Thursday's mail yet, so I put it on top of today's mail. Anything else I can do for either of you this afternoon? I was planning on taking the afternoon off to go shopping with my daughter, who's in town this weekend."

"Go ahead, Janet. We'll be fine. I'll go through all the mail this afternoon, I promise. Have a nice weekend!"

As Conner closed the door, without saying a word Charlie returned to the workspace he'd been using earlier.

Leaning back in his chair, Conner looked out at the bright afternoon sunlight and pondered everything Ashley had told him that morning. Anthony was moving up in the world despite his many handicaps. He deserves it. Always a hard working young man, his illness seemed to push him forward instead of holding him back.

With part of his mind assessing the situation with Ashley's company, Conner began to review Thursday's mail. Janet always had every piece open with the envelope clipped to the back of the correspondence for date reference, if necessary. After reviewing several letters and making the appropriate notations, the next piece brought his full attention back to the present.

Immediately, he called for Janet. After several rings, Rosemary answered the phone.

"Sir, Janet's gone for the day. I thought you knew. Is there anything I can do?"

"Rosemary, I need to know if the deposits were made for yesterday, and if a check for ten thousand dollars from a Jeffrey Lewis was included. Quickly, please."

Conner glanced at Charlie, only to find the young man comfortably ensconced in a leather chair with his eyes half-closed.

Despite appearances, Charlie was very much awake but showed no outward reaction at the mention of Jeffrey Lewis' name. He was watching as Conner glanced in his direction but decided to wait for Conner's next move.

Conner reread the document, much more thoroughly this time.

Jolted by the intercom, he listened intently.

"Sir, there was a cashier's check. We endorsed it and deposited it in our standard bank account around two o'clock Thursday afternoon."

"Thank you, Rosemary. Please have a copy made for me at your convenience."

Should he tell Harden, or did attorney-client privilege protect this correspondence? Postmarked and mailed from Dulles International on the day Robinson was murdered, Lewis was apparently the one who killed him. Conner could not let this go.

Conflicting thoughts were interspersed with the obvious.

I must inform Harden in private. They're apparently trying to bind my silence with a retainer, making me executor of their estates. Where did all that money come from?

Conner was still aligning his thoughts when the phone rang.

"A Mr. Harden Kelly is on line one, sir."

Rosemary hung up the phone, remembering the copy Mr. Hayes had requested.

"Conner, I don't know if it's connected in any way, but my friend just got word that there's a new drug on the streets. First signs are of heavy usage in the area of the thirteenth precinct in Chicago.

"We know that Lewis and Long were involved in a drug transaction in Abdali last week. The strange part is that this drug is a white powder similar to cocaine, but drug-sniffing dogs can't detect it. It has no odor and no taste and, because of that, it's much easier to transport. The street price is about half the value of genuine cocaine, but it seems to duplicate the effects. The FBI is analyzing a sample to find out its chemical components.

"Lewis and Long must have received a substantial financial reward for the gravity of their break. If you hear anything, let me know."

Harden paused for a moment. Conner was unusually silent.

"Let me talk to Charlie for a minute, if we're finished."

Conner finally spoke.

"I need to see you again. Can we meet at Maloney's in about an hour?"

"Make it thirty minutes. I'm not far away. Now, let me speak to Charlie."

Harden had noticed a slight elevation in Conner's voice.

Something's going on, Harden thought to himself while he waited for Conner to transfer the call.

"This is Charlie."

As always, his voice was firm and confident.

"Anything new, Charlie? Hayes seems a bit anxious."

"Do you think this line is clean? Give me a minute to attach the scrambler."

Reaching into his pocket, he removed a small device that screwed into the mouthpiece of the phone. At the same time, Harden was attaching his unit to his own handset. Both men required only seconds to complete this task.

Charlie turned away from Conner, discreetly making himself more comfortable in the chair.

"I overheard Hayes mention Jeffrey Lewis by name. It had something to do with a piece of correspondence on his desk. I haven't pursued this matter yet. That's all I know. It only happened within the past ten or fifteen minutes."

"I'm going to meet him at Maloney's in thirty minutes," Harden said. "Make some excuse not to come. See if you can identify the correspondence while he's gone."

Harden hung up and Charlie deftly replaced the original mouthpiece on the unit.

There was a soft knock as Rosemary peeked in the doorway and waved a piece of paper.

"I have that copy you requested, Mr. Hayes."

She handed the document over and turned to leave the office.

"Thank you, Rosemary," Conner said as she closed the door behind her.

Conner selected another document from the stack on his desk and folded it around the copy Rosemary had given him, carefully inserting them both into the pocket of his suit jacket that was hanging behind him.

Just as he stepped back to his desk, he received another call. Distractedly he picked up the receiver.

"Hello—Conner Hayes."

"Conner, this is Ashley. My secretary tried to contact Janet, but I gather she's gone for the afternoon. I have no plans for this evening, so I was wondering if we could meet for dinner. I could bring the hotel reservations and the airline tickets along."

Conner couldn't believe what he was hearing. If not for the current circumstances, he would have pursued that very thing.

"I'd love to, Ashley. Where would you like to meet?"

Conner was already picturing the alluring young lady from Wednesday afternoon and again that very morning. Although he had remained a highly eligible bachelor since the death of his one true love, he had dated only infrequently. Ashley was fascinating, mentally as well as physically. Tall and gifted, with seemingly perfect measurements, she glided across the room like a model on a runway, without the obvious affectations.

"How about that Aqua Restaurant where we had lunch?" Ashley replied. "Dinner should be more relaxing, and we can take our time. Is seven agreeable with you?"

Subconsciously she was seducing him with her voice, naturally soft and velvety smooth.

"It certainly is. Thanks for calling. I'll see you in a little while, Ashley."

Conner held the phone momentarily as he thought of seeing Ashley again so soon.

The beeping of the dead line brought him back to the present.

"Charlie, I'm going over to Maloney's to meet Harden Kelly. You can stay here, if you don't mind."

"That's fine, Mr. Hayes, uh…Conner. I'll catch up on some phone calls I need to make. You plan on coming directly back to the office, right? My job involves being with you at all times, and I intend to do my job."

"Certainly, Charlie."

A moment later, Conner was out the door.

36

As Jeff was reviewing the financial statements of both Brantley Chemical and Jennings Pharmaceuticals, Beverly Wilson paged him on his speakerphone.

"A Mr. James Zachary is here to see you, sir. Shall I send him in?"

Before she had finished her announcement, the door opened and Aubrey walked in.

"Hello, partner. A lot has happened since I last saw you in Roseau. Things are moving much faster than I anticipated," Jeff said.

Aubrey held up his hand to caution Jeff as he removed an advanced transmitter detector from his briefcase. He circled the room thoroughly, checking phone equipment, lamps, picture frames and furniture. After satisfying himself, he returned the apparatus to the briefcase.

"The room's clean. Let's talk. Monday afternoon we need to make another trip to the Abdali area for Mr. Jones. I'm hoping it'll be a much cleaner transaction this time around. We'll have reservations to Rome under our current identification as employees of Brantley Chemical.

"Once we're there, everything changes. We need to rent a vehicle for the drive to Amalfi, and then we'll catch a flight to that airfield in Warbah. Alberto will be our pilot again. We pick up four boxes of fertilizer at the UPS terminal in Rome, which we'll bring with us to Amalfi. These are four-by-six by one-foot-high crates, so we'll need a small truck for the drive to Amalfi. Alberto will have people there to handle the crates. Take a comfortable change of clothing in case things get out of hand. Otherwise, a suit will be appropriate. Weapons of choice will be waiting for us. We definitely don't want to make this meeting unarmed. I'll meet you here on Monday at 1300 hours. A company car will take us to the airport. I may see you between now and then, but I'm going to get on the Internet and find out if there's a casino around here somewhere. See you then."

"See you Monday. Good luck."

As soon as Aubrey was gone, Jeff's mind started to churn.

What have I done with my life? Using my government-trained skills to murder people! Those Delta Force guys! Robinson! When I worked for the company, using those skills had a purpose, a reason.

Jeff dragged in a deep breath of air to fill his lungs and let it out through pursed lips as if blowing out a candle. He shuddered as a chill hit him, and then repeated the process several times for relaxation. He rubbed his finger against the corner of his eye and felt moisture.

I've always been in control before. What's happening? Those guys had no reason to die. They were just doing their jobs. But it's too late now. I have a job to do as well.

Meanwhile, Aubrey was walking to his car, whistling and enjoying the freedom of his new identity.

* * *

Conner walked into Maloney's and looked around for Harden.

No longer hit by bitter memories of Liz, his thoughts were of Ashley and their dinner later that evening. With Harden nowhere in sight, he selected a booth against the back wall so he could keep an eye on the entrance.

His thoughts drifted back to Ashley, hardly noticing the arrival of the intimidating shadow across from him. Harden held his hand out across the booth.

"Good to see you again, Conner. I really do mean that. Sometimes we get so caught up in our everyday business that we forget what's truly important in this world, lifetime friends like you."

As he reached his hand out in turn, Conner got caught up in the sentiment.

"Thanks, Hard. After this is over, let's get together and talk about old times, leaving business behind us for a while."

"That would be great. But, for now, what is it you had to talk to me about?"

Harden had already switched gears back to the current problem.

"I have something to discuss with you, but only on the condition that it not go beyond the two of us. I'm ethically bound not to tell you what I'm going to tell you. That's the reason I need your promise as an old friend."

Conner paused and looked into Harden's eyes.

"I'll do my best to treat what you tell me as confidential information," Harden replied. "But you realize I have principles and responsibilities that go beyond our friendship."

"I trust your judgment, Hard. After lunch today, I sorted through the mail that came in over the past two days. A document had arrived on Thursday from Jeffrey Lewis."

Harden seemed to show no reaction to this name.

"A cashier's check for a substantial retainer was enclosed and deposited by our accountant on the day it arrived. My secretary clipped the envelope and the document together and put it on my desk right away. I didn't look at the mail until this afternoon. It seems he's retained me as executor of his estate, thereby contractually binding me to confidentiality. Janet always removes the checks and deposits them because I'm a real procrastinator about sorting through my mail.

"To get down to the facts, the envelope was mailed from Dulles International Airport on the day Robinson was killed. That would tie Jeff Lewis to the general vicinity when the incident occurred.

"No doubt he was counting on the fact that the check would be deposited before the document was reviewed, thereby contractually securing my confidence. I realize whom we're dealing with, but I still feel that we need to take a quiet approach with our response."

"Conner, I told you that Charlie Reynolds was a good man. Well, he's already told me that he overheard the name Jeffrey Lewis mentioned in the interchange with your secretary. This document may take some of the pressure off. It may also be a diversion to make you let your guard down and become careless. Let's leave Charlie around for a few days just to make sure. Meanwhile, we can keep this conversation confidential between us."

Conner was somewhat relieved that he had revealed the correspondence to Harden, but also perturbed with his careless handling of the situation in his office. He was fastidious about corporate ethics, especially where it concerned a client's personal affairs. However, he normally did not have a government agent in his office, observing his every move.

"Conner, why don't you go straight back to your office from here? I don't want anything happening to my old friend before he gets a chance to buy me that drink when this is over."

Conner was impressed with the current Harden Kelly, with his calm and confident approach to very real problems, just as he had always been impressed with his old friend's ability to fend off hardship with laughter and common sense.

"I'll be good, Hard. By the way, Sunday afternoon I'm flying to Cleveland with a client for a Monday morning meeting, a very interesting meeting. Anthony Riley is involved. If you're free for a couple of days, why don't you tag along? Afterwards we can renew old acquaintances. I'll let Charlie know the flight number and the time. If you can make it, you can get the information from him. Otherwise, I suppose you'll want Charlie to make the trip, right?"

"Anthony Riley, huh! That would be interesting. What's he doing in Cleveland? I thought he was still in D.C."

"Well, this might also be privileged information from my client. I may have gone too far telling you about Riley, but he's an old friend. Please join us. Our meeting shouldn't take too long."

Now that Conner had time to think about the reunion, he was anxious for the 'Three Kings' to fill in the blanks of the past seven years since they had last all been together.

"One of us will be there. I'll do my best to make it. In the meantime, be careful."

Harden was the first to leave.

Conner felt excited about seeing his old friend, but his thoughts quickly returned to Ashley. As he walked back to his office, he sensed he was being watched. Somehow he knew it was Harden, which made him feel safe. He still had two hours before dinner, so he returned to the task of dispensing with his correspondence.

Janet would certainly be busy come Monday morning.

During Conner's absence, Charlie had had enough time for a thorough search. However, he found no document with Lewis' name on it, which meant that Conner must have taken it with him.

37

As Jeff opened the door to his room, all those earlier questions continued to vibrate inside his head. Hanging his jacket carefully in the closet, he headed for the service bar. Stocked full each day, the small freezer/refrigerator had a varied selection. On the way across the room he picked up a glass, removed the plastic wrap that protected it, and tossed the cellophane into the trash. Several dark green bottles of Tanqueray gin were on the shelf, right in front. After dropping two ice cubes into his glass, he emptied two of the small drinks into it, followed by a shot of tonic. There were no limes available, so he stirred the drink as-is and took a long swallow.

Plugging in his laptop, he called up the Neuhaur National Bank and keyed in his account number and password. Selecting the option for balance information, the seven-digit figure stared back at him.

So much had happened in less than two weeks.

Again his thoughts went back to the Monday before last. One more long drink, and his glass stood empty. He repeated the process with two Grey Goose vodkas plus a small shot of tonic. Seated in the lounge chair close to the minibar, Jeff took another drink and closed his eyes.

Deltas Three and Four were staring back at him with startled eyes as he fired his weapon. They seemed to be silently suspended for an interminable amount of time before finally falling to the sand. The shock in their eyes still haunted him. Blinking his eyes chased away one memory, only to have it replaced by another. JAG officer Robinson was now staring at him with pleading eyes as he fell into the street.

Jeff staggered back to the bar for another attempt to erase these scenes from his memory. Two bourbons, this time with just a little ice to dilute them, soon disappeared from his glass. After a few hours of ransacking the minibar, Jeff collapsed across his bed. Now the two special ops hovered over him, joined by another figure with a similar-looking uniform, only with Robinson's face.

Jeff tossed fitfully. An old man appeared in disarray, torn apart by explosion and fire. Jeff recognized him as the owner of the Amalfi print shop. Even Delta Five appeared briefly in the picture. Each man had been an innocent victim, their lives taken by Jeff and Aubrey over the past two weeks.

What have I done with my life? That was his final thought before falling into oblivion, his tormentors chasing after him.

* * *

As arranged beforehand, Charlie planned to stay in the background at the Aqua Restaurant on Friday evening. He sat at the far end of the bar, facing the table where Conner awaited the arrival of Ashley Jennings. Charlie had shown his credentials to the maitre d', and the two of them had made an agreement with the bartender that would allow Charlie to remain in that spot, sipping on Perrier, until Mr. Hayes and his guest had finished dining and were ready to leave the restaurant.

Suddenly she appeared in the foyer, no longer dressed in her business suit and projecting her businesslike demeanor. Wearing an off-white cocktail dress topped by a soft pink jacket, brushing her hair back into place after its exposure to the soft San Francisco breeze that wafted in off the bay, Ashley was a striking figure as she approached the restaurant host. He glanced over his shoulder and saw Conner rise from his chair.

"Miss Jennings, I presume? Would you follow me, please?"

By then Conner was already at her side, smiling broadly and obviously taken by her beauty.

"Good evening, Ashley. Our table is right over here."

She slipped her arm through his. With a slight squeeze she whispered, "I'm glad to see we're alone tonight, Conner. Charlie's a nice guy, but…"

She left the sentence hanging as they arrived at their table. Conner slid her chair back into place as she took the seat across from his, thus sitting with her back to the bar that was on the other side of the room.

"Conner, you're staring at me. I hope I didn't forget something when I got dressed for the evening. I was a little rushed."

Her smile was naturally seductive, but only in the way it felt whenever a beautiful woman focuses her smile in your direction.

"I can't help it, Ashley. I was so impressed when I met you on Wednesday, and even more so when we met this morning. But tonight you're stunning. You remind me of someone I knew a long time ago."

Conner's demeanor was impressive and commanding when required but, so far, he had maintained the youthful smile that had charmed the young ladies ever since his high school days.

Ashley, too, was always in control, often complimented on her cool and reasonable resolution of business problems. But now she could feel a warm flush spreading over her face that needed some of that control.

"Sounds like there's a story there, Conner. I'd like to hear it sometime, whenever you're ready to tell it."

The waiter interrupted their brief reverie.

"May I bring you something to drink? Wine, perhaps? Or, if you are ready to order dinner…"

He paused to appraise their reaction.

"I would like a glass of Chablis."

Ashley was the first to answer.

"Make that two, please."

As the waiter left, Conner gazed again into Ashley's bluish-brown eyes and took her hand in his across the table.

"I haven't dated much lately, not seriously anyway. I hope I haven't made a fool of myself by staring at you. It seems like forever since I last wanted to do that. I realize tonight isn't officially a date, but I'd certainly like to correct that in the future."

"Conner, the tickets were just an excuse to see you this evening. I was so impressed by your attentiveness and, of course, your smile, that I found myself hoping you weren't attached."

The flush was returning. Just then the waiter returned carrying an ice-filled bucket out of which a pale green bottle peeked. They managed to switch their attention to him as he wrapped the head of the bottle in a white towel and removed the cork. Without saying a word he poured a small amount and presented it to Conner. Conner swirled the liquid, took a sniff, and then tasted the wine.

"This is fine. Please pour. Thank you."

They both agreed with the waiter's recommendations for dinner. After he had taken their orders and left the table, Conner continued with his story.

"Thirteen years ago, I did fall in love. She was the daughter of one of our partners at the time. The very morning after she accepted my proposal, she was murdered while sitting at her desk. That was in New York City. She worked at a legal defense office for people who needed representation but couldn't afford a private attorney. She had become fiercely protective of her people. But one of them, blinded by some kind of drugs, came into the office that morning and started shooting randomly. After wounding the young woman at the first desk, he fired several times at Liz. She died instantly."

Conner paused reflectively.

Ashley squeezed his hand.

"Conner, I'm so sorry."

He could feel her sincerity.

"Well, that was a long time ago. I was letting it destroy my life until one of my coworkers found a way to bring me back to the real world. I'll always be grateful to him for that. You brought back memories of the way I felt when I first met her. Please don't be offended. I mean that in a very good way. You've aroused feelings in me that I've been covering up for years. I would very much like to continue seeing you. You've made me feel alive again."

"Conner, you're making me blush. You're saying things that I felt myself when I first met you."

The food went virtually untouched as they talked, telling each other about their personal lives. The envelope with the reservations and tickets sat unmoved beneath her purse. Charlie observed from a distance as the time passed, showing no signs of impatience as he shifted positions and sipped on his drink.

As Conner looked up for the waiter, he caught sight of Charlie and realized that this night could go no further. After signing the check, Conner took Ashley by the arm as they left the restaurant.

"I have to return to the office for a while, Ashley. I'll meet you at the airport on Sunday. You made this evening unforgettable."

Just as the cab pulled up, Ashley slid her arms around his waist and moved her lips to his, softly but passionately. She parted her lips, looked into his eyes, and then slipped away from him to slide in through the open cab door.

As the taxi drove away, Conner stood there staring after it, wondering what Ashley was thinking about the way the evening had turned out. A moment later Charlie was beside him, and they both walked silently back to the office.

38

Jeff finally pulled himself together on Sunday morning. After shaving and showering, he dressed in one of Henry Atwell's new business suits and left the room. Pulling off the freeway at the first exit, he was looking for a place to have lunch. On the next block he saw the twin spires of a church. As he came closer, he saw that the area was virtually deserted. Mass apparently was over for the day. Jeff pulled over to the curb, a few doors up the street. Without knowing why, he found himself getting out of the car and locking his door. Slowly he walked the short distance to the church. The name Church of the Annunciation was emblazoned on a sign in front. He lowered his head and discovered his shoes ascending the steps to the front door.

As he entered, his hand automatically dipped into the holy water.

He started to bless himself but instead stood staring at his wet fingertips. He went over to the right-hand aisle and was reminded of the church in Rosslyn where there lives had changed. Taking a seat in the rearmost pew, he could see the entire church before him. His eyes assessed the situation out of habit. The only people he saw were two elderly ladies, one kneeling about halfway down the center aisle, and the other standing beside her in hushed conversation.

The statues, the altar and the crucifix were beginning to spin around in dizzying circles.

"What am I doing here? I don't belong here," he nearly shouted as he rose from his seat and hurried to the exit, his head still spinning.

Back at the hotel, he noticed Aubrey sitting in the dining room of the hotel and joined him. Hunger tore at him again. He had not eaten a meal since his binge that began late Friday and lasted all day Saturday. Although it was lunchtime, he ordered a breakfast of scrambled eggs, hash browns, wheat toast and black coffee.

Aubrey was waving a big wad of bills in front of him.

"My luck continues, partner. There isn't any gambling around here so I took I-90 east, all the way to Niagara Falls, and then crossed the bridge to the casino on the Canadian side. I think I've mastered this blackjack game."

He accentuated his point by again flashing the stack of currency that looked to be hundreds of dollars.

"They 'comped' me a room, so I slept a few hours before driving back this morning. What have you been up to?"

It appeared to Jeff that Aubrey was adjusting to this new life better than he was.

"I just had a few drinks in the bar, did some reading, and then had a good night's sleep."

"I'm still trying to find a way to get to Anderson," Aubrey said. "Once he's out of the way, they'll pretty much stop looking for us. That last connection will finally be broken."

Aubrey showed no remorse whatsoever for the murder of innocent people.

More killing! Jeff thought to himself. Again, the Delta ghosts and Robinson's blank stare flashed before his eyes. He shook his head and rubbed the corners of his eyes with his thumb and index finger.

"Starting tomorrow, we'll be getting busy again. Anderson will have to wait. I have a morning meeting with Mr. Riley. I'll be ready to leave from the office as soon as you get there."

Jeff was looking forward to more activity and less time to brood over the direction his life was taking.

Aubrey rose to leave.

"I'm going to take a nap. All that driving made me tired. I was up most of the night at the casino and didn't get much sleep. See you tomorrow."

Both Aubrey and Jeff recognized the importance of being well rested when preparing for a mission. It was dangerous and potentially fatal to let the other side have the advantage.

Jeff finished his breakfast and asked for a coffee to take back to his room. Noticing Aubrey had dropped three twenties on the table before he left, Jeff thanked the waitress for the coffee and went upstairs. Tomorrow was an important day in this new life of his.

* * *

Conner and Ashley boarded a 10:40 United Airlines flight to Chicago, which continued on to Cleveland. Anthony Riley had suggested that they stay at the Sheraton Airport Hotel for convenience, since they would only be in Cleveland for a short time.

Although amicable enough, Conner detected a slight detachment in Ashley's mood since meeting at the airport that morning. While pretending to read through the financial statements Ashley had furnished, he noticed her big eyes looking at him several times during their flight. The bluish-brown tint he recognized brought back those few magic moments when they were staring across the table at each other on Friday night. That night had gone unbelievably well until he remembered that Charlie would not let him out of his sight, and he was not free to discuss those reasons with Ashley.

Ashley remained quiet. She wondered what had happened to bring what looked like a promising evening to such an abrupt end. Every now and then she glanced over at him to see if she could read anything in his eyes.

Finally, Conner could take it no longer. He certainly was not going to let this second chance fade away without a fight.

"Ashley."

She turned, and he looked deeply into her eyes. Although no tears were visible, there was an extra moistness there.

"I need to apologize for ending Friday evening so abruptly, without an explanation. I wanted to stay with you that evening, more than anything in the world, maybe even spend the night if you would have let me.

"But I'm involved in a case right now that's so confidential, I shouldn't even be telling you that there is one. I couldn't figure out a way to be alone with you, even for a few hours. Things were out of my control. But this will be over soon, and I'd like to see a great deal more of you, if you still want me to."

He almost wished he had not said that last part, half fearful of her answer.

She looked up at him and then pressed her lips against his briefly. A moment later she settled back into her seat with her eyes closed, but with so great a sense of relief that she felt her heart flutter for an instant.

Conner laid his head back, now content. At least he had taken the opportunity to express how he felt. Her lips said she had similar feelings. Those few kisses reminded him of a new song he had recently heard on the radio. It was titled, "Heartfelt," a piece of country music written by a fellow graduate of St. Xavier High School—his alma mater—with the cooperation of a Nashville artist. The line he specifically related to was "My heart runs wild, like a child, every time we kiss." Ashley had caused that effect every time they kissed.

By the time they reached the Sheraton, they were laughing and talking as if there might be a future for them. While checking in at the front desk, the attendant had a message for Conner.

"Mr. Harden Kelly wanted me to tell you that he was in Room 210, and would like you to give him a call as soon as you arrived."

Again, this was a diversion that caught Ashley's attention.

After checking into their rooms, 303 and 305 respectively, they decided to have a casual dinner somewhere that did not require a change of clothing. Their rooms were interconnected, and Ashley asked if she could leave the door open between them.

After the porter left, and while Ashley was busy unpacking her things, Conner picked up the phone and dialed Room 210. Harden did not answer. Conner left his room number so that Harden could return the call. Evidently he was going to be able to attend the meeting. Riley would be surprised to see them both. When he cradled the phone, Conner was anxious to leave before Harden returned the call so that he could be alone with Ashley for a while.

"Are you ready to go?" he asked.

She appeared in the doorway almost immediately.

"Were you able to get in touch with your friend?"

"No. He wasn't in, but I left him a message. Let's get out of here before he calls back."

She latched onto Conner's arm, and he pulled the door closed behind him as they left the room.

39

"Henry! Henry! Open the door."

Aubrey was pounding on the door, yet he remembered the protocol of using the proper identification.

"What is it, Aubrey? We just talked a little while ago."

Jeff had been either sleeping or drinking. His eyes were not quite open.

Aubrey slipped inside and closed the door.

"Guess who I saw just out in the hall. Is this a coincidence or what? And when I tell you, remember that we were seriously cautioned against ever believing in coincidences."

"Damn it, Aubrey. Who did you see?"

Jeff was both tired and impatient.

"It was that JAG attorney you sent the documents to in California. You know—Conner Hayes. He was with a really good-looking woman. Neither of them was wearing a wedding band, so it's apparently not his wife. I checked with the front desk to be sure. He's staying in Room 303. This could be the perfect time for us to get rid of him, once and for all."

This was turning out to be a tumultuous weekend for Jeff Lewis. Every time the subject of killing showed up, either in his head or in conversation, his ghosts returned. Sometimes they were dressed in special ops uniforms, sometimes they were wearing business suits, and sometimes it was only their heads staring at him.

"What's the name of the woman with him?" Jeff wanted to know.

"Jennings. That's what they told me at the front desk."

The name caught Jeff's attention.

"That's the name of the woman Riley and I are meeting with in the morning. I wonder what the connection is between Hayes and Jennings. We'd better let Mr. Riley in on this before we take any action that might jeopardize our position. We can talk to him before ten tomorrow morning."

"All right, but we'd better not let Hayes see us before then."

* * *

"Damn!"

Harden had just listened to the message on his phone. He had spent the last half hour in the exercise room, working out the stiffness from the flight Anderson had arranged for him. There was not much reaction to the documents Jeff Lewis had sent to Conner Hayes. These papers were not going to help find where the two men were right now. There was no question that they were gone from Dulles. That place had been thoroughly searched for either Jeff or Aubrey immediately after Robinson had been attacked.

He dialed Room 303, and then 305. There was no answer at either room. Next he dialed Conner's cell phone from his own cell phone. One had to make special arrangements for long-distance calls from this hotel.

"Hello."

Conner was in the habit of picking up immediately so he would not miss any urgent calls relating to his cases or from his mother, as he spoke to her so rarely.

He recognized the deep voice right away.

"Conner, you know my cell phone number. I was down in the exercise room. Just wanted to let you know that I was here, and that I'd like to see Riley again.

"I flew up here on a military flight. Where are you? I don't think

Anderson wants me to let you out of my sight in case that document was sent to put you off guard."

"Ashley and I are at an Applebee's restaurant just off the airport highway. But, frankly, Harden, we'd prefer to be alone. There can't be any danger in Cleveland. No one knows we're here. This lady is special, Hard. I mean, really special."

"Fine, Hayes. Just don't stay out too late. You don't want to underestimate the ability of your adversaries. Those two men completed their courses well enough to make me nervous about any sort of encounter. I'll ride in with you two in the morning, if you don't mind. Just ring my room when you're ready. See you tomorrow!"

"Good night, Hard, and thanks!"

Conner had the Santa Fe chicken salad and Ashley had the oriental chicken salad. Between bites, Ashley was able to extract many of the details of Conner's earlier love interest. There were some sad moments as Conner recounted her death, but he had long since learned to appreciate the time he did have with Liz. He was ready to put that behind him forever. Ashley Jennings brought hope and laughter back into his life.

It was Sunday night and the demand for their booth was not pressing, so they talked for several hours, sipping refills on their Diet Cokes. Finally, Ashley insisted they get some sleep before the meeting the next morning. Feeling guilty about the excessive use of their waitress' stations, Conner handed the young lady a fifty-dollar bill and told her to keep the change.

Conner and Ashley hung onto a deep, lingering kiss before Conner finally forced himself through the connecting door and into his own room. When he finished his nightly bathroom ritual, the door between the rooms had been pulled closed, but not all the way. He convinced himself that the kiss would hold him until morning. He could hear the shower still running in the other room as he turned out the light and stretched his long frame across the bed.

A few minutes later, the door between the rooms opened wide. Ashley drifted toward him slowly, tentatively. Conner was not yet asleep. He slid off the side of the bed and stood to meet her. Feeling her warm body through the thin silk of her nightgown, he heard her gasp as he held her as tightly as he dared. Then her lips were on his as they both sank onto the bed. She was fumbling with his pajama bottoms even as he was slipping the gown up over her shoulders. Her breasts pressed firmly against his chest as they kissed again and again. By the time they fell exhausted to the pillows, they had explored all the nooks and crannies of the human body. The last thing Conner knew before falling asleep was that he wanted to hold her in his arms for the rest of his life.

40

Anthony Riley was seated comfortably behind his desk. The previous year he had a chair designed specifically for his needs, with padding and curves that fit the cruel malformations of his body. Without an occupant the chair appeared twisted, as if it had gone through a tornado. Nonetheless, all the gadgets and buttons added by Anthony's design gave the monstrosity a certain level of sophistication.

Jeff and Aubrey came in thirty minutes prior to the meeting to tell Anthony about the man who would accompany Miss Jennings.

Anthony had shown no outward signs of recognition at the mention of Conner Hayes. But internally, he was analyzing what this news meant regarding their upcoming meeting. Conner occupied an office in San Francisco the last time they had spoken, so the connection could either be as legal representation for Jennings, or purely social.

"Henry, I want you back in my office for this meeting. Walk in only after you're sure they've arrived. James, please wait in the conference room. Have a weapon with you and listen in on the intercom. Make certain it's activated before their arrival so they won't notice the click."

Anthony was careful to call them by their assumed identities to avoid accidental slips in the company of others.

Both men left by way of the conference room to await a cue for making their reappearance. Jeff (Henry) wore glasses and was dressed in a conservative gray business suit, accented by a gray striped tie. Aubrey (James) wore a loose-fitting sport coat over black slacks, his holstered weapon positioned in the area where his left arm hung slightly away from his body.

Anthony sat back in his chair and planned his reaction for Conner's surprise appearanc. His concentration was interrupted by the intercom.

"Miss Jennings is here to see you, sir."

"Send her right in, Margaret."

Anthony was adjusting his personality to remain upbeat for the meeting. However, when the door was opened and two gentlemen instead of one appeared with Miss Jennings, he was unable to mask his surprise.

"Conner. Harden. It's great to see you both. What a pleasant surprise!"

Jeff and Aubrey had told him about Conner Hayes, but there was no way they could have identified Harden Kelly...*the 'Three Kings' together again*, Riley mused.

"What brings you to our fair city? Are you both working for Miss Jennings now?"

Although he could not rise to greet them, he leaned forward in his chair and extended his hand across the desk.

Harden was the closest. He extended his huge right hand and gently buried the pale, but surprisingly strong proffered hand.

"Always good to see you, Anthony. When Conner told me he was coming to see you, I cleared my schedule to join him. But I still work for the government."

"Hello, Anthony. Good to see you again. It's been a while."

Conner came around the desk and hugged his friend as he had in high school.

"When Ashley told me you were involved in their organization, it brought back some good memories. We three have been friends for a long time. Our firm is doing some legal work for Jennings Pharmaceuticals, and I jumped at the chance to see you again. I understand you're doing quite well here at Brantley."

"Things have worked out fine. This is an interesting business right now. There are many opportunities for an individual with the insight to follow through on them. I guess I was in the right place at the right time."

Riley paused. The energy required for him to accomplish long conversations in a clear voice tired him quickly.

"And Miss Jennings, it's always a pleasure to see you. You mentioned some shareholder reports. Why don't we get that out of the way so I can visit with my friends?

"I suggest we go over to the conference room to review your documents."

Anthony Riley had already started around his desk, maneuvering his custom-made chair expertly, toward the door on the opposite wall where his guests had made their entrance a few minutes earlier. The door opened electronically to facilitate the power wheelchair.

As Anthony took the position at the head of the table, all three guests made a note of the gentleman who waited beside him.

Ashley took the initiative.

"Good morning, Mr. Atwell. This is Conner Hayes, an attorney from San Francisco who represents our firm. And this is an old friend of Mr. Hayes and, apparently, of Mr. Riley as well—Harden Kelly."

Although he knew only the name as it was brought up in conversation with Ashley, Conner was certain he recognized the face. He offered his hand in greeting, hoping that his initial reaction had escaped notice.

"It's very nice to meet you, Mr. Atwell."

Harden followed suit, but the momentary change in Conner's facial expression upon entering the conference room had not gone unnoticed. Harden made a mental note to ask him about that once they were alone.

Always mentally alert, Anthony also recorded the change in expression, brief as it was. Ashley was apparently the only one not to have seen Conner's reaction, as Henry Atwell suppressed a smile at the incident.

While Ashley spread out the financial documents for Anthony to review, Conner spoke quietly to Atwell.

"Have you lived in Cleveland long, Mr. Atwell?"

Admiring Conner's astute recall, Jeff decided not to take the bait on what was so obviously a fishing expedition.

"Mr. Riley hired me as chief operating officer about two years ago. I think our performance over that period would indicate that we've formed a mutually beneficial relationship. Wouldn't you agree, Mr. Hayes?"

Riley decided to cut this off before it went any further.

"Henry, I think these reports reflect fairly the operations of Brantley for the period. Would you give us your opinion, please?"

Jeff was cool, especially when under pressure.

"Yes, sir. I would say that they certainly give a fair reflection of our operations. But I must also include the fact that the numbers we've furnished remain conservative, as has been our practice in recent years."

Anthony decided he had made a wise choice, considering the way Jeff handled himself. Smiling broadly, he concurred.

"We always take a conservative position in projections, so that the final outcome will not be disappointing."

After thirty minutes of discussion and review, the meeting was drawing to a close.

"Mr. Riley, you've shown such success here at our Brantley subsidiary that we'd like for you to review the techniques at our other facilities. There may be opportunities there as well. If you could give Mr. Hayes and me a tour of your research facility and manufacturing operations, perhaps we can learn from your success."

So here's the real reason for the visit, Anthony thought to himself.

He knew the report review was too mundane a subject to have warranted a trip all the way from California to Cleveland. Suspecting that such observation was inevitable, Anthony had installed a walkway high above both the processing facilities and the research and development area. From this vantage point, workflow could be observed without getting anywhere near the product.

Aubrey was waiting on the other side of the door until his services were needed. Before, when Anthony had started toward the conference room, Aubrey had slipped quietly into the hall, leaving Jeff alone as their benefactor had requested.

Anthony had two problems. The first, and likely most dangerous, was the fact that Conner had displayed a glimmer of recognition upon meeting Jeff in the conference room. Second, the parent company would insist on seeing the operating facilities in detail. This second problem Anthony had hoped to dissuade until he gained controlling votes on the board of directors of Jennings Pharmaceuticals. Perhaps that presented a task for Aubrey in the immediate future. Mr. Jennings had stood in the way far too long.

However, the path of least resistance at present was to lead the tour, even inviting Harden to join in, to make a magnanimous gesture toward the sharing of information that might be beneficial to other elements within the corporation.

"I only have a short while, but let me show you our little operation. We're extremely proud of our efficiency, but also extremely protective of our methods from the dangers of industrial espionage. Our competitors are everywhere. Please follow me."

His self-designed, motorized chair moved out toward the elevators.

Harden was impressed.

"Anthony, you must have created that chair to your specific needs. You're able to operate doors, elevators and whatever, combined with highly flexible maneuverability."

"Well, Harden, I simply wrote up an analysis of my needs as opposed to my physical capabilities, and the engineers took over from there. With only a few minor changes this is really a product of their ingenuity, not mine."

The elevator cabin fit all five of them comfortably. As the number four lit up on the panel, the elevator rose swiftly without any apparent change in air pressure. When the door slid open, Anthony led the way down a long hallway toward a frosted, glass-walled enclosure.

"As we proceed through this doorway, we'll be looking down on our research department. It's small, but adequate for our needs. There will be four associates working on the floor when we pass through."

To open the door, Anthony entered a code into a digital access panel on the wall. The three guests were surprised to encounter a uniformed, armed security person stationed immediately inside. Ignoring the guard, Anthony stated the obvious.

"As you can see, we take our industrial secrets very seriously. From here we can circle the operation and proceed on to the processing facility."

As they stepped out onto the catwalk that skirted the laboratory from four floors up, Conner whispered to Ashley.

"We won't be able to see any detail from this height, but at least we'll get an overall view of the operation."

The lab below had the appearance of a clean room. As Anthony had previously indicated, there were four technicians working on the floor, cloaked in white from their hairnets to their shoe coverings. The walls were painted white and the floor appeared to be made of white marble, patterned with a scant gray tint throughout. Twenty feet above the floor hung five huge stainless steel tanks. Four lines ran from each tank, one to each of the four vats near the floor. These vats appeared to be fermenting or boiling some combination of ingredients released from the tanks above. A thick white mush filled the conveyor carts that were parked next to the vats.

"Is this how fertilizer is manufactured?"

Ashley had never been even this close to the operation.

"This is how our new sales phenomenon, TR-7, is produced. When we first entered the room, you noticed the three long tables where all of our chemical analysis is performed. That is our research department. The total department consists of the four chemical engineers who developed the TR-7. They continue to experiment, working to improve both the cost and the quality of our products. Now, if you will follow me please, I need to return to my office. My doctors have insisted that I have a short period of rest in the morning, and one again in the afternoon."

As they completed the circuitous walkway, all three guests leaned over the rail to see the research lab, which they had so quickly bypassed on their way in. Ashley recognized the equipment on the tables as being typical of the research labs at Jennings Pharmaceuticals. Conner performed a visual sweep of the area as well, and then moved behind Ashley who was already at the door through which they had entered.

Harden was puzzled. The only lab he had ever been exposed to was not for the production of fertilizer, no matter how sophisticated.

That lab had cooked and processed cocaine in large enough quantities to finance a terrorist group in the Sudan; that is, until Harden's group finally located and destroyed the facility. What caused Harden to take a second look was the fact that this equipment had the general appearance of the equipment they had destroyed in the Sudan.

As he was sorting out his thoughts Harden noticed another man, dressed in a sport coat and slacks, leaning on the rail opposite him. Feigning interest in the operation below, the man had his hand inside his jacket as if reaching for a cigarette, yet maintaining a vigilant watch on Harden.

Aubrey walked out onto the walkway just as the other party was reentering the building from the other side.

Why is that big guy staring at the lab so long? Aubrey wondered.

The question was both silent and rhetorical. No answer was required. He reached inside his jacket to loosen the snap on his shoulder holster, just in case easy access to his weapon might be necessary. He kept his head down but his eyes focused on the curious stranger.

Harden had seen enough. He moved through the doorway and followed the others back to the elevator. As he caught up with them, he found his curiosity had overcome his reluctance to interfere in Ashley's business.

"Is there any way we can get a closer look at that operation, Anthony—from floor-level, perhaps? Your results are really fascinating."

"Maybe next time, Harden. Now, let's get back to my office for a cup of coffee and some catch-up conversation."

The elevator had arrived. Everyone boarded except Jeff, who excused himself to take a phone call.

As the door closed, Aubrey was hurrying toward him.

"Did you see that big guy staring at the lab? I swear he suspects something. Who is he, anyway? Did you ever find out what connection he has with Jennings?"

"Calm down, Aubrey. I believe he's an old friend of Mr. Riley who just happened to be with Hayes. However, I think Hayes may have recognized me. He asked me how long I'd been in Cleveland. Also, when Riley introduced me, I thought I caught some spark of recognition, just for an instant. If they leave soon, we can talk to Riley for a few minutes to find out about the other guy."

They both returned to the first floor and Anthony's conference room.

* * *

Anthony and his guests had returned to his office to reconvene.

Jeff and Aubrey heard voices as they entered the conference room and realized, quite fortunately, that the speaker was still on. The office was quiet momentarily, as everyone appeared to be busy sipping on the delicious Peruvian coffee that Margaret had provided. Meanwhile, everyone was harboring different thoughts.

Ashley's smile shielded her strong disappointment at not being able to examine the manufacturing procedure more closely, and to touch or even see the TR-7 product.

Conner knew they had been buffered from actually learning anything useful about Brantley, and he was curious as to why. After all, the two companies had combined interests for their stockholders.

Harden, on the other hand, had similar questions but a different methodology. Realizing that their tour had intentionally circumvented the process, Harden was automatically driven to find out why.

"Anthony, where's the men's room? I believe that this strong brew is running right through me."

"Sure, Harden. Just take that door back to the reception area. When you leave Margaret's office, take a left down the hall. It'll be on your right."

Harden excused himself. Back in the hallway, he turned right and hurried down the long corridor in the same direction they had gone on the fourth floor. From inside the conference room, Aubrey opened the door a crack, just in time to see Harden slip around the corner.

The corridor ended in a solid concrete wall, with a single door on the far left side. A security panel on the wall beside the door required the proper sequence of digits in order to enter. Harden tried the door anyway. A buzzer alerted the guard on the inside, who then slid a small viewing panel aside to see who was there. Harden tried to exaggerate mouthing his words through the thick glass.

"Just looking for the rest room."

Harden threw his hands up as if in frustration.

Disgusted at being disturbed from perusing his *Penthouse* magazine, the guard gestured with his index finger.

"Back that way, sir."

Harden hurried back the way he came, past Anthony's office to the rest room. Just in case anyone was listening, he went through the process of flushing, washing and drying before exiting.

When he returned to their host's office he found Anthony begging their leave, using the earlier excuse of doctor-prescribed rest.

After thanking him for the tour and vowing to see each other more often in the future, Ashley, Conner and Harden made their way out of the building before resuming their conversation.

Suddenly, they all wanted to speak at once. Obviously, everyone had some reaction to convey. Ashley went first.

"That tour, although impressive, was useless. At best, I expected a fractionating of the various steps in the process to see if any of it was applicable to our other plants. At worst, we should have been allowed to view the equipment up close and examine the product."

Conner concurred.

"That was just an overall view that could have been presented to any tour group without danger of revealing any secret ingredients or procedures."

Harden, of course, agreed with these obvious conclusions.

"Let's take a look at the plant from the outside. A digital access code as well as a security officer guards the door on the first floor. I'm curious to see what security they maintain on their outside doors and the loading dock. They must have some access point for the delivery of raw materials and for shipping."

Taking a casual pace, Harden led the way along the right side of the building as they pretended to be engaged in animated conversation.

Walking past the last office window, they found a solid wall that ran the entire remaining length of the building. Continuing their mock conversation, they rounded the far corner.

Jeff and Aubrey watched the trio from the main entrance's glassed-in foyer.

"I'll keep an eye on them, Aubrey. Why don't you make your way back to shipping as fast as you can?"

Immediately, Harden and his companions found what they were

searching for. A UPS van was backed up to the overhead door, where the driver and one of the white-clad engineers were busy loading a shipment.

Harden estimated the plastic boxes to be about two feet by four feet, and about a foot thick. They did not appear to be heavy. The boxes were marked in large letters with the name Brantley Chemical, but additional small print was impossible to read from that distance. He counted four boxes in all. Just as they were about to turn away, Harden caught some movement out of the corner of his eye, and he turned in time to see a man slipping back into the shadows of the loading dock. It was the same man who had been watching him inside the plant.

On their way back to the car, Conner spoke

"Hard, that Henry Atwell could be Jeff Lewis' brother. Were you listening when he evaded my question about how long he'd been in Cleveland? He had those eyes. That's the part I remember most, back when I represented him at JAG. Only now, besides the intensity there's a confidence there, maybe even something taunting. It was as if he knew I recognized him. I could swear that Henry Atwell is Jeff Lewis, but I saw no sign of the other man, Aubrey Long."

"Can you give me a physical description of Long? Do you remember him well enough?"

"As I remember him, Harden, he was at least an inch taller than Jeff, maybe more. He was more muscular in appearance, with dark brown hair, cut very short at the time. Handsome face, but you could sense there was no feeling left in him. He was hardened, even at that young age. His smile was not cordial—more of a sneer, as I recall."

Harden had the pieces of a puzzle and was determined to fit them together.

After the others catch their flight tomorrow morning, I'll stay over one more night. Charlie can meet them back in San Francisco and continue his observation. Was it possible that both of the men I've been following around the world are right here in Cleveland? I doubt that either Ashley or Conner saw the other man either on the walkway or the dock. I'm sure those plastic containers were the same as the ones I saw at the airfield in Warbah.

All these thoughts ran through his head, seeking assimilation, as the three of them made their way back to the Sheraton Airport Hotel.

41

Who is that big man, the one you didn't know about in advance?"
Aubrey and Jeff had walked back into Anthony's office.

"He's just an old friend from high school. His name is Harden Kelly. Now, I'm tired and there are two things we need to do. First, Henry, I have a document here that you'll fly to San Francisco and deliver to Mr. Jennings for his signature. I have a flight reservation for you for tomorrow night, after you return from today's adventure. Second, James, I want you to be thinking of ways to improve our security at the research and processing facility. Now, you both had better catch that flight. This delivery must go smoothly for all of us to benefit."

Henry, as Jeff was called within the four walls of Brantley Chemical, was hastily reviewing the document.

"He'll never sign this. He transfers all his voting rights to you so that he can back off from the everyday hassle of running the companies. That sounds ridiculous, even to me."

"Henry, if it was that simple, I could handle it myself. Why do you think I hired you? Improvise, however necessary. Just get it done."

Jeff had seen eyes as cold as that only once before, at a time when he had put a hole right between them. His mind drifted back.

There had been a government-sanctioned operation to break up a terrorist group being formed in Cape Town, South Africa. After he and Aubrey had eliminated several security people, he had surprised Khali Hamad in his office on the fifth floor of the downtown Djorstad Building. The man had turned quickly with a weapon in his hand.

Jeff had stared at pure hatred in the form of two black dots surrounded by chilled white ice. Those dots had simply served to outline his target. Blood trickled from the small hole between the eyes as Hamad's weapon had fallen to the floor. He stood staring at Jeff for interminable seconds before dropping slowly to the thick pile carpet. The cushioning effect of the carpet was probably the reason that Jeff had been able to surprise the man.

Now Jeff saw those eyes again, only this time on the man who was his employer.

"That sounds like carte blanche to me. You'll have his voting rights, I guarantee."

Jeff turned to leave, and Aubrey followed with a wave of his arm to Anthony, who had already closed his eyes to rest.

* * *

Everything was going as planned as Jeff and Aubrey arrived in Amalfi. Alberto had met them as arranged and drove them to the airfield. Serena was there to greet them.

"Good to see you again, gentlemen. There are glasses and ice on the counter as well as an assortment of snacks. Please help yourselves to whatever you choose."

Aubrey managed to slide his hand down the back of her short skirt, touching her leg, before Serena hurried into the pilot's cabin. Even if there was a larger tip this time, she was not going to let that larger man anywhere near her on this flight.

Jeff and Aubrey had been furnished with Glock handguns. The new polymer frame made them light and easy to handle. Both men checked over their weapons as the Lear jet glided gently down the runway.

Aubrey had visited the luggage compartment before boarding to ascertain that the four plastic containers had arrived and been loaded.

Everything was in order for their meeting. Jeff leaned his head back and shut his eyes to devise a plan for the following evening's mission. Aubrey moved toward the bar.

They had already dined, so he was looking for some good bourbon. He tossed three cubes of ice into glass, followed by a generous portion of Knob Creek, a brand of small-batch bourbon named for Abraham Lincoln's boyhood home in Kentucky. The distinctive sweetness and rich, full-bodied flavor belied the 100-proof strength of the drink.

Aubrey grabbed the handrail and sampled the liquid. The soft burning sensation as the nectar splashed across his tongue and down his throat was just the tonic he needed.

After refilling his drink, he returned to his seat. Jeff was aware of this activity but decided not to say anything to upset Aubrey. He needed to have a sober partner when they made the transaction at Warbah. Again the demons were visiting his sleep as he dozed off in the plush cabin chair. This time Kafu and Al-Sufa decided to join the nightmare. Disembodied heads and eyes swirled through his dreams, along with the ever-present deceased Delta team and the old man from Amalfi.

Khali Hamad made an appearance as well, but this time his eyes were made of fire, not ice. In the dream Hamad had both his hands outstretched and was shaking Jeff.

"Hey partner, you were freaking out. Do you have visitors in your sleep, too?"

Aubrey stood over him.

"What you need is one of these."

He held up his now-empty glass.

"Thanks, maybe I will."

Jeff quickly regained control and followed Aubrey over to the bar. His nightmare must have lasted longer than it seemed, as he felt the plane begin its descent for landing.

Aubrey and Jeff straightened their ties and used the palms of their hands to smooth the wrinkles from their suits. Checking their weapons one more time, they were ready to deplane.

The plastic containers, while bulky, were surprisingly lightweight. Jeff brushed off Alberto's offer to help as he and Aubrey set the four cases onto the makeshift tarmac. They both came to attention at the approach of two stout-looking men in suits, each possessed of an obvious bulge between their left-hand pockets and their armpits.

One of the men carried a small suitcase. Little conversation was necessary. Both visitors examined the labeling on the plastic containers. Satisfied with the Brantley label marked TR-7, they presented the suitcase to Jeff, who stood closest to them.

The older man looked hard and dangerous. The younger man was nervous; his eyes kept darting in all directions. But their demeanor reflected how tired they were, and it was obvious that they were anxious to finish this transaction. Jeff placed the suitcase on top of the plastic cases and inserted the key that the older man had given him. The lid popped open. Jeff raised the black leather cover to reveal bundles of U.S. hundred dollar bills. Flipping through the bundles, Jeff quickly determined that the currency was consistent throughout. Then he closed the case.

"Thank you, gentlemen. See you next time."

Jeff turned to board the jet. Aubrey remained facing the two men until they addressed the plastic cases. The older man just stood there while the young one walked away to get the truck. Aubrey then boarded the plane.

"Let's go, Alberto."

The jet began to taxi down the runway.

With the exchange behind them, both passengers slept through the return flight, tensions relieved at the smoothness of the transaction.

* * *

"Anthony didn't seem especially friendly, Harden. In fact, he appeared downright uncomfortable with our presence, and certainly not excited to see us."

Harden had already decided that he would return to Brantley the following night, once Ashley and Conner were safely back in San Francisco.

"How about a nice dinner this evening? It's my treat."

Conner had hoped to have all of Ashley's attention that evening.

"Sounds great, Harden. Is that all right with you, Ashley?"

"Certainly, guys. Everyone will wonder how I rated two such handsome and charming gentlemen. Have you picked out a place yet?"

"I have a restaurant in mind, but I'll need to call for reservations. It shouldn't be a problem for a Monday night. How about we rest a bit and leave the hotel around six?"

They parked and parted company at the second floor. Conner had no more than said goodbye to Ashley at her door and entered his hotel room, when she appeared at the connecting doorway.

"We have three hours, Conner. Do you want to come over for a while?"

The invitation was not wasted. Conner was at her side in an instant. He put his hands on her waist and they looked into each other's eyes. She kicked off her heels and was suddenly a head shorter than Conner. His head bent down and met her lips as she lifted them toward his. He had thrown his suit jacket on his bed but still had a tie knotted around his neck. Her fingers made quick work of that before starting on the buttons of his shirt. Their lips and tongues were fiercely exploring while there hands raced to remove the items of clothing in their path. Now, with her blouse open and the clasp unfastened at the front of her brassiere, his lips moved down her neck to the valley below. His shirt was off and she opened his belt, helping him to remove his trousers just before his lips started to move south. Naked now except for a pair of silk lace panties, she threw her head back as his lips encircled the aureole of her stiffened nipples. She could feel his hardness against her leg as he gently laid her across the bed.

Two hours later, an exhausted Conner leaned over to look again into her eyes and, for only the second time in his life, repeated the words he had spoken so many years ago to Liz.

"I think I have fallen in love with you, Miss Jennings."

She raised her arms around his neck and gently squeezed.

"We had better start getting ready for dinner. Harden will be here before we know it."

Reluctantly, they parted. Gathering his clothing, Conner retreated to his room.

Promptly at six o'clock, Harden knocked on Conner's door only to have it swing open at his touch.

"We're ready, Hard. I left the door open for you. Tell us where we're going"

"I was able to make reservations at Parker's New American Bistro, down on Bridge Avenue. Even though this is my first time in Cleveland, I've heard good things about the owner and chef, Parker Bosley. He's well known for changing his menu to reflect whatever's in season. Fresh, seasonal cooking is definitely his forte."

Harden had picked the destination, so Conner tossed him the keys to the rental car and they were on their way. They took West Twenty-Fifth Street and, with light traffic, managed to arrive before six-thirty. Since their reservation was for seven o'clock, they decided to sit at the bar for a drink before dining. Harden felt as if he was imposing on the couple. No matter what the topic of conversation, they kept stealing glances at each other. He felt relief when the maitre d' arrived to tell them that their table was ready.

At their server's suggestion, Ashley and Conner both ordered the Chicken Papparedelle, while Harden chose veal medallions with a vegetable ragout. In the dining room, the atmosphere was completely changed. Harden and Conner talked about their boyhood adventures while Ashley listened intently, occasionally inserting a question when the stories became too vague for an outsider to understand.

On the way back to the hotel, they all agreed that the choice had been superb and vowed to duplicate this evening the next time they were in Cleveland. Harden said goodnight as well as good-bye, since the couple was catching an early flight the next day and he had other plans.

42

Harden ordered a rental car for Tuesday morning and had it delivered to the hotel. He ran several errands during the day, prior to his scheduled evening adventure. Since he had flown into Cleveland on a military flight, keeping his weapon with him had not been a problem.

Dressed all in black—trousers, sweatshirt and jacket—he picked up his satchel from the table and started out at 2300 hours, just as he had planned.

After circling the plant to make sure that no employees were present, Harden parked in an alley close enough to make a prompt departure, if that proved necessary. The only vehicle in the company parking lot was a red pickup truck that he assumed belonged to a security guard. Staying in the shadows, Harden made his way to the rear of the building where the loading dock was located. From the dark satchel he removed the multipick system he had acquired that afternoon, as well as a model MPN-50 blade holder, which was supposed to make the system foolproof. Selecting a pick, he inserted it into the MPN-50 and then into the lock. The soft vibration was noiseless as the pick searched out the tumblers, with no positive results. No sooner had he inserted the second pick than he heard one click, followed by another. The lock was open.

Raising the overhead door a fraction of an inch, he slid a plastic card along the bottom edge until he found the alarm release. Removing a lead weight about the size of a man's fist from his satchel, he set the bag aside. Holding the alarm button down, he raised the door about two feet off the floor as he lay on the concrete dock. With both hands free, Harden rested the flat end of the weight on the alarm button to simulate pressure from the door. Quickly he rolled under the door and was on his feet inside the darkened shipping area. He did not care if he attracted the guard's attention. Were he to deal with him now, he would no longer have that problem ahead of him. Carefully he walked toward the processing plant. He used his flashlight to locate the door to the plant while shielding the beam from being seen outside.

Surely this plant must have some additional security, he thought. *This door alarm is no more than what's basically used in homes, and there aren't any motion sensors out here.*

It was time to get the guard's attention so he could reconnoiter more freely. Harden extinguished his flashlight and rolled back under the door to the outside. He walked boldly up to the front entrance, which was brightly lit, and rang the bell beside the main lobby entrance. Before long a guard appeared, waving his arms to indicate that the office was closed.

"Can I use your phone? Car trouble."

Harden shook his car keys and pointed back toward the entrance. The guard waved him off and turned to leave.

"Come on, man," Harden pleaded. "At least make the call for me, O.K.?"

The stranger standing out front appeared to be alone, so finally the guard relented. After punching buttons on a security panel behind the receptionist's desk, he unlocked the door.

"Make it quick. The boss would fire me if he knew I let somebody in after hours."

Harden noticed that the man was nervous about letting him in and had rested his hand loosely on the Smith & Wesson holstered at his hip. The security guard was experienced and kept his distance as Harden moved to the telephone sitting on the receptionist's desk.

"Thanks, man. You don't know how much I appreciate this."

He pretended to reach into his pocket for a phone number, and the man carelessly moved to the side of the desk. In a blur, Harden gripped the guard's right wrist and used body leverage to spin him around. With a well-placed chop to the side of his neck, Harden laid the unconscious guard down behind the desk, where he would be out of sight from the exterior. Although he could not reset the alarm, Harden did lock the front door.

After glancing back inside to make sure no one could see the guard, he made his way down the long hallway to the plant's entrance. Before he reached the door, Harden suddenly remembered that he had left his satchel out back so as not to make the guard suspicious. Quickly, he ran back up the hall, unlocked the front door, and jogged over to the loading dock. He returned to his task just as quickly, satchel securely in hand.

Thanks to his equipment he was able to unlock the door but could not disable the alarm, at least not without more sophisticated equipment, or with the guard's assistance.

Returning to the reception area, he bent over the unconscious man.

A few slaps on the cheeks roused the man gradually. Harden was careful to unload the man's weapon before he was fully awake. Taking him by the arm, he led the guard back down the hallway.

"I want to take a look around the plant. If you'll punch in your alarm code, it'll save us both a lot of time, and save you a lot of trouble. I'm not going to steal anything, and you can forget I was even here. No one will be the wiser. Your job will be a lot safer than if you try to stop me."

Harden accentuated that last point by applying additional pressure to the man's left arm.

"Punch in the code. If the alarm goes off, you'll be in a whole lot of pain, and I'll be gone."

After pausing to mull over his options, the guard's fingers moved across the keyboard. A green light appeared on the left side of the panel.

"Now, open the door and we'll walk through the plant together."

Moving quickly through the doorway, Harden led the guard around ahead of him and began making mental notes of everything he saw. In the lab area he picked up an empty, corked test tube from a supply cart that sat next to one of the tables. Harden slipped it into his pocket. With the machinery shut down for the night, he learned little more than he had from the walkway tour the previous morning. However, the last bin in the procedure was still half-full of TR-7. Hastily, Harden uncorked the cylinder that he had stashed in his pocket and dipped it into the white powder.

Filling the tube nearly all the way, Harden was ready to make a quick departure.

He retrieved his satchel at the hall entrance. Still pushing the guard in front of him, he removed the lead weight from the overhead door alarm at the rear of the building. He pulled the door closed and walked the frightened guard back to the front entrance. Harden slipped his .357 Magnum out of his jacket and held it in front of the man's face.

"Stand in the light of this doorway for five minutes. Smoke a cigarette, or at least pretend to smoke in case anyone sees you. If you do that, we can both forget this incident ever happened. If not, I'll be back to see you."

Harden turned and disappeared between neighboring buildings, leaving the trembling guard to study his options.

* * *

The papers Mr. Jennings needed to sign were in a briefcase Jeff was carrying with him, as his United Airlines flight made its way to San Francisco.

He'll never sign this document. There's no reason to. My choices are to either threaten his daughter or to kill him. I could do that by faking a break-in and injecting some of this kurari into his system, which would make it look like he died of a heart attack or a stroke. Or I could just tell Mr. Riley that he wouldn't sign it.

Jeff was still mulling over his options as the jet taxied to the terminal at San Francisco International late on a Tuesday evening.

Margaret had made his flight and car reservations on Monday morning. Jeff caught her in time to put them in the name of Robert Tobias, another alias he had acquired thanks to the old man in Amalfi. There was no logical reason for Henry Atwell to be visiting San Francisco today.

Jeff was well prepared. He had studied a photograph of the old man, memorized the route to his home from the road map, and read through the document several times in order to have some persuasive arguments handy. He had learned that Mr. Jennings employed a combination housekeeper and cook who left by seven every evening.

It was almost ten when he pulled his rental car into the driveway. The lights were still on in the hallway, in one room off to the right side, and in an upstairs room as well.

Jeff rang the doorbell and waited. He preferred not to break in unless he was forced to do so. With no immediate response, he rang the chimes once again. It was probably late for someone to be calling on a Tuesday evening, so Jeff tried to anticipate the man's reaction. The huge door opened a few inches, the security chain still in place.

"Henry Atwell! What are you doing here?"

The old man had a good memory. They had met briefly at the last directors' meeting. The door closed and Jeff could hear the chain being released. Then the door opened wide to reveal a tall man wearing black trousers, plus a white shirt and tie covered by a red smoking jacket, loosely buttoned to complete the ensemble.

"Hello, Mr. Jennings."

He extended his hand and was surprised by the strength and the warmth of the handshake.

"Mr. Riley had some papers for you to review. I guess they were important enough for me to deliver them to you personally."

"Come in, Henry. My office is just off to the right here."

He touched the light switch to reveal a small but comfortable-looking room, with an old cherry desk occupying a good portion of the available floor space. Two leather chairs, looking almost too cozy for business, faced the desk. Jennings motioned for Jeff to sit down. Moving around the desk, Jennings sat in his chair and leaned forward.

"Let me see what you have, Henry."

Having used multiple names on this trip, Jeff had learned to respond to any of them as naturally as possible. Although there was only one document in the briefcase, Jeff pretended to move things around inside as he searched for the correct paper.

"Ah, here it is!"

He handed the document to Jennings.

It did not take long for Jeff to see a frown extend across the man's face, one that eventually turned into a mock smile.

"What is this, a joke? Riley knows I can't sign this. My daughter will get all my voting rights when I'm through with the company. I admire what he's done with Brantley and hope he has similar success with the balance of the corporation, but this is a ridiculous request. I'm sorry you made this long trip for nothing, Henry."

He attempted to hand the document back to Jeff.

"You don't understand, sir. I'm to see that you sign this paper before I leave tonight. I'd hoped you would do so voluntarily. Mr. Riley would be disappointed to think that you didn't value his impact on the company enough to let him run it."

Jennings began to rise from his chair.

"I will not sign this. Tell Mr. Riley to come and see me if he has anything further to discuss. Meanwhile instruct him that, as chairman, I hereby remove him altogether from the board of directors. The paperwork will be prepared in the morning to update the minutes. Now, you'd better leave."

"Sit down, Mr. Jennings."

The menacing tone in Jeff's voice made the older man settle back into his chair.

"You can sign this document in recognition of the accomplishments Mr. Riley has made, and as encouragement for the future growth of Jennings Pharmaceuticals. That would be as a reward for his efforts to date."

With the old man back in his chair, Jeff relaxed his demeanor somewhat.

"I recognize Riley's effect on our balance sheet, but I will remain in control of my company," Jennings repeated. "This meeting is over."

Again, he started to rise.

"Please remain seated, Mr. Jennings, until you've heard me out.

"I see that I must be quite frank with you, sir. You mentioned your daughter. You know, she could have a serious or even fatal accident, perhaps as early as this evening. Then what good would your decision be?"

Jennings reached for the telephone. With a quickness that belied the persona of Henry Atwell, Jeff slapped his own hand down on top of Jennings', locking the receiver in place.

In a much colder tone of voice he said, "Sign this document and everyone will be fine, sir."

Now it was Jennings' turn to review his options.

I could sign the paper and call the police when this man leaves. It should be obvious that the only way I'd sign away my rights would be under duress. I could try to subdue Henry. He wouldn't be carrying a weapon if he'd just arrived on a commercial flight. Or I could continue to refuse and get immediate protection for Ashley when Henry leaves. This is certainly not the Henry Atwell we all met at the last board meeting. What's going on, anyway?

Jennings sorted through these thoughts as Jeff released his hand from the receiver. He could not take any chances with his daughter's life. The first choice was the only viable one.

"Let me see the document again, please."

Jeff placed the paper in front of him. After rereading the paper in disbelief, Jennings opened his pen and affixed his name on the appropriate line.

"You have what you want. Now, leave."

With his eyes locked on Mr. Jennings, Jeff returned the document to his briefcase and removed the dart from its vial, sliding it into the coffee stirrer that he had brought along expressly for this purpose. He snapped the briefcase shut and, leaving it on the chair, rose and extended his right hand to Mr. Jennings. Jennings reflexively gave his hand and immediately regretted having done so.

Jeff grasped his hand and spun him to the side. In the same motion he raised his left hand and blew the deadly missile into the now-exposed neck tissue. Jennings' muscles contracted automatically, but he could not free his right hand to remove the missile. His eyes popped wide open, his face froze with a wild stare, and then he slumped heavily to the floor.

Jeff had been careful not to touch anything, including the chair he had used. Bending over the man, he carefully removed the dart and placed it in his pocket. He wet his index finger with his tongue and wiped a drop of blood from the entry point. The wound was no longer visible.

Retrieving his briefcase from the leather chair, he moved quickly to the front door. He opened the door with his handkerchief and carefully closed it behind him. With the handkerchief still in hand, he wiped the doorbell clean and calmly walked to his car.

Later that evening, "Robert Tobias" returned the rental car to the Hertz representative, caught the shuttle to the terminal, and boarded his flight back to Cleveland.

43

As Aubrey pulled up in front of the office he saw the night watchman standing outside the main entrance, smoking a cigarette. Parking sideways across the handicapped spots nearest the entrance, he exited the car and headed up the stairs.

"Hello, Phil."

Surprised by Aubrey's unexpected return to the office, the still nervous guard replied, "What are you doing here, Mr. Zachary? I thought you were out of town with Mr. Atwell. I was just having a smoke out here. Don't want to get smoke inside the building. You know how Mr. Riley feels about that."

He's nervous and talking too fast, Aubrey thought to himself.

Aloud he said, "Anything unusual happen here tonight, Phil?"

Phil responded, "Everything is quiet, sir. I haven't seen anything unusual at all."

Aubrey was close enough to look the guard directly in the eye, which seemed to make the man even more nervous.

"I believe I'll look around the plant for a few minutes. You go ahead and finish your cigarette."

As he opened the door and moved down the hallway, more troubling thoughts occurred.

Why would he turn off the alarm and use the front door for his break? I know he often went into the loading area for a smoke to keep it away from Riley.

He entered four digits into the panel and unlocked the door. Both the lab and the production areas were kept spotless. Tonight was no exception. Trained to be highly observant, Aubrey walked slowly through the area, his eyes constantly shifting from one operation to the next. He saw no sign of a disturbance. However, just before exiting through the door to the shipping area, he noticed a thin trail in the white powder that remained from the last production batch, as if someone had run a finger through it.

Aubrey flipped the wall switch in the dock area. Immediately the entire floor was bathed in a bright light. He shut off the alarm before raising the overhead door. Although this area was kept as clean as possible, there were always footprints left by the drivers as well as the employees who helped them load. Curiously, he noticed that the area directly under the overhead door was wiped clean of footprints in about a five-foot-wide swath. Getting down on one knee, he examined the alarm button in the floor, pushing it in and out. Then he lowered the door from the outside and examined the lock. There were marks where metal had scraped against metal.

I'm probably being a bit too cautious here. Those marks could have been made by repetitive key usage. The floor could have been rubbed clean by pulling a shipping carton across it. That second guy yesterday morning certainly was giving the place a good look, but it may have been nothing more than curiosity. He wouldn't have a reason to suspect anything, I suppose.

Analyze and reanalyze. That was how he had been taught to handle unusual situations. Just as he was about to lower the door, he noticed a circular ring in the dust that surrounded the alarm button on the floor. The circle was about three inches in diameter. Again, he knelt on one knee as he ran his finger across the line that formed the circle. He stood, staring at the lock again and then at the floor under the door.

There are no coincidences. Isn't that what they taught us a long time ago. To reconstruct this, someone could have picked the lock, carefully set a weight on the alarm as they raised the door, then slid under the door so as not to attract the attention of opening the door all the way. If it happened that way, then who did it, and why?

Slowly and pensively, he lowered and locked the door, activated the alarm, and then walked back the way he had come. Returning to the production area, he got down on his knees next to the nearly empty bin. Tilting his head to better view the tiny scooped-out area, he imagined someone running a small container through the white powder to get a sample.

Rising to his feet, he decided he needed to have another talk with the guard.

44

Harden had seen the car pull into the lot as he sat in his car. Wondering what reaction the guard might have, he quietly returned to the side of the building to take a closer look.

The guard seems to know this man, he thought to himself.

Just then the man came alongside the guard and turned at an angle where Harden had no problem identifying him.

That's the same man who followed us through the processing tour. Then I saw him again on the dock as I went around the building. He was probably wondering what I was doing back there. But if this is one of the men I'm after, I'd better find out what he's up to here at Brantley.

Observing no reaction on the man's part, Harden thought it safe to assume that the guard had not related his earlier adventures to the man—not yet, anyway. Harden moved in closer as the man entered the building. While he was trying to decide whether to have another talk with the guard to get the man's name, the guard made the decision for him. Flicking his cigarette carelessly onto the lawn he reentered the building, locked the door, and set the alarm. Harden could see him sit down in the receptionist's chair as if waiting for the other man to leave.

As late as it was, everything was quiet. Suddenly Harden heard the overhead door open. He quickly rounded the building to get a better view of the situation.

The man appeared to be suspicious. He came outside and examined the door lock for an inordinate amount of time. As he raised the door to go back into the building, something on the floor caught his attention. Harden watched as he got down on one knee and examined the alarm button again. The man rose and looked at the floor under the door before closing it again, this time from the inside.

Harden returned to his previous spot, where he could keep an eye on the front door.

A few minutes later, the man came into view and walked up to the guard. Harden certainly wished he could read lips on this animated conversation.

Aubrey sat on the corner of the desk and looked the watchman squarely in the eye.

"What's going on, Phil? Who was here?"

Phil fidgeted nervously in his chair.

"What do you mean, Mr. Zachary? No one, sir."

The man was now outwardly trembling.

Calmly, Aubrey put his right hand on the man's shoulder. At the same time he removed the pistol from the watchman's holster with his left hand.

A quick glance told him that the gun was not loaded.

"You forgot to load your weapon, Phil. What would you do if you had to chase someone away from here? An intruder? A break-in?"

Aubrey slid the weapon back into the holster.

"Did he scare you or threaten you in any way?"

With his right hand still on the guard's shoulder, Aubrey could feel the man shaking. He knew he was almost there.

Harden viewed the exchange from his vantage point and could almost put words to the conversation. The guard was about to break. But, more interestingly, the other man was displaying skills that tended to reinforce Harden's earlier suspicions.

"Yes, sir! Yes, sir! A man broke in tonight just before you arrived. He threatened to shoot me if I told anyone. He had just left and told me to stay out front for five minutes and smoke a cigarette as if I was on break, or he would kill me. He was a big man, dressed in black pants and a black sweater, with a black jacket. I had just lit a cigarette when you arrived."

At this, Aubrey quickly turned his head toward the front of the building.

Was there movement out by the sign?

Whatever it had been, it was gone now. He turned his attention back to Phil, who was still rambling.

"He hit me on the head with a gun or something, so I don't know what he did while I was unconscious. Next thing I know he's slapping me around and making me punch in the alarm code so he can go into the back. I reached for my gun one time, but found out he'd unloaded it. I thought about hitting him in the head with it, but this guy was big. I don't know if I could have hit him on top of his head. Suddenly, he had enough and pushed me outside, there where you found me smoking a cigarette. Mr. Reilly won't fire me, will he? I tried. I really tried, but this guy was big."

Phil was beginning to repeat himself, so Aubrey's thoughts drifted back to the shadow he may have seen moving out in front of the building.

I was careless, thought Harden. *I think he saw me when his head suddenly turned this way. The guard is apparently telling this guy his story, maybe even embellishing it to protect his job. I can't blame him. Nobody wants to get fired.*

After fearing he had been spotted, Harden had returned to his earlier position behind a neighboring building. He could still see the two men, but from much farther away.

"Just one more question, Phil. Did you see him take anything from the building? I'm particularly interested in whether you saw him take a sample of the TR-7 fertilizer."

At that question, Phil began to perspire once again.

Can I get away with lying again? Will I have a better chance of keeping my job if I say no?

Reviewing his options in his uncomplicated brain, Phil needed only to look once more into Aubrey's icy blue eyes to reach his decision.

"He took one of those little corked containers from the lab as he shoved me along, almost knocking me down," Phil admitted. "Then, when we got to that bin that had a little fertilizer left in it, he scooped some of it into that container and put it in his pocket."

That was enough. Aubrey knew he needed to talk to Anthony tonight, if at all possible.

"Go to the washroom, Phil, and throw some water on your face. Pull yourself together. You still have a long night ahead of you. I'll be in Mr. Riley's office for a while."

Quickly, he was around the corner and out of sight. Phil heard the office door open and close before he stood up on his shaking legs and walked down the hallway, headed in the opposite direction toward the men's room.

* * *

With his protagonist gone in one direction and the watchman off in the other, Harden decided to wait it out and see what might happen next. In order to do so, he realized that standard operating procedure dictated he should have extra ammunition clips in his possession. With one last look at the now-deserted reception area, he moved quickly to his car that was parked about a half block away. After opening the trunk he pushed his larger suitcase aside and opened the smaller gym bag. From under the pile of clothing he retrieved two additional clips for his .357 Magnum and dropped them into his jacket pocket. He had already returned the satchel to its place when he caught sight of a car turning into the Brantley parking lot.

Reaching the decision that he would not need to break in again tonight, he closed the trunk and returned to his position behind the neighboring business. He saw that the reception area was still deserted. Harden sat down with his back against the wall, but at an angle that allowed him to see the front of the Brantley Building.

Aubrey did not want to sit in Anthony's crooked chair, so he pushed it aside and rolled one of the other chairs in behind the desk.

After locating an emergency contact number for Anthony, he waited for someone to answer.

After twelve rings, a gruff voice on the other end answered.

"Mr. Riley's phone. Who is this?"

No polite answer—no "please." It was easy to identify Mandrake, even over the phone.

"This is James Zachary, Mandrake. I need to talk to Mr. Riley. Believe me, this is important or I wouldn't be calling in the middle of the night."

"Hold on. I'll check with him."

Suddenly, Aubrey was on hold and listening to classical music while he tapped his fingers impatiently on the top of Anthony's desk. He could not help but admire Mandrake's reaction to pressure. A fairly gruff individual, he nonetheless seemed to maintain the same controlled response. Although he was a giant of a man and looked as hard as a rock, Aubrey was confident that he could take Mandrake down, should a face-off ever occur. Aubrey cradled the receiver and listened to the music through the speakerphone.

The minutes passed and Aubrey's thoughts turned to the identity of the evening's intruder.

Anthony thinks he knows him, maybe from somewhere in his past. I hope he has some current information. I wonder if that guy is still out there. Should I sneak out there to see if I could confront him?

Aubrey had no shortage of confidence.

A distorted voice croaked out over the speaker, "Aubrey, what's on your mind?"

Sleep had distorted Anthony's usual caution. James Zachary had once again become Aubrey Long.

"Mr. Riley, I'm here in your office. Jeff and I got in some time ago, and he's no doubt in San Francisco by now. I've already put the suitcase into the safe, as you requested. However, I checked my account after our return and saw no significant increase in the balance."

"James."

Now Riley was back in control.

"You could have gone over all of this in the morning. What's the reason for this call in the middle of the night?"

"Phil, the night watchman, was telling me about a break-in here tonight. It was that friend of yours from yesterday morning, the big guy. According to Phil, he succeeded in getting away with a small vial of TR-

7. In order to provide the services for which you hired me, I need to know the identity of this man, Mr. Riley."

"This is indeed very disturbing. I didn't realize we had such weakness in our security. But, on the other hand, we could not have been prepared for a man such as this. Have you ever heard of 'the company,' James? It's an organization of special services of the U.S. government. My friend's name is Harden Kelly, and he's been an employee of this 'company' for fifteen or twenty years. Are you certain that he's the perpetrator?"

Aubrey was still in shock. Harden Kelly was a legend in special ops.

He was the standard around which all training revolved. Unbelievable stories circulated, stories that certainly must have contained exaggeration about his strength, his courage, his hand-to-hand combat skills, his originality in methodology, and his mission successes. The stories about his abilities were mind-boggling.

The all-confident Aubrey Long almost smiled at the challenge that lay before him.

"If you're sure that he's the man who toured the plant yesterday morning, then I'm sure he's the man who broke into the plant tonight. Harden Kelly. I still can't believe it. I told you about our controller, Anderson. Well, this man has been Anderson's protégé from the time he was first recruited."

Anthony was quick to detect the awe in Aubrey's voice as he talked about his old friend, Harden. He had not realized how impressive his quiet friend's career had become. While it had been easy to keep up with Conner Hayes' activities through the media, where he was a much more public figure, Harden Kelly's clandestine activities never made it into the press.

45

Conner dropped Ashley off at her condominium on their way back from San Francisco International Airport. When they reached her door, she turned and kissed him passionately on the lips. By the time he caught his breath, she was already unlocking the door.

On the return flight they had spent almost no time talking about business. Instead they were like two school kids in love, excitedly discussing their future plans together.

"My dad will be so excited. He thought he'd be stuck with me forever. I just never found the right man until I met you."

Conner was equally enthralled.

"I haven't felt like this in a long time, Ashley. After telling you all about Liz, I hope you don't mind me comparing my feelings now with back then. If I say I'm experiencing the same feelings as I had, that's the ultimate for me. My love for you has become the most important thing in my life. I do love you."

Their flight had arrived in San Francisco sooner than scheduled. There had been no discussion of Harden, Anthony, or Brantley Chemical.

Now things were different. As she unlocked the door, she turned.

"I'm embarrassed to say that I forgot to tell you I really enjoyed meeting your friend, Harden Kelly. After the initial intimidation, I see why you consider him such a good friend. He has a wonderfully soft manner for such a huge man—friendly, courteous, and fun to be with."

"Whoa, Ashley. I'd better not let him get too close to you again. I didn't realize he was such strong competition."

"You know I didn't mean I liked him in that way. But he's one of the few genuinely nice people that I've met in my life. You have a good friend there. Now, I'd like to think I do as well."

"I couldn't agree more," Conner replied. "The only problem is, we don't see each other all that often. Our lives are worlds apart—literally."

"Can you give me a couple of hours to freshen up and put my things away? Maybe pick me up about seven?"

"I don't want to leave, but I'll force myself away for two hours."

They parted with one last brush of their lips.

On the short drive across town, Conner's thoughts returned to the Cleveland meeting.

Anthony certainly didn't want us to examine his process too closely. That catwalk he took us on was designed for hustling tour groups through a plant, not for giving members of the board a decent look at things. I need to talk to Harden about Jeff Lewis. I'm certain it was he that we saw. He even seemed to be taunting me with his little charade. I could be wrong, but I don't think so. If I know Harden, he's probably planning a return trip to take the plant tour that was denied to us yesterday.

There was so much to think about that he arrived home without realizing how long it had taken him to get there. Charlie was parked across the street, apparently waiting for him.

Harden must have arranged that, Conner reflected.

* * *

"Mr. Anderson, I have a powder sample I need to have analyzed as soon as possible."

Early Wednesday morning, Harden had caught a ride on a military jet back to San Francisco.

"There appears to be a possible connection with Lewis and Long, but I don't have enough information just yet."

"Since you're back in San Francisco, see Admiral Jesse Shaffer at the

Hunters Point Naval Shipyard. They're equipped to do military analysis there. I'm sure they'll have a lab equipped to analyze your powder sample. Is it an explosive powder, or what?"

"Well, it's supposed to be fertilizer. If it is, it certainly generates a lot of revenue for the company. I'll get back to you on that. Thanks!"

Harden still had possession of a black Chevrolet Impala he had signed out at the Presidio. Still too early to check in with Conner, he drove directly to the shipyard.

Security was tight. A sentry stood guard on either side of the entrance. Harden presented his identification and expected a quick approval. However, the young sergeant took his papers into the kiosk and carefully scanned them. Through the open doorway Harden could see a green light click on.

Apparently satisfied, the young man returned his papers and, with a salute, opened up the gate.

"Have a good day, Mr. Kelly, sir. Admiral Shaffer is expecting you. He's waiting in Building 408, two blocks straight ahead on your right."

"Thanks!"

Harden returned the salute as he drove through the gate. As usual, all military buildings were identified by nondescript numbers whether a commissary, a barracks or, in this case, a communications office. A short, stocky officer was waiting just inside the door as Harden entered the building.

"Mr. Kelly, sir, I'm Lieutenant Dorfmann. The admiral wanted me to show you to our lab. Will you follow me, please?"

Instead of leading Harden back outside, Lieutenant Dorfmann escorted him down the building's hallway and out the rear door to the adjacent building. Although the guard at the laboratory apparently recognized Dorfmann, the lieutenant still presented his identification. Kelly did likewise. A second steel door buzzed open, and the two men entered.

The night crew consisted of a young man and a slightly older woman. They were both bent over microscopes at facing tables as the two men came in.

"Hi, I'm Sally. You must be Mr. Kelly. We've been expecting you."

She extended her hand.

"May I see your sample, please?"

Harden was always amazed at Mr. Anderson's efficiency. Every request was met with a prompt response. Of course, he had earned Anderson's respect almost from the moment they had met back in Berea, Kentucky, so many years ago.

"Nice to meet you, Sally. I have this small vial of white powder. Be careful. It might be quite difficult to obtain another sample. I need to know its properties and its probable use, if you can do that."

Sally took the vial to her table, visually analyzing it as she walked those few steps. Holding it up to the light, she gently moved the powder back and forth in its container. Next, she poured a tiny sample onto a slide and covered it with a plain glass cover.

"If you'll give me a few minutes, Mr. Kelly."

Harden took the hint and had Lieutenant Dorfmann lead him to the employees' lounge, where there was always coffee brewing. Dorfmann excused himself and left Harden alone in the room. The chairs were comfortable, and he quickly dozed off without taking a second sip of his black coffee.

* * *

Conner Hayes had no trouble falling asleep once he finally reached his condo, in spite of the ever-present Charlie Reynolds in the living room. Once again he was enjoying the previous evening's events with Ashley, this time in his dreams, when the phone rudely awakened him. Before he could say hello, he heard her excited voice.

"Conner—Conner! My dad had a stroke or a heart attack, or something. The ambulance just left. I couldn't get a pulse. They wouldn't tell me, but I think he's gone. I just don't understand it. He was only sixty-one."

Conner caught enough of the conversation through the tears.

"I can get there in fifteen minutes to take you to the hospital. Please, just wait for me to get there."

Conner was pulling on sweats as he left the bedroom. Charlie was already dressed, having awakened right after he heard the phone ring. They left together with Conner driving, since he was more familiar with San Francisco geography. When they arrived, both men ran up to the house. Ashley met them at the door with her coat already on.

"San Francisco General Hospital," she managed to say as they immediately rushed back to Conner's car. "The address is 1001 Petrero Street."

Conner knew the place. Too many times he'd had to visit clients there over the years. Although it was easy to find the hospital, it seemed more difficult each time his relationship with his clients required him to return. It was not yet daylight, so traffic was light. Conner stopped at the emergency entrance, and Charlie agreed to take care of the car. Conner and Ashley hurried inside. Dr. Heywood was waiting for them.

"How did you get here so fast, doctor?"

Ashley was surprised to see him so soon.

"I was in the hospital on another matter, Ashley. Would you follow me? There's a small conference room right over here."

Ashley could not restrain her reaction to what she knew the doctor was about to say. With his arm around her shoulders, Conner could feel the trembling as tears again freed themselves from her bloodshot eyes and traveled down her cheeks, thus ending the trip that began all the way from her heart.

Heywood took her hand in his at the table.

"He had a massive heart attack, Ashley. It was quick. He died before he reached the floor. I am so sorry."

"I want to see him, Dr. Heywood."

Her voice was soft and quivering. Conner offered silent support with his hand on her elbow as she rose from her chair.

"We anticipated that. Follow me this way, Ashley."

With Conner remaining behind, Heywood and Ashley left the conference room and walked quietly but purposefully down the corridor through the emergency room. Dr. Heywood held the door open on Room E-10 and, after he was satisfied that she was strong enough for the moment, closed the door gently behind her.

"Daddy, Daddy, what am I going to do without you? You weren't supposed to leave us so soon. I have so much to talk to you about."

211

Ashley had initially grabbed her father's hand, but it was already cold to the touch. Now she could only hold onto the bed rail as she released all her emotions in words and tears. Then, gathering the strength her father had instilled in her since childhood, she began to compose herself. Ashley spoke to her father about Conner, and from that effort she gained even more control. Suddenly thinking about the angioplasty he postponed because he had been too busy with his job, the mental anguish she felt caused tears to fall once again. By taking a deep breath she composed herself once more, and then bade him farewell.

"I'll do my best with the responsibility you entrusted to me, Daddy. If I start to crumble or weaken, please be there to give me a push in the right direction. I love you, Daddy."

She bent forward for one last kiss and, as her lips touched the cold flesh, she knew that he had already gone to a better place. She turned and left the room, no longer with slumping shoulders and tears, but with upright stature and determination in her eyes.

Heywood and Conner had waited to offer their support, but were surprised to find it was not needed.

"Will there be an autopsy, doctor?"

Ashley was uncertain as to the proper procedure for patients who had been transported to the emergency room.

"The cause of death was heart failure, Ashley. An autopsy is not required when death is due to natural causes."

"Good. I would hate to see his body abused any more. I just want to see him put to rest. If I can use that office again, I'll start making the necessary arrangements."

Conner was concerned.

"Do you feel up to it, Ashley? I can make the calls for you."

"These are things I need to do for Daddy. I appreciate the offer, but I really do want to take care of this myself. He seemed to have held on to one last bit of strength, waiting for me to get here. I know he had already died, but I felt a surge of energy come over me as I said goodbye. It was his last gift to me."

Again, they entered the small conference room.

46

Harden sensed someone approaching and immediately came awake. "Mr. Kelly, sorry to have taken so long. We analyzed your material and tested it on lab mice to record their reaction. My original thought was that we have here a very pure form of cocaine. Contrary to that, our chemical analysis reveals that there is no residue whatsoever from the coca plant. This substance is totally manmade, but the end result is the most pure form of artificial cocaine that I've ever encountered.

"It's certainly not used for fertilizer. It would be economically unfeasible, not to mention impractical. Plants absorbing this compound into their root systems would burn up within an hour. Whoever arrived at this combination of substances, and in these exact quantities, must have been a genius of a chemist.

"The bottom line is that this product has the intensifying, hallucinogenic effect of the strongest drugs on the market today. Such a combination of substances appears amazingly inexpensive to produce as well. That's why I said that this is a breakthrough drug, either produced by accidentally combining the proper ingredients, or else designed by a master chemist. It's illegal as hell, by the way. I'll keep our analysis safely locked in our files, if you don't mind."

Harden was listening and arranging all that he had learned up to this point.

So, Brantley Chemical isn't producing fertilizer as their reports indicate. TR-7 is an illegal narcotic, produced to compete with cocaine at a lesser price. That means Riley is running this operation independently of the parent company, Jennings. The fertilizer containers at Warbah were actually illegal drug shipments. Riley must have turned Lewis and Long by offering them unbelievable payoffs. If he were to stand up to the established cocaine dealers, he would require all the services those two have to offer. Everything fits together after all.

Aloud…

"Thanks, Sally. Of course, I don't need the list of substances right now. They probably wouldn't mean much to me, anyway. Certainly I understand that you need to secure that information. Could this drug have medicinal value, or just street value as a hallucinogen?"

"Like I said, Mr. Kelly, this is a breakthrough combination of substances. Any medicinal value would have to be tested thoroughly before it could produce market value. With this being a new combination of chemicals, testing would take years."

That was the answer Harden wanted.

Brantley is making unbelievable profits today, so that rules out any medicinal value.

This final thought seemed to fortify his conclusion.

Now I need to talk to Conner, and then Ashley, about that corporation of hers.

Thanking Sally for her prompt services, Harden hurried to his car.

* * *

Anthony had made it perfectly clear to Aubrey that he was to prevent Harden from getting the sample analyzed. Hurrying to the hotel, Aubrey arrived just in time to see Harden throw his bag into the trunk of his car and drive away.

Without stopping, Aubrey began to follow what he assumed was a rental car, intending to make his move once Harden was inside the busy airport. He knew that, contrary to common belief, a brief encounter in a very public place could be more effective than waiting for a more private opportunity. This plan was necessarily abandoned when Harden entered through a guarded gate into the military section of Cleveland Hopkins airport.

Aubrey had no intention of exposing himself to that kind of observation. He parked in a no-parking zone and mentally reviewed the situation.

Where would he go to get the TR-7 analyzed? He seemed to have some business with that attorney Hayes, and he and Miss Jennings returned to San Francisco early Tuesday.

He realized his options were fairly minimal, at that. Driving quickly back to the hotel, he returned his weapon to his room and packed a small briefcase for the trip. The hotel clerk was more than happy to place a reservation on behalf of Mr. James Zachary on the next flight to San Francisco, dialing the number with one hand even as he pocketed the hundred-dollar bill with the other.

Aubrey was aware of all the military connections available to Harden Kelly, so when he arrived at San Francisco International, he drove directly to a shop in Chinatown instead of trying to locate Harden on some military base. That was forbidden ground to him now. Momentarily his thoughts returned to a better time when he had strutted these grounds with the respect earned through his former position. Both he and Jeff had the second-highest security clearance available to anyone in the military. They could move through any compound in the world with impunity. That had been a good feeling.

Aubrey's nostalgic thoughts were always brief, and this particular reverie ended with his arrival at the tiny shop. Locking the rental car, he stepped inside. In place of the man he had expected, Aubrey found a young Asian man standing behind the counter.

"I would like to speak to Cho."

That was the only name he had ever used in this particular shop.

"Mr. Cho is no longer with us, sir, but I am sure I can help you as well as he could."

Aubrey hoped that this meant what he wanted it to mean, or else there was likely to be another dead body discovered by a follow-on customer.

"What I want is something you've always had available in the other room."

The young man led him through curtains and a doorway to a back room filled with stinging vapors that clouded the air. Aubrey immediately showed his impatience with this new proprietor.

He almost shouted his exasperation.

"No! No! I want to buy a weapon. Let me see those now."

Aubrey stood closer to the young man, just in case he decided to bolt. Instead, Cho's successor led Aubrey back the way they came and slid aside a wall-mounted display case. Built into the back of the case were an equal number of shelves, each one packed with a variety of handguns. Aubrey immediately spotted a Glock; it was similar to those he had preferred for earlier work. He examined the weapon thoroughly. Surprised at the cleanliness of the pistol he loaded the weapon, added a shoulder holster and extra cartridges to his purchase, and then paid cash for everything. He did not like the young Asian's attitude, but he may need this source in the future so he had to forgo his initial inclination to significantly shorten the young man's life.

Wishing that Jeff could have been here to back him up, he decided to find attorney Hayes and hope that Kelly came to him. It was almost noon as he made his way to the financial district and the offices of Smith, Pitt and Alagia.

"Good morning! May I speak to Mr. Hayes, please?"

Aubrey had decided to find out if the attorney was in his office before going upstairs.

"May I tell him who is calling, please?"

Janet was always efficient. Before proceeding further, she first had the responsibility of identifying the client.

"My name is James Zachary. I only need a minute of his time. Can you connect me, please?"

"Mr. Zachary, I expect him in some time this morning, but he's not here yet. May I leave a message for Mr. Hayes?"

"No, thank you. I'll call back this afternoon."

There was no way that Hayes would recognize the name Zachary. Aubrey decided to wait just where he was and keep an eye on the entrance. After feeding additional quarters into the parking meter, he settled down to wait.

His patience was rewarded. After only fifteen minutes, he saw the man he recognized as Harden Kelly entering the building. He had apparently used the parking garage that occupied the south side of the block. The man was carrying a briefcase and walked in long, purposeful strides as though he had something on his mind.

He does have something on his mind, thought Aubrey. *He probably knows more about Brantley now than we can afford for him to know.*

He started to follow Kelly, but instinct told him to hold off until Hayes arrived as well. Kelly would no doubt decide to wait in his office.

Around one p.m., Aubrey spotted Hayes driving into the parking garage. Knowing that he would not see the attorney actually enter the building, Aubrey left his car. He fed two more quarters into the meter for additional time.

All these expensive attorneys have private entrances so their clients won't see them come and go. Surely, Hayes is no exception.

Again he thought of Jeff. Aubrey's cold heart had no room for fondness, only survival, but they were always much safer when they watched out for each other.

Once in the main lobby of the building, Aubrey found a less-trafficked corner and dialed Jeff's cell phone. He answered after two rings.

"Jeff, where are you? I could sure use some cover."

"Mr. Riley told me what happened. He sent me back here to San Francisco in his private jet to help you take care of the problem. I was just about to call you."

"I'm in the main lobby of Hayes' office building. They're both up there now. Do you know the address?"

"Yes, I have it. Wait in the lobby and we'll handle this together."

* * *

Conner Hayes pulled into his parking slot on the fifth floor of the garage and entered the main building through a locked door. The elevator was right inside the door. As usual, Charlie was with him.

This was a private elevator, designed for the exclusive use of occupants of the building's upper floors. Their nonstop trip to the thirty-sixth floor required only seconds. Again, Conner led Charlie through a private entrance, thereby avoiding the waiting room.

"Janet, I'm here now. Are there any messages?

Conner was already leafing through the stack of papers on his desk.

"Mr. Kelly is here to see you. Also, about an hour ago, a Mr. James Zachary asked to speak to you. He left no message but said he would call back later this afternoon."

"Show Mr. Kelly in right away, Janet. I don't know who this Zachary is. If he calls back, try to find out what he wants. If Miss Jennings calls, patch her through immediately. Also, arrange to have flowers sent for her father, from me personally. I don't know which funeral home he's at. We just left the hospital this morning—San Francisco General."

Just as Janet was assuring him that she would take care of everything, his office door opened and Harden walked in.

"Charlie, wait out there with Janet," instructed Harden. "Be alert to any strangers who come into the outer room. Work out a signal with Janet for her to make you aware of anyone she doesn't immediately recognize."

After Charlie left, Conner was puzzled at the exchange between the two men.

"What was that all about, Hard?"

"Well, several things, really. Let me lay it out. We can put it all into proper order later. First, I believe you were right about the two men at the Brantley Chemical plant. Second, I was able to pick up a sample of the TR-7 and have it analyzed. It's a combination of several synthetic chemicals, processed in such a way to duplicate the effects and even the appearance of cocaine. My source tells me that all of the ingredients can be bought in bulk at a rate that allows the producer to compete price-wise with the real thing.

"This product is definitely not fertilizer. That would account for the impressive cash flow and Brantley's improved balance sheet. I am afraid our friend—Riley—is masterminding the production of a whole new concept in drug trading. I still don't understand why he hooked up with a subsidiary of a major corporation instead of starting his own company. That would seem to invite problems."

Conner, while not totally surprised, was overwhelmed by the enormity of the situation and the effect it might have on Ashley's corporation, not to mention her personally.

"Riley must have seen this as an innocuous entry into the chemical production business, thereby achieving some level of legitimacy even with an illegal product. By taking controlling interest in Brantley, no one at that level could give him any trouble. He seems to have hired people commensurate with the activity he projected. Riley didn't take into consideration the level of interest his profit margins would generate in Ashley Jennings' mind, and her desire to employ his techniques at other subsidiaries. Ashley has already shown me Riley's steps for taking control of the board of directors. His only obstacles were Ashley and her father."

Conner's paused as he thought about what he had just said.

"Mr. Jennings passed away last night—heart failure. The doctor said it seems he suffered a massive heart attack and died before he hit the floor."

"What?"

Harden was clearly shaken by this news.

"Ashley found him early this morning. When he didn't answer the phone, she went over to the house. It was already too late."

"The only obstacle was Ashley and her father," Harden repeated. "Conner, are you thinking what I'm thinking? There's no such thing as coincidence. Everything happens for a reason. It's all cause and effect. Ashley may be in danger as well. It's probably a long shot, but I've found it's always better to play things safe. Where is she now?"

"I dropped her off at her condo to freshen up. She has a meeting with the funeral director at two this afternoon."

47

"Hello."

Jeff answered his cell phone just as he and Aubrey were entering the elevator, on their way up to the thirty-sixth floor. He recognized Anthony's distinctive voice immediately.

"Henry, I need both of you back in Cleveland right away. We're going to take a different approach altogether. I've scheduled an emergency board meeting for Monday afternoon, the emergency having been caused by the unexpected death of our chairman. Harden Kelly is with the federal government—special ops. He certainly wouldn't be involved in local police work. I want to see if we can effect a peaceful takeover of the board, based on the success of Brantley Chemical, and the fact that I now have Jennings' voting rights."

Anthony abruptly signed off, and Jeff quickly punched thirty-one on the elevator's panel.

"What did you do that for?

Aubrey was surprised by his partner's sudden decision to change floors. He was anticipating possible action as soon as the elevator opened on the thirty-sixth floor, counting on surprise to count in their favor.

"Riley canceled this part of the operation. He wants us back in Cleveland right away. His jet is still at San Francisco International, waiting for us."

The elevator door opened on the thirty-first floor. Both men stepped out, looking around them as they exited the elevator. Aubrey pushed the Down button as the unit they had been in carried on to the thirty-sixth floor.

"That guy recognized us," Jeff explained. "He's not going to just drop this. If they're looking for us, then they undoubtedly know everything we've done, including Robinson, but especially that special ops unit."

Aubrey was bitterly disappointed that they had lost the opportunity to end this, here and now.

On the express ride back to the first floor, the faces of their previous victims again haunted Jeff. The dropping motion of the elevator dizzied him for a moment, allowing these dead-yet-undead images to swirl about the tiny enclosure. He shut his eyes and shook his head back and forth to clear them away, but to no avail.

Only their sudden arrival at the first floor, with daylight spilling in as the door opened, brought him back to reality.

As they exited the building Aubrey looked at him, puzzled.

"What happened in the elevator, partner? For a minute I thought I lost you there. You were acting kind of crazy."

"I guess that sudden downward acceleration got to me. I'm fine now. Let's get to the airport."

He did not tell Aubrey that this time the images never completely ended their visit, but were still lingering against the back of his skull.

They were able to keep their weapons on them since they were flying on a private jet. Under present conditions, both men felt more secure having that familiar bulge beneath their jackets.

* * *

When they arrived back at Brantley Chemical, Anthony was too busy to see them but he had left instructions for them to wait in Henry Atwell's office. After stopping for a cup of coffee in the employee lounge, they settled in comfortably to sip their drinks and wait.

"Do you think he has this office bugged yet, Jeff?

Aubrey wanted to talk.

"I don't believe he saw any need for that, but I don't have a kit to check it out right now."

Jeff leaned his head back against his chair, trying to force the demons out so he could think clearly again. He threw his feet up on the desk and closed his eyes.

"What if we took off right now, Jeff? We both have well over a million dollars in our accounts. We could get lost and not have to worry about Riley's problems anymore, just concentrate on our own."

Although he had his eyes shut, Jeff heard every word. Having had similar thoughts this very day, he was tempted to jump up and leave, just as Aubrey had suggested.

"For starters, we could go back to Roseau. From there we could make plans for even deeper cover. I have a feeling that this will all blow up in our faces if we don't get out soon."

Aubrey had always trusted his instincts for survival.

Jeff opened his eyes to respond.

"That's certainly tempting, Aubrey. But maybe we should give Riley a chance on Monday. He's provided us with some big paydays so far. One more would certainly help."

The potential for adding another half-million dollars to their bank balance for so little work proved irresistible to them.

Unbeknownst to Jeff and Aubrey, Anthony Riley was making arrangements of his own to offset a potential disaster come Monday afternoon.

* * *

Samantha Chandler nearly bumped into the two men who were hurrying off the elevator at the ground floor, apparently absorbed in their own thoughts. However, she noticed the bulge under their jackets and even got a glimpse of a holstered weapon as the larger man's jacket flew open when he strode past her.

As the elevator quickly skirted the lower floors, her thoughts went back to the previous day's call from Mr. Anderson. He seemed to think it was urgent that Harden have backup, as he may have accidentally run across the two men they had been trailing through the Mideast and Europe. Since she was already assigned as Harden's partner on this case, she was the obvious choice to make the trip. Sam had seen enough by now to know that Harden Kelly held a special place among Mr. Anderson's collection of special agents.

The door opened onto the lobby of the Smith, Pitt and Alagia law office. Only two people were there. One was the receptionist, who immediately greeted her.

"May I help you? Do you have an appointment with one of our attorneys?"

Sam noticed that the other occupant of the room had risen from his seat as soon as she entered, positioning himself casually behind her and to the right while he leafed through a stack of magazines.

"Mr. Conner Hayes, please. My name is Samantha Chandler. The man with Mr. Hayes will recognize that name if you will please announce me."

The young man who had been looking at magazines was suddenly at her side.

"May I ask what business you have with Mr. Hayes, miss?"

He was rather young but very intense, and apparently armed as well. Janet was speaking on the phone with someone as Sam turned slowly to face the man.

"I don't see that being any of your business. Who are you, anyway?"

Charlie was about to answer when Harden opened the door that led to Conner's office.

"Sam!"

He rushed over to give her a hug.

"I wanted you to be here but I didn't know how to persuade Mr. Anderson that I could use my partner."

She was again reminded of how wonderful it felt to be smothered in this huge man's arms. But she also noticed that the other man had backed off.

"I see you've met Charlie. He's been working with Conner Hayes during the times that I wasn't here. Charlie, this is Sam Chandler. Anderson sent her."

That was just an assumption Harden had made, but it would do for now.

Charlie stepped forward again, this time showing off his natural, youthful grin.

"Nice to meet you, Sam. Sorry I was so abrupt earlier."

He did not know how much of the situation she was aware of, so he stopped right there. Sam grasped his outstretched hand firmly.

"No problem, Charlie. It's a pleasure to meet you."

At that, Harden led Sam back into Conner's office and closed the door.

"Conner, I want you to meet Samantha Chandler. She was my partner while we were chasing Lewis and Long all over Europe. More than that, she and I have become very close friends."

Conner and Sam both noticed the coloring change in the big man's face as he spoke that last sentence. Sam had never heard Harden say anything publicly about their relationship, and she grabbed his arm with an acknowledging squeeze.

"Since we were already partners on this case, when Mr. Anderson found out that our two men may be involved here as well, he sent me as backup for Harden."

"Don't let her appearance fool you, Conner," Harden explained. "She completed her unit training with very high credentials and has proven herself in the field over the years."

Harden had difficulty discussing his personal relationship with Sam, but the way his face lit up when he spoke of her professionally was more than enough to satisfy Conner.

Conner came around his desk to give her a hug. He did not have Harden's problem with being personable.

Sam liked the man immediately. His natural charm and good looks, combined with his brilliant smile, gave a first impression that would be acceptable at any level.

"Samantha, it's wonderful to meet you. I thought this big lug was made out of stone. I'm glad to see his better half."

Sam glanced up at Harden and was pleased to see that he was still beaming in spite of Conner's remarks.

Settling around Conner's desk, Harden filled Sam in on the events to date, including the fact that Charlie occupied the outer office to serve as perimeter security. When Harden had finished his dissertation, Sam seemed to be absorbing all the information before she spoke.

"On the first floor, just as I was about to enter the elevator, two men came out of the car in an awful hurry. I avoided a collision only by stepping to the side at the very last moment. They were both carrying weapons under their jackets. One man was maybe six feet tall, the other a couple of inches taller. They were both dressed in dark business suits. The larger man's jacket flew open as he dodged me, and I actually saw the weapon. The other one had an obvious bulge under his left sleeve. Could there be a connection?"

Harden had already moved to the window to look down on the street below.

"Are you certain they were leaving?"

"They were headed for the street before the elevator door closed on me. After that, I don't know."

Harden was pleased with Sam's instinctive observation of details.

"Was one of them wearing glasses?" Conner asked, thinking of Henry Atwell.

"The smaller man did have glasses on when he passed me."

The two men were unsure what to make of this latest news.

48

With the immediate threat apparently removed, Sam and Harden accompanied Conner to Ashley's condominium. Ashley remotely released the security lock from upstairs and, as they entered, Sam made certain that the door closed firmly behind them before she followed the others to the elevator.

Ashley was waiting with her door open. She greeted everyone with a warm smile and a hug.

Noticing hesitancy on Harden's part, Conner put his arm around Sam's shoulder.

"Ashley, this is Samantha Chandler. She works with Harden. She came to California to assist him on this case."

"She's also my very best friend."

With considerable effort, Harden had succeeded in finishing the introduction. Surprised by this last remark, Sam slipped her hand into his and squeezed it gently.

Ashley was already on her with arms outstretched.

"So nice to meet you, Samantha. I haven't known Harden Kelly very long, but certainly long enough to know that any friend of his is also a friend of mine."

Sam could feel the sincerity in the hug and knew, at once, that she would be honored to have this woman for a friend.

"Thank you, Ashley. I feel like I already know you. On the ride over, Conner told me all about you. They were all good things, I assure you."

With introductions complete, Ashley led them to comfortable seating to discuss the day's events.

"Mr. Remagen, the funeral director whom I met this afternoon, was very competent. My father's funeral service will be Saturday morning, with visitation Thursday evening and all day Friday."

Ashley dabbed at both her eyes with a tissue.

"I didn't think I could make my way through all the decisions that death necessitates but, with Mr. Remagen's guidance, everything got done.

"But there was a rather upsetting message on my answering machine when I arrived back home. Anthony Riley called. Here, let me play it for you."

Pressing the message button with her right index finger, an unmistakable voice echoed forth.

"Miss Jennings, although I will not be able to attend your father's funeral service, I certainly want to express my condolences for your loss. My physical limitations impact my ability to function, except under controlled conditions. Please accept my regrets."

After only a brief pause, the message continued.

"With the passing of your father, we have a corporate crisis of some magnitude regarding the board of directors. I have called a meeting for Monday afternoon to resolve this crisis. Your attendance would be appreciated. Your absence would be understood. Again, I offer my sincerest condolences."

"Can you believe that? My father isn't even buried yet, and that man is already making a push for control of the corporation. I'll be at that meeting to keep things under control. Conner, I could use some backup, though. Can you arrange your schedule to be there with me?"

"I can do that."

Conner glanced at Harden to see if he had the same reaction. They seemed to make eye contact with the same thought in mind.

"Ashley, Harden and I have uncovered a very regrettable situation. Has Mr. Remagen sent for your father yet, or is he still at the hospital?"

"What is it, Conner? Mr. Remagen said he would arrange transportation by the end of the day. Why do you ask?"

Ashley was inquisitive as well as intelligent and felt as though she might already know the answer.

"We suspect that your father's death may not have come by natural means," Conner began. "There is reason to believe that Mr. Atwell and another employee of Brantley are the same two men Harden has been chasing for the past few weeks. If so, they're very capable of murder to achieve their end. Even more serious is the fact that Anthony Riley has these men in his employ. We have a number of pieces to this puzzle, but not a complete picture.

"Ashley, it would help us clarify the situation if we knew for certain that your father died of natural causes," Harden added. "The two men that Sam and I are looking for have killed before, using a poison that paralyzes almost instantly and simulates heart failure."

Harden and Conner did not receive the response that they had expected. Instead of shock and tears, Ashley came back fighting mad.

"If your suspicions are strong enough to request an autopsy, let's do it. If my father were murdered, I'd want to know that. Then I'll want to know who was responsible for his murder. How do we initiate an autopsy?"

Conner was already dialing the phone.

"May I speak with Dr. Heywood, please?"

"One moment, please."

Before the receptionist put him on hold, he could already hear the doctor being paged in the background. After an interminable delay the operator finally came back on.

"I'm sorry, sir. Dr. Heywood must have left the…"

Suddenly her words were cut off.

"Hello, this is Dr. Heywood."

"Dr. Heywood, this is Conner Hayes. I met you this morning with Ashley Jennings. Ashley is with me now, and she has decided that an autopsy would be appropriate under the circumstances. If it's not too late, we'd like for you to prevent the funeral home people from removing Mr. Jennings until an autopsy can be arranged."

"Can I speak to Miss Jennings, please?"

Conner handed her the receiver.

"He wants to speak to you."

"Hello, Dr. Heywood. This is Ashley Jennings."

"Ashley, are you sure you want to go through with this? Your father had severe heart blockage, which I'm sure is what precipitated this massive attack. An autopsy is always very difficult on the family."

She could sense the genuine concern in the old doctor's voice.

"I'm very sure, doctor. Would you arrange the proper paperwork? We'll be on our way over in a few minutes."

"Excuse me a moment, Ashley."

Dr. Heywood had caught sight of the one person in the hospital who could handle this situation expeditiously.

"Dr. Mirimar, do you have a minute?"

Sujee Mirimar closed the folder she was reviewing and looked up.

"Certainly, Dr. Heywood."

Heywood quickly outlined the request and its resultant urgency.

"I'm just completing a work-up on another case. If you send the patient to my lab and have the paperwork prepared, I could be with you in about an hour."

Even Heywood was amazed at how well things were falling into place.

"Ashley, I've just spoken to Dr. Mirimar, and she's willing to perform the procedure so long as we make the appropriate arrangements. She'll be available in about an hour. How long will it take for you to get back here?"

"We can be there in thirty minutes. My attorney, Mr. Hayes, will be with me. Good bye, doctor, and thank you very much."

Within minutes, all four were back in the car. Their destination was San Francisco General Hospital.

49

J on, I've notified my bank to transfer twenty million dollars into my account there. Please verify that it has arrived. I also want to be informed if there is activity in either of the two new accounts of Mr. Lewis and Mr. Long—immediately! Of course, there will be a substantial bonus for your services."

Mandrake sat quietly as Anthony Riley completed his arrangements.

Jon Heydn was basking in his good fortune. It was no coincidence that he had been selected to service the accounts when the two Americans showed up the week before. Elizabeth had been instructed in advance that he would be their account manager.

When the strange man, Anthony Riley, first made arrangements with him for a private account a little over a year ago, he had no idea of how his life would change. For special facilitation over that period, he had twice received considerable bonuses. The first was for fifty thousand dollars for enabling Mr. Riley to open and gain direct access to his account, bypassing stringent banking regulations.

The second time was much more rewarding financially, but also illegal. Mr. Riley had offered him one hundred thousand dollars for the account numbers plus password access to the accounts of Jeff Lewis and Aubrey Long. The first incident only involved stretching the conditions for opening an account. The second was clearly a violation of national banking laws. Although financially rewarding, Mr. Riley did not leave Jon any choice in the matter when he made an almost unnoticeable inference to his previous transgression.

One more bonus like that and I can tell Mr. Riley I am through doing his dirty work. Then he can call on someone else.

Jon was feeding courageous thoughts to his ego, although he knew his only hope of escaping Mr. Riley's demands was to disappear. Despite his greed, Jon was a caring family man and truly understood he had no way out.

Mandrake sat back in the comfortable leather chair and listened, alert to any need that might arise from Anthony, as the disabled man placed three more long-distance calls.

Finally finished with the telephone, Anthony Riley leaned back in his specially constructed chair, deep in thought, his crooked fingers forming a misshapen parapet.

As he watched this genius of a man who displayed a bitter perspective on life, Mandrake thought back to the day he first met Anthony. As a young man, Mandrake "Manny" Speagle had repeated run afoul of the law. Having never known his father, Manny doubted whether his mother knew him either. He was aware that his mother loved him, but the long periods of loneliness while his mother was away molded the angry, brooding young man. Manny was left on his own from an early age, especially at night, while his mother earned enough money to support the two of them. He tried to envision her alternately as a hard-working hotel maid, as a cleaning lady, or even as an aide in a hospital, but he knew better. She always came home with enough money to support the two of them comfortably, so he had never questioned her profession too closely. He satisfied his curiosity with mental images of her working hard at her job at a nursing home or a hospital.

The inner city of Washington, D.C., was a poor place to grow up with no one for guidance or direction. Manny had been involved in many incidents throughout his early years where he was forced to use his size and strength to defend himself, and to defend his less-gifted friends. In prison, he developed the habit of observing as opposed to engaging in the inmates' discussions. Always a loner, he spent long hours in the gymnasium, primarily lifting weights and using other kinds of exercise equipment.

Staying out of trouble in prison allowed him to become eligible for a work-release program. Moving heavy equipment, plus placing and installing new equipment, he became intrigued by the inner workings of the National Weather Service. Although not aware of it, he was being observed by the local director, a thin, twisted man in a wheelchair, someone who looked much older than his thirty-nine years.

Anthony Riley had befriended Manny and showed him how to extract data from the various machines that he had been handling.

Having selected the young man for his future plans, Anthony insisted on using his formal name, Mandrake, and even suggested that Manny consider changing his legal name to that name alone. Before separating himself from the weather service, Anthony schooled the young man in personal hygiene and professional manners.

Buoyed by the attention given to him by the director, Manny chose to follow his instructions and soon found himself assigned as Anthony's assistant. That was the final stage of preparation for separation from government work for the two of them. Anthony had succeeded in grooming this young giant to meet his demands, including having him wear a business suit to work every day. For Mandrake's part, he was grateful to Anthony Riley for forcing him to develop pride and self-confidence in himself.

"Mandrake."

Anthony had finished his thought processes and was leaning forward to relay those plans to his faithful assistant.

"I need you to do a few things for me on Monday."

When he was sure to have caught Mandrake's attention, Anthony laid out his contingency arrangements that included himself, Mandrake and Sean Pfister, the brilliant young chemist who had been principally responsible for the development of TR-7, based on Anthony's broader ideas.

"The three of us will fly to San Francisco in the corporate jet, early Monday morning. I want you to work with Sean to see that ten containers of TR-7 are shipped to this address, even if our two men have to work all weekend to get it ready."

He handed Mandrake the information.

"Don't use our usual carrier, but choose a dependable one. Leave no paperwork here on the premises for this shipment."

He now had Mandrake's undivided attention.

"Be sure to pack whatever personal belongings you may need for an extended trip. I'll do the same tonight, with your help. Make sure the pilot refuels the plane immediately after we land so that it'll be ready for another flight that same afternoon. Although I'll ride to the board meeting in a limousine, I want you to charter a helicopter for a short flight, to arrive no later than noon. Have them land on the Jennings Pharmaceuticals rooftop helipad. Come alone and make your way to my side of the boardroom. Be prepared for any emergency. Atwell and Zachary will be there as well. Atwell will attend the board meeting with me, and Zachary will wait in the adjoining room. Go—make these arrangements. I need to rest now."

As he left Anthony's office, Mandrake glanced at the strange address written on the piece of paper. It was a place he had never heard of before—Ramkin Island.

* * *

Dr. Heywood had been successful in averting the collection of Mr. Jennings' body by the mortuary. However, he remained puzzled as they made their way down the corridor to the elevator.

"Ashley, what caused you to change your mind regarding the autopsy? I can assure you that your father's heart attack was of sufficient severity to have caused his death."

"I understand that, doctor. There have been some events involving our company that suggested taking the precaution of an autopsy to eliminate any other possibilities."

Arriving on the hospital's lowest level, the elevator opened onto a stark hallway, brightly illuminated but absent any decoration. Dr. Heywood led them into a large, refrigerated room furnished with several stainless steel tables, where these specialized surgeons performed their work. Dr. Mirimar was waiting for them at a small desk just inside the entrance.

"Hello. I am Sujee Mirimar. I shall be performing the autopsy. Do you have the paperwork completed and signed, Dr. Heywood?"

After flipping through the documents to confirm the proper signatures and authorization, she stood up.

"This should take about an hour. Of course, if I find anything unusual, it might take longer. If you have not experienced this before, I would advise that you wait in the break room down the hall, back in the direction of the elevator. You are welcome to stay, but…well, it is up to you."

Ashley had already said her goodbyes to her father and was certainly willing and relieved to move on to the waiting room.

"Although the paperwork will take time to process, I will come and speak with you of what I find. Dr. Heywood has indicated that this was some sort of an emergency, so I volunteered to help him out. Please be patient."

She turned in the direction of the coolers. When Mirimar began to twist the handle release, Ashley had seen enough. In anticipation of this, Conner was already holding the door open for her. Only Harden held back.

"I'll see if I can assist the doctor somehow."

Taking his cue, Sam knew instinctively that she was to stay with the group to ensure their safety while Harden was away. She took pride in the fact that he trusted her with this task. Both she and Harden had been required to show their federal identification cards at the door in order to bring their weapons into the hospital. The small group proceeded to the break room.

Heywood chose not to enter the room with them, instead hanging back in the hallway.

"I have surgery scheduled in about an hour, so I'll leave you now. You're in very capable hands, and I hope Dr. Miramar can alleviate your anxieties."

"Thank you so much, Dr. Heywood," Ashley said. "Thanks for all you've done, and for being my dad's friend over the years."

Heywood returned her hug before continuing down the hallway.

The three of them sipped coffee from stoneware mugs as they sat in silent commiseration, awaiting the verdict.

50

It was late afternoon, and Jeff's patience was wearing thin. Quietly, he opened the door to Anthony's office. The lights were turned down low and the man was apparently sleeping. Jeff gently closed the door and returned to his office.

"Aubrey, he's sleeping and left us sitting around waiting for him. I don't care who he is, I'm…"

"Henry."

The intercom interrupted his dissertation on hurt feelings.

"Would you and James please come in here for a minute?"

Aubrey patted his partner on the back as they left the office.

"It's not like you to blow up like that. We've had many less comfortable waits together. Calm down. We'll make this work out, with or without Riley."

"This will only take a minute, gentlemen," Anthony instructed. "We will fly to San Francisco on Monday morning. I want you to pack personal belongings for what may be an extended trip. If things do not go well on Monday, we may need to make a quick exit."

The two men showed no outward reaction, but they were absorbing every word.

"Have no qualms about carrying your weapons, as all travel will be aboard my private jet. James, there's a small office adjacent to the boardroom. I'd like for you to wait there in order to avoid a further opportunity for identification. If they were suspicious of your real identification, it'll be more confusing for them as long as we're not seen together. Henry, you need to be in the boardroom with me, since we've installed you as a director."

Anthony paused as he contemplated how much information he should give these two men.

"If things should go awry at the meeting, I've made contingency plans. Please be attentive at all times so that you may follow my lead."

Jeff and Aubrey left the meeting feeling more alive than they had in a long time. Another assignment was about to take place on Monday, and they could feel the excitement building within them. Buoyed by their confidence in themselves, the thought of an adverse ending to this confrontation never entered their minds.

They would be ready.

* * *

Harden came bursting through the door.

"There was no invasive entry or wound. However, Dr. Mirimar has taken a blood sample directly from the heart and is in her lab now to analyze it."

After pouring a half-cup of coffee into a mug, Harden sat down between Sam and Conner, facing Ashley.

"Conner, do you remember when I told you about the JAG attorney who was killed by a dart that had injected a type of curare poison into him? In sufficient strength, this poison paralyzes the heart muscles and simulates a heart attack. That was about a month ago. Well, the doctor found a red dot on Mr. Jennings' neck. It turned out to be a speck of dried blood.

"That's when I asked if she could do a rush analysis on the blood, just in case we have a similar incident."

"Oh my god, Harden! Was my father murdered?"

"We don't know that yet, Ashley. We're just exploring every

possibility. The mark on his neck could be from shaving, or from some other innocent cause. I asked Dr. Mirimar to interrupt the process to see if there are any unusual substances found in his blood, before she continues."

The four of them sipped their coffee in silence as they waited, each developing their own conclusions to this new information.

The phone on the table between Harden and Conner rang so abruptly that everyone was startled to attention.

"Hello."

Conner had reached for the phone, while Harden had paused in deference to his long-time friend.

"This is Sujee Mirimar. Could you all come down the hallway to my lab? I may have something of interest for you."

"She wants us in the lab."

Conner took Ashley by the hand and, as they left the room, he put his arm around her shoulders. Harden's long, hurried stride enabled him to reach the lab ahead of the others, with Sam right on his heels. Holding the door open, they stood aside and let Ashley enter first.

"For years now, we have been using an extract from a tropical vine that is grown in South America for its sedative effect," Miramar began. "In larger doses, this extract sedates the heart muscles to such an extent so as to paralyze and thereby cause almost instantaneous death. The scientific name of this plant is Strychnos toxifera. Although it is not a perfect match to this extract, your father did receive a sufficient dose of a very similar poison. With the advantage of an autopsy, I was able to take samples of blood from the suspected entry point in the neck, and from several other places as well. Evidence appears to indicate that your father had received some sort of injection in the neck which precipitated a massive heart attack, resulting in almost immediate death."

Tears flowed again, but anger as well.

"Why would someone do this to my father? He never hurt anyone. Everyone who met him liked him. I don't understand."

"You realize I will now have to complete the autopsy and notify the authorities of this unnatural cause of death. I will stay tonight to finalize everything so that your arrangements may continue as planned unless, of course, the police wish to delay the burial. That would be out of my control."

On the ride home from the hospital, Conner stated that he would remain with Ashley, at least for the night. Harden and Sam insisted on staying over as well. Although not spoken aloud, they both had to consider the possibility that Ashley's life could be in danger for the same reason as her father's.

Alone in the condominium, Harden, Conner and Sam sat in the living room to discuss what they had learned.

"Why can't we go get them, right now?"

Conner wanted to do something immediately. When he conceived a course of action, he was anxious to proceed.

"Conner, we can't be sure that Anthony and his people are responsible. Besides, they're coming to us on Monday. Let's set up a plan to react to whatever likely scenario might take place Monday afternoon."

Conner was impressed with Harden's experienced take on the situation.

"Dr. Mirimar's results will not be assigned to a detective until Monday morning. It'll take her at least that long to submit an official autopsy report, and the police won't do anything until the proper procedures are in place. They will, however, seal off the Jennings residence, probably tonight. Maybe they already have.

"Sam and I will attend the board meeting on Monday afternoon with you and Ashley. I know they always have chairs set up against the wall for subordinates who might be there to supply additional information. Conner, you and I will sit directly behind Ashley. Sam will act as our surveillance team to scout out adjacent rooms and corridors."

"Hard, I'm impressed. You seem to have everything covered. Now, if we can just make it through the weekend without further incident."

* * *

Deltas Three, Four and Five stood only a few feet away. All three had their automatic weapons pointed directly at him. Their faces were distorted by death, a combination of anguish and confusion. The old shop owner had also made the trip all the way from Italy to harass him as he slept, tossing and turning in his bed.

Having arrived back at the hotel fairly early, Jeff had gone directly to his room to freshen up. After showering, he felt the excitement of the new assignment pumping up his adrenaline level. Later, after checking and cleaning his weapon, he was restless. The Tanqueray gin still sat on the bar counter. Over three cubes of ice Jeff poured a generous portion of gin, adding a splash of tonic. Two hours later he found himself lying on the couch, the empty gin bottle on the coffee table beside him. He stumbled his way to bed, and the nightmares that had dwelt there this past week began again.

They swirled around him now, including images he did not even recognize that were evidently stirred up from his subconscious. He could feel the bullets tear through him even before the flash from the weapons struck his eyes.

His body twitched and contorted as the rounds kept coming—hundreds, even thousands. He could not avert his eyes from the blank stare in the eyes of his victims as the missiles continued to tear at his body. They were all around him. He had nowhere to hide.

Upon arriving in his room, Aubrey changed into swim trunks and a robe, grabbed a towel, and headed for the exercise room and the adjacent sauna. He could be charming when he tried, and the opportunity soon presented itself. Two young ladies entered the sauna shortly after him. Aubrey guessed that they were in their early thirties. They were fascinated by the stories Aubrey told, not believing for an instant that any of them was true. Before long, one of the women left to go for a swim in the nearby indoor pool. With his beaming smile and perspiration glistening on his tanned, muscular body, the other young woman soon found herself leading Aubrey down the hallway to her room.

Jeff jerked to an upright position, realizing he could not spend the night in his bed. His past had taken and fortified that position, intent on destroying any trespasser. He dressed quickly and left the room.

Just outside, he met Aubrey coming from the other direction.

"Where are you going, partner?" Aubrey asked.

Jeff noticed traces of blood on the sleeve and collar of Aubrey's white robe. No doubt there was a female involved. Because of his rough treatment of women, who invariably left with obvious wear and tear—some more serious than others—Aubrey had trouble sustaining a relationship beyond the initial rendezvous.

"Can't sleep," Jeff said. "I thought I'd go over to Brantley and see if anything was up."

"Give me a minute to change and I'll go with you."

Instead of being wasted from tonight's interlude, Aubrey appeared wild, disheveled and perhaps even energized.

"I'll wait for you in the lobby, over by the coffee pot. Hurry. I want to get out of here."

Jeff's statement was sincere. He wanted to get away from there before someone else discovered what Aubrey had done this time.

51

Aubrey pushed the button to alert the guard of their presence before sliding his card into the slot to unlock the door.

"That old fool has a gun and might get off a lucky shot if we surprise him."

Phil came hurrying down the hall, still fooling with the zipper on his trousers.

"Mr. Atwell. Mr. Zachary. I weren't expecting you back tonight."

Disgusted with his grammar as well as his mannerisms, Jeff pushed past him.

"We'll be here for a while. Make sure the front door is secured."

Before reaching his office, both Jeff and Aubrey's attention was diverted to the far end of the hall, where lights were burning brightly both in the lab and the plant. Simultaneously they released the snaps on their shoulder holsters, prepared for any contingency.

Aubrey wondered if the infamous Harden Kelly was back again.

The door was locked. Aubrey still had his key card in his jacket pocket and quickly retrieved it, releasing the lock. Almost immediately they ran into Mandrake, who was coming from the direction of the plant.

Surprised to see Mandrake without Anthony present, Jeff asked, "Is Mr. Riley here, Mandrake?"

"No! He wanted me to take care of some last-minute work before the meeting on Monday. He's home in bed."

He paused, as if thinking things over.

"What are you two doing here this late?"

Before Aubrey could respond, Jeff intervened.

"We just wanted to pick up a few things from my office, but the lights in the shop caught our attention. What's going on back there?"

Mandrake saw no harm in telling these two men. He knew that they had passkeys to the entire facility, anyway.

"Mr. Riley requested that ten containers be prepared and shipped by Monday morning. He wants me to make sure this happens. He wants Sean to go with us on Monday morning."

"Will you be able to accumulate ten containers of TR-7 in time to ship on Monday morning?" Jeff queried.

"Sean is back there now. He and that other guy said 'no problem.' He was a little surprised to hear that he was flying with us, though."

Jeff and Aubrey were satisfied and turned back toward the office.

"That was more words I've heard out of Mandrake's mouth than in all the time we've known him," Aubrey mused.

"I think there's some excitement involved about this possibly lengthy trip on Monday."

A few minutes later, they were back in Henry Atwell's office. Jeff leaned back in the desk chair, and the soft leather soon reminded him how tired he actually was.

"Aubrey, I'm satisfied that we have all the information available at this time, so I'm going to try to take a nap. I couldn't sleep in my room—too many nightmares."

He closed his eyes.

"O.K., partner," Aubrey replied. "I'm going back to the hotel. See you sometime tomorrow."

* * *

Just as Harden had predicted, the police cordoned off the Jennings house as a crime scene as soon as they received the report from Dr.

Mirimar, courtesy of the county medical examiner. The funeral arrangements had gone as planned, although delayed a number of hours initially for the autopsy.

Now it was Monday morning and everyone waited impatiently for the board meeting to begin at one o'clock. With his coffee mug in hand, frozen somewhere between his lap and his lips, Harden was staring at Sam. She had dressed in a charcoal business suit with a loose-fitting jacket open in front, and a tight-fitting white cashmere turtleneck sweater beneath. As his eyes scanned the area from her firm and shapely thighs, past her short, matching skirt, up to her breasts, accented by the white sweater under the black jacket, Harden allowed himself to dream of a better future.

He loved this young lady, and, even more satisfying, she had made it obvious that she felt the same way about him. As Sam reached for her coffee, her weapon was partially revealed, jolting his mind back to the present and the confrontation that lay before them.

She realized she was being appraised, and the slight blush on her cheeks made her even more appealing. She turned her head in his direction and smiled in a manner almost imperceptible to anyone but the big man, for whom it was solely intended.

Their private moment was interrupted as Ashley and Conner completed their review of the reports on the financial condition of Brantley Chemical, as well as the previous year's minutes. As Conner stood and stretched his long arms, Harden could assess at a glance that his friend had found time in his fast-paced career to dedicate some attention to his physical condition as well.

"Ashley tells me she ordered in some ham-on-rye sandwiches and salad with balsamic vinaigrette dressing. There's only an hour before the meeting, so no time to go anywhere. Is that satisfactory with you two?"

Neither Sam nor Harden had ever indulged in heavy meals immediately prior to an operation, so they found the offer quite agreeable. They could eat as much or as little as they chose.

At that moment a young man entered carrying a tray of food, including a pitcher of iced tea, and set it on the coffee table in front of Harden and Sam. Harden abruptly stood up. After an initial, still-framed reaction at the man posed before him, the delivery person was gone.

"Thank you very much."

Harden's expression of appreciation hit him in the back as he left the room.

As Ashley and Conner moved to join them, Harden managed to divert Conner over to the desk. With his back to Ashley he removed a small, pocket-sized Glock from his jacket.

"Conner, I know you had tactical training a while back in Missouri, so I think it would be worthwhile for you to carry a weapon here. If you'll slide it into your belt in the back, with the clip just above the waistline, it should stay in place under ordinary movement."

Conner accepted the weapon without hesitation, and found that it fit comfortably under his belt just as Harden had predicted. His training had been so complete that the feel of the weapon in his hand immediately recalled from memory all the proper handling and firing procedures.

"It's my understanding that only board members can sit at the table. We'll sit directly behind Ashley in the auxiliary chairs. If anything goes wrong, you take the responsibility of covering her and getting her underneath the table. If I can count on that from you, I'll be better able to handle any adversary."

"I'll be ready, Hard. Thanks!"

They rejoined the ladies for lunch.

Harden had already apprised Sam of his plan to arm Conner in order to cover Ashley. She was to wait in the adjacent office until needed.

* * *

Everything appeared normal as the four men entered the corporate headquarters of Jennings Pharmaceuticals. Some eyes turned in the direction of the young, well-dressed giant who was bending over the twisted figure in the custom-made wheelchair, but quickly turned away upon catching a glance from the third man with the cold, steel blue eyes. Expertly maneuvering the electronic controls, Anthony entered the elevator first, followed by the balance of his entourage.

Having made this trip several times in the past, Mandrake knew to select the fourth floor, where the boardroom was located.

With just the slightest gesture, Anthony indicated the office where Aubrey was to position himself. The other three men moved toward the next door, to the boardroom itself. More as a statement of authority than for wheelchair accessibility, Anthony positioned himself at the end of the table, closest to the door. Jeff, as Henry Atwell, took the first seat to his right, adjusting his jacket as he sat to be certain that his holstered weapon remained inconspicuous.

After placing his briefcase on the conference table, its top snapped open to permit easy access to its contents, Anthony again gave a dismissive wave of his hand. At that signal, Mandrake left the room without a word. Jeff did not let this escape his attention. He immediately rose and checked the door to the adjoining office to be sure that it was unlocked. Feeling satisfied in seeing Aubrey pacing back and forth, he closed the door and returned to his seat just as three men in dark business suits entered the room.

"Good afternoon, Mr. Riley. What's this meeting about? I received no agenda."

The tall, thin man did not like to be surprised.

Ignoring his inquiry, Anthony removed several papers from his briefcase and looked impatiently at the door, anxious to proceed.

Though agitated, the man knew better than to press the issue and let his body fall into the chair, conveying his irritation to everyone present.

At exactly one o'clock, Ashley Jennings entered the room. Anthony, while not surprised, was nonetheless bothered by the attendance of the two men who had befriended him when he need it most, the formative years of high school. Instead of an odd couple, they had formed an odd trio throughout their four years together. Conner had always been brilliant but encouraging. Without that encouragement, Anthony would never have achieved second honors and his ensuing successes. Anthony, himself, had dubbed them 'the three kings'.

Subsequent exposure to the harsh realities of his physical condition, however, had warped his mind beyond repair. Without his two companions to lean on, he had fought both his disability and his peers throughout college and his ensuing career. Unable to contend with the cruel stares and overheard mutterings, Anthony had learned to harden his heart against the world. No longer bothered by a conscience that interfered with his methods, his well-tutored brain hungered for knowledge as a substitute for his inability to mold friendships. Bitter memories soon overrode the nostalgia that resurfaced upon seeing his old friends.

With eyes scanning the potential combatants in this confrontation, Harden was somewhat surprised at the absence of Mandrake. Though relieved to find that he and Conner were the only observers at the board meeting, prior experience warned him not to relax his attention until the situation was contained.

"As acting chairperson, I would like to bring this meeting to order. Since you requested the meeting, Mr. Riley, I will yield to your agenda."

Conner admired Ashley Jennings as she stood straight and tall in fulfilling her newly acquired responsibility.

52

A s Sam entered the adjoining office, she was surprised to find that it was already occupied. She immediately recognized the man as one of the two who had nearly run into her in the lobby of Conner's building. Evidently the man did not have the same cognizance of her.

"What are you doing here, beautiful?"

He stared at her as she entered. Now his icy, blue eyes reflected the light from overhead as he turned toward her.

"I was about to ask you the same thing, sir. Miss Jennings asked me to wait in here in case my services were needed at this meeting."

"I could use your services right now."

He was now close enough for his hand to stroke her cheek, which he did. She cringed at his touch but chose not to retaliate. Deciding instead to play along with the man, she thought she might learn more about him while they were waiting. Gently, she removed his hand and turned toward the desk.

"Not now. Maybe later. I told you why I'm here. If you're here for the board meeting, why are you in this office and not in the boardroom?"

She glanced at her watch.

"The meeting is just about ready to begin," she observed, ignoring the fact that he had not yet answered her question.

He was still watching her every move as Sam took the chair positioned behind the desk. Feeling encouraged at not being turned down outright, Aubrey's eyes were distracted enough by her shapely breasts, wrapped in soft, white cashmere and protruding from her open jacket, that his professional training failed him momentarily. He did not even notice the additional padding under the jacket on her left side, where her weapon was concealed.

"Mr. Riley asked that I wait in this office as well. I wasn't expecting to share it."

He moved toward her again. She gave him her most provocative smile.

"Miss Jennings told me to turn on the intercom button for this phone so that I could hear the proceedings. That way she won't have to dictate a lengthy report later. I wanted to alert you because they'll also be able to hear anything said in this office."

She pressed the button.

Since Sam had successfully delayed his advances, Aubrey took the chair across from the desk where he still had an appreciative view, from her crossed legs all the way up to her teasing smile.

Realizing that she had succeeded in diffusing the situation for the moment, Sam sat quietly and listened to the activity in the other room. The only immediate sound over the intercom was the shuffling of chairs.

She could still feel the intensity of this man's eyes moving up and down her body, but at least they had established a temporary détente.

Harden had briefed her on all the details of this case. She fully realized that this man was the suspected AWOL operative responsible for the deaths of three trusting agents. The only thing in her favor was the fact that he did not know her true identity. The flirtation was intended to enable her to maintain that advantage.

* * *

When jeff observed the seating arrangements of Miss Jennings and her companions, he immediately pushed his chair back and moved to the other side of the table, this time to Anthony's left. From there he had the advantage of facing his potential adversaries, as well as having the heavy walnut table between them.

"Miss Jennings."

The croak in Anthony's voice seemed even more pronounced.

"I have before me a proposal to establish an additional operating facility for Brantley Chemical in Savannah, Georgia. The site we have selected has access to major waterways that would facilitate cost-effective overseas shipping. We all know that the financial performance of Brantley demands that we allow our subsidiary to unleash its potential for further growth."

Anthony pushed the copies toward Jeff who, under the guise of Henry Atwell, seemed somewhat preoccupied. Nonetheless, he managed to retain one copy and distribute the others around the table.

"As you can see, we've been able to limit the cost of this expansion to 1.2 million dollars, well within our budget.

"Based upon the success of our Cleveland facility, I would like for each of you to review the documents for a few minutes so that we can bring it to an immediate vote. Time is of the essence, if we are to be able to control the property and construction estimates contained in the proposal."

Ashley scanned the document quickly. The urgency of the additional plant was not the issue. The real motive behind the timing of this proposal was the resolution of the emerging power struggle for control of the corporation. If Anthony succeeded in winning this vote, there would be no way to stop him from also assuming the chairmanship. Ashley knew that the time to stop him was now, backed by the added strength of her father's shares.

"Mr. Riley, we all appreciate the success of Brantley Chemical over the past three years. However there are other, more pressing issues at hand. I'll need a little more time to analyze this motion. I know you won't mind if we table this discussion until the regular meeting at the end of the month. Is there any further business that needs to be brought before the board this afternoon?"

"Miss Jennings, you can't dispute the successes of Brantley Chemical, as evidenced by the audited financial statements over the past three years. The very life of this proposed expansion depends upon our immediate attention. Again, I would like to see a vote on the issue this afternoon."

Anthony, while gracious, was becoming somewhat more aggressive.

"I can assure you, Mr. Riley, that the vote will not be in your favor if you continue to press for this afternoon. With my father's shares we can control the outcome, as you already know."

Ashley was trying to maintain control of the meeting.

"Madam Chairman, I am sorry to hear of the recent loss of your father, and I certainly appreciate your appearance here today. However, this other document, signed approximately two weeks ago…"

Anthony paused in his speech to push another set of copies toward Jeff, who seemed to appear even more distracted. Mandrake, who had returned to the boardroom, stepped in to move the papers around the table.

"…by your father, acknowledges the success of Brantley Chemical by stating his confidence in my ability to run the corporation. In other words, Miss Jennings, he has given me power of attorney to administer the voting rights of his shares while, of course, maintaining the beneficial ownership thereof. I would like for you, as current chairperson, to call for a vote on my expansion proposal."

Ashley was stunned. Conner stood at her back, one hand resting on her shoulder.

"Hold on a minute, Anthony. The death of Miss Jennings' father is now being investigated as a homicide. The court will freeze all recent correspondence, transactions and documentation until this issue is resolved. Speaking as Miss Jennings' attorney, I must advise you that if any documents involving Mr. Jennings' signature are used in a course of action before the aforementioned issue is resolved, such action will undoubtedly be overturned by a court of law, pending resolution. Now, strictly as an observer and as your long-time friend, Anthony, I suggest that this matter can wait a few weeks."

Taken by surprise at Conner's outburst, Anthony was rearranging his thoughts to address this latest setback.

* * *

Already distracted by the appearance of Deltas Three, Four and Five in the chairs to his left, the haze that clouded Jeff's brain seemed to thicken at someone's mention of Mr. Jennings' death. Throwing his phony glasses to the table, he bowed his head and ran his fingers through his hair, shaking his head back and forth as if to clear it.

This unsettling episode escaped neither Harden's attention nor Conner's. Turning abruptly to Harden, Conner whispered quietly.

"It's him, Harden. It's Jeff Lewis."

Harden reached inside his jacket.

As old man Jennings floated out in front of him, his hands outstretched as if to strangle him, Jeff reached for his gun and fired twice at the apparition. Swinging to his left he fired three more rounds in quick succession. As a red circle appeared on each of their chests, the three Delta agents fell forward onto the table. The only mistake that Jerry Fox and the two Riley-appointed board members had made was to show up at today's meeting. This proved to be a fatal error for them all.

There was one more shot fired. Jeff looked down at his own chest. There was a hole through his tie, and he realized that it was slowly turning a darker shade of red as blood began to pump through the opening in his chest. His arms were still thrust forward from the impact of the bullet. His right hand clutched his weapon as he crumpled in slow motion back into his chair, and then onto the floor.

Conner had pushed Ashley to the floor at Harden's first warning, having drawn his own pistol.

Since he was the person closest to the door that led to the boardroom, Aubrey appeared first from the adjoining room, his gun in his hand, just in time to see Anthony's motorized chair race for the elevator as Mandrake led the way. At the same instant, he watched Harden fire across the table at his partner.

Sam caught up to him and slammed the handle of her Glock hard against the back of his head. The blow glanced off as he had heard her footsteps and anticipated the aggressiveness of her move. Aubrey backed into the hallway with his weapon pointed at Harden. This mission was over. He had to clear the scene. With some regret, he knew he had to take care of the big man before he could leave. Looking again toward Harden, he was suddenly dropped to the floor by two shots from the left. Before his eyes finally closed, he caught one last sight of the beautiful young lady in the white sweater, both her hands gripped tightly around a gun that was pointed in his direction.

Jeff and his demons were gone from this life. With him he took the three board members Anthony had installed. All three lay with their heads between their hands on the huge walnut table. Their only serious transgression had been their transformation to Deltas Three, Four and Five in the troubled mind of the fallen Jeff Lewis. Aubrey Long lay on the tiled floor, his sightless eyes frozen in the direction of the vision in white, the conquest he had hoped to make once the meeting had ended.

"He was going to shoot you. I had to do it."

Harden was holding her tightly, her moist face pressed against his chest.

"I love you, Samantha," he responded.

He knew she had just saved his life. Given the opportunity to shoot, Aubrey would not have missed. Jeff's fire had been just as deadly for the three weak, but otherwise innocent souls at the table. As for the two holes in the ceiling, no one doubted that Jeff had been shooting at some past demon that still haunted his mind. Ashley would never know that her father had wreaked a form of revenge, however unwittingly, on his murderer.

As the police entered the room to assess the damage, Harden presented his identification to the officer in charge and requested that the police block all the exits to search for a man in a wheelchair.

After immediately acknowledging Harden's identification card, the officer barked out the order into his radio.

53

Anthony was already planning his departure after hearing Conner's impressive argument. When he caught sight of Jeff falling apart, he motioned to Mandrake that it was time for them to leave. Mandrake ran to the door to hold it open for Anthony's wheelchair, then raced down the hallway ahead of him to take the elevator off hold. He had previously locked the elevator open and taped a sign to the front indicating it was out of service. By the time Anthony entered the lift, Mandrake was ready to push the button for the roof exit. They heard shots being fired as the door closed.

The helicopter was waiting as arranged, its rotors turning. The pilot helped Mandrake lift the man and his chair into the wide opening and took off immediately after strapping him in. Anthony Riley made his plans thoroughly, and he paid well those who ensured their completion.

They boarded his private jet without delay or interference, which indicated that no order had yet been issued to stop him. Their departure and the flight itself went flawlessly. His chemical genius was on board, along with Mandrake, himself and the pilot. Anthony felt badly about losing the two young men. His original plan involved bringing them along for future use. That would have completed the team.

* * *

Sipping his drink on the balcony of his small mansion, looking out on the blue Mediterranean Sea, Anthony contemplated his options.

He felt safe here on Ramkin Island, situated off the coast of Tripoli, or Trablos as some people called it. The island was quite remote and there had been no shipping papers created or flight plans filed that would have revealed his ultimate destination.

With his money safely transferred and his shipment of TR-7 stored in the basement, he had time to plan. Although it had cost him another substantial bonus to Jon Heydn, the balance in the accounts of Lewis and Long had also been successfully transferred to his own. Nostalgia intruded as he watched the huge cruise ship sail past in the distance. He wondered if he would ever see his two old friends again, or if they were even still alive.

* * *

Cruising in the Mediterranean Sea on her honeymoon, Ashley was relaxing alone on deck. Conner was resting in his own way, lying across the bed in their stateroom. Jennings Pharmaceuticals had survived but no longer enjoyed the Brantley boost to its corporate balance sheet.

With Harden Kelly's credentials opening the proper doors, Conner had successfully managed to work with the U.S. Food and Drug Administration to dismantle Brantley Chemical. The cash that remained after Anthony's disappearance was employed to settle the debts of the company, including paying the substantial FDA fines levied on the illegal activity.

After Anthony's takeover of Brantley, the only business he had retained was the manufacture of its primary product, TR-7. The beneficial result was that this operation enabled him to lower their overhead drastically, thereby turning Brantley into a cash cow, albeit an illegal one. With the expeditious closing on the sale of the property, Conner was able to terminate the subsidiary with no net ill effect on the remainder of the corporation.

After saying goodbye to Sam and Harden at the airport, Ashley and Conner had set off for Athens to enjoy a ten-day cruise of the eastern Mediterranean. Mr. Anderson had another assignment for his two favorite operatives but, of course, they could not disclose their destination. After promising to keep in touch as best they could, the couples separated to pursue their own agendas.

Mr. Anderson had managed to take possession of the bodies of the two renegade operatives, thus providing closure to the incident which greed had initiated such a short time earlier.

Dr. Mirimar had taken a trace sample of fluid from the entry wound in Mr. Jennings' neck. The one mistake Jeff Lewis had made was to wipe away blood from that spot with his own saliva. The resultant DNA evidence had been conclusive.

Now, from the deck of the *Athens Princess*, Ashley had her binoculars trained on the beautiful little islands off the coast of Tripoli, with their old mansions that sported wide verandas overlooking the sea. Finally relaxed, the glasses slid to her lap as she fell asleep on the padded lounge chair.

PART 2

1

Anthony Riley let the binoculars slide down to his lap. The Cruise ship had maneuvered between the Islands so as to move the object of his attention from his field of vision. Upon sighting the beautiful young lady on the deck only moments before, he was certain that not only was she the daughter of the deceased Chairman of the Board of his former Company, but that she was also looking directly at him from her lounge chair on deck. *Surely, her lenses were not as strong as mine.* His were of his own unconventional design, patented especially for the handicapped user. But he continued to feel a chill as though his secret recluse had been discovered.

Anthony had been attempting to relax all morning as he worried about Mandrake handling a new assignment. Maneuvering his custom built wheelchair through the portal between the ornate French doors, he had just begun to feel that he had everything under control.

He had moved in to the big house several weeks prior, and rather abruptly, with Mandrake, his personal assistant, and Sean Pfister, a chemical engineer who had been in his employ. Flooded with applicants from the small seaside village below, his household staff was soon complete.

Now, his nerves were on edge and he knew why. Looking out over the balustrade, which formed a protective boundary around the parapet from which he had been viewing the surrounding area, had certainly not eased his tension. He pulled the afghan closer around his shoulders. Hundreds of feet below was the small seaside village in which resided ninety five per cent of the diverse population of Ramkin Island. For the past three weeks he had felt like a King overlooking his peasantry from high up on his balcony.

Suddenly, old fears returned, and along with them came a late morning chill from the direction of the cruise ship far out in the Mediterranean Sea. He had always had someone to look after him. Throughout his early years, he had been befriended by two of the most popular students in school. Then came four years of torment as he made his way through Bellarmine University in Louisville, Kentucky, seemingly, without a friend. Soon after, he had worked himself in to a position of authority, with lesser employees to do his bidding. Now, he found that he had to buy both loyalty and assistance. One proved to be more expensive than the other.

His plans had begun a year in advance, selecting the secluded island of Ramkin, off the coast of Tripoli, expecting never to see again the people he most feared. The old mansion he had purchased after much negotiation was to be a safe haven from his past...a place where he could start his life and his business anew. Now, that was all in jeopardy, as he sat quietly, eyes wide open but seeing nothing. His mind was formidable and he now had all cylinders working on the potential consequences of sighting one of his recent foes. The wind seemed to increase and he pulled the blanket tighter around his misshapen shoulders.

The malformation of his body from birth had been the cataclysm from which he had always been forced to struggle, even to the extent of cursing his mother for choosing to carry her poor child full term. At the same moment in which Anthony had exited the womb, his mother had succumbed to her weakened condition, and unwittingly deserted her son when he needed her the most. Faced with the death of his wife and the arrival of what he considered an abomination for a son, his father had disappeared from the face of the earth.

The place of his birth, St. Anthony Hospital, had been the source of his name. After months in pediatric intensive care, Anthony was allowed to go home with the elderly nurse, who had stepped in when the father stepped out, to take him as her own foster child. She had been a very strong and devout Catholic lady, who had been widowed for twenty years, and she welcomed little Anthony as a gift from God. In her fifties at the inception of this relationship, Mary Bentley had managed to see Anthony through college and to the National Weather Service before her age and weakening heart had taken her from him.

With few friends, and no social life, Anthony Riley spent endless hours at his computer. Overwhelmed by the knowledge it contained, he found his system growing with his enthusiasm. His cutting edge equipment allowed him to travel in to restricted areas of this new world, often losing himself in the adventure. As his fortuity expanded, his expertise at covering and diverting his trail had expanded as well. Anthony looked upon his travels within the confines of the nineteen inch flat panel monitor as one would view flying down the highway for a vacation in faraway places. He found the Government had many doors to be opened and he enjoyed the formidable challenge and ultimate victory in finding the key to these doors.

The source of his renewed tension, Ashley Jennings, had become the new Chairperson of Jennings Pharmaceutical after the unexpected death of her Father. Anthony's coup attempt had failed violently. After managing the meteoric rise of the subsidiary, Brantley Chemical, from a fledgling producer of several minor substances which enhanced the performance of fertilizer, to the multi-million dollar success that had become the driving force of the Jennings enterprises, his world had collapsed.

At great expense, Anthony had researched and recruited two well trained operatives from the Government special services. After enticing them in to his employment, however, he found that he could not control them as stringently as he had planned.

With Brantley Chemical as the star of the Jennings Balance Sheet, Anthony had sent Jeff Lewis to Ralph Jenning's home in San Francisco to coerce the old man's signature on a Power of Attorney releasing his voting rights to Anthony Riley in recognition of his performance at Brantley. Although his employer had authorized threats against Jennings and his daughter, Jeff had also been instructed to get the document signed before returning to the Cleveland office at whatever cost.

After his daughter's life had been threatened by the intense young man standing before him, Ralph Jennings had signed the paper, with full intention of rescinding the document the following morning. Jeff Lewis had returned the signed document to his briefcase and, as he turned to leave, he saw the shadow of the cane rising above his head. Surprised by the strength of the old man, he nonetheless was able to avoid the blow and shove Mr. Jennings back in to his desk chair. Prepared for the situation, he removed a dart, coated with Kurare poison, from his pocket, and with a small coffee stirrer, blew the dart in to the exposed neck of his now heavily breathing adversary. Carefully he removed the dart and wiped away a drop of blood with his own saliva. Kurare paralyzed the central nervous system and caused the heart muscles to go in to trauma, simulating a heart attack. *Should have let it go, old man.* Jeff had little remorse.

When presenting the document at a Board meeting a week later, Anthony's old friend, Conner Hayes, a very successful attorney in San Francisco, had successfully refuted the legal consequences of the document in representation of Ashley Jennings.

With his conscience battered by recent killings, Jeff Lewis finally cracked at the meeting and began firing his weapon at his demons. Although his ever efficient planning had enabled Anthony and his assistant, Mandrake, to escape the melee, Aubrey Long and his partner, Jeff Lewis, did not survive the episode.

2

"Mandrake! Mandrake!"

Dressed in white, long sleeved shirt and black pants, the man was at his side in an instant. Anthony's personal assistant was a huge man, who, with patient grooming, had also proved to be quite intelligent as well. His broad chest and arms with protruding biceps and pectoral muscles accented the fitted shirt and narrow hips.

Since Anthony had taken him under his wing four years ago, Manny Speagle had evolved from a rough, troubled young man on a work release program into a well groomed, soft spoken and better educated human being then anyone could have expected. He also proved to be intensely loyal to his new friend and mentor, Anthony Riley.

Somewhat abashed and embarrassed by his panic attack, Anthony had again gained control. "My friend, I am tired. Would you help me to my bed? I need to take a brief nap."

The early afternoon air had an ominous foreboding as the Sea blew its late summer breezes across Ramkin Island.

"I need to rest a while and then I will need you to help me with some research."

Anthony had much to think about. *Had the young lady seen me as well? Will*

I have to move again? What was the name on that cruise ship?...Athens Princess. I can get the manifest on my computer system.

With his twisted body, confined to a wheel chair, dependent on others for even the most menial tasks, he found that he could be a master at manipulation, despite his weak body, in the world of his own computers. Back in High School, while his best friends, Conner Hayes and Harden Kelly, excelled on the athletic fields, he had delved in to the intricacies of the computer, and discovered his niche. He deftly manipulated the mouse and persistently invaded private files with immunity from prosecution. Expert as he was, covering and diverting his trail was a deliberate and automatic function at the conclusion of each excursion.

His body was tired and consequently he was concerned that his thinking was influenced by paranoia. *I need a clear head to sort out all of these questions and to start Mandrake on his new responsibilities.*

After clamping his chair to the lift, the ascent was smooth as always.

Mandrake helped him into the King size bed, in which he invariably worked his way to the center. One of Anthony's greatest fears was simply falling off the side of the bed on to the floor and remaining there, helpless, for any period of time. Just the thought began shivers of panic rampaging through his system, even if the episode would only last for minutes. He so feared his inadequacies that he felt the need to control everything that touched his life.

3

Ashley's eyes opened only to find her husband of two weeks standing above her simply staring down at her reclining form.

"I'm sorry if I startled you, Hon, but I need to absorb every moment of you before we both have to return to the grindstone. Have I told you today how much I love you?"

"Not since lunch...but I will never get tired of hearing it."

The space between her eyes began to wrinkle as her face took on a thoughtful, business look as it had the first time they had met at his office.

"Conner, after you left for your nap, I was enjoying the breeze and salt air here in this lounge chair." She paused. "See that island, not the one straight out from us but the second one to the right. Before I dozed off, I was exploring the islands with my binoculars when a rather large, white stone house came in to view. On one of the parapets or balconies, I saw an old man in a wheelchair who was also looking through his binoculars, apparently in our direction. Mine were not powerful enough for a very clear picture, but seeing the man reminded me of Anthony Riley. He had the same appearance of a twisted, uncomfortable body. Anyway, I was wondering how your old friend ever got caught up with those horrible men who were his associates."

"Anthony never had many friends. You really had to work at being his friend…and not many people were willing to do that. Perhaps, if they had, things may have turned out differently. I have always believed that it was because of his speech impediment as well as his disquieting appearance. Although I scored slightly better than he managed to do in high school, I think his brilliance grew as his handicap turned him more and more into a recluse"

Conner Hayes had become Valedictorian of his senior class at St. Xavier High School in Louisville, Kentucky, and Anthony Riley had achieved second honors in the same class. Conner's address had been in praise of his classmates as a whole, and Anthony in particular. Harden Kelly, Conner's best friend since those early days, stood to cheer his friend after the brief speech. His six foot six inch muscular frame stood out even when all the other classmates joined in. All three friends had a copy of a picture somewhere, showing the three widely smiling faces in their caps and gowns, with Anthony in his chair dwarfed by Conner on his right and Harden on his left, both with their arm around his shoulders.

"I believe he simply hired people to be his arms and his legs after he had accumulated sufficient funds to enable him to do so. Anthony probably thought that he could also control their actions as well. This obviously worked on people like Mandrake, but Lewis and Long were a different matter. These were highly trained operatives, with skills honed to act and react to situations. It was not likely that a man in a wheelchair, however brilliant, could manipulate their every move. Obviously, Anthony got involved with the wrong people that time."

"I saw glimpses of him, Conner, when he was charming, gracious, even pleasant. He could have used that mind for any number of more beneficial endeavors than the course he pursued."

"You know, he did that at first. With his facility on computers, he worked his way to the top position at the National Weather Service in Washington, DC. as National Director. He never seemed to be satisfied with his accomplishments. Maybe it was greed. I believe he had already envisioned a greater plan when he started buying out Brantley. That Chemical Engineer, Pfister, was already associated with him when he first joined the Company. According to the personnel records, they both showed up at the same time."

Conner had familiarized himself with all the Company records in order to work out a settlement for the surviving parent, Jennings Pharmaceutical, after the collapse of Brantley. Anthony had, however illicitly, built an empire at Brantley. Using a new drug combination, created by his employee, Sean Pfister, he had produced that product exclusively, calling it a new miracle fertilizer, TR7. The clear white powder, as effective as the purest cocaine, had soon developed a simple distribution network for Anthony to use as the manufacturer. These channels inherently exposed him to a new genre of customer, which led him to hire the well trained, but avaricious, operatives to oversee all the transactions.

Conner settled in to the chair next to Ashley, both staring out at the passing islands, deep in thoughts of the recent events as well as the possible impact if it was indeed Anthony Riley in the eye of Ashley's binoculars. Conner made a mental note to find out the name of that island.

4

The Kuwaiti government and the Italians, as well, will have to deal with those illegal airfields and unrecorded flights. We have done all we can do in that area. Now, I have another assignment for you."

Anderson was as terse as ever, always getting directly to the point. Harden Kelly had had the same Controller since being recruited at the Boone Tavern in Berea, Kentucky, upon graduation from Eastern Kentucky University. The secrecy of the meeting stood out in his memory, approaching the man waiting in the back booth, twenty miles south of his Alma Mater. Working for the US Government on such important assignments had been a source of pride for him ever since day one. Anderson had recently confided in him, referring to him as the son he never had, but had always wanted.

Harden had worked himself through all the situations which he had to confront, with the tremendous satisfaction of accomplishment, until he was now considered the Company's finest operative. Although he was in line for a Controller position himself, Harden was still young and healthy enough to be of even more importance in the field.

His most recent assignment had been locating and neutralizing two renegade operatives, Jeff Lewis and Aubrey Long. These two men had been responsible for the deaths of three Delta Force Agents in southern

Lebanon, at which point Harden and his partner, Sam Chandler, had followed their trail of blood through Syria, Iraq, and into northern Kuwait. The trail had dried up in a small old resort town in Italy, named Amalfi, where the two men had negotiated additional identities and subsequently murdered the old proprietor and obliterated his shop with an incendiary grenade.

As fate twisted the events that followed, both Lewis and Long surfaced in Cleveland, Ohio, at Brantley Chemical, beneficially owned by Harden's old friend, Anthony Riley. The trail then led to San Francisco to the parent company, Jennings Pharmaceutical, which was owned by a Miss Ashley Jennings and her father. As it turned out, their attorney was Conner Hayes, Harden's best friend since high school. After the now infamous shootout in the Jennings Boardroom, Riley had disappeared with his assistant, Mandrake, and his Chemist, Sean Pfister, leaving both Lewis and Long lying dead on the boardroom floor. Three other members of the board had been shot by Jeff Lewis in some kind of fit of disillusionment. Sam had saved Harden's life that day by shooting Aubrey Long as he swiveled his weapon in Harden's direction.

Three weeks later, Harden and Sam had acted as witnesses when Conner and Ashley recited their wedding vows. Now, he was sitting in Building 132, at Rosslyn, Virginia, awaiting their next assignment.

"Harden, have you ever been to Afghanistan?"

Anderson already knew the answer, being familiar with the service record of all the operatives under his control.

"Sir, I have been there several times, achieving maybe a seventy percentile of operating familiarity with the region."

"There is extensive opium trade in the region. Through surprisingly elaborate labs within Afghanistan and the surrounding countries, the opium is being processed into what amounts to eighty or ninety per cent of the entire heroin used throughout Europe. The Afghan people are poor. About fifty per cent of the population lives below that country's recorded poverty level. The rest is obvious. Opium is a great source of money; money buys food; therefore the people don't starve. They have no knowledge or concern for what happens to the crop when it leaves their tiny farms."

"Our concern is more direct. This crop also funds terrorists with unimaginable resources. This is the part that concerns us and is the basis of your involvement in the area. The idiocy of this situation is that the United States and its allies are funding terrorism, indirectly of course, through their citizens who spend unknown millions of dollars for the purchase of cocaine each year."

Harden knew that the funding was not that indirect, however unintentional. If there was only a solution to cut the demand, the crop appeal would dry up with the unerring laws of economics, and, subsequently, alter the financing of terrorist's organizations around the World.

5

"Mandrake, you wanted to become more involved in our business and I am willing to make that opportunity available to you." Anthony had awakened from his nap and was now dining with his trusted assistant.

Through these many years, Mandrake could still not force himself to become accustomed to the croaky voice, although his audio perception had almost perfected the interpretation of what his employer was attempting to relate. Now he was being indoctrinated for additional responsibilities and, of course, additional compensation. Mandrake had become well aware of the activities required of the two men who had preceded him. He sincerely hoped that no killing was necessary in his new position. He was not sure if he could handle that…or…maybe he could.

In order to cover the loss of Mandrake's constant attention, there had been a steady stream of applicants for the three eight hour shifts to attend to the needs of the man in the wheelchair who lived in the mansion on the hillside. Most of the residents lived by the Sea, but Ramkin was a small island so travel was no obstacle.

Three ladies had been selected.

Mosa was in her late thirties, clean and neat, and known as a good worker. Lobeth was forty years old and rather plump, but agile enough to handle the job. Chrisimminia was the youngest at twenty-nine years of age, and still fairly attractive and definitely ambitious.

With Anthony's speech impediment, the third one had unwittingly undergone a name change. Immediately her name had been shortened to Chris. Mandrake had been sent down to the development by the Sea to research the candidates and played a great part in their choice.

Providing sexual favors was certainly not a factor in the position. Anthony had long ago shut that door, and locked it securely. In his twenties, he found the desires and lack of satisfaction to be a quandary he could not tolerate and thereby directed his attention to the things he could control.

The women were sworn to secrecy with a penalty of immediate dismissal if they were to divulge anything that occurred at the mansion to their ever curious neighbors. The generous pay assured at least a short life to this binder. The stronger assurance came by way of a not too veiled threat to their well being.

"We need to begin doing business, again, Mandrake. I have thoroughly briefed you on your responsibility in this transaction. Now, I am prepared to give you the details. My helicopter will fly you to Kuwait City with two containers of TR7, tomorrow, at nine in the morning." Anthony had arranged for loading of the remaining production of TR7 product into his private jet before departing the Mainland. "The pilot, who is also armed, will stand by while you rent a van large enough to carry you and the two containers to the Sheraton Hotel on Soor Street. The Hotel is expecting you and your freight and has adequate storage facilities for your vehicle and containers of that size."

"When you are in your room, stay there. For food or drink use the room service provided so as not to miss a very important phone call. You have met Fez and should have no trouble recognizing him. He will phone your room when he arrives at the dock in his boat. When you receive this call, leave immediately. Retrieve your rental van with the merchandise and simply follow the street directions that Fez will have given to you. Fez will load the two containers on his boat. You can be certain that he is familiar with the safest route to Warbah. Stay with the containers until the money changes hands at the airfield on Warbah

Island. There is no need to count the money as I have dealt with these same customers before.

After you receive the satchel with the money, return to the boat and Fez will take you back to Kuwait City. Take a cab directly to the airport where our pilot will be waiting. Board immediately and return here. You are armed with the weapon you preferred and trained in its use, although I can not imagine why you chose a Glock. Do not hesitate to use that weapon to deter anyone, I repeat, anyone, from opening either the TR7 containers or the satchel."

They had gone over this several times, and Mandrake was anxious to get started. His stomach muscles were churning in nervous anticipation. His share for this additional exposure would certainly enhance his bank account although he knew that it was not equal to the share his predecessors had received. The grooming and training, which Mr. Riley had insisted on early in their relationship, served also to create an appetite for a better life than he had endured in his formative years.

"Mosa will be here from seven until three, then Lobeth. You should be back early the following day, definitely while Chris is still on her shift. I want to be awakened when you arrive and I will make the girl aware of this as well."

"Yes, sir. I am ready."

Mandrake was ready in more ways than one. He had overheard the transaction conversation whereby the accounts of Lewis and Long had been transferred to Mr. Riley's personal account, after their unexpected demise. He dared not open his bank account with Jon Heydn. The Swiss banker was tied too closely to Mr. Riley. Concerned at how adept his employer was at controlling people, Mandrake wanted to distance his account from any easy access by either of these two gentlemen. Inadvertently, he had made it even a more simple procedure for Anthony to access his account, if necessary at some time in the future, without the necessity of compensating Heydn or anyone in a similar position. He had long ago taken a tour of his assistant's computer and extracted all the information necessary to transfer the balances if something should happen to Mandrake.

In his short span of service with Mr. Riley, the young man had been exposed to perhaps more information than his employer intended. He knew how much his predecessors had been paid as bonus for successfully completing each of these missions. He was promised what he knew was only a tenth of their compensation, although his employer seemed to be unaware of his knowledge of those numbers.

That is ok with me. He will soon see how valuable I can be. When I get this first delivery behind me, Mr. Riley will surely have more confidence that I can handle this part of the operations. If I have to use my weapon, that may help convince the man of my worth. I could do it...I may even look for the opportunity.

Greed was seeping into his pores, a natural consequence of his environment over the past few years. If the mind controlled the greed, it could be used wisely for self progression. However, like a cancerous growth, the greed would soon control the mind, altering wise decisions to result in ultimate personal disaster.

6

Conner and Ashley Hayes had decided to move into Ashley's condominium because it was larger and better suited for two people. Before the cruise ended, Conner had questioned the Captain about the island which Ashley had described.

"That must have been Ramkin Island. There are a dozen or two old mansions on the hillside, with most of the population living closer to the Sea. Half of the mansions are closed because of the expense of upkeep. However, several have been renovated and are currently being used as summer homes, maybe even permanent residences."

"Is there somewhere I can get a list of the homeowners on the Island?"

"I doubt that a list is available. Local realtors are very protective of their clientele. People that wealthy are very concerned about their privacy."

Conner had dropped the subject, seemingly at a dead end, at least for now.

Their attention was now diverted to Monday morning and what lies ahead at both their Companies, Smith, Pitt and Alagia and Jennings Pharmaceutical, respectively.

As they sat their luggage on the floor of the prodigious walk in closet in the master bedroom, Conner gently slid his arm around her waist and felt her warmth beneath the smooth silk suit. She turned, and they held each other, with no haste or urgency, but with the soft contentment of knowing that they would be together forever. Without a word, they prolonged the moment with silent satisfaction in the life they were beginning together.

With reluctant release, Ashley gazed into his eyes. It was late Sunday afternoon and they both had commitments at the office in the morning.

"I need to freshen up before dinner...shower and change."

With both hands still on her waist, Conner eased back to revel at the beautiful young lady before him.

"With all that fancy cuisine on the cruise ship the past two weeks, I was hoping we could just fix a salad here at home."

"Oh, Conner, I am so glad you said that. I am ready to get back to normal again."

With three gourmet meals set before them each day for the last two weeks, they both agreed that was sufficient for a while. The only way they could stay in shape on the cruise was their daily jog on the upper deck track.

In the weeks following the infamous board meeting, they had joined Harden and Sam for a daily run. It proved to be miraculous therapy after their recent ordeal. Impressed with the conditioning of his best friend, Harden Kelly, Conner swore to himself to allot adequate time each day to maintain some modem of physical fitness. He had discovered that Ashley had already established a regimen of jogging for exercise several times a week.

As Ashley exited the master bathroom with her satin gown wrapped securely around her body, parts of the gown clung to the still damp portions accenting her sensuality. However, this was partially offset by the turban like wrap around her head, expertly held in place by a soft knot in the back.

As she entered the kitchen, she was surprised to see that Conner had just about completed their salads, sprinkling shaved pecans over the top.

Balsamic vinaigrette dressing was standing by, as well as a gently percolating coffee pot.

Since they both had demanding positions which required adequate preparations each morning, it was agreed that Ashley would continue to use the master bath while Conner would use the guest bathroom which opened into the master bedroom as well as the guest room on the other side. Conner had taken a quick shower and hurried to the kitchen to have things ready for

Ashley when she arrived.

Now, she was standing in the doorway, and his eyes were riveted to her beauty. Her right breast, still slightly damp from the shower, was accented through the thin material and did not fail to get his attention, although he found himself laughing softly at the makeshift contraption on her head.

"Dinner is served, my lady."

He bowed slightly as he spoke.

"It looks wonderful, Conner. How did you beat me to it? I hurried as best I could and, yet, you still were the one to prepare our first dinner together."

Trying to divert his eyes from the nipple highlighted in the moist cloth of her robe, Conner felt himself becoming aroused at her beauty. He turned away to retrieve the coffee pot and successfully managed to pour a cup for each of them, despite the distraction.

After their gourmet repast, they rinsed the dishes and sat them in the dishwasher. Throughout the meal, Conner was thankful for the loose fitting terry cloth robe he wore as it managed to obscure his arousal. Now, as he entered the bedroom, he found Ashley standing at the foot of the bed, her robe had slid to the floor and the early evening light through the window silhouetted the apparition before him.

He closed the distance between them without even being aware of moving. With his hands softly cupping her cheeks, he tilted her lips to his and they touched, gently at first, until the urgency increased. His hands slid down and slipped the flimsy straps from her shoulders. With no resistance whatever, the thin negligee fell to the floor. He cupped her breasts as his lips descended to her neck and then the valley below. His pace quickened as he felt her hands on him, making his arousal complete.

7

As Mandrake watched carefully, Fez easily lifted the two TR7 containers into his boat. The boat looked sleek and powerful and Mandrake was anxious to get this first adventure completed. He would be much more comfortable after the experience of this first mission was finalized.

Fez was a giant of a man, dark complexioned and muscular. With cutoff shorts and a white, collarless shirt with the sleeves cut out, he still reminded Mandrake of a genie, as he always wore his namesake little round hat with the tassel securely squeezed around his shaven head. As tall as Mandrake was himself, the thought of a confrontation with this giant kept running through his mind. *Perhaps this could be the man I will have to shoot…and I will, if he tries to interfere with my opportunity…my job.* Mandrake was trying to buoy up his courage, his nerves still on edge over this first mission for Mr. Riley.

Purchase of the boat was arranged by Mr. Riley, originally. With the promise that Fez would eventually become the owner of this expensive vessel, Riley had insured his loyalty. After his previous assignment directly for Mr. Riley, Fez sped away from the departing helicopter, promising himself that he would now be able to arrange the forged documents necessary to show the police patrol boats on the inside waterway, between Bubiyan Island and the mainland.

He was tiring of the longer trip through the open sea on the East side of Bubiyan. With the documents securely in his onboard safe, Fez had been able to show off his prize possession to his unbelieving friends along the docks of Kuwait, a fringe benefit that meant much to the once struggling dockworker.

With the promise of the boat, Mr. Riley had not paid him much in the way of cash, realizing that his loyalty would remain much stronger until the man was able to secure ownership papers. Buying these documents from an independent entrepreneur was much more expensive than the already exorbitant rates charged through legal channels.

Although fully aware that this man had undoubtedly achieved ownership through some devious means, the Patrols were always satisfied after viewing his documents, even appreciating, to some degree, his success.

The boat, itself, belied the fact that a man like Fez could be the owner.

As they rounded the northeast coast of Bubiyan, they began to circle around the eastern tip of Warbah Island toward the West and their final destination. Even with his proper documentation, he dared not gamble with the Police Patrols while carrying his current cargo.

Backing expertly in to the makeshift dock, they were somewhat surprised to see another old ferryboat already docked. The old man on board eyed them curiously as they tied up and began to unload. There was a limousine waiting, appearing to be an old funeral car, black and shiny under a light coating of dust. Fez quickly loaded the two containers in the back of the car and returned to his boat for a drink and to wait for Mandrake's return. They had spoken few words on the trip, but had exchanged many furtive, cautious glances at one another. It was difficult to place complete trust in anyone with whom you associated in this business.

After being satisfied that his containers were safely stowed, Mandrake slid effortlessly into the front passenger seat. The driver, dressed in Arab garb, drove the short distance to the waiting jet in silence. He had learned long ago that few of his passengers could communicate in Arabic, and he knew very little English, hence the silence. Although hesitant about using the weapon, Mandrake had felt less anxious with his right hand inside his jacket, touching the Glock, a position he had nervously maintained since first boarding the boat with Fez.

Mandrake and the driver quickly unloaded the two containers and placed them by the freight doors of the aircraft. Two men in suits watched intently until the activity was complete. The older man, somewhat paunchy,

but with an air of confidence, made a show of examining the merchandise then signaled the younger man forward. As the pilot came around the front of the plane to help the younger man load the containers, the first man approached Mandrake with a briefcase, as wide as a small suitcase.

At his approach, Mandrake became nervous. However, he was instructed to also move toward the man with the briefcase to acknowledge his responsibility and to receive payment. Hoping that his anxiety did not show on his face, he reached for the case with his left hand to leave his right hand free to retrieve his weapon if necessary.

Though Al Molini had handled these transactions many times before, he was somewhat wary of the way this huge man filled out the custom made suit. *I believe I would much rather have this guy as my partner then this smart ass wimp I got stuck with.* He couldn't help but smile slightly as the young man hefted the heavy bag effortlessly from his grasp.

The smiled allayed some of the anxiety Mandrake felt as he came up next to the stranger. Without a word, he took the bag and with several steps backward he lengthened the distance between them. Doing this, he was able to see the other man turn and hurry to the passenger door. He caught a glimpse of a black haired young lady in a short skirt, with a white blouse tied around her slender waist. The sun shone off a piece of jewelry at her bare midriff. She smiled and waved as she pulled the door closed.

Fez was already standing by the rope, anxious to return so he could show off with his buddies on the dock without worrying about this young giant. Fez had always been proud of his strength, but was often dismayed when confronted with someone of equal or greater stature. *I know I can handle this man. That bag is full of cash. I wonder how much. That guy is young and nervous...makes him more dangerous. Mr. Riley would not have sent a man he could not depend on. Oh well! I have my boat...best to get rid of this guy as soon as possible.*

They sped out into the open sea, so intent on each other that they failed to notice that the entire transaction had been watched by a casually dressed, but intense, young man from the other vessel.

Charlie Reynolds was instructed to observe, but not to interfere at this time. When he reported the obvious exchange to Mr. Anderson, he would receive further orders on how to proceed. After spending the past two months with the old man on the ferry boat, he was finally rewarded with something to report. The participants never even noticed him as he raised and lowered his miniature Sony camera, capturing each person involved with 6 mega pixels and 10x optical zoom. Raising a cigarette to his lips as he palmed the camera and recorded the images of the two men on the arriving vessel and the driver who met them, he had successfully obscured his primary function.

He then jogged the mile distance to the storage shed, keeping the tall shrubs between him and his quarry at all times. Charlie Reynolds prided himself in his physical condition, and smiled as he arrived at his objective before the limousine. From this vantage point, he quickly recorded the two suits waiting at the Lear jet. When the pilot disembarked to help with the freight, he was also captured on film. As the young lady appeared at the top of the stair casing, she also entered the collection. Charlie could hardly suppress a complimentary *wow!* as the scantily clad but classy young woman came in to view.

Now realizing that he was holding a great deal of cash, Mandrake's nerves tightened another notch, but this only served to make his senses equally wary. The return had gone smoothly and he was now boarding the waiting helicopter for the flight to Ramkin Island. *That wasn't so bad.*

Though drowsiness was beginning to overcome him, Mandrake did not dare shut his eyes until he handed the briefcase over to Mr. Riley.

8

G ood morning, Mr. Hayes. It is good to have you back."
Janet knew that her boss, Conner Hayes, was an attractive man, but with the wide smile on his face and even tan on his exposed features, he looked more handsome than ever.

"Good morning, Janet. Did I miss much excitement while I was away?"

"No excitement…but a lot of correspondence. I have it arranged on your desk in chronological order as well as order of importance. You will see there are two rather large stacks."

As he entered his office, the view was as refreshing as ever through the corner window. From thirty six floors up, the view of San Francisco and the Golden Gate Bridge was unparalleled. He had used it often in a casual manner to impress his clients with the resources of his firm, Smith, Pitt & Alagia. They were now a National law firm with overseas connections.

Funny to walk into my office and not see Charlie Reynolds over there on the couch, patiently researching a couple of huge law volumes from my shelves. Charlie Reynolds had been an associate of his old friend, Harden Kelly, whom Harden had assigned to keep a protective eye on Conner as a potential target while the two renegade agents were still at large in the area.

Charlie had been a constant companion for about a week, even accompanying Conner to his home for the night. The young man was pleasant, neat, friendly and efficient, but Conner could never accept the syntax of having a baby sitter. His friend, Captain Bill Robinson, had remained with the Judge Advocate General's office long after Conner had decided to leave. Robinson had represented then Private Jeff Lewis and Conner had defended Lewis's adversary, Private Aubrey Long.

After years of special training and complicated missions, Lewis and Long had since become inseparable, each depending on the other with confidence born of necessity.

Too many missions and too much killing had turned their fervor and loyalty to the corps into a cold and logical analysis of their own situation. A promise that would turn their hard earned retirement fund into an unbelievable cash opportunity, offered by the emasculated but avaricious Anthony Riley, led to their bloody separation from the Corps while on a mission in southern Lebanon.

In an effort to erase their past, the two men found it necessary to delete their files and eliminate their former Jag Attorneys, William Robinson and Conner Hayes. When Robinson was murdered, Harden Kelly immediately assigned one of his men, Charlie Reynolds, to attach himself to Conner.

With his musing over, Conner returned to the present, pulled a wooden hanger from the closet and soon had rolled up his shirtsleeves to peruse the waiting stacks of documents at his desk.

Across town, at Jennings Pharmaceutical, a similar scenario was taking place.

"Good morning, Ashley. Good to have you back."

Although Mary Grayson had been her assistant for only six months, Ashley had insisted on a first name basis in their relationship.

"Mary, hold my calls so I can sort through all the accumulated paper on my desk...unless, of course, if one of the callers is my husband."

"Will do, Ashley. Let me know if there is anything I can do to help you. There is an unbelievable amount of paperwork accumulated on your desk."

Mary had not been exaggerating. For the next three hours, Ashley sifted through the documents, dictating responses and sorting financial data.

The burden was all hers, now. *How I miss him! But his strength will get me through this.* Her father had been gone now for almost two months and, somehow, she still expected him to appear in her doorway, with his smiling face and loving greeting. His demise at the hands of Jeff Long had broken her heart, but, as she said goodbye to her father, she extracted some of his strength, the strength she needed to go on with her life and the ensuing responsibilities.

9

To Harden, there had always been another world out there, a world for other people, ordinary people, people for whom it was his job to keep safe from the evil elements encircling the globe. For the last few weeks, hard as he tried to be one of those ordinary people, shouting 'Honey, I'm home,' each evening after work, he knew in his heart that it would never be. Anderson already had another assignment awaiting their attention.

After attending the wedding of his best friend, Conner Hayes, to the stunning Ashley Jennings, he and Samantha Chandler had been married in a quiet ceremony in San Francisco, attended only by those two, before Conner and Ashley set sail on their honeymoon cruise of the Mediterranean. The service was held in the small chapel at the Presidio, an old military facility dating back before WW2.

While Harden and his new wife enjoyed a week long escape in Las Vegas, his Controller and mentor, Mr. Anderson, had arranged new quarters for them in Rosslyn, Virginia, where they intended to make their home for the near future. Rosslyn had been their home base for so long now that, when not on assignment, they both enjoyed the familiarity of their surroundings.

As he gazed out the window on the twenty fifth floor of the Flamingo

Hilton, he found he could still be impressed by the glaring lights below. With a room facing the famous Strip, Caesars Palace and the Mirage, as well as all the other brightly lit gaming establishments seemed to beckon to them with their illumination. Both he and Sam worked beyond the real world. It only seemed fitting that they should vacation in the illusory world of Vegas.

Harden enjoyed playing the simple game of chance, feeding quarters into the mouths of the awaiting predators. With just a small amount of luck, he found he could spend some relaxing hours shifting around the room to the variety of machines. Even with his size and powerful aura, he managed to meld in to the flow in the crowded casinos.

In their room of shadows, lit only by the lights through the open drapes, Harden turned his eyes back to his sleeping wife. With the blanket kicked aside, revealing her smooth, long legs, and her breasts pushing against the thin fabric of her nightshirt, it was hard to realize that this young lady had become one of the top operatives in the Company over her ten years with the Government. The emotions aroused in him just holding her in his arms found their culmination in sincere love when she held him in response. No longer would they have to rely on chance encounters or joint assignments in order to be together.

Anderson had again expressed his concern over the intimate involvement of two of his top agents, however, he relinquished his concerns when he saw realized how necessary it was for them to be together. It would be a battle he could not win. His fatherly concerns could not be as easily abated. He knew only too well the dangers of their mutual occupation.

Now, they were back home in the familiarity of Rosslyn and the time had come to return to work.

"Sam, I just had a meeting with Anderson. We have a new assignment."

They had just returned from the firing range, which they visited monthly, honing their skills on the training course laid out for Special Ops Agents.

"There will be a lot of travel involved, but, of course, it seems like there always is. We are going to western Afghanistan, where the main crop has become poppy plants, used to manufacture opium. The poverty level was so extreme in Afghanistan that when provided the opportunity of using their sparse land for raising this cash crop, the decision had nothing to do with the drug trade, only that they could now provide food and shelter for their families."

"Why is the Company so concerned with those people?"

"Well, it seems that a great deal of money from this crop is being used to finance terrorists, not only in Afghanistan, but throughout the region. Our objective will be to trace the opium from the original source to the ultimate payoff, and then try to create some damage to the flow."

"I am ready to get back to work, Harden. Although, when we get another chance at vacation, I would like to return to Las Vegas. That was like a brightly lit playground...a fantasy land. Of course, it may not seem the same the second time."

"To most people, our world would be the fantasy. Although it is more than real to us, the general public probably never gives it a thought with the exception of when the news media interferes. With technology so advanced that the average person can watch live war maneuvers from the comfort of their family room television, it has become much more difficult to keep our operations from public scrutiny." Harden was becoming perplexed.

"Our country's efforts to provide an organization with the sole purpose of defending our country by offsetting the affronts of envious individuals or groups, intent on disrupting our freedoms and way of life, could not exist except in secret. Public exposure would mean total loss of effectiveness, and would endanger the lives of our agents around the world.

It seems that everyone should realize that, and have confidence that these operations are necessary to protect our constitution, not infringe upon it. They must be convinced that these are good people involved."

"Harden, that was the longest speech I have ever heard from you."

She gently put her arms around his waist.

"And, of course, I agree with you. Now, when do we start?"

10

It was seven in the morning as Mandrake entered the front hallway to the chimes of the great Filmour Grandfather clock with its golden oak finish and a beautiful pediment featuring a cerejeira panel bordered by a raised shell and vine overlay. The strength of its chime never failed to catch his attention. However, this morning, sleepless and feeling the stress of his previous day's adventure, Mandrake was startled by the sudden outburst.

With his huge left hand wrapped tightly around the grip of the valise, he made his way directly to Mr. Riley's room. Although hesitant to awaken his employer, he had been directed to do so upon his return. He passed Chrisimminia in the hall, apparently just having left his room.

"Is he awake yet, Chrisimminia?"

Of the three women in attendance, she was his favorite, even entertaining thoughts of developing a more personal friendship when he had the time.

"Yes. He just asked if you had arrived yet. You better go right in." Of course, the fact that Mandrake always used her full name did not escape her attention. She smiled at him, her eyes lingering a little longer than necessary for the exchange.

Gently opening the door so as not to disturb his patron, Mandrake was surprised to see him already in his chair at the computer. Riley raised his hand over his head in a gesture meant to silence whoever had entered while he completed his task.

The keyboard was engineered especially for his use, requiring only a touch of the letters or commands on the screen to activate their function. It was held in place by small suction pads on the bottom to offset any awkward bump from his unwieldy limbs. Anthony's fingers seemed to glide over the commands causing the screen to hone in on his target, the manifest of guests on the Athens Princess for this past week's sailing.

His efforts were rewarded as he came across the names that confirmed his anxiety. Of course, this information was not accessible to the general public. To Anthony Riley, this was just another door that people tried to lock, always in vain. Conner and Ashley Hayes were indeed on the ship and it meant that he had looked directly into the eyes of his recent adversary.

As his hand relaxed from the keys, he motioned Mandrake to come over. Having noticed his shadow reflected on the screen as he processed his search, Anthony already was aware of who had entered the room.

"I have the satchel, still latched as I originally received it. No one has touched it or even attempted to do so." Mandrake laid the heavy load on the desk.

"Mandrake, I need you to open the bag and lay the contents on the desk where I can reach them."

Seemingly disinterested in the sum total that lay before him, Anthony's mind was busy calculating and scrutinizing the bundles of bills as Mandrake emptied the briefcase. Taking one bundle aside, he quickly counted off five one hundred bills and presented them to his assistant.

"This is for your loyalty and successful completion of your first assignment in your new position. Hopefully there will be many others."

Mandrake's huge hands swallowed the bundle of Hundred Dollar bills as he accepted his cut of the payoff. Putting half of the stack in each of his front jacket pockets as deftly as possible under the circumstances, he knew he would have to make a trip to the mainland later that day to meet with his banker. *What a nice ring that has to it!...My banker.* He was finally getting the financial recognition from Mr. Riley for which he had worked so long and hard. Next time, he would get a larger share.

"Now, would you put the remainder of this cash back in the bag and follow me to my safe."

Anthony turned his chair and started moving toward the door, trusting his request to be honored by his faithful assistant. Mandrake was beside him, carrying the refilled satchel, before he reached the door. At the head of the stairs, Anthony backed into the lift clamp and heard the familiar click as his chair was locked in place. He pressed the button for the slow descent with Mandrake pacing himself on the stairs to stay at his side.

Once inside the room furnished to be his office, Anthony removed a tiny remote control from his pocket. Entering a short series of touches to the unit, a panel on the wall next to the fireplace slid aside exposing the door to a large metal safe. With a few more touches on the remote, that door also began to slowly turn on its hinges outward toward the two men. The exposed room was large enough for Anthony to enter in his wheelchair. He motioned for Mandrake to come in also, and directed him to again unload the currency and stack it neatly on the stainless steel shelves lining the wall.

With this operation complete, both men exited the small room, closing the door behind them. The click was audible as the ten inch thick door locked in place. Touching one button on the remote, the panel slid into place and the room was as it had originally appeared.

"Keep the briefcase in your room until we need it again." Having already observed the tired eyes of his assistant, he was ready to let the young man get some rest. "You had better rest now. We are finished for today. Before you leave, will you make certain to send Chris back in, please?"

11

Charlie watched as the two big men sped away in the cruiser without realizing he had moved in to the field of vision of the older man standing on the top step of the boarding platform. Al Molini lowered the glasses and yelled for his partner as he quickly descended the steps to the tarmac. The young man caught him before he reached the car. The driver had the seat fully back and was smoking a cigarette with his eyes closed. The music was blasting from the radio so loudly, that he did not hear the two men approaching.

"Get back to the dock, quick, Bud." Al Molini left no room for question as he jumped in to the front passenger seat and roughly jostled the driver back to the present. His young partner, Joey Bono, had already closed his door and drawn his weapon.

As the limo threw gravel and sand into the air, the driver was turning the wheel and accelerating at the same time. Shaken back to reality, he had seen both men drawing weapons as they entered and slammed the doors almost simultaneously.

"There's somebody on that ferry that don't belong here, and he has a camera. We got to find out who he is and what he is doing here. When this guy stops the car, you get out fast and go around the back to the other side of the car. I'll get his attention from my side. Have your weapon ready, Joey, and stay behind the car door."

Charlie turned his attention from the speeding boat when he heard the approaching vehicle. The limousine slid to a stop at the edge of the dock and doors on both sides opened immediately. Charlie could see two men with their guns pointed in his direction.

"We want to talk to you, fella. Get your ass over here, now." Molini had been in many similar situations in the past and did not want any margin for error as he shouted his command and pointed his weapon.

This location had been perfect for these large transactions and if anything went wrong, he was not going to let it be blamed on him. He had a clean history with his boss and at fifty six years old, he knew he was being considered for a position with much less travel and much better pay…he would get a cut of all the action in his area. *What's this guy waiting for?*

He fired a warning shot at the hull.

Charlie secured his camera in his jacket pocket with one hand and drew his P99 Walther with the other, while shouting to the old man to get the boat out of there. His weapon of choice was nine millimeter with a fifteen round capacity per clip. He was not to engage, but, of course, he had to defend himself if necessary. When the first bullet struck the hull, with a piercing scream as it glanced off, the old man finally had the boat moving out of the dock. The large ferryboat was bulky and slow picking up speed. *At least we have water between us, now.*

Just then, a shower of bullets whistled in their direction. Al Molini had realized his command was being ignored, and shouted to Joey to forget the old guy and get the young one for sure. Charlie Reynolds was an excellent marksman and showed the calm response borne of having been fired upon before. Dropping to one knee behind the side rails, he fired one shot at each adversary. The one on the driver's side of the car was a huge target as he stood well above the open door. Charlie's first shot impacted just inside Joey's open jacket as he paid for his lack of experience, which now would never be realized.

Al had experience and had crouched behind the open door for cover, as the second shot simply shattered the window on the passenger side, spewing shattered glass shards on to his shoulders. Between the open door and the frame, Al Molini fired five more times in rapid succession at the now receding target.

"Joey, let's get out of here." The driver was still wedged between the steering column and the floor as Al jerked him up by the cloth on his shoulder. The passenger door on the driver's side remained open, and Al repeated his command. This time he pulled himself up to look over the back of the seat and saw his young partner sprawled on the ground. Al again jerked his door open and ran to the other side where he found Joey lying on his back with an ever widening circle of blood right in the middle of his chest, gasping for breath.

"I'm sorry, Al." Molini could barely make out the choked whisper coming from his partner's lips. With his eyes still staring, his head dropped to the side.

"Me, too, Joey. Me, too." The latter was no more than a whisper to deaf ears. Al was sincere…he had always felt responsible for the younger guy he was training, even if he did make derogatory remarks about his youthful partners. Pausing only briefly, he slammed the back door and ran to the front passenger side and clambered in to his seat. "Let's go."

That order was not to be ignored. The driver spun around to avoid Joey's body and sped back to the plane. Neither partner carried any identification while on these transactions, but, nevertheless, Al felt bad about leaving his young protégé. He pulled out five hundred dollar bills from his pocket and laid them in the waiting hand of the driver. Without releasing his grip on the money, he gripped the open hand tightly.

"Bury my young friend as soon as we leave. Do not let me down or I will find you. You know I have been here many times and I *will* find you.

Thanks!" He turned and ran to the stairs without looking back. All he heard was…"Yes, Sir, Yes, Sir, Yes, Sir, Yes, Sir" until he could no longer here the fading voice behind him.

As he sat back with the Old Forester over ice cooling his dry mouth, he wondered what his superiors would have to say about his report…however, the transaction was a successful one and the product would be delivered on time. After one last goodbye thought to Joey, his mind started writing the career affecting report…always a verbal report…always in person.

12

I hit one of them. He fell away from the door...he wasn't ducking.
Charlie was reconstructing in his mind what had just happened. He peered in at the Captain, who was still visibly shaking, as the old man guided the ferry west through the channel between southern Iraq and Warbah Island toward the Kuwait mainland. The Police patrol boats operated principally in the channel between Warbah Island and the Kuwait mainland, a very busy waterway which led south to Kuwait City, so it was not likely their boat would be stopped in this northern channel.

Hamad had been very vocal on the way over when Charlie had first engaged his ferry for the trip to Warbah. Having been a widower for the last ten years, he worked and lived on the boat. Two or three bookings a week were more than enough to buy gas and food for himself, and there was very little traffic in this channel.

He complained that all his wife did for their last ten years together was to give orders and now he was free to do whatever he wanted to do...and this was it. Charlie Reynolds could tell, beneath the gruff exterior, that the old man still missed his wife very much.

We will be lucky to make it to the mainland without the old man having a heart attack. It was not my intention to expose him to danger in any way. Of course, missions had gone awry in the past. Now, he had to call Anderson and let him know what was going on. Dialing the answering machine from his cell phone, as the mainland came into view, his brief message was, "Reynolds reporting."

Before leaving the boat, he entered the cabin. Touching the old gentleman on the shoulder, they shook hands. With his left hand, Charlie folded three one hundred dollar bills into the crease between their handshake.

"This will be my last trip, Hamad. Be careful of that place. But, I assure you that it was not you they were after, so you should be in no danger."

Having been paid in advance for this trip, Hamad managed to smile at the additional tip. He did not ask questions so he had no knowledge about who the young man was or why he had made these daily trips to the airfield.

Hamad had a reputation for not prying into the business of his customers. Though curious, he managed to avoid getting into trouble by continuously talking about himself and his hard life, and never asking questions.

Hamad watched as the young man hopped the side of the boat effortlessly on to the dock. He attached the two ropes, and dropped the ramp across the opening. The large ferryboat was docked, and the Captain had nothing else to do until another customer showed up out of nowhere. Climbing into his jeep, his passenger drove ashore and probably out of his life forever. *Strange young man, but he certainly knows how to handle himself. Two weeks every day, and now it is over. That plane must have been what he was watching for.* All his customers, as well as all the people going and coming from that airfield, carried danger with them, some better encrypted than others.

Charlie Reynolds felt the vibration and flipped his cell phone open as he raised it to his ear.

"Anderson, here." As abrupt as ever, his controller was ready for his report.

"First, I have a photo of everyone involved so I will not waste time describing them. The plane arrived about an hour before the cruiser. A young man in a suit disembarked the boat and, with the help of the large man with him, loaded two containers in to the trunk of the limo. These looked like plastic containers, each one about four feet by six feet wide and about fifteen inches deep. They did not attempt to close the trunk. The suit jumped in to the front passenger seat and a man in Arab attire drove the short distance to the airstrip where a Lear jet was waiting. This is where I had to use binoculars. Two more suits met him and loaded the two containers in the freight compartment of the plane after exchanging the briefcase they carried, a rather thick briefcase. The limo driver then returned the first young man to the cruiser and drove back to the airstrip. I watched as the other two men went up the steps to board the plane. My attention was diverted back to the departing cruiser as it took off in a rush. I wanted to see in what direction they headed. They had arrived from the East, and went back the same direction."

"As I was watching their direction, the limo returned with the two air passengers. When they called to me to come ashore, I simply signaled to my pilot to take off. The man on the passenger side fired his weapon one time, apparently as a warning, as the round glanced off the hull. Then all hell broke lose. When they saw me loosen the tie and the boat started moving, they fired a barrage of rounds…this time at me. I dropped to one knee to take advantage of the boat rails, and fired one shot at each man. With the water between us lengthening, I did not continue to fire. I am fairly certain that I hit one of them, as he seemed to fall back too quickly."

"Did you see any markings on the containers?"

"No. I could not read anything on the label, but I snapped a picture of it thinking that maybe it would become legible with enhancement."

"Well, forward the photographs to me as soon as you reach our base in Kuwait City…and, Reynolds, I am certainly relieved that you were not hit."

Charlie knew he had not mentioned to Anderson that none of the rounds had hit him, but, that was as close to empathy as he would get from his Controller. Without further comment, the connection was broken, and Charlie was speeding west to Abdali, where the road turned south to the air base.

13

Harden Kelly and Sam Chandler arrived in Amalfi. On the surface, a growing tourist town by the Sea, Amalfi was also the home of an unusual flight service to unusual destinations.

It was from Kuwait that the two of them had first arrived at this unlisted airfield. They had traced the two renegades, Lewis and Long, as far as Amalfi, when their trail had dried up. Now that they were aware of this service, Harden had suggested to Anderson that they fly in to Farah, the provincial capital of the province of the same name, by uncharted airline. A United States military plane would broadcast their arrival, and it would be to their best advantage to operate undercover.

Anderson located another agent, who was in Italy at the time, and he managed to secure a phone number for the unlisted service.

After seven futile attempts over two days, Alberto finally answered the phone. He had just arrived back from the small airfield at Warbah Island, and had quickly ushered his one remaining passenger from the plane along with his freight. Al Molini did not like being hustled, but his mind was too involved on his delivery back home to even notice. However, he had enjoyed the attention of the sultry stewardess, Serena, on the return flight. She helped take his mind off his young assistant, who, of course, did not make the return flight.

He did not know how his boss was going to take the loss of this young guy. Joey Bono had an uncle somewhere in the organization who had arranged for him to train for this job. Their could be repercussions. With all of this on his mind, Al Molini was deftly managed off the jet and in to his waiting transportation, along with his freight. *Good Riddance!* Alberto was relieved. He had witnessed the melee at Warbah and was nervous about his surviving passenger.

Serena, on the contrary, saw opportunity. Her attention had been well rewarded by the now subdued Molini, thereby assuring her full attention all the way to his vehicle.

"Come back soon, Al." Serena offered one last seduction as his vehicle prepared to depart.

Alberto was now confronted with another opportunity. As always, these bookings created concerns but that was the nature of the business.

"Stay where you are. My partner and I will be right over. Service and refuel for about the same length flight. We will only be going with you one way."

Harden's strong commands had frozen Alberto in place.

As the vehicle pulled on to the runway, Alberto and Serena were ready. Serena had been briefed as much as possible under the circumstances as Alberto described the big man and the young lady who had flown back from Warbah with them about two months ago. Alberto could still subconsciously feel the imprint of the strong hand on his shoulder holding his attention at the end of that flight.

"Afghanistan! My God, man, we could get shot down." The wary pilot had a strong reaction to their destination.

"Farah is a provincial capital and is located in the midst of a farming community. They have an airfield which will accommodate your jet, and, since you have no markings, we do not expect anyone to take particular notice of our arrival. Kabul is three hundred miles east of there but much more closely watched by interested parties."

The jeep had also been stripped of any identifying features and a German license plate applied. The vehicle barely fit into the freight area. Harden had to fold the mirrors inward to keep from scraping the frame of the hatchway as he backed up the ramp. Sam had the job of observing the pilot and attendant until their departure.

Alberto had disappeared into the small office at the site to secure flight coordinates for the exact location of their destination. He was not happy. Entering an area he was not familiar with disturbed him, especially after just witnessing a firefight at Warbah. *There is never any letup. It seems every flight is more dangerous than the previous one. I don't know how much longer I can do this.* The fact that he had accumulated enough money to start thinking of leaving this business had altered his thinking. When he first agreed to fly independently, he was young and brash and saw the opportunity to become wealthy quickly. His desire to take these risks decreased proportionately with the increase in his bank account.

Locating the coordinates he needed on the flight map in the office, he felt a little better. The flight would be somewhat shorter than Warbah and he could hold enough fuel to take off immediately after unloading his fare, limiting his on ground exposure to approximately a half hour. Now, all he wanted to do was get this job behind him.

No further identification was necessary as Harden and Sam took their seats on the aircraft. After closing the hatch, Serena gave them her full attention. Samantha could well understand the glances the flight attendant received from her husband. Serena had the body of a model and most of it was exposed. Dressed in her normal attire with a very short skirt and a white blouse with ends tied just below her breasts, her exposed midriff was highlighted, this time, by a tiny, glistening sapphire dolphin dangling from a golden ring.

Sam was somewhat relieved to see Harden lean his head back and close his eyes.

Both she and Harden had dressed in casual clothing purchased in Amalfi, with an Italian label, to attempt to obscure the fact that they were Americans. Both their passports and credit cards were issued to Charles Bogart and Mary Bogart, who surreptitiously owned a fertilizer company in Stuttgart, Germany. They were combining business with pleasure this trip as they explored this community for possibly marketing their products.

14

Anthony Riley had just closed his cell phone after a disturbing call from his contact in New York City. Things had not gone as well as his assistant, Mandrake, had indicated. The decision had been made to eliminate Warbah Island as a point of exchange. As well, his customer seemed somewhat reluctant to continue their relationship, indicating that the leak was on Riley's end of the transaction. Anthony could never adjust to the kind of ruthless intelligence displayed by these people and always thought he could outwit them. However, he was discovering that, under a very gruff exterior, lays an intelligence not encumbered by principles.

Hanging on to the last thread of what had proved to be a rewarding relationship, Anthony had successfully negotiated for the sale of the remaining eight crates of TR7. After drastically reducing the price as well as changing the location, he still would realize a substantial profit. Holding the weaker position in the negotiation, Anthony forged the best deal he could to clear his house of the last remaining drugs. Feeling that his customers had used his weakened position to take advantage of him, Anthony vowed to even that score at a later date, when leverage returned to his side of the table. Plans were already in progress for a new venture. The only problem was that these new plans still required the services of Sean Pfister. With the value of this shipment enhanced by the shipment of eight containers instead of two, Anthony decided he must accompany Mandrake on this exchange.

Painfully aware that he could not handle the task himself, Anthony furnished Mandrake with a detailed list of the size and quantity of the containers as well as his chair and the number of passengers who would make the trip to Kuwait. This information would empower him to secure a lease on a helicopter with the capacity to transport both weight and distance. The water taxi carried Mandrake and the pilot to mainland Beirut.

Security was visible everywhere as armed military police patrolled the streets of Beirut. Mandrake was alarmed because he did not want to relinquish his weapon. After much practice on the Island under the tutelage of Mr. Riley, his confidence had grown along with the comfort of having the weapon available.

Jim Dixon, the pilot, was also a worry for him. Mandrake knew that his license was forged. After recording over two thousand hours in Army helicopters, Jim had gradually experimented with drugs to the extent that he was finally discharged with cause. Jim had become a very talented and aggressive pilot, and the Army did not turn lose of this asset easily. They had run the man through drug rehab several times before finally realizing they could not solve his problems for him. The potential consequences of keeping the man in uniform eventually exceeded the potential benefits of having him available. They gave up on him. His job opportunities were soon dried up as no jurisdiction would license him when they discovered the nature of his discharge.

One of his remaining friends had recommended him to Anthony Riley when Anthony was first exploring the possibility of owning a helicopter. Anthony had been his salvation. Requiring a blood test before each flight forced the man in to a lesser habit. Anthony paid well and Jim knew that he could do no better. This worked equally for Anthony. He could do no better, as well. The nature of his helicopter usage precluded a legally licensed pilot.

As their taxi maneuvered the busy streets, Mandrake could feel the wary eyes of the uniformed men all along the way. Not only did Jim Dixon carry a forged license, he also carried a weapon...and Mandrake did not trust him with the weapon. His wild eyes were glaring at each armed man they passed. Mandrake did not know what to fear most…Jim firing at them or a nervous guard with his finger already on the trigger. Each time the vehicle stopped in traffic, he tensed, ready to restrain the man if need be.

Not wanting to enter the main terminal where there weapons would have to be turned in to the authorities while on the premises, Mandrake directed the driver to go directly to the office at which they could make arrangements to lease a helicopter. The operation was more impressive than anticipated. They arrived at a two story office building with a small lawn in front, nicely landscaped.

Mr. Riley had already made financial arrangements. After the attendant had photographed both Jim Dixon and his license, another young man led them to the recommended freight helicopter, resting on the tarmac about fifty kilometers from the building. After running his tape measure along the freight bay, Mandrake did the same at the side entrance from which Mr. Riley would board. Satisfied with the capacity, he confirmed also the weight limitations of the vehicle.

The young man shook his hand and presented the key to Jim Dixon, well satisfied with the deal he had made. The customer on the phone did not even barter a discount from his suggested lease fee. This would move him up another notch with his supervisor.

Dixon quickly familiarized himself with the instrument panel as Mandrake took the passenger seat beside him. Fascinated by the man's dexterity with the equipment, Mandrake enjoyed the return to Ramkin Island much more than the nervous ride through Beirut. Jim Dixon's entire personality changed when he had the controls in his hand. Mandrake even spotted the beginnings of a smile as the powerful engine lifted them effortlessly from the ground. Jim Dixon was back in his element and it felt good.

15

The days had been about one hundred and twenty percent occupied since Conner Hayes had returned to San Francisco. Besides the backlog of cases, Thomas Alagia, the senior partner of Smith, Pitt and Alagia, had been in town overnight the week he had returned.

The widowed Mrs. Francis Carpenter had invited a gathering of friends to her Napa Valley home for the weekend and among the invitees were Thomas and Martha Alagia. Her deceased husband had been one of the clients that Conner represented on his many trips from the New York office, before opening the San Francisco Branch. Though eminently satisfied with Conner's performance, the Carpenters were extremely wealthy and required the appearance of one of the founding partners from time to time. Their Sorrento West Winery was one of the oldest in the Valley.

Though they did not have to spend the weekend, Conner and Ashley were requested to attend the Friday evening soiree. Conner found that the Carpenters regular list of guests included several other clients of his firm as well. Ashley was charming and never lacked for attention as Conner was continuously extracted from her side by guests with inquisitive conversations into the legality of certain potential operations by their various companies. Conner was all too familiar with this type of gathering at which the guests manage to work the conversations toward getting free legal advice or opinions. He deftly averted direct answers and managed to pass a business card on the more serious queries, without seeming to upset any of the guests. His down to earth mannerisms and charm had always made it difficult to dislike the young man.

Now, it was Saturday morning and they had just finished a run together and were sharing a bottle of orange juice in the kitchen.

Conner seemed pensive.

"Penny for your thoughts...or a quarter, dollar, ten dollars...according to how interesting they turn out to be."

"I was just thinking again about what you said on the cruise...that you may have seen Anthony on one of those islands. I am going to take the rest of the orange juice and visit my computer for a while."

"Hey, wait! I need another drink first." Ashley quickly turned the small bottle over and drained the contents. With an exaggerated thrust of her tongue, she licked her lips. "Umm, that was good."

Conner grabbed her around the neck as if to strangle her but, instead, met her lips firmly. She responded enthusiastically and they tasted still fresh orange juice as their tongues explored the lingering kiss.

"Conner, I am all sweaty. I need a shower. Want to join me?"

Glancing briefly at the computer, he already knew the priority in this decision.

* * *

Later that afternoon, Conner sat down at his computer. The note he had made when he talked to the Captain on the deck of the cruise ship was still held firmly by the small paperweight on his desk...Ramkin Island.

That was a start. He started a google search for the Island and was instantly rewarded with the choice of several hundred sites. After finally narrowing the results to a map and even a photograph of the Island, there was no evidence of any residency whatever. Further inquiry revealed a small development by the Sea which caught his interest.

After looking under Real Estate in the Beirut directory, he finally chose a company with a prominent advertisement and pulled out his cell phone.

"Hello, I am looking for another home, either for investment or for vacationing and someone recommended Ramkin Island. Do you have any listings that you think would interest me?"

Conner found the connection extraordinarily clear. He must have found a legitimate broker on the first try.

"My name is Sara Naiser, and I think I can help you. But why are you interested in Ramkin? That Island is small and almost deserted. There are a few homes at the higher elevations that could interest you. You need to realize that these homes would only be suitable as a place to get away from civilization. Any thing you would need to furnish the place would require a trip to Beirut, including food and supplies. There are several other islands in the area with much better facilities."

"Ramkin sounds like exactly what I am looking for. Are many of those homes presently occupied?" Conner still did not know how he was going to work this conversation around to Anthony, when Sara startled him with her next comment.

"I do not receive many inquires about Ramkin. As a matter of fact, about a year ago, I sold a piece of property on the Island, sight unseen. Although, I was able to send a full set of photographs to my client. He lived in Cleveland, Ohio, in the United States. He bought the property for cash and even enlisted the services of our contracting division to customize the residence to suit his needs…it seems he was restricted to a wheelchair."

Conner almost dropped the phone. *Almost a year ago…Anthony would have made contingency plans. He could not rely on a quick exit if things went wrong with his business.*

Realizing that several seconds of dead air had ensued, Conner quickly recovered. "Sara, I think I may be interested in the Island as well. I have your name and number and I will call you back after I discuss this with my wife. By the way, did the gentleman in the wheelchair ever take up residency in his house?"

"Oh, yes, sir. I believe it was about a month ago that one of our agents met him at the house with the keys. Oskar remarked that it was a strange assembly...three men, one much younger than the other two. I could have Oskar call you if you want." Sara was trying to secure a contact so she could pursue this potential client but Conner was not about to reveal his name or number.

"I will get back with you, Sara. Thanks for the information. Have a nice day."

16

Harden's cell phone vibrated against his shirt pocket.

"This is Anderson. Harden, I want you and Sam to fly in to Shindand directly instead of Farah. We still have forces there and they will be expecting you. Colonel Jack Sanders will brief you both on your arrival. They have maps of the area and can answer your questions before you set out on your mission. The Soviets operated a major military airbase there until it was taken over by the Taliban in 1997. Our forces have been in joint control with the Afghans since 2002."

"Yes, sir. I will tell the pilot."

"Good luck to you two...stay in touch." Anderson was gone.

Two healthy strides and Harden was entering the pilot's cabin. At six feet six inches tall, he had to duck and turn to the side to enter. With the agility of a cat he twisted his body and lowered himself in to the co-pilot's seat. Alberto was intent on his instruments and paid no heed to his visitor.

"There's been a slight change in plans." Harden watched for a reaction and admired the wiry pilot for outwardly taking this in stride. "We are going directly to Shindand. They are expecting us. Change your coordinates and take as direct a line as possible, bypassing Farah."

At this, Alberto did glance over at the other man, trying to read something in his eyes for a split second before returning his attention to the instrument panel. Deftly, he hit the autopilot switch as he studied the map folded beside him. Keying in the correct coordinates for the Shindand base, he resumed control of the flight.

Alberto was familiar with the area. He managed to stay well informed regarding changes that occurred in the various countries and provinces from Amalfi to the East. Two years earlier a recon helicopter had been shot down just east of Shindand. Just before that, a med vac chopper was hit just north of the city. Although the United States, in cooperation with the Afghanistan National Army, controlled the cities, there were still pockets of insurgency in the area. He closed his eyelids for a second to clear his head. *I do not want to die this way…just a few more years and I will be set for life.* Under control again, he looked out at the world below as they passed over Iranian countryside, avoiding all heavily populated areas.

* * *

They began their descent as the Lear jet crossed the border into Afghanistan. Shindand was only about one hundred kilometers away. Alberto was already in contact with the tower and was not surprised to be talking to an American as he identified himself and the passengers he carried. Their flight was cleared for landing immediately. *Man, they were expecting us…these two must be some kind of bigshots.*

Harden had remained in the cockpit for the balance of the flight. He did not want any surprises as he checked the coordinates on the map with the control panel. Alberto was an experienced pilot and the jet set down with no discomfort whatever. Harden maneuvered out of the seat and through the door. He knew that Anderson would handle payment to the airline.

Alberto jumped up and followed him out. He was going to have to refuel after all. The change in destinations had altered his plans. Harden turned as they entered the main cabin.

"Thanks, Alberto, you did a fine job. Share this with the attendant."

He thrust ten hundreds into his hand as he slapped him on the shoulder. *We could have taken a military flight, but the cost probably would have been even higher. If we are seen arriving, this private plane would be more discreet.*

The first thing they sensed as they stepped off the plane on to the stair ramp was the hot, dry air blowing in their faces. Summer highs reached over one hundred degrees Fahrenheit almost every day. Today was no exception. An American officer and driver were waiting at the foot of the ramp. Sam went to the freight bay to retrieve the jeep as Harden walked over to the man who had come to greet them.

"Good afternoon, Sir. I am Captain James Blalock. I want to welcome you to this hell hole. The alias won't be necessary right now. Mr. Anderson called and needs to talk to you on a secure phone…a last minute change in assignments."

The uniform bore no indication of rank. Higher ranking officers were primary targets for snipers and suicide bombers. Harden began to appreciate the fact that they were in civilian clothing…the weather and the rank recognition.

"This is my partner, Sam Chandler. As you can see, we brought a civilian jeep. You lead the way and we will follow." Sam had pulled the jeep up beside the two men and gave a salute that was more of a wave of acknowledgement. Without her uniform obscuring her femininity, Samantha had both men staring for a moment. "Let's go, gentlemen."

She felt it was her responsibility to cut this off and get down to business.

Both vehicles pulled to the side at the door to Building 11. Harden and Sam followed the Captain inside. "This is our Headquarters Building. It is not labeled as such for the same reason as not wearing rank on uniforms. As a matter of fact, we rotate buildings at irregular intervals."

"If you will follow me back the hall, we have a room set up with some marked-up maps and a secure telephone. The walls are soundproof."

Entering the room, Harden and Sam were immediately introduced to the Colonel. "Hi. Jack Sanders. Anderson called and set this up and I believe we are ready to go." The Colonel shook hands with both Sam and Harden before taking a seat at the table. After the Captain closed the door, Harden dialed Anderson's number. "Kelly reporting." He immediately put the handset back on the receiver.

Captain Blalock cautiously walked over to the table. "Mr. Anderson asked that I be present when you talked to him in order to save time later."

"Fine with us, Jim. If you have already talked to Anderson, then you know who we are." The phone interrupted his introduction.

Harden picked up the handset. "I understand that there is a change in our mission, Sir."

"Harden, I am glad that you both had a safe trip. Sorry for the confusion. I want you and Sam to divert your attention from what we discussed and lead an operation for me. If you will now put me on a speaker, we can avoid repetition later."

Harden hit the speaker button and dropped the handset into the cradle.

"We are ready, sir...myself, Sam, the Colonel and Captain Blalock."

"Jim has one more participant for this conversation. Please have Lieutenant Rasmussen come in please." Captain Blalock was already at the door and ushered in the waiting Lieutenant. Blalock took the initiative. "Ready, Sir."

"Harden, these two men are in Special Forces and their unit has been assigned to me for this single mission. Here is the layout. We have built a map showing the major areas of opium farms in Afghanistan. This should be on your table. As you can see, it generally covers about one third of the land area in the Country. We are not going to target these areas at this time.

Our primary interest lies Northwest of Shindand, about halfway to Herat. Along this road, you will find some very nice homes. A few are legitimate landowners who have lived in the area for generations."

"On closer inspection, the ones we are interested in become quite obvious. They have fences that are well fortified and armed guards at all vulnerable access areas. Hidden by the grand old homes are small factories for the mass processing of heroin from the opium plants delivered almost daily in season by the independent farmers encompassing the entire South Central Regions of the Country. This supply is inexhaustible. Our objective is to cut out the processing and warehousing, cutting off the demand from the farmers, thereby drying up the interest in producing the crop."

There was another map on the table that caught Harden and Sam's attention. It was a more detailed map obviously highlighting target areas.

"As you can see on the detailed map, the Colonel and I have clearly marked our objectives. Air reconnaissance has been extremely helpful in being able to put together these photos showing the entire layout of two separate operations. The garage facilities look exactly like their neighbors. This is a small area of successful businessmen's residences."

"There is one obvious distinction. On the photograph, you can see steady pillars of white smoke coming from chimneys on the roofs of the two garage facilities we are interested in. Our mission is to destroy those two buildings where the cooking is taking place as well as any product storage on site. There will be resistance. The time frame of choice is tonight. Good luck!"

Harden held his eyes on the now dead phone as he digested this latest information. Jack Sanders broke the silence.

"Through my previous discussion with Anderson, he suggested the following. The Special Forces unit assigned to this task consists of these two men, plus three other operatives. Blalock and Rasmussen will take two of these men and initiate a simultaneous operation with you, Chandler and the third man. Anderson made it quite clear that you are in charge of this mission and that this arrangement is simply a suggestion of the best split of the manpower available."

"Thanks, Jack. Could we just have something to eat brought in here in a little while. I would like Blalock and Rasmussen to stay and help us coordinate the details. This may take a couple of hours. Then maybe we could get some rest and be ready to go at Midnight."

"I'll have it taken care of. Good luck!" Jack Sanders left the room.

17

Sean Pfister was standing before his employer, wondering what he was to do next. He had felt like a prisoner on this Island for about a month now, bored almost to desperation.

"While we are gone, Sean, I want you to make a list of all the supplies and equipment that you need to start up our operation again. That large reception hall, which is practically devoid of furniture, will serve well as your working area. Call various businesses in Beirut to purchase these items, being careful to spread your purchases so that no one supplier could become interested in their purpose."

"This time we will keep it much simpler…we are not going to build a plant, as such, just an area sufficient for you to produce adequate quantities of TR7. Get what you need to get started, beginning right now. When I return from our trip, I want to see progress. Go, and get started." Anthony waved his hand in dismissal.

Sean felt the first twinges of excitement begin to build in his system.

As he hurriedly exited the room, his mind was racing with plans. *Man, I have Carte Blanche. I will get this going fast.* Presented with the opportunity to again earn his share of the operation which Mr. Riley had just authorized, Sean virtually ran to his room to start planning his requirements to rebuild.

Meanwhile, Mandrake walked along beside the wheelchair as they made their way to the Aircraft, a Sikorsky S-92 Helicopter. With three rows of seats removed from the rear of the aircraft, they were able to split storage of the eight remaining containers between the freight bay and this area. As the containers were not heavy, the weight limitations were never approached.

Anthony had not slept the entire trip as he tried to anticipate anything that could go wrong. The transaction was to be made at the same location just outside Abdali, where Jeff Lewis and Aubrey Long had aborted the last exchange and eliminated Kafu and Al-Sufa. This time, Jim Dixon, the pilot, was heavily armed as well as Mandrake.

The site was easily identifiable from the air, a clearing surrounded by a cluster of trees to the south and sand dunes to the north. Dixon expertly set the aircraft down as far away from the trees as possible without getting too close to the sand dunes. As the rotors slowed, Mandrake exited the helicopter and made himself visible to anyone waiting in the tree line. This time he wore a Kevlar vest under his suit coat, making him appear even more muscular.

The arrangement was that Anthony would not leave the aircraft and neither would the pilot. Jim Dixon now hovered in the shadows of the now open door by which Mandrake had jumped down, his weapon ready. A successful mission would benefit all of them…an aborted mission could cost them their lives.

After blinking their headlights two times, a 2 and ½ ton truck emerged from the shadows and headed toward the aircraft. As the truck pulled up to the freight bay, Al Molini jumped out with the expected suitcase, only, this time, he had one in each hand. Al was relieved when he spotted Mandrake with his binoculars from the safety of the trees. Two men jumped from the back of the truck just as the freight bay opened. Dixon had dropped to the rear of the aircraft to oversee the unloading, but remained hidden in the shadows.

Al handed both suitcases to Mandrake; smiling at the change of advantage as both his hands were now free as the other man accepted the exchange. Mandrake slowly backed to the passenger compartment and hefted the two cases where Anthony could reach them. Molini also backed away where he could watch the two men loading eight containers in to the back of the truck.

Mandrake stepped back in to the aircraft to assist Mr. Riley with the heavy cases. Snapping them open he held them up for Riley to see. Anthony ran his fingers through the stacks of bills only enough to assure himself that there was no false stuffing. Molini was back in the passenger seat of the truck and Dixon had closed the back of the aircraft just as a humvee came speeding around the sand dunes in their direction.

Evidently the drug lords from Umm Qasr had become aware of the exchange, as the men fired warning shots for the truck as well as the aircraft.

The driver of the truck slid into a horizontal position as opposed to the oncoming vehicle. Both the driver and Molini fired answering shots at the new arrivals.

Neither of the parties, nor Anthony Riley, himself, had expected the response from the highly trained pilot, Jim Dixon. Dixon jumped to the ground firing his Uzi automatic rifle at the approaching vehicle to give him cover in order to pull the pin and expertly aim the missile at the humvee. The vehicle exploded on the run scattering debris in all directions. As the men were thrown from the vehicle, Dixon aimed his Uzi and made final what the grenade had initiated, the need for accuracy offset by the rapid repeat of the weapon. What was left of the vehicle crashed in to the trees behind them.

Jim Dixon jumped in to the entry, dropped his weapon on the co-pilot seat and started liftoff, all in the space of a few seconds. Astonished at the pilot's reaction to eminent danger, Anthony Riley found new respect for his drug tormented pilot. Suddenly aware that he and Mandrake were sitting there with an open case of cash, Anthony closed and snapped the latch to protect his recompense from being lost in the prop induced wind.

As they lifted off the ground, they could see the truck disappearing in the distance. Instead of heading south to Abdali, the truck veered to the left, and the road leading east to the boat ramp to Warbah. *They were just trying to squeeze me…evidently they are still using the airstrip on Warbah, after all.*

Anthony smiled to himself, satisfied with this new found knowledge as well as the impressive performance of his employees.

18

"I have been trying to reach Harden this afternoon and all I ever get is his answering machine. He must have his cell phone turned off." Conner Hayes was pensive as he sipped his iced tea and stared off into space.

"I wonder if he and Samantha are on another mission. It seems like one of them would have called you back by now." Dinner was complete and Ashley was leaning back in her chair, stretching the stiffness from her arms as she raised them high over her head. "The workload has been tremendous since we returned to work. There are a million details to keep track of in order to insure that we remain in compliance with the court ordered reconstruction after that Brantley fiasco."

"I know what you mean. After our meeting with the new board members this afternoon, I do not envy you the tedious tasks of compliance with that Judge's ruling. Of course, we should be thankful that Jennings survived at all, considering the wanton disruption of Riley's company. It still bothers me that my old friend could be involved in drugs and blatant murder of innocent people."

"That is why I must reach Harden. He will know the best way to handle the Riley problem, particularly on foreign soil. I would call Anthony, myself, but I do not want to interfere and possibly drive him to another unknown location. Now that we know where he is living, we should settle this problem before it gets away from us again."

"Maybe you should call him, Conner. After all, you were very good friends until recently. It is possible that you could make him see past the money and power, and become his old self again."

"I still would like to talk to Harden first." He had just dialed Harden Kelly's number for the fourth time today. "Harden, I have some important information and need to talk to you as soon as possible." Again, the answering machine.

"Let's take a short run. You said you wanted to stay in shape after seeing the condition Harden was in and I can work out some of this stiffness. I must have been working with my shoulders slumped over my desk all day." Again, she stretched her arms in to the air as if reaching for the ceiling.

When Conner saw how these gyrations pressed her breasts against the thin material of her blouse, he had other ideas, but relinquished anyway.

"Let's go. I can take my cell phone with me in case Harden does try to return my calls. Give me three minutes to change."

"Make it five...I need to change as well."

19

The vehicle of choice was a Ford Explorer, with the windows shaded from the desert sun and a rental plate from a dealer in Shindand. All seven members of the team wore black, no one in the uniform of the United States Military. Harden and Sam rode in front, both with off white shirts worn loosely over their black tees, and white brimmed hats normally used to ward off the hot sun. The front windows were not shaded and they were trying to present the guise of tourists, at least civilians.

After memorizing the layout on the aerial photographs, they all recognized the first of the two mansions on the left. The property was surrounded by a six foot cedar fence, which looked as if it had been there since the homes were built. Installed above the wood fence was a combination of barbed wire and razor wire, enough deterrent to discourage any but the most determined intruder. The wrought iron gate across the entry drive was as tall as the fence and barbed wire combined and also had the combination of wire installed above it, to make it even less tempting to scale.

The second mansion came in to view. As they passed the gated entry, a slight glimpse of the garages behind presented itself between the two large houses in front. Though mostly hidden by the tall fencing, their destination was made more obvious by the security precautions. They continued on the Herat road around a bend which changed their direction to northwest. Immediately, a taller but totally functional storage building came into view. Not even visible from the front of the mansions, it was evidently built taller to accommodate the product because of the lack of property to build a preferable facility lower to the ground.

About a quarter mile up the road, Harden pulled to the side, hidden by some wild shrubbery which had grown to the size of small trees. "I have seen enough. Our best access is under that wood fence…I noticed that the lower sections are even rotted away in some areas. Aerial reconnaissance indicated that the motion detectors are located only on the four sides of the garage. The storage facility must have been built more recently."

"We will all go under the fence on this side of the facility so that the storage facility is shielding us from the motion sensors. Once inside, we will scale to the roof of the facility. From that higher vantage point, we will take out the four guards on the roof. Henderson and Johnson…you will take care of that while we put our gear together to rappel to the roof of the garage, above the sensors. Sam and I and Bronson will make our way to the far side and place the charges at intervals as we come back in this direction.

Blalock will start at this end with Rasmussen, Henderson and Johnson, and work your way south with the charges."

"When we are satisfied that we have the facility adequately covered, we will rappel back to the storage roof, and, after placing our charges on that roof, we will also place them down the out side of the building so as to avoid the sensors and yet maintain the objective of our mission. We will not do anything to deliberately damage the old mansions. However, if we come under fire from the additional security, we will have to respond in kind."

Arriving at the old wood fence on the northwest side of the storage building, they easily found decaying planks, rotted out by weather and insects. Bronson and Johnson soon had enough dirt and sand removed for passage under the fence for a man and his backpack. While they secured their trenching tools to their packs, Blalock and Rasmussen crawled through the opening and shot padded hooks to the roof of the barn. Harden and Sam were to be the first to climb the knotted ropes and they were soon peering over the edge of the roof. *Just as I thought, the guards cannot see us on this higher level.*

As they crawled low to the roof, they were soon joined by Henderson and Johnson, each cradling their sniper rifles with silencers installed. Harden raised his eyes to see over the low parapet of the roof and the four guards came into view. None seemed to be alerted to their presence. They were stationed at the four corners of the building's roof, two intently watching the ground below. The other two were nonchalantly smoking some kind of twisted thin cigarette, one man even sitting on the ledge of the building.

Harden held his right hand up slightly to deter the marksmen from firing. If the seated man should fall over the edge, all hell would break loose as he would no doubt set off the motion sensors, waking everyone in the barracks.

"Ana abgha inta hena!" Apparently the guard at the far end was in charge of this shift as he shouted at the seated man. The one with his legs dangling over the edge jumped to his feet immediately and walked swiftly to the other side of the roof. Harsh words were again directed at the miscreant, but in a quieter voice. The guard returned to his post, somewhat abashed at the reprimand, this time standing more alertly, but safely away from the edge of the roof.

Harden motioned the men to proceed. With no more noise than a puff of air, the two furthest men fell to the roof, quickly followed by the closest two. As he fell, the miscreant's final thought was of the severity of his punishment for smoking on the job. Harden and Sam were busy tightening the line to the garage roof, even as the last man fell. Quickly, they clicked on and slid to the roof below, followed closely by the rest of the team.

Along with Bronson, who was right behind Harden, they rushed quietly to the far side of the building. The packets were prepared with plastic explosives to be followed by incendiary explosives set with a timer set at twelve twenty five. This allowed no time for delays, as they followed their prearranged disposition procedure back to the center of the building.

The other team worked as quickly. The climb back to the taller building was not as simple, but all team members were in excellent shape and, shortly, all seven were placing their packets of explosives around the roof of the storage facility. Sam and Harden first retrieved their gear from the adjoining roof, and then rappelled down the ropes on the northwest side of the storage facility, placing explosives as they descended. By the time they reached the ground, the others were descending as well. As Blalock and Rasmussen retrieved their climbing gear from the wall of the facility, the others were crawling under the fence and jogging to the vehicle.

"Damn!" Blalock's hook would not disengage. Just as he heard Harden whisper "Leave it," the hook came loose and slithered to the ground. Harden had remained at the opening in the fence to be certain that he counted six team members leaving the facility before he, himself, crawled through the dirt under the fence. In silence, they jogged back to the waiting vehicle. Both he and Sam donned their hats and shirts in case they should be spotted on their return trip.

At twelve twenty one, they were racing south on Herat Road. Passing the two mansions, they detected no signs of commotion to indicate their presence had been discovered. One mile further south, the sky lit up with the detonations. Under the existing conditions, the explosive packages had been perfectly placed to destroy the manufacturing facility building followed by incendiary devices which were then able to combust on the interior, with molten flame dissolving everything inside. Both buildings were successfully eradicated.

No longer concerned with detection, they raced southward to the base.

20

Waking from an unusually good night of sleep, Anthony found that Chris was already in his room, anticipating his awakening. Anthony was not a heavy man since his taste for food was directed more toward culinary pleasure from exquisite preparation and presentation rather than consumption. Chris had no difficulty easing him into his waiting chair so that he could make his own way to the bathroom for his early morning regimen.

By the time he returned, the bed was made and his clothing was laid out awaiting his approval. Anthony found that Chrisimminia was very attentive to detail and he seldom objected to her selections. After seeing him successfully to the lift and overseeing his downward flight, Chris returned to the master bedroom to complete her daily chores.

Before retiring the night before, Anthony had requested that Jim Dixon have breakfast with him at eight. While Anthony picked at his fresh fruit tart and poached egg, topped gently with home made hollandaise sauce, Jim was busy with a three egg western omelet, with thick Italian sausage on the side. The coffee was rich and fragrant as Anthony seemed only to wet his lips with the smooth black elixir. Dixon, again, was a differing story indeed, as he took long drinks of the superb coffee.

"Jim, I want to congratulate you on the way you handled the disturbance, yesterday, and by way of thanks, I want you to have this."

He picked up a small bundle from his lap and passed it across the table.

Dixon half stood to accept the package from his employer and was immediately distracted by the hundred dollar bill at the top, his mind quickly calculating how much a bundle of that thickness would amount to in total. "Thank you, Sir." Jim Dixon did not talk much but he was well educated and knew how and when to be well mannered.

"That bundle is five thousand dollars." Anthony knew it was important to clarify this fact immediately before Jim's mind anticipated a larger amount, thus avoiding disappointment as opposed to appreciation of this bonus. Jim had not smiled often since accepting the position as Pilot for this strange man…and the smiles did not linger very long. Anthony thought he detected the formation of the lips into what sufficed as a smile on Jim Dixon's face and was satisfied that he had achieved the desired result.

"That is only the beginning. You have shown that you can be a very valuable employee. As you know, I have recently lost two men who provided very adequate security for my business. Eventually, you can earn a hundred times that amount if you are willing to provide the services you displayed yesterday for me as the need arises."

Jim was well aware of whom Mr. Riley was speaking. He had been the pilot sitting on the roof of Jennings Enterprises with the rotors going, awaiting a quick departure of Anthony and his entourage. Those two did not make it to the roof that day.

"For that kind of money, my services are available, the sooner the better."

Anthony smiled to himself, again witnessing the power that money possessed over humans. "There is one condition. You will have to remain drug free to be of any use to me. Otherwise, our relationship will have to exist at its current level."

As Jim again concentrated on his breakfast, fresh, new thoughts raced through his mind, perhaps the first time in the last ten years. *I can do this.* He had already discovered that, with vigorous mental effort, he could force himself to abstain from drug use for short periods.

Bored with his breakfast after just a few tastes, Anthony left the room, satisfied that he had found an adequate replacement for the more expensive operatives he had recruited from the Government.

He met Sean Pfister almost running through the hallway, nearly colliding with the wheelchair. "Mr. Riley...uh uh...I am just about ready to start processing again, maybe by tomorrow."

"Fine, Sean, Fine. When you can make projections on the completed product, let me know. I would like to schedule some shipments as soon as possible."

Sean had a similar goal. The sooner he became productive again, the more money he would make personally. Mr. Riley started moving again and Sean hurried back to his lab.

Passing the kitchen, Riley caught just a glimpse of Mandrake and Chris abruptly ending an embrace. *What is going on here?* Not completely surprised, his mind started working over the pros and cons of a relationship between those two. *Mandrake has always been loyal to me. Maybe some of that will rub off on the girl. I will have to keep an eye on that little matter.*

21

Harden and Sam were just leaving Officers Mess when they were intercepted by Captain Blalock. It was in the morning just the second day after their successful excursion to the north.

"Harden, would you accompany me to see the Colonel. Something has come up just now and it involves you." Although it was phrased as a question, the answer was assumed to be affirmative, as the three of them made their way to the same building in which they had met on their first day. Jack Sanders was waiting for them and ushered Harden and Sam in to a small reception room adjacent to the conference room.

Upon entering the building, both of them had noticed two official Afghanistan Government vehicles parked near the front. With the basic orientation of their unit geared to undertake whatever clandestine activity beneficial to the United States Government, Harden was leery of open discussions with other Government officials. *Anderson should be in on this.*

"Mr. Kelly. When we enter the conference room, I would advise you not to offer any response to what you are about to hear. There will be time enough for that later."

Somewhat puzzled, they followed the Colonel into the conference room. "Ladies and gentlemen, this is Harden Kelly and his wife, Samantha."

On the other side of the table sat an Afghan woman, who appeared to be about thirty to forty years old, and obviously a Begum. Dressed in traditional garb, including the veil, she was apparently a Muslim woman of high rank. On her left was a middle aged man. He presented a furtive appearance, with his eyes mostly downcast but at intervals dashing around the room. The man wore a flashy European style suit and no headdress. He appeared nervous and wary of his surroundings.

"Harden, let me introduce you to our guests. This is Sa-ina Kalemi. She is the Minister for Women's Affairs for the new Afghan Cabinet. On her right is Abdul Haddiq, the Minister of Light Industry." Their were two other uniformed individuals, who appeared to belong to the Afgan Military or Police. When introduced, neither individual proffered any form of acknowledgement or greeting. The woman had soft features that were presently locked in to an expressionless block of granite. She appeared to be here under duress…as if she had an unpleasant duty to perform.

"Mrs. Kalemi has recently become a widow and has a surveillance photograph of the man she claims murdered her husband. The photo is quite clear. She has taken her story to Mr. Haddiq, who is her neighbor, and he suggested that they come directly here to our base. Her home is north of here, near Herat."

"According to her story, some thieves broke in to their residence by using explosives to enter by way of the garage. Her husband, a locally respected businessman, was parking his car in the garage at the time of the attack and was killed by the explosion. She claims that they were home alone at the time and, without her husband's protection, the thieves were able to take many gold items as well as her husband's wallet with several thousand dollars in U. S. currency."

"Although she claims their were several perpetrators, the obvious leader of the group was caught on camera while standing at the opening that had been cut in the fence, as the group made their exit." Jack Sanders passed the photo, which he had been changing from one hand to the other as he was giving his dissertation, across the table to Harden Kelly.

Harden could feel all four sets of Afghan eyes on him as he looked down at the photograph. Surprising clear for the conditions of the night before last, there was no doubt as to the identification of the person in the photograph. Showing no outward reaction, Harden placed the photograph down on the table and surveyed their visitors with a scrutiny not essential upon their original introduction. Now, it seemed a desideratum in respect to the direction this meeting was likely to pursue.

Sanders continued. "The widow, Mrs. Kalemi, has come here accompanied by Minister Haddiq and the two members of the Afghan Police, to take you into custody awaiting trial by proper jurisdiction in Herat." The two persons seated across the table did not take their eyes off Kelly while the Colonel was talking. Sa-ina Kalemi now appeared somewhat less assured as she gauged the strength in the eyes of the big man across from her. Her gaze returned to Minister Haddiq and then to her folded hands, weakened by the intense scrutiny of the man's steel blue eyes. Meanwhile, Abdul Haddiq continued to fidget nervously, as each time his eyes would meet another of the participants, he diverted them immediately.

"They insist on searching your quarters while you remain seated at this table. I cannot justify denying their request, based on the evidence they presented. We, of course, will have Captain Blalock and Lieutenant Rasmussen accompany them on your behalf. Do we have your permission, Mr. Kelly?"

Without breaking the intensity, nor turning away from the two officials, Harden affirmed. "Certainly." He was carrying the fake I D's in his pocket and there was nothing else in the room except basic military gear. Sam had seen the photograph as Harden held it at such an angle to present it to her without being too obvious. Alertly, but without showing emotion, she absorbed every word, every glance and every movement at the table. She could not betray Harden by showing concern over the uncomfortable, potentially dangerous, position in which he now found himself. The two Afghan Officers left the room with Mr. Haddiq as Captain Blalock appeared at the door. The widow remained seated, eyes now downcast.

Jack Sanders now acted as host to preclude allowing more people in to this confidential circle. He poured and distributed coffee to the remaining four people, including himself. Harden knew that Anderson would not permit him to be taken into custody by local officials. Company protocol would require whatever means necessary to avoid one of their agents falling into foreign hands. He did not yet know, however, if it would be left up to him to make certain that this did not happen...or did Sanders already have this eventuality covered. No one had asked Sam or himself for their weapons and there had been no attempt on their part to conceal same.

Looking at Sam for confirmation, he saw that she, also, was alert to the situation if any aggressive action was to be required on their part. Her hand slid across the shoulder holster almost unnoticed except by Harden. He passed his hand similarly over his weapon in affirmation.

With the Minister temporarily out of the room, Jack Sanders took the initiative once again. "Madam Kalemi, can you furnish us with any more detail as to the alleged break-in." He knew that by addressing the woman, she would be forced to either respond or, at the very least, to raise her eyes from the table.

Looking once again in to the non-threatening, but icily intent eyes of her adversary, her voice was not as strong or assured as she responded in very fluent English. "My husband was murdered two nights ago..." her eyes dropped again to her hands on the table..."and this man was seen clearly by our camera trespassing on our property that same night." She now lacked the assuredness she had exhibited in the presence of her three fellow countrymen.

Captain Blalock stepped into the room, looking somewhat perturbed.

One of the Afghan Police Officers crossed the room and showed an expensive gold necklace, embossed with diamonds, to the now distraught widow. Her reaction was to the recognition of the stolen item, holding it partially responsible for the death of her husband. Her acting was not as convincing as her appearance. Her reaction as well as her response had been rehearsed.

Haddiq seemed reluctant to assume the role of spokesman for the group. "This piece of jewelry was found in the quarters indicated to be assigned to this man." He pointed his finger accusingly at Harden Kelly.

Although he was trained to respond mentally before physically, Harden could hardly resist grabbing the accusing finger and effecting damage in one of the hundred ways he knew possible. Instead he let the scene play out before him, constantly analyzing his situation.

Sam watched and waited as she, too, displayed no response.

Haddiq continued. "My Government insists that we be allowed to take this man in to immediate custody. The evidence proclaims his guilt and since he is not even a member of your military, we hereby place him under arrest." His two Officers, although appearing disinterested in the proceedings, were attentive to Haddiq's position, therefore, willing to follow his orders. They started slowly around the table to the accused.

Captain Blalock was anxious to respond but was held in check by a glance from Jack Sanders. "Hold up, Gentlemen. Based on the evidence that you have presented, we will place Mr. Kelly under house arrest here at the base, awaiting further proceedings. You may go now. When the proper paperwork is processed, you may serve me as Commanding Officer of this base."

The two Officers stopped in their tracks at Sander's orders and looked swiftly at Abdul Haddiq for further instructions.

"My Government insists…" Haddiq's response seemed weak as he was cut off.

"No way, Mr. Haddiq. This preliminary hearing is adjourned." Jack Sanders was exhibiting why he was placed in command of the thousands of Military assigned to him at the Shindand base.

Without assisting the now quiet widow, Haddiq gestured his men that it was time to leave. Sa-ina Kalemi slowly pushed her chair back and rose to follow, casting a sideways glance again in Harden's direction, only to be again caught in that questioning gaze. Head down, she left the room with the others.

22

"What happened? How did Umm Quasr find out about our exchange? I cannot risk that kind of exposure. I am not well enough to do any physical exchange. How did they know to be there?"

Anthony was upset. The man on the other end of the conversation did not seem to have any answers or any sympathy for the situation.

"Listen, Riley. We are as puzzled as you. Our men and our money were at risk as well. That was just another close scrape but it is over...forget it. Let's get on with business."

"You say you are now in a position to fill future orders for TR7. We will make arrangements for a future meet and let you know when and where...probably within the next few days. We need to keep the street happy or the demand will dry up. I'll call you."

Anthony was left with a dial tone. The brusqueness and lack of concern for what he considered important bothered him greatly but he had not yet been able to formulate a plan which put him more in control of his buyers. They had been in business for a much longer time and had perfected their operation through trial and error...a process that was still viable at present.

Sean had arranged to acquire containers similar to the ones used at Brantley so that Mr. Riley could better manage the sell price of the material. Although Brantley was now non-existent, he had the containers embossed with the name 'Brantley Fertilizer Company' anyway. The product could be shipped through normal freight channels as fertilizer. Dogs had not yet been trained to distinguish this drug as it did not arouse their olfactory organs as did cocaine and opium.

Riley smiled in spite of the ingratiating attitude of his partners. *Business as usual...until I can find a way to eliminate the middleman from my operation. They do not show me any respect. They do not even know me except as a source. But they will.*

Sean Pfister interrupted his contemplations. "I ran a small batch for testing. We are ready to roll. How much should I produce at a time?"

Sean was not being completely honest. *Something is different...I ran all the tests...checked all the ingredients in my head...something is different but no one will ever know it but me.* Sean was anxious to expand his income and did not dwell on the variation he had detected in the test batch.

"Have four containers ready by Monday. I expect to hear from my customer by then and they will want immediate delivery. They do not allow any advance notice in order to protect the security of the transaction. Good work, Sean. You will be adequately compensated for your timely setup for production." Anthony turned away from his desk, heading for the balcony to enjoy the view and contemplate how well things were going.

I have three men, now, that I can trust. Dixon was quite surprising with his reaction and response to eminent disruption at Abdali. Mandrake has always been faithful to me and has displayed an adequate competence in handling transactions on my behalf. I am still not certain how he will respond if the use of his firearm is required. Pfister has gathered the material and supplies to set up production much faster than I anticipated. I will have to make certain that they are rewarded for their performance after this next transaction.

Anthony closed his eyes with one last thought. *I wonder if that was Conner's wife that I saw on the cruise ship. I wonder if I will ever have occasion to see he and Harden again.*

* * *

"Harden, I know this looks bad, but I have talked to Anderson about the situation. He asks that you remain on base for a while to allow him time to formulate a plan. Right now, the Afghan government still thinks you are Charles Bogart, a German National. Anderson is going to have to decide whether he wants it to remain that way." Tom Sanders was trying his best to placate the now furious Harden Kelly.

"Why did you call me in to this meeting unprepared? Why did you even honor their request at all? Those two people know who I am...or at least what I am. That is the reason they came here. They want to show how much power and influence they have in the newly formed Government. That Haddiq is a pawn for someone else...someone who doesn't want us to repeat our attacks on their business. The woman is just being used as well. I do not understand why you gave any credence to their story in the first place. There is an unbelievable amount of money involved...evidently enough to buy a Minister or two."

"Calm down, Harden. We all know that what you did was lead a raid on a cocaine producing plant by our forces with the mission to destroy it and all its supply. You realize that the United States has over a hundred thousand men in uniform in Afghanistan and with that many individuals there are some transgressions. We have had incidences of rape, murder and theft. That is why we must respond to this accusation with some kind of cover story...we do not want you to be a scapegoat for that operation."

"Scapegoat! You have got to be kidding. Just get me out of here and the matter will die. I don't care how you do it...just do it."

Although he did not know what rank he held, Jack Sanders was certain that Kelly carried a higher one than he. "Anderson agrees with us at this point. He wants you and Chandler to stay put until the plaintiffs make another move."

* * *

"We found the man in the photograph. He seems to have a great deal of influence, however. We may need some pressure from higher up." Haddiq was filling in the man who had waited in the car. The windows of the Minister's car were darkly shaded. He was certain that no one even knew that he had been waiting in the car. The Begum was being completely ignored...she had served her purpose.

Sa-ina Kalemi had been taken from Herat to work in the household when she was still in her late teens. That had been twelve years now and, although she had never been seriously mistreated, she felt like a prisoner there. With the free time allotted her when the men were away, she had read almost every book in the house's library as well as every magazine or periodical found on tables or desks. She had no husband. The only fatalities that night had been the four rooftop guards. Lying was strange to her…it was strongly forbidden by the Qur'an.

From all the literature that she had read, Sa-ina had discovered that many things expected of her were not that acceptable to women in the outside world. They seemed to have as much freedom and independence as the men…and she liked that. Now, she listened intently to the conversation as they drove north to the house.

"We can probably develop a story from this that will prompt a response from our newly elected President. We do not need much, just a suggestion that a legal inquiry be made."

"Can you do that?" Haddiq was impressed.

"No, you will." That was no question. Abdul Haddiq was silenced for a moment. These men had selected him for his background and education. He had no inclination toward running for the new Legislature in his homeland. They had prepared the speeches and the advertising propaganda that had gotten him elected. His family was wealthy…he did not want any new responsibilities. In fact, he had not wanted any responsibilities at all. They treated him well and he feared their wrath if he ever failed them.

"How do I do that? I do not even know him very well."

"You just get the audience with him. We will prepare the documents that will initiate the inquiry. His signature will be your responsibility. If need be, we will send the grieving widow with you."

Sa-ina heard every word. *Why do they want this man so badly? This is all a fabrication. I think he could see it in my eyes. I had to look away.*

Haddiq looked at her nervously. Her eyes told him that she was stronger than he was. Again, he looked at the man across from him in the limousine…immediately diverting his eyes from the icy cold glare of the man in contrast with the smiling face. *I will have to go through with this. Why can't they just leave me alone? I do not need their money.*

23

Those Americans think they can get away with anything. I will show them. Haddiq can get me a warrant signed by our President, General Fakir. When we have him in one of our prisons, preferably in Herat, we will see what a big man he is. Al-Zaquari has told us about this man and now we almost have him in our custody. With that incriminating photograph, Fakir cannot refuse our request for a hearing in our local court.

Abdullah Amin was feeling quite confident of his plan for revenge, as well as taking this adversary out of the picture permanently. Revenge was the guiding force. This man had completely obliterated his operation including his enormous supply of raw goods on hand, for which he had already paid the local farmers. His buildings were burned to the ground. He had lost four good men. There was nothing left of his plant.

But conjuring up the most hatred in his heart was the remains of his 2004 Rolls-Royce Phantom and 2001 Mercedes-Benz S Class, his most prized possessions from his years of exposure in this risky business. The smashed vehicles were barely visible under the debris in the garage. Amin could see enough to know that they were now worthless pieces of garbage and would be indiscriminately picked up by the backhoe as it removed the debris for rebuilding. He had been forced to rebuild before...but not at such a shattering loss.

Five years ago, when he had moved over here to Western Afghanistan from the Iraqui coastline, he found the supply inexhaustible and the demand almost equally so. His associates in Umm Qasr had sent him here to operate independently as one of their primary suppliers. Now, he was temporarily out of business. They would be upset if he did not rebuild quickly…they expected an uninterrupted flow through them to the vast Western European market. *Oh, well…laws of economics. If the supply gets short for a while, they will simply raise the price…same net.*

When he entered the house, the woman was nowhere in sight. Abdul Haddiq was on the phone. He had just faxed his story and the photograph to the Minister of Justice in Kabul and was awaiting a reply. This was the result of his brief conversation with the new President, General Fakir. *Why did he brush me off so quickly? We used to be friends. At least he transferred me to the person who can get me a warrant for this Harden Kelly's arrest and get Amin off my back. Come on…come on.* His nerves as well as his patience were wearing thin. *Amin is just upset about those automobiles, anyway. Why doesn't he just rebuild and get on with his business.* Haddiq knew this would never happen. If he did not pursue this to the limit, Amin would never let him rest…maybe, permanently.

The fax machine started printing. "I am forwarding the warrant signed by General Fakir. I do not think he paid much attention to the case. He was in a hurry, as always. Be careful with this. I do not want to turn in to the scapegoat if this case backfires." The Minister of Justice was an old acquaintance of Haddiq, but he was quite concerned about the accuracy of the facts in this case. He knew the man who was Abdul Haddiq's patron.

Abdullah Amin grabbed the paper as soon as the printer ejected the soon to be notorious document into the tray. His smile reflected cunning as well as evil. He had been well educated, having qualified for two years as an exchange student at UCLA, in the United States. Now he would get even with the American who had disrupted his life and destroyed his prize possessions.

"Abdul, I want you to contact that Commanding Officer at Shindand and get another meeting tomorrow. This time I expect you to return to Herat with Kelly in custody. I will be waiting there. He may try something to avert arrest so take at least four police officers with you. I believe Jack Sanders will advise him to go peaceably based on this document signed by our new President. Keep me advised." With this, Amin returned outside to supervise the waste removal which had already begun.

Haddiq was visibly shaking. *What if that man, Kelly, resists. I would probably be his first target. How did I ever get mixed up with this man?* The answer was obvious, even if Haddiq tried to deny it to himself. Amin was responsible for getting him elected Minister…a position of which he normally took pride. The benefits were unbelievable…a good salary, a limousine and even a driver. He had been clerking in a law office in Herat when Amin had spotted him. Weak, well educated, but with a total lack of ambition, Haddiq would make the perfect pawn.

Without being forced to reveal possession of the warrant, Jack Sanders had agreed to meet again with the Minister at ten in the morning. Harden Kelly would be present. *Kelly was right. They do know who he is. I wonder why he wants to meet again so soon…they could not have processed any paperwork this quickly.* Jack Sanders was puzzled by the request, but too busy to dwell on it.

24

Anthony Riley's thoughts were interrupted by the incessant ringing of the phone. He started his chair back into the house to the nearest phone. It was his own fault. Because of the nature of his business, he had instructed Mosa, Lobeth and Chris to not answer the phone regardless of how many times it rang. They were to call it to the attention of himself or Mandrake, in that order.

He almost ran into Mosa as he passed through the French doors.

"Phone, Mr. Riley…phone." Her superfluous pleadings were certainly not necessary considering that Anthony was already hastening to his desk but he calmly responded. "I know, Mosa. I know. Thank you for letting me know." Analyzing the current situation on the balcony had enhanced his attitude based on the recent performance of his three aides.

"Hello. Riley here."

"Mr. Riley, we have not talked before but please do not hang up. I have a proposal which should prove extremely beneficial to both of us."

"I'm listening." Anthony was intrigued, not only by the opening line but by the Middle Eastern accent.

"Some mutual friends in New York City have furnished me with your number so I could make this proposal to you, with their approval, I might add. I understand that you may be ready to make available a few containers of your product at any time now. Based on the information our friends have given me, I would like to arrange the purchase of four of these containers right away. If this interests you, I will furnish the balance of the necessary details." Saddam Akbar had been upset upon hearing from his source in Afghanistan about the delay in production. Abdullah Amin had let him down when he needed him. He could deal with that later. Now he needed product to satisfy his Western European dealers right away. The market did not understand or tolerate delays. Someone else would step in and he would be forgotten.

"Since you were able to locate me through our mutual friends, I will assume your call is legitimate. We are interested and capable of handling your request as long as the price is right."

"I am offering you fifteen percent more than your previous sale. If this is satisfactory, I will furnish the details of the exchange." Akbar was not going to reveal his operation until he was satisfied the transaction would go.

"Proceed." Anthony was intentionally brief, but could hardly conceal the excitement streaming from his greedy heart.

"My name is Saddam Akbar. Please deliver by sea to Umm Qasr, South dock, Pier eleven. My man will meet you and exchange U. S. Dollars for your product, in cash. I would like to make this happen at Midnight, tomorrow."

Taken slightly aback by the mention of Umm Qasr, Anthony quickly recovered. *Akbar was recommended by New York. I will have to have Sean increase production. This will take most of my available product.*

"I can meet that schedule. Consider it done." Without salutation, the other man was gone.

"Mandrake. Mandrake. I need you, now." The big man kept himself in excellent condition and came jogging into the office at the sound of his name.

"Prepare Dixon for a flight tomorrow afternoon. I want you to fly again to Kuwait City and meet Fez at the same dock as before. We will skip the hotel room and phone call this time. I will see that he is expecting you now that you are familiar with where he docks. Be prepared to leave at about two in the afternoon. Fez will deliver you and your freight to

Umm Qasr, where the exchange will take place. I do not wish to write anything on paper, so remember this location...South dock, Pier eleven."

"I will take care of it, Sir." Mandrake was feeling the confidence born of the healthy bonus he expected as well as the proficiency he had gained with the Glock he had chosen.

* * *

Saddam Akbar was feeling a few degrees better than he had when he first heard from Amin. *What an inopportune time for those agents to strike.*

I needed that delivery. Thanks to our contacts in the States, it appears that the catastrophe can be avoided. I will have to make certain that this exchange goes without mishap. I may need him again. However, I will not forget that it was his man who disrupted my last incursion into Kuwait. We could have intercepted that product and had no need for this meeting. It was good that we did not risk any of our key people. But, on the other hand, if we had sent more capable personnel we may have achieved our objective.

If this exchange works out without a hitch, we will just store that information for later.

25

The next morning, Harden told Sam that he wanted to make this meeting alone in order to belie the importance of the meeting from his point of view. Samantha reluctantly visited the firing range at the exact time of the meeting in order to work off her frustration at not being there.

Present were Jack Sanders and Harden Kelly. This time the visiting entourage consisted of Abdul Haddiq, accompanied by four Afghan National Guardsmen.

"Mr. Minister, what is this meeting you requested about?" Colonel Sanders made it abundantly clear that he had no time for nonsense.

Haddiq nervously fumbled with the catch on his briefcase before he finally produced an official looking document. "Since we are dealing with Americans here, I had this document produced in English. As you can see it is an indictment signed by the President of our Country, General Fakir. Based on the seriousness of the alleged crimes committed by the U. S. National, Harden Kelly, this document was prepared by our Minister of Justice authorizing me to take Mr. Kelly into immediate custody. If you have no further objection, my men will escort the defendant to our vehicle."

Haddiq had practiced this speech numerous times on the road South from Herat, where he had picked up the armed Officers. Now, he felt his nerves trembling on the inside as he awaited the outcome.

"Wait a minute, Minister. I told you yesterday that Mr. Kelly was being held here under house arrest. It will not be necessary for you to take him into custody."

"Please read the document carefully, Colonel. It states specifically that the defendant is to be placed in the custody of our National Police without delay."

Sanders reread the document...this time, much more thoroughly. He read it again, slowly. There was no mistake that Haddiq had secured official authorization before returning to the table. His mind raced. He could not turn Kelly over to these men. "I need to make a phone call. Would you please wait in the reception area? As you can see, there is no other way out besides through that door." He ushered all five men into the next room.

"Harden, I need to call General Graven. He can straighten out this mess. I think it has gone beyond my authority." He began to dial from memory. Harden had been in worse situations. He waited patiently to see what the outcome would be.

"This is Tom Sanders at Shindand. I need to speak to General Graven right away. It is very urgent and very immediate." Pause. "Thank you."

After what seemed an interminable delay, Harden sensed a response on the line. "General, as you are aware, we had two agents arrive to conduct operations against the local drug producers. I am pleased to report that these operations were imminently successful. However, Harden Kelly was caught on a surveillance tape as he waited for his men to make their way from the compound. We have since had a visit from a Begum, who claims she is the wife of a man killed by this intruder. We had a visit from the Minister of Light Industry who accompanied the wife. He insisted on searching Harden's quarters and came up with a valuable piece of jewelry that the wife identified as stolen that night. Of course, it was placed there by the Minister or one of his men. Now, the Minister has returned with an official indictment against Harden Kelly, signed by the new President, General Fakir, and processed by the Minister of Justice. They want to take Harden into custody awaiting trial. What do you think I should do?"

"Tom, I know Fakir and I also know that he probably signed the document in a rush because the Justice Minister put it before him. We have had a hell of a time appeasing this new Government because of the transgressions of some individuals in our Military. Although it is a false indictment, it would appear very serious to the uninformed. I believe we should let them temporarily take Harden into custody. We will get him released in a couple of days and out of the Country. No doubt, he would be held in Herat. I will confer with General Fakir about the incident and explain the true circumstances. Let me speak to Kelly."

"Special Agent Kelly, I have heard a lot of good things about you from Anderson and others as well. In order to maintain the delicate balance we have in this new government, I think it best for you to go into custody for a couple of days until the heat dies down. We will then get you freed and moved out of the Country."

"Yes, Sir. I will cooperate unless things get out of hand before the two days are up."

"I will get in touch with Anderson and we will get you out of there as quickly as possible. Good luck, Son."

Sanders ushered the Minister and his Officers back into the conference room.

"Mr. Minister, we agree for you to take Mr. Kelly into temporary custody."

One of the Officers snapped cuffs from his belt and moved toward Harden. In order to avoid any altercation, Haddiq stepped in. "I do not believe that will be necessary."

Harden found himself escorted to the waiting limousine, leaving his weapon with Sanders until he returned.

26

Wishing to further distance his prisoner from the base at Shindand, Abdullah Amin used his puppet, Haddiq, to bribe the district judge in Herat to transfer Harden Kelly further north to the town of Towraghondi, on the border with Turkmenistan. The judge issued official documents transferring the prisoner to a higher security location based on the seriousness of the charge. The trial date was set for two days hence, again prompted by Amin.

* * *

Charlie Reynolds burst into the reception room so abruptly that it startled Janet for a second until she recognized the young man.

"Janet, I need to see Conner right away. I only need a few minutes. Tell him it is urgent." Janet was on the intercom before he finished speaking.

"Mr. Hayes, Mr. Charles Reynolds is here to see you. He says it is an emergency." Conner could tell by the higher pitch of her voice that he should see the man right away.

"Send him in, Janet. Also, would you bring some hot tea for Mrs. Alamang while I talk to him?" Then to his alarmed client... "Mrs.

Alamang, I need to talk to this gentleman for a few minutes. Janet will bring you some tea while you wait. I will be right back."

Intercepting Reynolds as he entered the office, Conner ushered him into an adjoining small conference room and closed the door. "What is going on, Charlie. I haven't heard from you since our bodyguard episode. Also, I have not been able to contact Harden Kelly this past week. I need to talk to him."

"That is why I am here, Conner. Mr. Anderson asked that I make a special request of you. Kelly has been taken into custody by Afghan officials on a trumped up charge of murder and theft. We know that you have had vast experience in International Law as well as previous experience in Military Law with JAG. Mr. Anderson urgently requests that you represent Harden in court on Thursday, the day after tomorrow, in Herat."

"Thursday! My God, Charlie. What is going on?"

"All that I know is that Mr. Anderson wants you there. He thinks that you would be the best man to represent Harden under the circumstances. I can fill you in with the rest of the story on the way there. We would have to leave this afternoon."

"Certainly. Certainly. I'll do it." Conner's mind was racing a mile a minute as he juggled his schedule mentally. "I need to call Ashley right away and stop by the condo for some things. I can call her from the car."

Conner immediately summoned Janet to the conference room. "Janet, please appease Mrs. Alamang some way and reschedule our appointment for next week…better reschedule the next few days as well. I will contact you as soon as I can. I need to be out of town for a while."

The urgency in his voice precluded questions. "Yes, Sir. I will take care of everything." Glancing briefly at Reynolds, she exited through Conner Hayes' office. They heard the first words of gentle coercion as she took care of Mrs. Alamang.

"Let's go this way." Conner led the way out the other door and down the hall to the private entrance reserved for discreet arrival or departure for the Attorneys employed at Smith, Pitt & Alagia. As they waited for the elevator to arrive at the parking level, Conner dialed his wife.

"Ashley, I have an emergency and I need to leave town for a few days beginning this afternoon. Harden Kelly is in trouble."

"Oh, Conner...I am so sorry to hear that. How about Sam...is she alright? I am going with you. Where can I meet you?"

"No! No! Hon. This problem is in Afghanistan, and..."

"All the more reason. I *am* going. Now, don't delay further, just tell me how I can meet up with you." Her secretary, Mary Grayson, was seated opposite her at the time and was already busying herself with rescheduling and clearing the slate for the balance of the week after overhearing the conversation.

Conner relented rather than waste more time. "Charlie Reynolds and I are headed to the condo as we speak. Meet us there and we will leave as soon as we get packed. You know you don't have to go, Ashley."

"Oh, yes I do, Conner. If I can help you in anyway, fine, but I need to be there for Samantha. I am on my way. I can probably get there before you do."

After closing the cover of his cell phone, Conner glanced over at his passenger. "She is going, too." Charlie Reynolds knew from experience that you had to take everything in stride and his expression showed no inflection.

Ashley was already in the bedroom packing as they arrived.

"Something to wear in court, but, otherwise, casual clothing for a few days is what Charlie advised." Conner threw his things together rapidly and they were ready to go.

"We have a jet waiting at San Francisco International. Do you want me to drive?"

Conner had made numerous trips to the Airport, sometimes with little time to spare. "I'll drive, Charlie." Taking off quickly, he intended to bend the speed limits as much as caution would allow. "Just fill us in on the problem...as much detail as possible."

Charlie was still talking as they pulled into the Airport. "Let me guide you from here, Conner. Stay to the right and you will see a guarded gate just a little ways up. Turn in there."

The gate was closed and they were immediately approached by one of the uniformed guards. "Can I help you, Sir?" Charlie Reynolds flashed his identification. After close scrutiny, he quickly responded. "If you do not mind moving over, Sir, I will drive the rest of the way. They are expecting you."

Conner acceded as the gate slid open to allow them through. Their driver then drove up beside a waiting Military jet, with the crew already on board. "Here you are, Mr. Reynolds. I will take care of parking the car until you return." Charlie helped Ashley with her luggage as they hurriedly boarded the plane.

As the door closed, the Captain must have been alerted to their arrival. The speaker softly activated. "Welcome aboard, Gentlemen. Our flight plan has already been recorded. We are on our way. Try to make yourselves comfortable. I am Lieutenant Colonel Johnson and I will be your pilot on this flight. On my right is Lieutenant Bill Carroll. He will be acting as co-pilot and navigator."

The jet veered north as it left the ground, taking the shortest route possible to their destination, Shindand, Afghanistan.

27

Mandrake had arranged for a rental truck to be available upon their arrival in Kuwait City and soon had the four containers transferred to the truck. With each job, he was becoming more comfortable with Jim Dixon, who had willingly helped him move the freight. His contact with Dixon never obviated any drug use nor was there any discussion about the subject. Jim Dixon was cleaning up his act and also building up his bank account, the latter evidently incentive enough to control his addiction.

Driving directly to the dock area, he was able to spot Fez from a block away. The man made an impressive appearance, bare bodied from the waist up, his dark and muscular figure accented by the tiny Fez on his head. Mandrake was getting accustomed to this man as well.

Fez did not offer any salutation. "You can park the truck right over there until we get back. Let's get this stuff aboard quickly." With the two large men working on it, the freight was soon stored out of site in the forward bin. Mandrake parked the truck and jogged back to the cruiser.

As customary, very little conversation ensued as Fez expertly guided his boat East into the Bay and out to Sea. Although the trip covered more miles, the timing was about the same as he could accelerate much more speed in the open Sea as he turned North around Bubiyan Island. Even equipped with the proper ownership credentials, he continued to avoid the coastal channel where Police patrol boats were more commonplace.

The trip took them North around Bubiyan, then West again, with Warbah Island looming large on their left. Fez expertly maneuvered the remaining waterways into Iraq and the docks at Umm Qasr. They were soon pulling up to the South Dock, Pier eleven. Two swarthy gentlemen, dressed in Western European suits with the favored kefiyyah covering their heads, were patiently waiting when they arrived. Each carried a large briefcase in their left hand, leaving their right hand free to fondle the weapons hidden under their jackets.

This fact was not lost on Mandrake, who, also, felt for his weapon before exposing himself to this encounter. Fez jumped ashore first and secured his boat. Mandrake joined him and they unloaded the freight quickly. After a cursory reading of the inscription on the containers, the two men walked over to Mandrake and each man handed him their briefcase simultaneously. Mandrake faltered for an instant as he realized that this exchange would leave him without a free hand if needed. With his left hand, he accepted each case in turn, setting the first on the dock beside his left foot before accepting the second. The first man issued a barely camouflaged smirk at this distrust before turning to help his partner load the merchandise on their vehicle.

With his huge left hand, Mandrake grabbed both cases by the handle and boarded the waiting vessel just as Fez released the second tie. The motor roared to life and without further incident the cruiser was speeding South then East, again to the open Sea.

As always, Fez mentally replayed the odds of overpowering Mr. Riley's representative, weighing in the fact that this man was obviously no longer a novice at his job. Mandrake opened a cold Coca Cola from the cooler on deck, maintaining constant surveillance of the briefcases at his feet and the Captain of the boat, whom he had not yet fully learned to trust.

Pulling into Kuwait Bay from the East, they were more or less ignored by the Police patrol boats, who were accustomed to Fez and his powerful boat coming and going at unusual intervals. Fez had learned from his colleagues dockside to share some of his benefits with select members of the constabulary. This proved to allow much freer access to the Bay and the coastal channel then the itinerant pilot might receive.

Mandrake was relieved to put his feet on the dock at Kuwait City. With a raised hand he bade the Captain a silent farewell before driving back to the airport to the waiting helicopter. He was again relieved to see Jim Dixon apparently sober and ready to go. Much more comfortable with Dixon, he had yet to learn to relax around the irascible Captain Fez. Since there was no risk of losing the briefcases on the return flight, Mandrake managed to doze at intervals.

Touching down on the Ramkin Island estate, Mandrake found Mr. Riley waiting in his office, having heard the approaching chopper blades.

Opening the cases which his assistant had placed on his desk, Anthony thumbed through the stacks of currency. Apparently satisfied, he turned to his young aide with a carefully counted stack of hundred dollar bills. "Again, a good job, Mandrake. You are handling your new responsibilities remarkably well."

Mandrake accepted the bundle and viewed this as dismissal as he stuffed the money into his two jacket pockets as he exited the room. He could not wait to share the news with Chrissimminia. But, first, he needed to arrange a boat to take him to the mainland and his secret banker to make this new deposit and review his balance as well as the investments made on his behalf.

28

Neither Conner nor Ashley found any time to sleep on the long flight as Charlie Reynolds brought them up to date on exactly what happened and presented a copy of the indictment against which Conner must defend his old friend, Harden Kelly, in a foreign court with, undoubtedly, an unsympathetic jury. This he needed to do without being allowed to reveal the real reason for Kelly's presence on the private property, nor the identity of any of his co-conspirators on that mission.

With his hands virtually tied by these restrictions, Conner foresaw only a bleak outlook for his friend. *What does Anderson think I can do? The truth would release Harden…but the truth cannot be used. I may have to use some of it anyway. I can't let my friend spend unwarranted time in Afghan prisons.*

They were welcomed warmly by Jack Sanders, who had been alerted to the arrangement by Anderson in advance of their arrival. Conner immediately noticed the lack of rank indication on the uniforms. Of course, the reason was obvious. Higher rank presented more imminent targets for the ever present enemy.

Colonel Sanders led them to his office, where he repeated, with few exceptions, the information furnished on the flight over by Reynolds.

"Could we see Samantha Chandler, now, Jack?" Ashley was anxious to console her recently acquired but very close friend.

"Well, there is one last thing I need to tell you. The trial has been set up for tomorrow morning at ten, but that is not the worst part. It is now to take place in Towraghondi, a small district capital. That is where the district judge is presiding this week. I do not know how or why they created such urgency for this trial, but someone has strong connections to the new Afghan Government. Tomorrow's trial could well be a farce with a predetermined outcome. Whatever the conclusion, we will get Kelly out of there, even if we have to use force."

Conner was still digesting the information when they arrived at Sam's quarters. She had just returned from the firing range, a frequent diversion for her since her husband had been gone, relieving frustrations and tuning skills. She threw her arms around Ashley, surprised that she had accompanied Conner to this isolated piece of the World. It was then that the tears released. Ashley held her until the tremors subsided. "Everything is going to be alright, Sam. The Colonel assured us that he would take whatever action proves necessary."

Sam, however, knew that the Colonel would have to follow protocol in his position as Base Commander and allowed little hope in that venue. Anderson was a different story. He would be the one to take whatever means necessary to extricate her husband…and she would insist on being part of that operation.

"Why don't we get back to that conference room, all of us, and see what kind of strategy we can devise for tomorrow morning." Conner had tossed a couple of reference books in his luggage dealing with problems arising between the military and civilian populations on foreign soil. He maintained a set of these reference books in his library in order to be prepared for just such an incident. His years with the Judge Adjutant General's office remained vivid in his memory banks, available for instant recall.

Six somber faces surrounded the large oblong table. Jack Sanders was on one side with Captain James Blalock. Across the table sat Sam Chandler Kelly and Ashley Jennings Hayes. Conner Hayes sat at the point of the table, where he could best prompt information from the participants. Charlie Reynolds sat unobtrusively at the other end.

"As you are aware, Mr. Anderson requested my presence in behalf of

Harden Kelly's defense. I recognize that we cannot dwell on the actual mission at this trial but I need to know what actually happened so that I can better understand what is fact and what is façade. Captain Blalock, would you start from the beginning of that evening's activity. I would also request that Sam Chandler interrupt to insert any missing pieces as they come to mind."

Captain Blalock looked at Colonel Sanders for authorization. "Go ahead, James. All of these people have been cleared for secrecy by Mr. Anderson."

"There were seven of us involved in this operation. We dug under the old fence and proceeded to the roof of the warehouse. From this vantage point we eliminated four security personnel who were guarding the roof of the lab. Working from both ends of the lab, we installed incendiary explosives at proper intervals to level that facility as well as the storage building, without any peripheral damage to the houses. My grappling hook got stuck on descent, and Harden Kelly was evidently caught facing the surveillance camera because he was doing the count off and I was late getting to the exit point. Otherwise, I am sure that we would have all had our backs to the camera at all times and Kelly would not have been subjected to this phony charge. The timing was perfect concerning the operation itself. We passed south of the facilities on our return before the timers activated. Aerial surveillance later confirmed that the mission was successful. I think that sums it up."

"I might just add that one of our directives was to cause no damage to the housing compound whatever because of the chance of civilian casualties. Therefore, no one was anywhere near the houses proper. Our operation was concentrated on the rooftops of the two cocaine producing buildings and the fence beyond." Sam clarified that none of the participants had any opportunity to enter the housing complex.

"This was not an official military attack on an enemy facility. I have been ordered by the highest command in Afghanistan to maintain the position that this operation was not sanctioned by the United States Government. We have all the problems with this fledgling Government that we need involving individual crimes by our personnel including rape, murder and theft. Special Ops agents are aware of the potential consequences if they are apprehended." Sanders had been given the official position of non-involvement. "I am sorry but my hands have been tied."

"This does not leave us much in the way of defense. Could I use this room for the afternoon? I want to make some notes and do some extensive research of our options."

"Do you need any help, Conner?" Samantha barely managed to hold her voice steady after the turn of the meeting.

"Not now, thanks. I can think better alone. The rest of you better get some rest. We have a big day tomorrow."

As everyone rose to leave, Jack offered one last appeasement. "I will have a helicopter ready to fly you to the town in the morning...o eight hundred hours.

29

Al Molini thought he was a dead man. Even after another successful meet with their supplier, Joey Bono's uncle was adamant about avenging his death. He blamed Molini, saying the older man should have protected his nephew and not put him in harms way since he was just learning the operation. Now, Joey was dead and Al feared he might soon be as well.

He quickly discovered that his years of service had not gone unappreciated. Having successfully completed every job requested of him, his boss did not want to lose him. Instead of a death sentence, Al was overwhelmed to find that he had been secretly transferred to Las Vegas.

"Juliano does not know of this. For his information, we have just made you disappear. Don't let me down. I want you to continue to work for me just like you have, only from a different base. Never contact me. I will let you know when I have something for you. We will arrange for you to have a little more money...I hear it is quite a bit more expensive out there."

That was just yesterday and already he was flying back to Kuwait to make another buy. He had a new partner. Though not a Cary Grant himself, Al considered this guy a little sleazy, in appearance as well as personality...another Joey...Joey Gondolfo was from the West Coast and probably selected because he had no contact with the New York crowd.

Thank goodness, the guy doesn't talk much...to me, anyway. Their destination had changed slightly to adjust for the problems at Warbah. It was not that different. They were to rent a truck and drive just across the border of Iraq, to Umm Qasr, South dock, pier eleven. This was suggested by their supplier and approved by New York. *I don't know what kind of friends they could have in that God-forsaken place, but he told me not to worry about a thing. There would be some people watching over us. I would rather know who these people are, but who am I to question them. They have been good to me, even after Joey's death.*

* * *

This sale was for only two containers, but Anthony Riley was pushing Sean Pfister to increase production as the orders came in. Mandrake was upset because he did not even get a chance to take his money from the last venture to his bank on the mainland before Mr. Riley called him back into his office.

"I need you and Dixon to make another delivery tonight, same place, and same time. Fez has already been alerted and assured me he would be there to meet you...only two containers this time."

His disappointment in not being able to bank his money was superceded by the opportunity for earning even more. Mandrake had hidden the undeposited cash in his room, and had entrusted Chris with its location so she could keep an eye on it for both of them. With the influx of cash, they had begun to make plans for their future together.

Dixon seemed like a changed man. Not knowing whether to credit the new financial opportunities presented to the pilot or the wake up call that occurred on their last trip to Abdali, Mandrake decided to just let it go.

They landed in Kuwait City without incident. The rental truck was waiting. This time, however, Jim Dixon came up with a little surprise.

"Is it OK if I join you on this run, Mandrake? There is nothing to do here at the airport and I like to stay busy...keeps me out of trouble. I won't get in your way."

"Sure, I guess." Mandrake was not certain how Mr. Riley would take to this change in procedure. "Are you carrying?"

Dixon used his hand to pat the small of his back two times, revealing the bulge under his jacket.

Neither man spoke on the short ride to the dock. Fez was waiting as promised. With Dixon taking one end of the containers and Mandrake the other, the freight was loaded in less than two minutes. The Captain closed the compartment and freed his ropes. They were ready to go. To this point there had not been a word spoken. This had become an accepted protocol with Mandrake and Fez, with only occasional wary eye contact as acknowledgement. This seemed to fare well with Dixon, who felt dwarfed between the two other men.

Fez did not ask and Mandrake did not offer any explanation for the additional passenger. However, appraising stares were exchanged as each man sized up the other. With his extensive military training, Dixon had developed a confidence in his own abilities that precluded fear from physical confrontation. Contrastingly, Fez had no fear of the stranger, knowing that he could squash him like a bug if he wanted or needed to do so.

Again, the route was East to the Sea, then North around Bubiyan Island. When they turned west again, Mandrake could see Warbah in the distance to his left. *I wonder why we don't use that place anymore...we would be there by now.* Mandrake had not been informed of the altercation that had resulted in the death of one of the men to whom he had made the previous delivery. He fully expected to be dealing with the same two men on this exchange since he was told that the customer was the same one he had encountered at Warbah. *I kind of liked working with the old guy. He was not a smart ass...just doing his job like I was doing mine. I think we got along pretty good. He even smiled a little.*

Reminiscing was over as they pulled in to the South dock at Pier Eleven. Fez had become quite efficient as he docked the boat and immediately jumped ashore and tied down. Al Molini was waiting, alertly watching the new man as Dixon and Mandrake unloaded the two containers from the freight compartment to the dock. Recognizing the big man in the suit, Al was relieved to be making the exchange with the same person. *I trust that guy. There is something about him...just doing his job.*

This time, Molini approached Mandrake with the satchel in his left hand, reaching out with his right hand in greeting. "Good to see you again."

Hesitantly, Mandrake's huge right hand encompassed the short, stubby grip of the old man. *Could this be a trap? When I accept the satchel with my left hand and shake hands with my right, I will be extremely vulnerable.* Cautiously eyeing the new man still standing in place by the truck, Mandrake managed a smile himself. "Good to see you, again, too. You have a new partner."

"Yeah. I noticed that you do, too." Neither man offered any explanation for the fluctuation in personnel.

The exchange had been made and each man returned to their transportation. So quickly did this transaction transpire that Fez was still standing by the stanchions to which the boat was tied. Slipping the loops free, he was back on the boat about the same time as Mandrake, sliding comfortably behind the wheel for the return trip.

As they pulled the cruiser into Kuwait Bay, nearing the point of land protruding out in the water with the promise that they had almost arrived at the Kuwait City docks, a Police cruiser pulled alongside. Shutting down his powerful engine, Fez went to the starboard side to meet them. Mandrake and Dixon experienced some anxious moments as the two men had a verbal exchange in their native language, occasionally gesturing in the direction of the two passengers. Fez had immediately pulled his ownership papers from a small compartment beside the wheel before meeting the Officer. Returning to the compartment a second time, he removed a well used envelope and returned to the conversation. Fez seemed upset. Then the Officer took his turn at flaring up. Finally, Fez removed what looked like U.S. currency discreetly from the envelope and handed it to the man. The Officer returned to his cruiser, now smiling broadly. Fez was not that happy as he again started up his engine with a roar, making one last statement to the departing Police cruiser.

Mandrake was relieved, anxiously watching his companion as well as the heated exchange. He feared Dixon would respond violently as he did at Abdali. This situation was much different. They still had to get to the airport in order to leave this country.

The balance of the trip was made without incident and they were soon on their flight back to Ramkin Island.

30

Conner Hayes was allowed to meet with Harden Kelly in a miniscule room with no windows and one door shortly before the trial was to be held.

Looking none the worse for wear, Harden was still dressed in the sport shirt and slacks that he had worn to the conference room for the confrontation. No grooming accouterments were made available to him, so he had not shaved nor bathed since being taken into custody. Neither man said a word aloud as the security guard closed the door behind him. Conner laid a legal pad and pencil in front of Harden. On his own pad, he wrote.

This place is probably bugged. Do not talk aloud...just write. Good to see you again, Buddy...terrible circumstances.

Harden had already concluded the same. *Hey, Conner, good to see you...Anderson...right?* He concealed his surprise amazingly well under these conditions. *Do we have a plan for my defense yet?*

Conner surmised that their silence would be frustrating to the listening ears. *Not sure...can't use the truth...we came up with a few ideas. We will have to see how it plays out. Just follow along and do not say too much.*

Harden did not seem perturbed in the least as he calmly wrote on his pad. *I really do not have anything to say, anyway. We all know that if you are apprehended on any of these missions, you play the cards you are dealt.*

Sanders cannot officially sanction our incursion so we have to come up with something else. He has to plead ignorance to our operation to appease this new Government. We disrupted the flow of farming goods to the manufacturing facility, upsetting a lot of people in the process. However illegal in our eyes, these people were just making a living. Harden tore out the first page and handed it to Conner, who, after reading the message, folded it behind the last page of his pad.

The silent conversation continued. *Harden, you know that whatever the result today produces, this is not the end of it. There is not much of a case for the defense without the truth.*

The door opened abruptly and two men in uniform entered. The one with the braid of Captain spoke. "We have to end this meeting, Gentlemen; the Judge is ready for us." Apparently frustrated with the silence, Haddiq and Amin had heard enough of the chairs scraping and decided to end the meeting. They were not going to learn anything of the defense strategy.

Conner returned both pads to his briefcase and shook hands with Harden before leaving his friend in the care of these uniformed strangers.

* * *

"This court is now in session...Honorable Judge Tajik Kahn presiding." The little man had a powerful voice as he used his authority to quiet the room, even to copying phrases he had picked up from television.

Western European attire seemed to be the preference of anyone who was in a position to afford it. The Judge was of average size and wore a dark suit with traditional headdress. "What are the charges against this man?"

Abdul Haddiq was seated at the table with the prosecuting attorney as well as the alleged widow, Sa-ina Kalemi. No one on the defense would recognize Abdullah Amin as he positioned himself three rows back behind the defense table. He wanted to be in a position to hear everything that was presented today as well as possibly overhearing anything discussed at the defense table. He was incensed, seething, with difficulty holding back his hatred of this man. Yet, none of this had surfaced. Also, from this vantage point, he could watch the bereft widow and had made certain that she knew he was there as he made his entrance.

The defense table seated Harden Kelly, Conner Hayes and a public defender provided by the court for assistance in translating language or procedure. In the first row behind them sat Charlie Reynolds, beside Sam Chandler, then Ashley Jennings Hayes. No United States military were present, thus distancing themselves from this purely civilian case. Charlie would keep them apprised of the situation.

"The charges are as follows. First degree murder, grand theft, assault with a deadly weapon and wanton endangerment."

"Thank you, Counselor. May I ask why Minister Haddiq is present at your table?"

"Sir, he is present as a co-claimant, being a good friend of the deceased and his widow, Madame Kalemi."

"You may proceed, Counselor."

"My first witness will be Minister Haddiq, on behalf of the distraught widow Kalemi."

This part of the job, Abdul Haddiq relished, playing out his newly appointed position in front of an audience, as he made his way to the witness chair. After being duly sworn to tell the truth, Haddiq began his story, which, of course, was what happened that night according to Abdullah Amin, his benefactor.

At the appropriate point, the prosecuting attorney submitted the surveillance photograph into evidence. On stage, as it were, the newly appointed Minister of Light Industry played out his story in great detail, adding great emotion at the death of Mr. Kalemi and the bereavement of his poor wife, left to fend on her own. Sa-ina Kalemi was a woman of stature in the community and was now left without any visible means of support. Her Ministry position was a position of necessity only with no remuneration. Haddiq gestured in the direction of the grieving widow at appropriate intervals.

Minister Haddiq could be extremely verbose when presented with a forum that gave him ample opportunity. His dissertation lasted in excess of an hour, with only brief pauses when his emotions overwhelmed him momentarily. Upon completion, he was excused and returned to his seat at the table with his head down, a perfect picture of the humble servant of his constituency.

"Your Honor, since Minister Haddiq so eloquently described the circumstances of that terrible night, we do not feel it necessary to expose our only other witness, the Widow Kalemi, to what would certainly be a heart rending and unnecessary, debacle. The Prosecution rests its case."

The Judge was not stupid but the facts were so stacked against the defendant, he knew he had no choice of verdict unless the Counsel for the Defense could refute the Minister's story.

Turning his attention, now, to Conner Hayes, "You may call your first witness, Counselor."

Conner could read the Judges mind to some degree. He only had two possibilities working in his favor, and they were both very weak.

"Your Honor, I wish to call the Defendant's wife to the stand...Mrs. Samantha Chandler Kelly." Conner had asked her beforehand if she would be willing to testify. Her testimony had been rehearsed and there would be no surprises on their part, but she would be exposed to cross examination by the Prosecutor if he so desired. Samantha took the stand and was sworn in.

"Mrs. Kelly, where was your husband on the night in question?"

"He was with me from dinner on through the night. We were never out of sight of one another. The Base Commander was nice enough to offer us adequate sleeping quarters at Shindand for the length of our stay. Being visiting U. S. Nationals, he was concerned for our safety if we were to stay off base." They had formatted her testimony so that it was entirely true, trying to add credence to the fact that Harden Kelly had not had any opportunity to be the alleged perpetrator. "We had dinner together on base and then we were left to ourselves the remainder of the evening. When we were asked to attend a meeting with Mrs. Kalemi and Mr. Haddiq, it came as quite a surprise. That was when we first became aware that Mrs. Kalemi had lost her husband in such a tragic intrusion. My husband and I were both very sympathetic at her loss until Mr. Haddiq insisted on implicating Harden in this incident."

"Thank you, Mrs. Kelly. That will be all for now."

The Judge turned his attention to the Prosecutor. "Do you wish to cross examine, Counselor?"

After conferring with Haddiq, momentarily..."Not at this time, Your

Honor. We would like to reserve our rights for cross until later, if necessary."

"You may step down, Mrs. Kelly."

Conner breathed a sigh of relief. He had been able to present to the Judge without objection, and without outright lying, the image that the Kellys had spent the entire evening from dinner on in their furnished quarters.

"Based on the testimony just presented, Your Honor, I would like to impinge on the reliability of the somewhat distorted surveillance photograph presented in evidence. I submit that my client could not possibly be identified, without a shadow of a doubt, as the person in this photogram." Conner was attempting to further discredit the likeness of the image by downgrading it to a shadowed photogram. He only had two shots at the prosecution's case and he was trying to make the most of them in presentation to the Judge.

The Judge picked up the surveillance photograph for another look then turned his eyes toward Harden, staring for what seemed an interminable length of time.

"Do you have any response, Counselor?"

"Your Honor, we are prepared to project this image from the tape on to a screen at twenty times its original size. I think you will then agree that there is no doubt as to the identity of the person you will see." He then was handed a projector by his assistant, who appeared out of nowhere. The enlargement filled the screen…Harden Kelly waiting for his last man to pass through the fence. Since the others were filmed from the back only, identification was impossible. Harden had counted off five operatives and had just turned to tell Blalock to leave his grappling hook when it finally fell loose. This was the only frontal image projected so it was the one that Amin was going to prosecute.

"Would Counsel approach the bench, please?" Conner sensed that his case was falling apart upon hearing the Judge's request. "Gentlemen, there is no doubt in my mind that the defendant is the person in the photograph. Unless you have further defense, Attorney Hayes, I must rule in favor of the prosecution. In addition, it appears that his wife is in contempt and subject to charges based on her testimony."

"No. No. That will not be necessary, Your Honor. She was simply defending her husband." The prosecutor had what Amin wanted; besides, the case against the wife was not one they could win.

"Your Honor, I wish to file an appeal." Hayes was grabbing at straws.

"On what grounds, Counselor?"

"I'll reserve that, Your Honor."

"Sentencing will take place exactly one week from today."

Harden did not seem particularly surprised or perturbed at the outcome as the guards cuffed him and led him out. Sam managed to make eye contact with a subtle assurance that he would not be there long.

31

Anthony was feeling more than generous, having had such rapid turnover of the TR7. However, instead of giving Mandrake fifty thousand as he had planned to compensate him for the additional risk, he deducted ten thousand dollars for Jim Dixon. He certainly did not want Dixon's bonus to come out of his share. Both men were nonetheless elated at their share...this time.

As he left Mr. Riley's office, Mandrake found Chris and asked her to come to his room for a minute. "We are almost there, Chrisimminia." He much preferred her given name to the shortened version. "I am going to make a trip to the mainland in a little while and I will get an up to date balance from my banker. Can you come with me?"

"I would love to, Mandrake. All morning I stayed and waited for you to return. I was watching your room to make sure no one went in there just like you asked." Mandrake and Chrisimminia, very formal, but very much in love.

As Anthony presented Sean Pfister with his bonus, he promised even better things to come, encouraging him to step up production of TR7 in anticipation of the increase in demand...two huge customers, now.

* * *

Almost a week later, Anthony picked up the phone in his office only to hear the same request from Saddam Akbar. "I need four more containers tomorrow, same place, same time and I assume the same price. We are establishing a good arrangement. Do not try to gouge me, Mr. Riley." The not so veiled threat was not even necessary. Anthony was ecstatic with the increase in business and his product was relatively inexpensive to produce. The more orders he received, the better for him and he was intelligent

enough not to jeopardize that position.

"Mandrake." One word on the paging system and his assistant was knocking on the door as he entered.

"Tomorrow afternoon, I need you and Dixon to make another delivery. This time, it will be the Arabs again…four containers. Sean will see that the freight is ready when you are. Take care of it for me, my good friend."

Mandrake whole body swelled with pride when his boss complimented him. "I will take care of it, Mr. Riley."

Now, as Riley sat again on his veranda overlooking the Mediterranean Sea, his thoughts wondered back to his old friends, Conner Hayes and Harden Kelly. *I wonder where they are right now. I wonder if they know where I am right now, or if they even care.*

The following day, Anthony received a duplicate order from New York. He was thankful that he had the foresight to get Sean to increase production.

Both deliveries were made without incident. His staff was complete. They had all proved their competence and exhibited capabilities that surprised even Anthony Riley.

32

Harden Kelly sat in his miniscule cell in an old stone prison built on the outskirts of Towraghondi contemplating his options. His big hand roughed the stubble on his chin as he realized he had not adequately washed or shaved since before the trial. *Those bastards wanted me to look the part of a renegade as well...made it easier to portray me as one. The judge did not have much to go on. Sam did an excellent job of describing our activities that night, evading the truth, yet not outright lying under oath. It was that photograph that did it. When they magnified that picture, I could not even lie about it being my likeness on the big screen. It was too obvious. Conner ran with the only two options he had.* With that, his mind wandered back to high school where he and Conner had run the option so many times on the football field. *Things were so much simpler then.*

Having already thought of the various ways he could break out of this prison, his only concern was planning what to do when he got out. His earlier training had resulted in the unobtrusive survey that he had made of the small crowd in the courtroom on the day of the trial. There was one man whose likeness kept returning to his mind. Seated in the third row directly behind him, he had caught the man's eyes. Registering his reaction for later use, Harden had been puzzled by the venom exuding from those eyes. Almost certain that this was the same man who rode in the front passenger seat when he had first been taken into custody, his mind began to release other images of the same man standing with the Minister at the other end of the corridor as he was led to the courtroom. Also, he had leaned as if to whisper something to Haddiq before crossing the room to sit directly behind the defense.

Was it possible that this man was the driving force behind the entire farce? Harden replayed the night of the incident in his mind. *There were four casualties. One of them could have been married to the lady, but I doubt it. They were four lackeys whose turn it was to draw guard duty at that unfortunate time. She appeared to be a Begum alright. Her carriage and her grooming indicated a Muslim woman of higher rank. Another thing that makes me doubt any of those men were her husband is the fact that she seemed not so much the weeping widow but more as an unwilling participant. Her eyes held no hatred, just nervous shifting, maybe even embarrassment at being forced to take part in this charade. Maybe we will never know, but I intend to visit that housing compound as soon as I get out of here. I would like to talk to her as well as that man who keeps showing up…him, particularly.*

He had been able to talk to Conner on two occasions since the trial. There were no grounds for an appeal. Conner had filed several motions, first questioning the location and timing of the photograph, attempting to cast doubt as to whether the photograph of his client was taken at another time or place. There were too many identifying objects in the landscape for this. Another attempt was made suggesting that Harden had been simply one of the men hired to keep watch as the leaders wreaked havoc. This was very weak as well. Harden Kelly was obviously the leader as he motioned to his men and counted them off as they exited the premises. The prosecutor had obtained just enough additional video in case such a premise had been brought up at the original trial.

Knowing better than to speak aloud of anything but a formal greeting, Harden and Conner had used several pads in their conversations, each time Conner leaving with all the materials used. Both times Conner had been accompanied by two Military Policemen from the Shindand Base for just that purpose. There was always the possibility that the guards at the Towraghondi prison would be instructed to detain Conner and search his person for evidence of the conversation. Tom Sanders had suggested that the two men go along to deter that from happening.

At their last meeting, Conner informed Harden that nothing would be done until after the sentencing. Anderson had indicated that their best opportunity would arise after the sentencing as the publicity would then die down as well. Through Conner, Anderson assured Harden that they would have adequate detail of whatever holding compound he was switched to after the Judge had read the sentence. Reynolds and Chandler would lead the team already assembling when the time was right.

Although reluctant to put it on paper, Harden had strongly advised Anderson that he wished to return to the scene before leaving the Country in order to get the answers he needed. *Why was this man so desirous of prosecution? Was it simply revenge for temporarily messing up his operation? Why didn't he just rebuild and go on? This guy is really making it a personal vendetta.* He also hoped to talk to the woman. She was obviously distraught, not over the death of her husband, but because she had been forced into a compromising situation not of her choosing.

When they met the day before the trial, Conner had released something into Harden's hand as they said farewell on this last visit…a tiny disc about the size of a collar button. Immediately recognizing the device, Harden waited until his friend had left before straightening his socks, while surreptitiously slipping the item into the space where the arch support of the shoe met his instep. This way he could constantly feel that the device was still there without causing unwarranted discomfort. Anderson was taking no chances on being informed of Harden's ultimate destination.

Preparations were being made. All parties involved fully expected the death penalty for the conviction of murder under Muslim law.

33

People are dying…our customers…three so far in France, two in Germany, five in Spain. What the hell is going on? You recommended this guy Riley and his new product. Now I am losing people as well as my reputation. We don't process anything strong enough to overdose on accidentally. You told me that you have been using his product for years without any problems." Saddam Akbar was upset and kept rambling on.

Tony Rubella, Al Molini's boss, just listened, mystified at the sudden turn in events. Riley had been supplying him his TR7 for the past three years without any problems whatever. That was what was so sweet about the arrangement…cheaper product with no reports of any fatal reactions to it. Now, he had heard of one death in New York and another in Chicago. He did not know whether to tell Akbar of these or not. The man was already upset enough.

"I will have to retool my entire organization. The demand will still be there but no one will buy from my people. Everyone is scared. I will have to move people around to look like a new supplier. This will cost me a great deal of money and I intend to get it from Riley, as well as some answers."

"Yeah. Yeah. Problems come up. You just have to deal with them.

Maybe you just found some users who were going to overdose on whatever they bought…maybe it isn't the product at all." Tony doubted there was any truth in this but he wanted to appease Akbar somewhat.

"I thought of that. I even tested it on a stray dog and a cat that had been hanging around the warehouse. Both exhibited signs of extreme pleasure before convulsing and dying. I just wanted to know if you were experiencing the same public reaction as we are. The next step is to get my money back from Riley…and I will."

"I will let you know if anything further develops here in the States. If the problem gets any worse over there, let me know before the newspapers do, so I can pull the product." Rubella was not overly concerned. There were always isolated cases of over dosing. The conversation was suddenly over. *I don't have time to listen to Akbar's problems. I have enough of my own.* Tony made a mental note to contact Riley about this, maybe run some tests, before he made another buy.

Saddam Akbar was still fuming as he hung up the phone. "Get my helicopter ready. I want to pay a little visit to that guy, Riley, in person."

His assistant had heard the entire exchange and immediately turned to leave the room. "Will we need any additional manpower, Sir?"

"Just you, me and the pilot this time. If we need to make a second trip, it will be a different situation." When the man had left, he opened his bottom right hand drawer and withdrew the Sig Sauer P229 SAS Pistol. Though he had not yet had to use this new weapon, the anti snag smooth release of the weapon from the shoulder holster had impressed him in practice. He ran his left hand over the smooth cold steel and his thoughts turned again to his errant supplier. *You two may get to know one another soon.*

On the intercom, Saddam summoned his second in command in to his office. "I need for you to take care of a few things today while I am gone. In any area where one of our customers has died, switch the people around. I want it to look like the remaining customers have found a new supplier. Do not even let them stay in the same area. Change countries if you have to. Use your own judgment."

At that moment, his assistant returned. "We are ready to go, Sir."

* * *

Tony Rubella had immediately dialed his most reliable Lieutenant.

"Al, what do you think? Are you hearing anything that I haven't heard? If we stop using TR7, we will have to make certain that no one else uses it. They could undercut us on price and steal our customer base. If we decide to stop pushing that product, we may have to eliminate the source."

Al Molini's thoughts immediately drifted to the powerful looking young man who made deliveries for Riley. He had taken a liking to him and would hate to see the arrangement end violently. Though not averse to doing whatever it took to perform his job, Al could still see his own young protégé, Joey Bono, lying on the ground with his life blood draining out. He still remembered Joey's last words. "I'm sorry, Al." Again, *me, too, Joey.*

"I have heard of several deaths in Spain and France. Is that our product that they are dying from?"

"I just talked to the man who supplies that area and he seems to think so. A few weeks ago, I needed a favor, so I gave him Riley's name in exchange. Now, I wish I hadn't. Let's just wait a few days and see if any more reports show up. We cannot wait forever. We will have to make a decision soon."

"Just let me know what you want me to do, Boss." Al was indebted to Tony for displacing him to Las Vegas. He would have certainly been a dead man if he had not.

* * *

Anthony Riley had just called Sean Pfister into his office to congratulate him once again on his splendid work. "I do not know how you set up so quickly for producing my TR7 here, but I assure you that you will be adequately rewarded as orders continue to pour in. Keep up the production schedule as I expect calls from both parties to keep coming in."

Sean was elated at his employer's praise as well as the generous bonus he had received on the last two orders. The defect in the product that he had detected earlier had already drifted deep into the background as orders continued to flow in. *Now is not the time to bring that up. Finding the problem would delay orders and cost me my bonus and possibly my job. I have not heard any complaints, anyway.*

Not realizing the serious consequences of the problem, he had not considered the possibility that the mistake could also cost him his life.

34

Jack Sanders had shown Sam Chandler to a secure phone located in a small soundproof conference room adjacent to his office. He was aware of why she requested a secure phone but did not want to be made aware of the conversation that ensued. Sam had gathered all the affected parties into the room, contacting them by cell phone as soon as the Colonel had left. Anderson had requested that Charlie Reynolds and Conner Hayes be present for the meeting as well. However, he did not figure on the strong willed Ashley, who insisted on accompanying her husband to the meeting. Her intuition told her that this meeting was called to discuss alternate measures to be enacted after tomorrows sentencing of Harden Kelly.

Samantha dialed Anderson's number by memory on the secured phone as soon as everyone was in place around the small table. Detailed maps of the area of interest were laid open on the table. "Agent Chandler reporting, Sir." After recording this message on an answering machine, she placed the phone on to the base. They sat in silence waiting for the response. Though it seemed interminable, the response came in less than a minute. Sam pushed the button for the speaker phone after she had determined that the call was indeed from Anderson.

"Before you speak, Sir, I want to apprise you of the conditions here.

We are in a small soundproof conference room just outside Colonel Sander's office and we are speaking on a secure unit. Present, as you requested, are

Agent Reynolds, Attorney Hayes and myself. But, also present is Ashley Hayes, the wife of Conner Hayes. She insisted on being present."

There was noise of paper shuffling and after a brief pause Anderson began the meeting.

"First of all, I am familiar with the accomplishments of Ashley Jennings Hayes. Besides proving capable of managing a large corporation, I have been informed that she stays in great physical condition by running and exercising. Harden informs me that, since losing her father recently, Attorney Hayes has tutored her in small arms fire, in which she has qualified as expert, a significant accomplishment."

"Mrs. Hayes, if you still insist on accompanying this unit on its designated mission, you will undoubtedly need both of these skills. I, for one, feel that all we need to do is put a weapon in Kelly's hands and he will find a way of extricating himself from this situation. However, this time he does not need to do it alone. Our mission will be to bring him back with as little collateral damage as possible."

"I have complete faith in Chandler's ability and she will take the position of Delta One. Reynolds will be Delta Two. Sam, do you have our other participants standing by?"

"Yes, Sir. They are waiting right outside." Captain Blalock and Lieutenant Rasmussen jumped up as Sam opened the door and requested that they come on in. "All present, Sir."

"Stop calling me Sir…Anderson will do just fine. These two of our men have been stationed there with customary rank because of the potential need in that area. Their orders had officially transferred them back Stateside on the day of your mission up North, making them disappear on paper. Since they no longer exist in that area, we can put them back to work again. Agent Blalock will be identified on this mission as Delta Three and Rasmussen Four. As stated before you came in, Agent Chandler is in charge."

"Attorney Hayes was successful in passing the locator module to Kelly on his last visit. It is working and we know that his present location remains Towraghondi prison. When he is transferred tomorrow to his final destination, we will plan our move accordingly. Chambers will furnish all of you with the details of our operation when that location is known. We will refer to Mr. and Mrs. Hayes as Delta Five and Six respectively. Just one last reminder…absolutely no personal identification is to be carried on your person during this mission. Good Luck, Gentlemen."

Sam assumed her position. "Stand by, people. We will reconvene immediately upon word of the new location…and thanks for coming."

Looking in on Sanders as the meeting broke up; she was not surprised to find his office empty. As ordered, he was distancing himself from the newly formed team. As she, Conner and Ashley headed back to their quarters, Sam again turned anxiously to Ashley.

"You do not have to do this, Ashley. We have all been training all our lives for just such an incident. Even Conner received extensive training in individual combat maneuvers while at MANSCEN."

"I do need to, Samantha. Everything I do pales in comparison. I have an opportunity to accompany my husband and accomplish something really significant for a very dear friend. Nothing else matters right now. I will not get in the way and I am not afraid to use my handgun if necessary."

35

Mandrake heard the helicopter approaching and knew there was no other destination feasible on this desolate island. Anthony Riley was in his chair behind his desk. Quickly summoning Dixon to Mr. Riley's office, Mandrake drew his weapon and positioned himself on one side of the open French doors, with Dixon on the other side, both obscured by the drapery.

As soon as the helicopter sat down on the wide expanse of the stone courtyard, a heavyset man emerged from the front passenger seat. Dressed in a dark suit, his head adorned with the traditional kefiyyah, he began walking in the direction of the open doors. The pilot and another man followed on each side. The rotors continued spinning. Obviously, this was intended as a short visit.

As he neared the doorway, Saddam Akbar recognized Anthony Riley from the description passed on to him from his referral in New York. "I am Saddam Akbar and we need to talk." His agitation had built up on the flight over. His lower back was bothering him from sitting in that uncomfortable position for so long and, besides, he felt like he had every right to be mad. "Your product has cost me business and therefore has cost me money. Fifty of my customers have died using your TR7…maybe more. I want my money back and I want it NOW." Saddam Akbar was not adverse to exaggeration if it suited his needs.

Akbar had not even noticed the two armed men now behind them but his assistants had, as they fidgeted nervously, maneuvering their hands closer to their weapons.

Riley was caught completely by surprise at this accusation. He had never met Akbar but recognized his voice from their previous telephone conversations. "Calm down, calm down. What in the world are you talking about? Our product has been extensively tested and out in the market for years. If any fatalities were going to occur by its use, they would have happened long before now. Let me call my expert chemist in and he will be able to give you all the assurance you need."

Not wishing his two men to lose their advantageous positions, he simply paged Sean Pfister on his intercom.

Sean entered the room smiling, expecting more congratulatory praise from his employer. When the heavyset man glared in his direction, he almost collapsed. Now he wished that he had ignored the summons. "Yes, Sir. What can I do for you?" Managing a strong front, the quaver was still obvious in his words. *Did something go wrong? Did someone find out about the defect? It was insignificant…no one could possibly notice.*

"Sean, my customer here says there is something wrong with our TR7. I assured him that was not possible. Our product has been on the open market for over three years without a single complaint…and much praise. Please help me convince the man that the product is safe." Expecting an enthusiastic response, all Anthony received was an uncomfortable moment of silence.

"I assure you, Sir, that this product is safe. I have even tested it myself. The result should be a very pleasant high that rises for about ten minutes until it reaches its peak. No sickness or uncomfortable after effects follow the high. I do not understand the problem."

Since Anthony Riley was not rushing off to return his money, Saddam realized that he did not have the upper hand at the moment. "Here is a sample of the product that we have been pushing. Examine it and let me know then if there is a problem. If there are any more deaths among my customers, I will be back…and we will get this matter resolved." He threw the bag on the desk and turned to leave.

Anthony waited until the men had reached their helicopter before he spoke. "Now that we are alone, Sean, is there a problem that I do not know about? Speak freely. I do not want any more surprises."

Sean glanced at Mandrake, then at the crazy pilot. "No, Sir. I will take this sample and analyze it to let you know if it got contaminated."

"Do that, Sean." The hesitancy did not escape notice this time. *I thought he was just intimidated when he first came in. Maybe he knows of some problem and is afraid to tell me.* The ringing of his phone broke his concentration.

"Riley here." He recognized the other voice immediately.

"What's going on, Riley?" Tony Rubella was no longer taking the situation lightly. "I got a call from Akbar this morning…this afternoon I find that I am losing customers left and right. Seven deaths so far…the Feds have been called in to support the investigations in both New York and Chicago. We had to pull our stuff off the street before they got a hold of it. Tell me what is going on."

"We are investigating the problem ourselves at this very moment. Akbar came to see me a little while ago. He left a sample and we are analyzing it right now. I will get back with you later today, as soon as I have something."

"You better, Riley. I need answers. I have people to answer to as well. Let me hear from you today or you will hear from me tomorrow."

"Try to calm down, Tony…" Anthony realized he was talking to a dial tone.

"Mandrake, get Sean back in here."

36

Harden had to appear before the Judge to hear the predetermined sentence. "Harden Kelly, I hereby sentence you to death for crimes against the Afghan people. The sentence will be carried out one week from today at the Towraghondi prison complex as the Qur'an directs."

Walking quietly back to his cell, Harden had already made a mental picture of his surroundings and could call up any doorways or hallways at will. Now, sitting on his bunk in his cell, he moved his right foot inside his shoe to make certain that he could still feel the device he had put there earlier. There were always two or three policemen hanging around the office at the other end of the hall, only one outside his cell. Meals were served through a flat cut in the bars about waist high. The cell had no windows. The guard outside his cell was carrying a key ring on his belt loop. His only weapons were a pistol in a holster at his waist and a billy club hanging from a strap next to the holster.

This does not present an insurmountable problem but what would I do when I got out. The shortest route out of the country would be North to Turkmenistan...but then what would I do...best to wait a few days. Harden slouched his shoulders and hung his head, playing the part of a prisoner resigned to his fate.

The next day, he found that the meals had improved significantly. Evidently they fed condemned men very well. Even the water was served in capped bottles. Harden picked at the dry food then screwed the cap off the water, hesitating momentarily as the cap gave no initial resistance. Lifting the bottle to eye level, he could see it was full and had no discoloration. *Why would they poison me anyway? They are going to execute me next week.* He tasted the water, and then took a long drink. He did not want to get dehydrated, knowing he would need all his strength and alertness when the time came.

Abdullah Amin strode purposefully down the hall. Two heavily armed men accompanied him. All were dressed casually. The guard was not at his post, nor was there any in the office down the hall. Turning the key, the cell door opened with a squeal. It did not wake the reclining Harden Kelly. *The big fool drank the water.* He motioned to his accomplices and they pulled Harden from the bunk, looping one of his arms around each of their shoulders. With the initial weight of the man, they both fell backward and were sitting on the bunk, Harden slumped between them. Pulling the right hand of one man and the left of the other, Amin soon had them upright again. The men groaned and complained all the way down the hall and out the door to the waiting van.

After managing to set their prisoner on the edge of the van floor, one man jumped into the truck and pulled him by both arms until he cleared the rear doors. He jumped back out and locked both doors before joining the other two on the front seat. "What are you doing up here? What if he wakes up?" Amin was disappointed with his men. They did not think.

"That's the problem. I do not want to be there if he wakes up." Maybe they were thinking after all. Amin just snorted in disgust.

Obviously Amin had spent a great deal of money to clear the jail complex so he could abduct the prisoner. Now they were taking the short drive to his home just South of Herat.

* * *

The team headed by Sam Chandler was housed in a deserted residence in Towraghondi, studying maps and watching the monitor. "Hey, he's moving." Charlie Reynolds was charged with watching the screen. The locator dot started moving slowly southward on the screen.

"OK, let's mobilize." All six members grabbed their gear and hastened to their SUV. Conner and Ashley sat in the rear seats, with Blalock and Rasmussen in front of them. Reynolds drove, as Sam, following the moving dot, acted as co-pilot. She directed Charlie through the maze of streets to the highway south, constantly following the beacon. Reynolds maintained a safe distance, realizing that, if they could see the vehicle that they were following, that vehicle could see them. There was no way they were going to lose them anyway. They were hoping to avoid collateral damage completely and, therefore, did not want to confront the Afghan Police, preferring to wait until they arrived at their final destination.

When they bypassed Herat, Sam became suspicious of that destination. According to the map on the locator, the vehicle they were pursuing stopped at the housing complex where the incident originated.

"Something has gone wrong. Those can't be Police we are following. They would not take a condemned prisoner to a residence the week before his scheduled execution. Pull over where we parked for the drug operation."

She had to show Charlie where to park as he had not been on the first visit to this location. "Since you are familiar with the point of entry used before, Jim, why don't you and Andy lead? Charlie and I will follow close behind. I will have the locator until we pick up their exact destination. We do not want to lose them now. Ashley, why don't you and Conner guard the vehicle?"

Conner and Ashley objected simultaneously. "You do not know how many men you will be facing. We will take up the rear. We will not interfere with your operation. Ashley and I can take care of ourselves."

The hole under the fence had not even been filled in…access was simple. Rasmussen ran a small metal detector over the surface before entering to detect any booby traps. Then he enlarged the opening to facilitate a quicker departure if necessary. After they were all on the inside of the compound, Sam took the lead.

The previous mission proved to have been an unqualified success as they passed through the rubble. Judging from all the crushed pipe and equipment, the lab had evidently taken up most of the garage area. There were also the remains of two vehicles. The stench remained...the unmistakable odor of burnt opium.

The back of the house stood before them. There was a van parked by a rear entrance.

37

Sean, I want you to find out what is wrong with the TR7 that you have manufactured here at your new lab." Anthony Riley was worried. These men did not make idle threats.

"Mandrake, you will see that he goes directly to the lab and starts to work analyzing the problem...then return here."

When both men had left the office, Anthony made his way over to his wall safe. Since there had been two recent transactions, there were over forty thousand one hundred dollar bills still in the safe. As he was mentally projecting his next move, Mandrake returned. "He is back in his lab working. You scared him, Mr. Riley. He won't let up now until he finds the answer or you have left the house."

"Good, Mandrake, good. Now, help me put this cash back into these two large briefcases." The cases were bulging and heavy when the task was done. "Lay them on my desk, Mandrake...then I want you to pack all my things, and yours as well. We are moving again. This time Sean will stay here. Do not let him know what is happening. You have about two hours before we take off."

Mandrake was not particularly surprised by the move, just the urgency of it. He and Dixon had witnessed the Iraqi man's threat. Hesitant about mentioning Chrisimminia...Mr. Riley was too agitated right now...Mandrake hurried off to do as he was instructed.

Riley was already back at his desk on the phone. "James, I need the helicopter ready to go in two hours. Pack all your belongings as this will be an extended trip. Also, file a flight plan with the Beirut Airport for our jet to leave Lebanese air space as soon as we arrive. I do not care what destination you use to accomplish this, just head west. Have it fueled and ready to go. I will let you know our final destination later. Arrange for storage for the helicopter indefinitely."

Dixon was excited. There was nothing to do on Ramkin Island except visit the small seaside village and drink and gamble with the locals. *I hope this time it is a larger city where I can have something to do and make some plans now that I have a little money to do it with.* Dixon, as well, had been instructed not to discuss this with anyone.

Sean was working feverishly in his lab when Mr. Riley suddenly appeared. "Sean, I need to fly over to the mainland for a while. Keep working on this problem and keep me up to date on the results by way of my cell phone. Do not leave the Island until you hear from me."

"Yes, Sir." With his self confidence dissipating quickly, the beleaguered chemist did not know what else to say. Anthony's eyes scanned the growing inventory of plastic cartons full of TR7 with mixed emotions. *All wasted…Sean let something go wrong when he set the process up here. There is some kind of problem with the product…people are dying. I ought to make him use the stuff on himself to see what happens…tempting, tempting.* Already writing off the loss, Anthony left the room. *When whoever comes sees that he is still working in his lab, they will not suspect that we have gone, at least not right away.*

Two hours after instructing Dixon, Mandrake was walking to the aircraft beside Mr. Riley. *It is now or never.* "Mr. Riley, since Sean is not going with us, I asked Chrisimminia to come with me. We are going to get married. We can both still work for you just like now." The big man was almost shaking after his unexpected request. Chris was nervously waiting at the helicopter for her man to arrive, carrying a small bag containing all her belongings.

The possibility had already passed through his mind after seeing them together earlier so Anthony was able to suppress his surprise at the request. He looked into his assistant's eyes and could see how much this meant to him. *I need him and she is already familiar with my condition and my requirements. Maybe this will work out for the better...I am sorry I did not think of it myself.* Graciously, he assented to the request. "She is your responsibility, Mandrake. You will have to make certain that she does not get in the way of any of our operations."

Mandrake was instantly relieved. He put his huge arm around Chris's shoulders. "Yes, Sir. Yes, Sir. No problem. Right, Chrisimminia?" She nodded vigorously in agreement.

Anthony looked back at the mansion as they veered away from the Island, facing the inevitable, but regretting the necessity of leaving his ideal refuge by the Sea. *I can sell the place later if we are unable to return. I hope there is something left to sell after our visitors arrive tomorrow.*

Dixon again proved his efficiency as everything was arranged at the Airport by the time they arrived. His corporate jet from the Brantley Chemical era was fueled and ready to go. They boarded immediately, with Mandrake putting the most valuable pieces of luggage right beside his employer's wheelchair. The cabin of the jet had originally been custom equipped with wheel locks that snapped into place as the chair moved into position. Anthony much preferred, even required, the comfort of his self designed chair which accommodated his twisted body better than the most luxurious of airplane seating.

As Mr. Riley had instructed him to file a flight plan somewhere to the West, Jim Dixon had chosen Madrid, Spain. Now, heading West over the Mediterranean Sea, he needed a more specific destination. "Where to, Sir?"

"Our destination, Gentlemen, is Roseau, Dominica."

384

38

Harden tested the handcuffs while he eyed his three captors whispering together in the corner of the room. He had watched to see which man put the key in his pocket…the tall thin man…right front pocket. Cuffed to a small wooden chair, Harden saw no problem breaking the chair arm if he could get the right angle for a good kick. In order to do this, the men would have to leave the room for a few seconds. *This looked like some kind of setup all along. These men are certainly not Afghan Police…not even military. That guy who was watching me during the trial is obviously in charge. He is so full of hate that he must be the leader of this drug lab…sorry to bust up your business, Bud.* Harden half-chuckled to himself, the only restraint being the fact that he knew they intended to kill him.

Just then, the fourth man, the leader, came back into the room. He was smiling this time, an evil smirk, a vengeful smirk. "You destroyed my business, friend, but that I can rebuild. The reason I have you here is because you left my 2004 Phantom and 2001 Mercedes a pile of burned and twisted metal." The anger was returning. "For this, you must die. I just have not figured out your method of execution. Maybe I should have simply left you for the executioner and watched the show. No, I could not do that. I want you to know that it was me, Abdullah Amin, who arranged your death. Everyone will know what fate will face the person who interferes with Amin."

He turned to the other three men. "Ali, go and watch the back of the house."

Harden watched the man leave before responding to Amin. He knew that he needed to stall for time and playing to this man's ego seemed like the obvious path to take.

"So you are the head man here. What do your bosses have to say about losing your lab and warehouse? That was a big warehouse...probably lost a lot of stock, as well. You are not in very good standing with them right now, I would guess."

"I am the boss. I run this entire operation." Harden had hit the right button. "When we get finished with you, we may dump you on their doorstep down there at Shindand to show the world that they cannot mess with Amin."

Harden could see behind the mask. Amin was worried about answering to somebody for this disruption. "They are putting a lot of pressure on you, aren't they? But you didn't let them know how bad the damage was...you are out of business, Amin. If you start this back up, we will destroy it before you even release your first shipment."

"Shut up! Quit talking or I will just shoot you right now." For all his anti American spiel, Amin pulled his American made Stealth Warthog from his waistband and waved it in Harden's direction. Harden immediately noticed the new handgun's smooth black finish and night sights. *These guys are well equipped. No wonder he is so upset...no more cash coming in for a while. I had better change the subject.*

"You had quite a business here, Amin. Where do you have to ship? Is it in Kuwait or even further?" Harden thought that if he could get the man bragging about his operation, he may reveal more information.

"You bet I have a good business...over a million dollars a month. My customers can depend on me. Those Umm Qasr brokers think they own me...I own them." Amin was emphatic. "They couldn't make it without me. You Americans think you are some big deal. In my country, I am a big deal. I am an important man. I have influence...as you have found out. That piece of shit, Haddiq, thinks being Minister of Light Industry makes him a big man. He would not be there if not for me. That man owes me for everything he has. I put him there. He was just a washed up, drunken Attorney when I decided he could be of some use to me."

Evidently, Harden had managed to push the right buttons. *That explains how Amin was able to trump up these phony charges against me. Haddiq is just one of his pawns. I guess being three hundred miles west of Kabul pretty much gives him free reign.*

His thoughts were interrupted by the sudden ringing of a cell phone. Amin pulled it from his pocket. "Hello." He growled into the speaker.

"Amin, this is Saddam. I am having trouble with another supplier and I need your help. How soon can you supply me...same quantity, same price? I will take care of my other problem, but I need delivery this week." Saddam Akbar was in a bind. His voice had mellowed since his previous conversation.

Amin was surprised with the sudden request. Immediately, he began to register all the equipment he needed to order and then assemble before he could again begin producing. He could not admit over the phone that he could not meet the order. The American was listening. *I cannot let him know that he put me out of business.* "Give me a week...I will take care of it." *How am I going to do it? It will take longer than that to get the equipment I need...then I need the farmers to bring me more raw materials.*

If I cannot get it together by then, I will just buy finished product from Younis Stanzai in Zaranj. We have both done this before.

Amin was still standing too close to Harden, mumbling to himself. Harden was able to catch some of it...enough to know that Amin was in trouble. Also, he overheard the name Younis Stanzai in Zaranj as the drug supplier continued to mumble to himself. *That gives us another target if I ever get out of here.* Harden was trying to determine whether he needed to make a move now or if Anderson would have a team here soon.

39

Two helicopters were coming in fast and loud on the tiny island, landing quickly on the helipad which Anthony had built. Three heavily armed men emerged immediately from the first unit and two from the second. Saddam Akbar followed at a safe distance as his men entered the mansion. When they met no resistance, the drug lord entered Anthony Riley's office only to find it deserted.

"Search along the walls for a safe, behind pictures or whatever."

I want my money and I am going to get it one way or the other. "Find Riley or somebody. I need some answers."

Within minutes his men returned. A severely frightened Sean Pfister was held in tow by one of the men. Another had the puzzled, but resigned, Lobeth by the arm. She was accustomed to hardships and viewed this as just another piece of life gone rotten. Not knowing whether to fear rape, a beating or even death, Lobeth resigned herself to her fate. She was not strong enough physically or mentally to fight back.

"Where is Riley?" Saddam glanced from one to the other. Deciding that the man in the white lab coat presented the best opportunity, he focused his attention in that direction.

"I don't know. He said he had to go to the mainland for a while. Ask Mandrake. I don't know anything." Sean's quivering voice had raised several decibels under the circumstances. His knees would probably give way if the rough man holding him ever released his grip.

"Who is Mandrake…and where is he?" Sensing that he had already frightened the man enough, Saddam Akbar softened his tone somewhat. Directing his attention once again to his own men, he asked. "Are you certain there is no one else on the grounds?"

"Not unless they are hiding somewhere…there are no signs of anyone else on the premises. I would think our approach was too sudden and would preclude having time to think about concealing themselves. My men have covered the entire facility." His Lieutenant had evidently made a thorough search.

Akbar turned back to the trembling man in the white coat. "I need to talk to Mr. Riley. If this Mandrake can help me find him, then I need to talk to him, *now. Where is he?*" The emphasis on the question only served to make the already woozy Pfister pass out completely, falling limp in his captor's grip.

After easily rolling a chest, which covered part of the wall, out of the way, another man was calling to Saddam. "I found the safe. It is a big one and it is locked. We will have to blow it unless we find someone with the combination."

Saddam Akbar's eyes lit up at the size of the monstrosity before him.

"Throw some water in his face and see if he can open this. That maid certainly can't…and try to find this Mandrake. When that little guy wakes up, treat him nicer. We may get more out of him if he is conscious." Saddam had to pull a chair over to sit at Anthony's desk. Then he remembered that the wheelchair had been the man's desk chair.

He began to shuffle through the papers on the desk, looking for a clue as to Riley's whereabouts, when Pfister regained consciousness. "Young man, we need you to open this safe for us. Mr. Riley owes me some money and I assure you I will only take the amount that is due me if you open this safe."

"Mmmr. Riley never trusted me with the combination, Sir," stuttered the wobbly lab man. "I just work as his chemist…" Sean regretted the word as soon as it came out of his mouth. *My God, what have I done? This is surely the man who complained about people dying. Oh my God!*

His fears were not wasted. Saddam came out of his chair. "You are the chemist...you are the one who produced the TR7?" Saddam Akbar suddenly realized that the man standing before him was the one responsible for producing the product that killed many of his customers...the one responsible for his huge financial loss. He was fuming. Saddam turned and stared out the rear window as he contemplated his next step. If he faced that man another second, he would have circled the desk and torn his throat out with his bare hands.

"The woman says that Mandrake left with Riley, the pilot and one of the other maids earlier today. There never was anyone else living or working on the estate according to her." Though his Lieutenant spoke the bad news to his back, it nevertheless served to calm his thoughts. With the facts before him, Saddam could now rationalize his thinking.

"We will wait two more hours to see if Riley returns. Get some plastic from the chopper so we can blow the safe if he does not come back.

That would damage some of the contents so we wait the two hours before getting drastic. If he does not return, Riley has no doubt emptied the safe anyway. Now, let's get some use out of the woman...something to eat and drink while we wait. Tie that wimp to a chair where I can see him." When he motioned in Sean's direction, the poor man almost fainted again. Saddam again sat behind the desk, searching its contents for a clue.

Upon shading the imprints on the next page of the pad lying on the desk, he was disappointed to find only Riley's request for dinner that night. Nothing in the drawers shed any light on the situation either. Saddam decided to take a look at the lab. Impressed with the number of full containers waiting to be shipped, Saddam had arrived at a scheme to try to regain some of his lost funds. Returning to the desk, he directed one last question at the cowering chemist.

"Riley says he has been selling this TR7 for over three years. What is wrong with your current batch? What did you change?"

Maybe with some information he could appease the man somewhat.

"I do not know. That is what Mr. Riley told me to work on this afternoon. Give me some more time in my lab and I can probably figure it out." Sean hoped to be free of his captors long enough to get away from this horrible place. His ruse apparently worked.

"Untie him and let him return to the lab. Have someone stay with him all the time. You have two hours, Mr. Chemist." Saddam dialed his cell phone, apparently finished with that problem for now.

"Good Morning, Mr. Rubella." A quick calculation plus previous experience told him that it was still morning in New York. "I have come into several more containers of Riley's TR7 and I was wondering if you had any interest in taking it off my hands at a good price. I have more product than I have customers at the present."

"You son of a bitch…trying to unload tainted goods on me. My customers have been dying all across the country now and I have been forced to shut down and reopen with local stuff. I will remember this, Saddam. My men are on their way to visit Riley as we speak." Rubella hung up on him before he had time to utter another word.

To his Lieutenant…"We have to get out of here, now. Blow that safe immediately. Drop that chemist over the cliff or something. He cost me much money."

Faking a trip to the restroom, Sean exited through the adjoining bedroom and was running across the lawn in the direction of the village when one of the men spotted him. Grabbing a scoped rifle from the chopper, the man found Sean in the crosshairs and pulled off two shots.

Sean felt the push and heat from the first shot and managed not to fall until the second blast hit him. As he fell to the ground, his puzzled eyes dropped to the two round red holes in his chest. The last thing he heard was a thunderous blast coming from the house.

"It is open, Sir." The man stepped aside for his leader to enter.

Swatting away at the smoke and dust, Saddam knew as the dust cleared that his efforts were worth nil. The shelves were empty. *Riley has no intention of returning. I ought to blow this whole place to pieces so he can't sell it for even more profit. Wait a minute. That may well be our opportunity to find him. If he lists this property anywhere in the future, I will find him.* "Let's get out of here fast." He raced to the helicopter.

"What about the woman." By this time Lobeth was resigned to her fate. She had overheard the death sentence issued for the chemist and feared that she would fare no better.

"Leave her...she is of no use to us." Saddam Akbar was not in the habit of killing innocent people who had no effect on his business. Vicious czar that he was, it was all about business.

The two helicopters departed simultaneously leaving the stunned Lobeth behind.

40

After motioning Blalock and Rasmussen to move to the front of the house, Sam and Charlie approached the back door evidently used by the men who had custody of Harden. They were followed closely by Conner and Ashley. All had their weapons drawn as Sam tested the knob to see if the door was locked.

The knob turned easily in her grip as the door swung open without an alarm going off or even a squeak to alert anyone in the house. The locator beckoned them toward the front and off to the right. Quietly, she and Charlie led the irregular rescue team across the room. Conner gently closed the door before preceding Ashley, following closely behind Charlie Reynolds. Ashley took up the rear of the entourage.

Suddenly, Ashley was grabbed from behind so roughly that her shirt was torn and her bra snapped open revealing her right breast. The man had one hand around her neck and a pistol pointed at her head as the others turned. "Drop your weapons, *now*, or I will shoot her." At the shock of being attacked from behind, Ashley had dropped her weapon to the thickly carpeted floor.

Sam and the others lowered their weapons slightly, without dropping them as she analyzed the situation. The bearded, rough looking Arab had the advantage with a choking arm gripped around her friend's neck. She knew she could hit him with one shot but would his reaction be fatal to Ashley as well. Her marksmanship had brought her high honors when first enduring the rigorous training required of recruited operatives. She could put a shot between those dark foreboding eyes but with what consequences. Anderson had warned her of the risk of taking civilians on this mission…any mission. She had no choice at the time…she would have had to use force to keep them from accompanying her.

Seeing that he had them at bay for the moment, Ali let his eyes drop to the exposed breast. *I hope I do not have to kill this one. There are much better things we could do. She is a beauty, such curves.* Ali was letting himself become aroused by this distraction.

Feeling that she had failed Samantha, she had now let herself become a liability to the mission. The determined Ashley recovered from her initial shock. Knowing her weapon was out of reach, she looked for any other advantage she could find. Feeling the man's hot breath on her neck as his gun hand descended to her breast brushing her exposed nipple back and forth with the cold steel, Ashley put her left fist into her right hand and, exerting all the strength she could muster, forced her right elbow around smashing Ali in the right side of his jaw. The stunned man staggered back. Charlie was on him in an instant, slamming his fist into the left side of his face. Ashley turned away as Charlie grabbed the man around the neck just as the man had controlled her. She did not want to watch but as she turned away, she was able to hear the muffled crunch as the man fell silently to the floor.

* * *

"Badi, see what Ali is doing out there. He is making too much noise. Tell him to be quiet or he will be no good to us." Amin strode over to the handcuffed man in the chair, still with his Stealth Warthog waving through the air with every gesture. "You are no longer of any use to me. Look into the bore. See the bullet that will be coming at you shortly. See the blackness of death." The man was enjoying his taunting, salivating over his revenge. Instead of looking at the weapon, Harden looked into the man's eyes. A person's intentions are first revealed in their eyes and he wanted to know the most advantageous moment at which to hurl the chair at the ranting drug dealer.

* * *

Just as Badi opened the door to step into the other room, Jim Blalock had come down the hall from the front of the house and slammed him on the back of his skull with his Smith & Wesson 45. Rasmussen followed closely behind and quietly closed the door as Blalock's arm rose into the air. Hoping that no one on the other side of the door had noticed anything out of the ordinary, Blalock quickly dragged Badi to one side. He and Rasmussen stood guard at each side of the door with weapons ready just as Sam was leading the rest of the team down the hall, following the locator signal. She raised her right arm, motioning first to the device and then to the door, indicating that this room was their objective.

Ashley had recovered now and had secured the button on her torn shirt, repairing the damage momentarily. After the harrowing experience, she was surprised at the calm that had come over her as she followed the lead and pressed herself against the wall awaiting the next move. Conner was at her side and reached down to squeeze her hand just for a second. She gave him an acknowledging nod of her head as they watched Sam intently.

Sam motioned Rasmussen to follow her down the hallway toward the front of the house. Whispering quietly, she handed him a headset for communications. As she snapped her own over her ear she motioned for him to do the same. "Go back outside. Surely there is a window to this room. See if you can locate it and see what is going on in there. How many men and their exact location. Let us know before we break in on them. You will have a vantage point to cover us from the outside. Don't expose your position by shattering the window until you feel that the time is right. Let me know when you have any information." She returned to her position just outside the door. Even listening carefully, with her ear to the door, any sounds from inside were muffled by the heavy oak. *Hurry, Andy, hurry.*

The minute it took Rasmussen to reach the outside of the window seemed like hours to the worried Samantha. "I am in position. I see two subjects besides Kelly. He is seated in a small wooden chair, sort of sideways cuffed to the arm of the chair. This one guy looks disturbed…has a gun pointed right in Kelly's face."

"What is the position of the other man?"

"He is right next to the door, opposite the doorknob. He would be behind the door if you were to open it." Rasmussen was being very specific so not to confuse rights and lefts from a different perspective.

"Are you sure there are only two obstacles?"

"I can't be sure. The drapes are shielding part of the room from my view. Let me try to change my angle." Again, interminable silence. "OK, I got a look at the rest of the room by moving around a little…just two, but that one guy has a gun right on Kelly. Do not break in yet. It looks like he is talking to Kelly…the man looks wild. He may be ready to shoot him. Wait! Kelly appears to be talking to him now."

"Let us know if the man lowers the gun and we will come in immediately. We know the other man's position. You never did tell us the exact location of Harden and the man with the pistol."

"As you enter the room, they are both directly in front of you. Kelly is facing the door, seated in the chair. This other guy has his back to the door but is between Kelly and the door."

"Just say the word 'Now' at the exact moment, then break the window and take your best shot. We will be in there at the next sound of your voice."

"Jim, when we go in, you take the man to the right. He may be behind the door as we open it. I will take the man directly ahead. You two keep us covered in case there are more than two adversaries in the house. When I get the signal, we must be quick."

Sa-ina Kalemi had heard the unusual commotion from her bedroom and had been standing in the hallway upstairs just out of sight. She had witnessed the episode in which Ali met his fate and smiled inwardly. These men had all treated her badly ever since they had taken over her house. Now, she needed to know what was happening. With bare feet, she silently crept down the stairs far enough to peer around the jutting wall. She sat on the stairs as far down as she dared…and waited.

Sa-ina was not as discreet as she had intended to be. Sam had first noticed her as they made their way down the hallway after Ashley was freed. Now, without looking directly in her direction, she saw the frightened woman was crouched on the stairs anxiously watching their every move. The woman certainly posed no threat.

They watched and waited.

41

Back home again, the frustrated Saddam Akbar was leafing through Riley's telephone directory, looking for a clue to his whereabouts.

He had already called the Beirut Airport and bribed the flight controller into revealing Riley's flight plan…Madrid, Spain. *There has to be a better way to trap this guy.* He continued to flip carefully through the directory.

Sara Naiser, real estate agent…The name leaped out at him. *This is how I will find him.* Akbar smiled inwardly.

"Could I speak with Sara Naiser, please?" Using as pleasant a voice as he could manage, Saddam was initiating his plan.

"Sara, here. How can I help you?" A firm feminine voice came on the line.

"I am an acquaintance of Mr. Anthony Riley and I am interested in property in your area. I am particularly interested in Ramkin Island. Riley's place intrigued me so much that I would very much like to purchase his estate if it should ever become available."

Sara searched her memory banks and had no trouble remembering the twisted man in his wheel chair and the croaking voice which had actually frightened her upon initial contact. "Always happy to be of service, Sir. Could I have your name please, and your phone number?"

Saddam was prepared. He furnished her with a different number then the one Anthony had used. "My name is Abdul Haddiq." The first name that came to his mind was the weakling pawn of Abdullah Amin. *She certainly will not recognize that name.* "I would appreciate a call if Mr. Riley is ever interested in selling that property. You will let me know right away, won't you?" The powerful drug czar surprised even himself sometimes with how gracious he could be when he wished.

Not realizing that the Riley property may be eminently available, Sara tried to interest her buyer in other property. "I certainly will, Mr. Haddiq. If you do not care to wait for that particular property, I have many other choice parcels available right now. There are several more old home sites on Ramkin Island. They are old mansions and need a lot of work but the price is right and they have large lots."

"I appreciate your time, Sara, but I am infatuated with Riley's layout and would prefer to wait until his becomes available. He had indicated to me that he may be moving soon. Let me know if you here from him in this regard. I will see that you are well rewarded personally for your efforts."

Sara was surprised to hear about the Riley property possibly becoming available again so soon. "Oh, Mr. Haddiq, I will certainly call you as soon as I hear something." At the mention of a possible additional bonus, her ever sweet voice had become even more gushing.

"Thank you, Sara. Be sure you let me know exclusively…remember, you will be well rewarded for this information. Goodbye, for now."

Sara immediately dialed Anthony Riley's number. A woman answered in a hesitant voice. "Mr. Riley's residence." Lobeth was shaking. She did not know what to expect now. Mr. Pfister was still lying out on the ground where he had tried to run away from those men. She had been afraid to go out there. *What should I do! What should I do!*

"I am trying to reach Mr. Riley. Is he there?"

Upon hearing the other woman's voice, Lobeth began to get some control of herself finally. "Mr. Riley is not here right now. He was called away on business. Can I have him return your call?"

"Yes, please ask him to call Sara Naiser when you hear from him. He has my number. Thank you."

Lobeth printed the name on the pad lying on Mr. Riley's desk and hung up the phone. Composing herself somewhat, she devised a plan. *I will get Mosa to help me when she arrives. We could live here. I think Mr. Riley is gone for good. She will help me drag Mr. Pfister to the cliff. No one will ever find him…no one will even look for him. There is enough food stored in that pantry to last a year.* Visions of this unforeseen good fortune danced before her eyes. *We earned it. We both earned it…waiting on that horrible old man.* She was now twisting the facts to suit her fancy. Anthony had actually been extremely appreciative of their response to his requirements and had extended generous bonuses to all three of them at intervals to express that appreciation and to encourage them to stay.

When Mosa arrived promptly at seven that evening, Lobeth revealed her plan, describing the afternoon's activity. Mosa was at first shocked at the idea, then, after looking around her at the luxurious appointments that the place had to offer, she decided to go along with her friend's arrangement. "I will just tell that no good husband of mine that I have the opportunity to work double shifts since Chris ran off. He never even knows whether I am gone or not anyway."

Lobeth and Mosa were simple people, but hardworking. This did not seem complicated. They would just take up permanent residence until Mr. Riley returned or someone else ran them off. After all, they had not received any severance pay or notification so they did have the right to be on the premises.

Sean Pfister had been a thin young man and the two healthy women had no problem dragging him to the edge of the cliff where the drop off was over a hundred feet straight down to the breaking water. First glance had repulsed them, but they quickly accepted the two holes in his chest with now dried blood spread across his white lab coat. As they were nearing the edge, another helicopter circled and approached the helipad near the house.

Al Molini had never been to Riley's house before but had very specific directions. The pilot had no problem flying them over from the mainland. "Wait here. We won't be long." After directing the pilot to wait for them, Al, Joey Gondolfo and one more man sent along for additional muscle, strolled quickly to the open French doors. Upon entering the office, Al immediately noticed the obviously blown safe to his left. Motioning his men to draw their weapons, he peered at the empty interior of the safe. "Somebody beat us here." He spoke aloud but to no one in particular...more of an exclamation. "See if you can find anyone...anyone at all...and bring them here.

The men went off in different directions while Al, duplicating his predecessor's moves, rifled through the desk and its contents. Five minutes later, the two men returned having found no one else on the premises. "It is deserted, Boss. We spotted two ladies over by the cliff. They were just looking over here, probably curious about what we are doing." Joey had not been able to see the body lying between the ladies in the tall grass. "There are at least eight more containers of that stuff we got last time in some kind of makeshift lab, but no one is around. That stuff isn't worth anything. Is it, Boss?"

Al Molini did not take time to discuss important decisions with Joey Gondolfo. He was already dialing Tony Rubella to report. "Tony, the place is deserted, safe is blown, nothing left in it, no money anywhere. There is a large batch of TR7. Do you want us to bring it back with us?"

"Absolutely not, Al. That kind of inventory could tie us to multiple murder raps." Tony paused to think over the situation. "Find Riley's quarters and do a thorough search. There may be something of value there.

You can also ascertain whether the man has left for good or not. If you find anything worthwhile, call me back. Otherwise, just get out of there quickly."

Lobeth and Mosa anxiously watched as one of the men gave them a long look before reentering the building. Al and his assistants found nothing in the master bedroom. *Riley must know that stuff in the lab is worse than worthless. He took everything else of value.*

"Let's go, men." Al hated the fact that he had found nothing, not even a little something for himself. As they passed through the office on their way back to their transportation, he noticed the bar was still stocked. Quickly returning to the lab, he picked up an empty carton that he had noticed earlier. Selecting only unopened bottles, Al was beaming at this collection of expensive liquor. "Earl, carry this to the helicopter for me while I check the desk one more time."

Besides the convenience of having his assistant carry the heavy box, Al did think of one more thing that could be important. He looked all over the desk and the drawers but could not find any kind of telephone index or register. *Strange. He must have thought to take that with him. I thought that would score good with Tony. Oh, well!"* Grabbing the notepad with one name on it, he rushed out to the helipad and motioned for the pilot to go.

The two women waited until the helicopter was completely out of sight before continuing with their task. Since the man was quite thin, they had no problem swinging his arms and legs in an arc away from the edge and down to the angry sea below.

Mosa was upset. She had seen the heavy carton the man was carrying out of the building and was anxious to get back in there to see if her fears were justified. She ran immediately to Anthony's well stocked liquor cabinet, only to find all the prized bottles were missing. Unlike Al Molini, however, she was not about to dispose of any open containers or lesser valued liquor. Although extremely disappointed, she was happy to see that there was still a good quantity remaining for her and Lobeth.

42

"Badi, get back in here." Harden could see that Abdullah Amin was becoming a little nervous with only one man as backup. Without lowering his weapon or taking his eyes off Harden, he spoke quietly to his remaining accomplice, almost in a whisper. "Arif, lock that door, now."

Without question, Arif turned the deadbolt control and heard it click into place. The clicking sound was not lost on the waiting rescue team.

"Oh, oh, this may slow us down." Sam was whispering to the rest of the team. "Charlie, be prepared to put your foot against that part of the door when we get the signal. That means you will enter first so you take the man with the gun on Harden. I will take the other guy on the right. Harden may be in a direct line as you enter. Be careful."

Turning to her headset, she whispered. "Andy, they locked the door...must be getting suspicious. Keep in touch."

"I saw that. One of the men is still waving his weapon in front of Harden's face. He yelled something at the other guy before he locked the door."

"We heard that. He must have been calling out to one of these men that we have put out of commission. If you see an opportunity to take them without getting Harden killed, go for it."

Amin was becoming worried. "Arif, call out to Badi and Ali to come back in here…something is wrong." Arif shouted loudly for the two men but got no response. As his man yelled out to the other two, Amin crooked his head slightly, listening intently. Harden took advantage of the aversion to swing his chair off the floor and send it crashing in to the right side of Amin. With his prized Stealth Warthog sent flying across the room, Amin's right arm would not respond, hanging uselessly at his side.

While Harden sent the chair crashing against the other assailant, Amin ran for the bathroom. There was another entrance from the connecting room which also led to the hallway. At Harden's sudden movement, Rasmussen shouted, "Now," as he came crashing through the window. Reynolds almost simultaneously kicked the door in right at the lock location, catching Arif full in the back as he was veering back from Harden's assault. Sam followed Charlie into the room, followed quickly by the other three.

Quickly assessing the situation, it was obvious that Harden had taken care of the two men himself. "You OK, Hard?"

"Yeah…get that other man. He is their leader…went through that bathroom over there." Harden was pointing as best he could with the chair still dangling from his outstretched arms. Sam raced through the other door but the man was gone. "Jim, Andy, see if you can find him outside somewhere. I will try to follow him this way." She disappeared the same direction as Amin had a moment earlier.

Charlie was searching Arif for a key to the cuffs which still inhibited Harden from participating in the search. In his right front pocket were numerous coins…and a key. As the cuffs and the chair fell to the floor, the big man stretched his long arms to loosen the joints at the same time crossing the room to pick up the abandoned Warthog. Checking the clip, he followed the path which Sam had just taken.

* * *

Realizing that he could not get far with his right arm broken, Amin waited behind a large chifforobe, evidently designed for holding the coats and wraps of visiting guests, just inside the front door of the mansion. He heard the sounds of his pursuer carefully making his way in this direction.

With only the use of his left hand, he unfettered the blade from its leather sheath. *Allah. What did I do wrong? First, my orders are cut back by Akbar because he found another supplier. Then, my factory is destroyed, my inventory burned. My life is being destroyed by this devil infidel.* Amin refused to acknowledge the fact in his own mind that his avenging wrath was his downfall. For some reason, orders were flowing again from Akbar and the plant could be quickly rebuilt in order to commence business as usual. The money would flow again. *Even if it costs me my life, I must see that man dead.* Amin could not free his demons.

Stealthy footsteps approached. With her weapon drawn and ready, Sam's eyes drifted around the room as she approached the front door. Giving wide berth to the colossal antique chest standing in the hallway, she checked to her left before moving sideways in to the living room. With both hands on her weapon, she edged around until she could have full view of the rest of the hallway.

Trained reflexes did not desert her, as the bearded man lunged clumsily in her direction with a knife held high over his head. Her first shot was directly on target but the wild man kept coming. She squeezed once more on the trigger and the man finally swayed backward and with one last push swung the knife in a downward arc well short of its objective. Amin was a victim of his own mindless vengeance. The last thing Amin saw before making the final lunge was his own prized Stealth Warthog in the hands of the devil infidel. In the slow motion of inevitable death, he could see the missile approaching from the smoking weapon as he raised his blade for one last gasping attempt. He could get no closer as both bullets seemed to enter at the same time, freezing him in place, one from his own weapon.

Samantha did not take her eyes from the man on the floor as Harden draped his arm around her shoulders and gently nudged her against his chest. "You alright, Hon?" Finally allowing herself to feel the relief at seeing her husband again at her side, she holstered her weapon and let his arms now encircle her. She put her arms around his waist and pulled him close as the others began to gather in the hallway.

At the sound of shots, Andy and Jim burst through the front door and realized immediately that the rescue was complete. Charlie had followed

Harden as he ran in search of Amin and had witnessed his demise. Ashley and Conner crossed the room and stood beside their good friends as their nerves began to unwind. The sight of Samantha and Harden defused the tension that had held their muscles taut for the last several hours. A sense of relief flowed through them.

43

Lewis and Long. Only a month or two since they died. They were the best I could have hoped for…but difficult to control. Anthony Riley was sitting at a desk in his room at the Fort Young Hotel in Roseau, Dominica. He had heard of this place from his two former employees. The convenience of the location as well as the seclusion brought the place immediately to mind when another move was forced upon him

I have some very powerful enemies, now, and those two could make up for ten Mandrakes. Well, we carefully covered our path. No one should be looking for us here on Roseau.

Just before departing Ramkin Island, Anthony had made certain that Sean Pfister had run a copy of the TR7 formula for himself and given the original to Mr. Riley. Now, with the document spread before him, he tried to determine what problem could possibly have occurred when Sean started producing a new batch in his makeshift lab. Just before he resigned himself to the fact that he would never know the answer, he held the paper up to the light. Possibly something had escaped his attention. As he lowered the formula from the light, he noticed a decimal point between two zeros in the formula.

That is odd. Why not just leave off one of the zeros. Then he noticed that there seemed to be some surface to the decimal point. With his middle finger, he scraped at the dot and it popped off the sheet. . .a piece of dirt or grime or food or drink. *The fool. . .how careless! Instead of diluting the end formula with two hundred gallons of water, he must have only used twenty. No wonder those addicts died. There are probably many more all over Western Europe and the United States. I should have forced him to test this formula on himself. Makeshift lab. . .careless, careless, careless.*

Of course, in Sean Pfister's defense, the elaborate laboratory at Brantley Chemical mixed the distilled water with the powder as part of the process in the proper relationship before entering the dryer for the final step. With that complete facility available for the processing, there would be very little chance of error. *Poor Sean tried to duplicate a complicated procedure with makeshift materials and probably would have succeeded if not for that drop of whatever on the formula.*

Anthony was already dialing his former homestead at the mansion as the thoughts ran through his mind. After a seemingly endless series of rings, he heard a somewhat nervous voice on the other end of the line.

"Hello, this is the Riley residence. May I help you?" Lobeth was both nervous and annoyed at the frequency of the phone calls and the unexpected visitors.

"Lobeth, I need you to get Mr. Pfister on the phone immediately. He should be in his lab."

Visibly shaken, she did not know what to do. *Mr. Riley will fire me if I tell him about Mr. Pfister. It will completely ruin our plans, me and Mosa. What should I do. . .what can I do.*

"Lobeth, Lobeth. Are you there? I need Sean Pfister on the phone right away." Anthony was becoming impatient. He needed to get this matter straight before Sean wasted any more time or money. *Maybe I can sell this TR7 again, after all.*

"Uh, Sir. After you left, four terrible looking men came. They blew up your safe and shot poor Mr. Pfister. They rummaged through the whole house looking for something. They left me here by myself. When Mosa came, we worked together to bury poor Mr. Pfister.

It is so hot here, we were afraid to wait any longer."

"Calm down, Lobeth. What did these men look like? Were they American or Arab?" Anthony did not know if it was Tony Rubella or

Saddam Akbar who had decided to come for their money. His expectations had been accurate. *Good thing we left when we did.*

"Sir, the first men must have been the Arabs. They are the ones who blew your safe and killed Mr. Pfister. They were wearing the traditional headdress of Arab men. The man who told the others what to do went through your desk and his men searched the entire house before leaving. That man was mad at Mr. Pfister. He told his men to throw him off the cliff.

When Mr. Pfister tried to run away, they shot him in the back."

"First men? What do you mean?" Anthony already knew the answer. Evidently Rubella's men had also come.

"Then the Americans came. When they discovered there was no money here, they took everything else of value and left quickly. By that time Mosa and I were over by the cliff's edge burying Mr. Pfister. They saw us standing there but left anyway."

"Alright, Lobeth. Is that all you have to tell me now? I would like for you and Mosa to look after the place while I am gone. I will contact you from time to time to see if there is any more activity to report. I will see that you are paid for your services."

Lobeth was relieved to have authorization for what they had already intended to do…and even pay for doing so. She decided not to tell him about the phone message.

"Thank you, Sir. That is all, Sir." *Hang up, please hang up.* Everything was going to work out fine. She did not want him to say anything else that might ruin her plans. Her hands were shaking. The phone finally clicked and she placed the receiver back in the cradle.

Anthony set quietly with his thoughts. *This may work out for the best after Sean's critical mistake. I need to find a place here to set up a new lab and hire a man capable of interpreting this formula. That is, if I can convince Rubella or Akbar to accept more shipments after that disaster. I will have to contact them from some other location. If they found out where I am they would probably send someone to kill me as well. First, I need to find a new house here on Roseau.*

Anthony Riley almost smiled. Things seemed to have a way of working themselves out for him, which, of course, he credited to his superior intellect…certainly not chance.

44

Jack Sanders had arranged for Conner and Ashley Hayes to fly back to the States on military transport after their adventure up North had concluded. Both of them had successfully informed their offices of the delay in returning and satisfied several questions from their respective secretaries, without divulging their present location.

With their mission successfully completed, the entire team had returned to the Shindand Base. This time, however, Jim Blalock guided them to a little used gate at the outside of the complex on the opposite end of the Base, furthest from the public section of the airfield. The Colonel could truthfully say to any future interrogators that he had no knowledge of the incident.

Conner and Ashley had been returned to their quarters by jeep after saying their goodbyes to the team, especially Sam and Harden Kelly. Theirs had included promises to get together as soon as they returned stateside. The next morning they gathered their things together and went to see Colonel Sanders to find out about returning home. They looked around for Charlie Reynolds with no success. The man had disappeared.

On the drive south last night, Harden informed his team about another target at Zaranj run by a man named Younis Stanzai. Abdullah Amin had inadvertently set the man up in his ravings while waving the gun in front of Harden's face. Ever confident, Harden had simply registered the name and location for future use.

The area which Blalock had guided them to had comfortable quarters as well as secure rooms for planning additional missions. Blalock and Rasmussen had met Harden and Samantha for coffee and breakfast in one such room the next morning. Between bites of egg and sips of black coffee, the team was again perusing maps of the area. After Harden had made him aware of the additional site, Anderson had hung up to further research the man, Younis Stanzai, and his operation. Now the team was assembled as agreed awaiting his call.

They were not kept waiting for very long. Harden was the one to answer. "Kelly here."

"Harden, as I told you last night, I would rather get you and Sam out of Afghanistan. Both of you have established too high a profile to be of any further use there."

"Sir, I feel that I owe Amin one more debt. Since he thought I would be dead by now, I feel compelled to complete at least this one more mission here. After all, he did provide the target."

"I know. I know. You gave me a fairly strong argument last night. That is why I am consenting to one more job while you are there. This man is running a much larger operation and he has not even seen any reason to conceal it. Two very obvious facilities with smoke pouring from the stacks, well guarded, as well as another building which appears to be their storage facility set just outside of Zaranj, right on the border with Iran. He has undoubtedly been alerted to the incident at Amin's place and so we would expect additional security. Go in quick and low and get out fast. As soon as this mission is complete, there will be a jet waiting to remove both of you from Afghanistan. Jim and Andy have maintained a low profile and could still be of some use to us there. Good luck." Anderson was gone and Harden was now in charge of planning the mission.

"Alright, Gentlemen. We have all had SEAL training and with that introduction, you can probably tell where I am headed with this plan. I have looked at these aerial photographs off and on all night. Our orders are to shut down the plant with as little collateral damage as possible, as always.

Stanzai gets his cooling and processing water from the nearby mountains by way of a sixty inch galvanized pipeline which empties into a basin inside the compound. This is our entryway."

Harden continued detailing the incursion for the next hour before suggesting that his team members get something to eat and some rest before the evening's adventure. "We will leave here at twenty three hundred in order to have enough time to complete the mission and get out of there before daylight without worrying about additional security appearing on the scene possibly early morning."

Samantha and Harden left for their quarters as Jim and Andy headed toward the mess hall.

45

Ashley and Conner had comfortable seating aboard the Military Transport jet with the destination of Oakland Army Base nonstop. Both were floating at a natural high after their adventures in Herat.

"Getting back to the office is going to seem rather dull after all the excitement of the past week. Maybe we should consider changing our professions, Hon." Conner was joking, of course, but the excitement of that world was tempting.

"I feel wonderful that we were able to rescue Harden and I was able to be a part of it, but I think I am ready for things to get back to normal again...at least for a while."

"There is some unfinished business with Hard. I never got the chance to discuss Anthony Riley yet. When we get home, I am going to try to get Anthony on the phone...just see what is going on. Harden will probably get mad if he finds out but I simply cannot stand loose ends. I have his phone number and present location. Maybe I could call incognito...pretend I am someone else, possibly a realtor."

Conner was still sorting the possibilities of his new plan when the plane began its descent at Oakland. The Army Base is only seven miles from San Francisco across the Bay Bridge. They were almost home. A small limousine, a Military car with darkly tinted windows, was waiting to take them to their final destination. As they descended the stair rack, they found the limo driver had pulled alongside the Jet.

With only a brief greeting, the Captain who met them whisked them across to the limousine and instructed the driver to deliver them wherever they wished. With a waving salute, he closed the door. Conner gave directions to the Sergeant who was acting as their chauffeur and he was pulling up to the curb at their building a short while later. The driver also assured them that Conner's car would be delivered sometime during the night from the Military lot at San Francisco International.

"I think I am going to try to call Anthony now." Conner was drying his hair with a thick cotton towel as he called in to Ashley who was still in the shower. He dialed the number on his cell phone and after a brief silence it began to ring. Just as he was about to give up, a woman's voice answered.

"Mr. Riley's residence. May I help you?" Lobeth had been too nervous to answer and had coerced her ally, Mosa, into picking up the phone.

Conner was elated. His research had been accurate. He had found his old friend. "Could I speak to Mr. Riley, please?" Rehearsed greetings flew through his mind during the momentary silence. *How can I have a conversation with the man responsible for the death of my wife's father? What can I say? Should I be friendly or inquisitive?* Conner was beginning to have regrets already. *Perhaps I should have waited for Harden. This man is wanted for murder, illegal drugs distribution and Heaven knows what else.*

After talking it over with Lobeth, Mosa was again on the line. "Sir, Mr. Riley is not in at the moment. May I take a message?"

"No, I will call back later. Is he out of town or just not available?"

Again the pause. "He has left the Island, Sir. We do not know where he is or when exactly to expect him back. If you will leave your name and number, I will be happy to give the message to him when he calls."

Conner was deflated. He was probably no closer to locating his old friend then before he found out about Ramkin Island. "Thanks for your help. I will just call back later. Goodbye."

Ashley walked in on her pensive husband just as he was saying goodbye. "Was that Riley?"

"No, Hon. He is not there. I suspect he has left Ramkin Island for safer ground. Maybe that realtor told him that someone was asking about him. I don't know what to think. I just don't know." He felt the soft cotton of her robe against his back. She opened the robe wrapping both ends around his shoulders. Conner could feel the softness of her body against his shoulders and back as she leaned into him. His arousal was abrupt and Anthony Riley was soon forgotten…at least for the evening.

* * *

Lobeth and Mosa had pulled two softly cushioned office chairs over by Mr. Riley's liquor cabinet. With the clink of ice cubes, then the pouring of what was left of a fifth of Elijah Craig Single Barrel Bourbon, the two ladies sat down to commiserate on their troubles…as well as their good fortune. "There sure are a lot of people looking for Mr. Riley since he left. Good riddance, I say." Lobeth took a long swig of the mellow Kentucky Bourbon.

"I'll drink to that." Mosa raised her glass toward her friend for an instant before following suit.

46

Harden Kelly and his team arrived beside the huge galvanized pipe. Arriving by way of a four wheel drive Mercedes SUV with no markings, the four operatives had reached their destination shortly after midnight. "We can leave the car here behind these trees. We are far enough from the facility not to be detected. Let's get this over with."

As planned, Blalock and Rasmussen used torches to cut an opening in the top of the pipe large enough for them to enter. After cutting on three sides, they managed to bend the fourteen gauge metal back to form a doorway. They could easily hear the roar of the water descending through the stiff metal through the newly cut opening, splashing out as it passed the cut. They were prepared for just such a discovery. Quickly donning their wetsuits and waterproof packs, they formed a circle, each person checking the backpack of the one in front of him.

The last thing out of the back of the SUV was two non-military, UV-18 SAFT NiMH water scooters. The high level of water in the piping would prove to be an asset, allowing swifter and much quieter travel through the system.

With their oxygen in place, Harden dropped first followed quickly by Sam. Jim Blalock was close behind and paused to help Andy Rasmussen pull the steel shut behind them. They traveled two to a scooter, holding on to the first person's ankles. Their objective was estimated to be approximately two hundred yards distance.

They promptly reached a steel grate designed to keep large debris from entering the system. Harden and Sam quickly cut an opening large enough to pass through without tearing their suits. Ending in a large tank, smaller pipes could be seen carrying water deeper into the facility. Overflow was forced naturally out a huge opening cut to funnel the excess away from the plant and down the hill.

Harden surfaced the open topped tank first, prepared for the worst. Evidently there was no security at this point and no workers present at Midnight. The others followed. They quickly stowed the scooters and oxygen devices under a nearby tarpaulin, hoping to be reclaiming the equipment before anyone noticed.

With the layout memorized from the aerial photographs, Harden set out toward the front of the facility with Rasmussen in tow. Being second in rank, Sam Chandler proceeded toward the rear with Jim Blalock assisting.

If it proved feasible, their objective was to reach the furthest point undetected and set the combustion devices intermittently as they returned. This method allowed them to spot choice locations on their first pass and save time on the return.

In black wetsuits and blackened faces, they managed to maneuver unseen to the furthest points. Motioning with wrist motion, Harden pointed out the several armed men posted at the various entry points. "Cover me." He whispered to Andy before crossing to the far side of the warehouse. Harden slid the magnetic side of the explosives against the underside of the bin in order to avoid the telltale clank as the metal magnet gripped its target.

One of the men standing guard proved to be more conscientious than his companions and picked that exact time to make a perimeter walk of the inside of the storage facility. He actually walked between the two men hidden in the black shadows. Having preset the timers, the first one had already been set into motion in the warehouse. After circling the stored raw material ending up on the direct opposite side of the bins, the man had a full frontal view of the two intruders. However, the unsuspecting guard did not feel the need for a flashlight and was not able to discern their shadows from the blackness which enshrouded them.

The man looked from side to side before unzipping his trousers and relieving himself with the stream striking loudly against the far wall. Finally satisfied, he made his way sluggishly back to his companions. Harden looked at his watch. *We will have to hurry now and hope that we do not run into another delay.*

Quickly Harden rejoined Andy and motioned for him to set his devices on the other side making steady progress back to the tank. Making it a point to use all the explosive material before reaching their destination, their packs were now empty. Sam and Jim were anxiously waiting for them.

Sam gave Harden a thumbs up sign which he returned. Donning their oxygen gear again, they silently dropped into the water behind their scooters.

The electric motors were relatively quiet but the force of the water made the small devices strain as they pulled upstream. The return was much slower and Harden again checked the time. It would not be safe to be caught in this tunnel when the blasts occurred. The sudden increase in water pressure could render them unconscious before they reached the opening.

Rasmussen had marked the cut section before leaving with a green phosphorous paste that glowed quite brilliantly in the dark, but only for an hour or so. The paste was waterproof but there was the possibility that the force of the water running through the pipe may eventually wash it off the wall.

Just as the lead scooter began to sputter and miss, Harden spotted the glow. The galvanized steel bent outward the second time with much less pressure required. After forcing the scooter up through the opening, he formed a foothold for Sam as she seemed to step up and float out the opening. Her agility had always amazed him. Jim and Andy followed. Harden, at six feet six inches tall, had sufficient reach to grab the edge of the metal and pull himself through.

One more glance at his watch told him it was time to get out of the area. Quickly, they gathered their supplies and loaded the gear and themselves back in to the Mercedes. The four wheel drive SUV bumped over the rough surface as Harden hurried back down the slope to the road.

They had no sooner hit the road and turned North when the first of the explosions occurred. The air blast rocked their vehicle as Harden pulled over to the side to make sure the mission was successful. The blasts continued moving inward from both sides as the facility was shattered.

After counting twelve distinguishable explosions in sequence, Harden pulled back on to the road and sped north. They needed to return to the Shindand Base and disappear from the area for an undetermined period of time. As they sped away, they heard additional explosions in the distance as the fire reached other chemical storage. Although they would be better able to make the judgment after seeing aerial reconnaissance, all four of them felt that the mission had been a total success.

At that moment, they heard the rotors of a helicopter traveling North behind them, but at a much greater speed. "Is it possible that this guy, Stanzai, has a helicopter warship in his arsenal? We had better pull over."

Pulling in to the shade of a heavy cluster of low lying trees, they almost immediately saw the dust whirling on the roadway from the powerful rotors as the chopper passed too near following the highway north.

Harden could not believe his eyes. "That is an Iranian Military aircraft. They did not even hide the markings. Just two men aboard but they must be looking for us. No wonder Stanzai was not worried about his operation being in danger. He must be bribing those border guards stationed right across from his facility. They won't report an incursion but that won't stop them from doing what he has paid them to do."

"We won't be able to use this road, Harden. Did you see the armament on that thing? One of those missiles would make us disappear from the face of the Earth."

"Did anyone look at alternatives to make our way back to Shindand?" Jim Blalock knew that he had not as he posed the question.

"I have been down this way before. There are no other roads recorded on the maps." Andy had no solution. They were trapped where they were. Ground vehicles were sure to follow. They had to find a way North.

"We may have to confront that chopper…but let's get back on the road while we can. We need to put some distance between us and Stanzai's place. I believe there is a rocket launcher in back with two rounds. Jim, check that out for us, will you." Harden again pulled onto the roadway.

After going less than five miles, they heard the rotors off in the distance. "They have circled back, Harden…coming South. We had better pull off again." This time they were in an open area, mostly desert, with the nearest cover about a mile in the distance to the Northwest. Harden pushed the accelerator to the floor.

They all saw the road disintegrate from the automatic weapon fire before they heard the shots. Trying to dodge a second round of fire, Harden swerved to the right and then circled quickly back to the left, heading for the clump of low lying trees in the distance. With both vehicles moving toward each other, the chopper pulled up to come around for a finishing volley.

"Get that thing out, Jim. We will not get a second chance. I think that first volley was simply a warning for us to stop. When we did not stop, they had their answer. Now, they will come in for the kill."

With Andy's help, Jim had the launcher loaded and aimed through the open rear window. They were not going to reach cover. "Fire when you get the chance, Jim. It won't do us much good if they are able to get off a shot, too." Harden was headed over the uneven ground at high speed in the direction of the trees. The missiles were heat seeking so all they had to do was come close. Their adversary had the same advantage. The warship had completed its turn and was coming straight toward them, gaining rapidly.

Jim knew he could wait no longer and fired the missile. Andy immediately reloaded the weapon as the others watched and waited. When nothing happened, Jim fired the second time. Brilliant white light filled the air and shrapnel cut through the trees just as they entered the welcoming shadows. The noise followed as more pieces of the aircraft were flung vigorously at the ground. Instead of stopping in the shelter of the trees, Harden immediately turned back to the road to hasten north. Despite the uncomfortable ride, he tried to maintain maximum speed back to Shindand.

All four of them breathed a sigh of relief in unison as they pulled through the gate after presenting proper identification to the sentries. As promised, a jet was waiting. Everything they had brought with them had been put aboard the plane. Swift but emotional farewells were exchanged between the four team members. They had just completed another successful mission even with the unexpected accosting of the two Iranian Military. Jim Blalock and Andy Rasmussen had not been directly recognized as being connected to either operation so they had orders to remain on base. It was now even more dangerous for Harden and Sam to be found in this primitive country.

Their jet headed North over Towraghondi and across the border through the more welcome airspace of Turkmenistan. As the plane reached friendly space, their hands, which had been clasped apprehensively, fell softly to the deck as they finally gave way to much needed sleep.

47

"Mr. Hayes, Mr. Harden Kelly is on line one. Shall I put him through?" Janet was relieved to have her boss back in the office. Too many clients were pressing for answers that she did not have. A week had passed since the latest trip to Afghanistan and Conner was swamped with much needed responses and scheduled court appearances. Most important of all, he had already appeased Thomas Alagia, the principle partner in the firm, assuring him that the office would have his unerring attention for the foreseeable future.

"Yes, Janet. Please." Janet was fully aware that this man, Harden Kelly, was the principal reason for Mr. Hayes recent absences. Upon hearing his voice, she feared it was going to happen again.

"Hello, Hard. How are you and Samantha getting along? You are back home now, aren't you?"

"We are doing fine, Conner. We arrived back here at Rosslyn a few days ago…currently between jobs right now. I noticed that I have several messages from you prior to that last episode but you did not mention anything when I saw you last week. What is on your mind?"

"Well, we were busy with other things. I know we are not allowed to discuss that activity but I just wanted to let you know that Ashley and I both had a tremendously rewarding experience, one that we will always remember."

"You know, if I had been there, I never would have allowed you two to participate in the mission. You both risked your lives and I will always be grateful for having you and Ashley as friends."

Rather than pursue this line of conversation which was heading toward overly sentimental, Conner changed the subject. "The reason for those earlier calls may still interest you, Harden. I found Anthony Riley, again…we found him, actually. On our Mediterranean cruise, Ashley was lounging on deck, looking at the islands through her binoculars, when she spotted an old man in a wheelchair on one of the verandas on the hillside.

That man was looking through his own binoculars right back at her. Anyway, it reminded her of Riley. The ship was moving so the moment did not last long."

"Whoa, Conner. You said an old man. Riley is our age. That could have been anyone."

"You know me, Hard. I always follow through. I asked the Captain the name of that particular island and when we got home, it was a simple matter to find information on the island on the internet. There was no listing of residents so I contacted a realtor pretending to be interested in property on Ramkin Island. Sara Naiser was her name. She did not actually use Riley's name but in the conversation she mentioned Cleveland, Ohio, and a man in a wheelchair. That was proof enough for me, so I tried to get in touch with you several times."

"Interesting, Conner. I will see if Anderson has any plans to pursue Riley. He may just want to pass the information along to Federal authorities…see if the FBI is interested."

"Well, there is a little more to the story. When we returned home last week, I called his house. A rather nervous woman answered…told me that he had left the Island and she did not know when to expect him back. When I persisted, she said that he did not inform her of his destination."

"I would like to follow up on that…see what happened to old Riley. I have to check with Anderson first. I suppose that you and Ashley found plenty to do back at the office." There was a long pause.

"Harden, are you still there?"

"Uh…Thanks for coming to help me, Conner. I feel honored having a friend who would risk his life for me…and Ashley, too, of course. You could never know how much Sam and I think of you two. Thanks for being there. I hope Ashley is alright. Sam told me about the man grabbing her. She did a brave thing. She is a tough lady."

Conner remembered how hard it was for Kelly to express himself and felt an even stronger relationship after this emotional outpouring from his long time friend.

When she heard her husband struggling to find the right words to thank Conner and Ashley, Sam gently put her arms around his neck for support. "I have to go now, Conner. Stay in touch and we will do the same."

Conner allowed himself several moments to reminisce about the old friendship that existed between Harden and himself…and Anthony Riley…before returning his attention to the work at hand.

48

Purchasing this property on the side of the mountain, overlooking the Atlantic Ocean, had been a daunting drain on his assets. Anthony Riley was again enjoying what had become his favorite pastime. He was sitting comfortably on his balcony, overlooking the Sea. Here he could think clearly without interruption. He closed his eyes to concentrate.

I need to bring in some cash very soon. Sean would have straightened out that problem by now and we could be again producing TR7. I wonder if I can find a market for it again. First, I need someone knowledgeable enough to follow the formula. He began to prioritize the steps required in order to revitalize his cash flow.

First, I need to find out if there is still a market out there for my products. Second, I need to find a qualified chemist. Third, I may need to contact that realtor to sell the mansion for me, and maybe the helicopter.

Mandrake did not hover so much anymore. Professing his love for Chrisimminia, the couple had pronounced their wedding vows just the week before. Anthony had agreed to be a witness for his long time protégé and endowed them with a generous gift of one hundred thousand dollars. Mandrake was enraptured with his new wife and overwhelmed by his employer's generosity. As for Chrisimminia, she had already surpassed her wildest dreams before her husband even told her about the wedding gift. Riley knew that he had just bought their continued loyalty. Mandrake had hugged him so emotionally that Anthony had to finally push him away. The bride, as well, had thanked him with a tearful kiss.

When his services were required, Mandrake responded as quickly as ever, thanks to a recently installed intercom system throughout the house and grounds. Chrisimminia performed her chores as efficiently as ever. Anthony noticed that now she seemed happy most of the time.

Since he had forgotten to include the telephone directory which had always sat on the right front corner of his desk at Ramkin, Riley was forced to rely on the somewhat less complete pocket directory which he carried at all times. It was time for the first step. He dialed the number, after checking his directory, having just about committed it to memory.

He was using his cell phone, which he had programmed through his computer to be traced to a series of remote locations around the World.

"Could I speak to Tony, please? Tell him it is Anthony Riley."

Tony could not believe his ears when his man told him who was calling. "Rubella, here."

"Tony, if you can remain calm long enough for me to talk, I may have some news of interest to you." No response. "I have discovered the error that my man was making in the production of TR7. I can now produce this formula in its original state, just like we did from our plant in Cleveland."

"Go on, Riley. I am listening."

"Perhaps we would have to repackage the product and rename it, but think of all the profit we were able to make when it first came out. I can be in production within a week but I cannot afford to do so without firm orders. You are the first one I called because of our past relationship."

Tony could not believe the audacity of the man. With the FBI all over these OD cases, there was no way he could bring more of the product on to the market right now. They were even cooperating with Interpol because of the many similar cases in Western Europe. Before answering the phone, Tony had instructed his man to try tracing the call while he talked.

"Maybe, I'm interested, Riley. Are you telling me the truth when you said you had not contacted anyone else?"...had to keep him talking.

"I need for you to be sincere with me, Tony. If you are not interested,

I have several other potential customers who will be. Remember the initial profit margin…a deal like this would be hard to pass up."

"This time we would have to lower the price to cover the expense you caused us with your screw up. Are you OK with this?"

"We could negotiate. I am flexible." Now he realized that Tony Rubella was stalling, attempting to trace the call. "However, if you think that I am stupid enough to allow you to trace this call, then we need not be dealing anyway."

"Wait a minute, Riley. I wouldn't do that. We have always done business in mutual trust. Don't you trust me anymore?"…still trying to hold him on the line. "Boss, the call originated from Nome, Alaska. I got the location." Realizing he had been beaten, Tony changed his approach.

"You owe me a lot of money, Riley, and I want it. You got out of your house just in time. Did Akbar get any of his cash back? We are businessmen and I want that last payment we made to you back in full, *now*. You cannot hide from us forever. We are everywhere."

"I can see that you are not interested, Mr. Rubella." Anthony touched the end button on his phone. *I only had two customers and that is the end of one of them. I suppose there is no harm in trying the other."* Riley dialed the next number from his list.

"Could I speak to Mr. Akbar, please?" It was important that he reach Saddam before Rubella. Maintaining reliable communications was a necessary part of the business in which these men were engaged. Akbar was not difficult to reach.

"Saddam, here. Who is this?" The voice was gruff. He did not want his man putting through calls regarding the problems he was having in the Western European countries. They were paid well to keep unpleasant calls from reaching him personally and somehow one of his people had let this one slip through.

"Good Morning, Saddam. This is Anthony Riley. Do not hang up, I have some good news. I was able to isolate the problem with TR7 and we can now produce it in the original form that was received so well on the street. We can even rename it and repackage the product if you wish. Can I count on your interest? We can both recoup our lost money."

Saddam had no means of tracing calls, so he decided to take a more friendly approach. Quickly calculating, he could break even with just one of the cartons like he had purchased before but there would be new costs in renaming and marketing it as a new product. "I can use four containers similar to the ones you previously furnished. Change the name…somehow all the officials have become aware of Brantley and the TR7 logo…meet the same place as before at Midnight tomorrow."

Anthony was excited at the order but naturally suspicious of the Arab.

"I need two days to manufacture. Make it Midnight day after tomorrow and we will be there."

"One more thing, Mr. Riley. In order to recoup my losses from your defective product, you will cut your price by forty per cent on this delivery only. As a sign of good faith, I would also like to see you there at the buy."

Is this a trap? Well, I have gone this far so I may as well go all the way. "I will agree to your terms for this one shipment only. Just be sure to hold up your end of the agreement." Anthony Riley was trying to show some of his past assertiveness.

Who does he think he is…giving me orders? Oh, well, he will be a dead man in two more days and I will have his product and my money. Before he dies, I am going to find out where his factory is located.

"It's a deal, Riley…Midnight, day after tomorrow."

49

Anderson had decided to send Charlie Reynolds to investigate the Ramkin Island estate purported to belong to Anthony Riley. Reynolds could handle himself and at the same time avoid bringing in local authorities unless the situation demanded their presence.

Lobeth and Mosa had established a favorite pastime, seated comfortably in Riley expensive chairs and sipping on his wide assortment of liquors. Al Molini had not taken any open bottles and with the many brands stocked by Mr. Riley, many had been accessed simply for a taste. The two ladies found they had a substantial supply even after the men had ransacked the place

Now they heard the rotors approaching yet again. *Will these people not leave us alone?* Lobeth managed to arouse Mosa, who had dozed off in the other chair. She awakened with a start at the sound of the helicopter as it settled on the pad. This time, however, they were not as easily frightened.

A single young man stepped out, bowing low under the blades.

Dressed in a dark gray suit and matching tie, Reynolds did not appear as a threat to the ladies. Even so, his gait and carriage also indicated a capable and confident young man. The two ladies wiped their faces and straightened their clothing before greeting the young man at the French doors.

His efficacious smile had the desired effect. "Good afternoon, ladies." Lobeth and Mosa responded with their most gracious smiles.

"Good afternoon, Sir. What can we do for you?" Lobeth had never sounded so sweet...even earning a sideways glance from her friend.

"Well, could we step inside and talk for a minute. Perhaps it would be more comfortable." Without waiting for any further invitation, Charlie entered Riley's office, taking in everything as he did. Nothing had been done about the damaged wall safe, but the furniture had been cleaned and dusted since the blast. As the two women watched apprehensively, he found a chair behind the desk and sat down, appraising everything on the desk as he did so.

"I would like to speak with Anthony Riley, please. Would you see if he has time to visit with me?"

Lobeth and Mosa returned, with faltering steps, to their favorite chairs and settled in to the soft texture. Lobeth was no leader but she seemed to be forced into being spokesperson for the two. "I am sorry, Sir. Mr. Riley is away on business. Is there anything we can do for you?"

Charlie moved down the list of names he had memorized from the earlier incident in San Francisco. "He had an assistant name Mandrake. Could I speak to him, then?"

"Sir, there is no one here but the two of us. We are employees of Mr. Riley and are to take care of the house while he is away." Immediately, she regretted revealing their defenseless position, even to this nice young man.

Charlie Reynolds was persistent. "There was one other person that I should ask for. Is a man named Sean Pfister here?"

Becoming annoyed, Mosa finally spoke up. "Sir, we already told you that no one else is here. Now, if you will kindly leave us alone and go back where you came from, we will inform Mr. Riley of your visit." Lobeth looked over at her friend, relieved to have corroboration of her story.

"Does that mean that you know where Mr. Riley is? You indicated that you would inform him of my visit."

Mosa had stepped in to the verbal exchange. "No, Sir. When he calls in we will give the message to him. We have no way of reaching him."

"Since I came all the way over here only to find that the man to whom

I wished to talk is not here, may I at least look around the premises a bit? It is such a fantastic place." Charlie was again using his most engaging smile.

Ignoring the mess caused by the blown safe, Charlie began to step toward the hall, registering admiration as he went. Mosa and Lobeth were standing now, but with no way of stopping his progress. They decided that this young man could do no further harm to the place. In whispering voices, they agreed to let the nice young man look around. There was not much the two of them could do to stop him anyway.

Entering the hallway, Charlie could faintly detect the subtle fumes of chemicals. He continued in the direction of their source, casually complimenting the décor as he proceeded. Down the hallway, the source became obvious as the odors intensified. He turned in to what had been a library but now all the furniture was pushed to the walls. Tubular pieces of glass and chemical stains were everywhere. Someone had totally destroyed what had obviously been a makeshift laboratory. *Probably the same ones who did the safe. I wonder if they found what they were looking for.*

Then his eyes came across several containers over to the side of the room. Under the watchful eyes of the two shadows behind him, Charlie gathered intact test tubes as he found them strewn across the floor. With four of them in hand, he opened the containers and filled a test tube from each, carefully sealing the caps. *Obviously, no one was interested in this product. I may have found the source of the problem the FBI has been looking into…all those OD's from some strand of drug. I better call Anderson to see what he wants me to do…can't leave this evidence unguarded.*

"What happened here, Ladies?" Charlie waved his hand around the debris. Lobeth and Mosa watched closely as he took the samples, wondering how that might affect their stability at the house.

"Some men came after Mr. Riley had departed in his helicopter."

Lobeth decided to tell partial truth since the outcome was quite obvious. "They blew up the safe looking for money. I do not think they found anything of value because the man in charge got mad and did this." She decided not to mention Sean Pfister, limiting her explanation to what the young man could see for himself.

"What did these men look like? Can you describe any of them?"

Mosa spoke up. "They were Arabs, foreigners, Iraqi or Kuwaiti. I couldn't tell which. The boss man was wearing a Kefiyyah." Lobeth simply glared at her friend as the unnecessary words ebbed from her tongue. She was sending a mental message. "Do not tell him anymore than we have to."

Charlie was disappointed. He had hoped that the woman would describe the men he had seen at Warbah Island. That would have been something with which he could relate. *If Riley has left the Island and taken all his money with him, he must not have plans to return anytime soon.*

"Has anyone else shown up since Mr. Riley left the Island?" He realized the women were holding back something, answering only what he had already surmised. The sand dusted onto the helipad showed traces of multiple activities. *I guess Riley's, his visitor's and my tracks would account for that much activity though.*

The simple women were becoming intimidated by the young man's inquisitiveness. Their answers had not been enough to make the man go away. They were becoming confused, not certain of what information they had already been forced to divulge. "Sir, why don't you just let us have Mr. Riley call you? He can answer your questions better than we can." They attempted to resume the posture of subservient maids.

Their non-answer had possibly been informative. *They could have just answered in the negative. Does that mean someone else has been here?* "Can you tell me who left on the helicopter with Mr. Riley?" The question surprised Lobeth and she answered too quickly.

"Just Mr. Riley, Mandrake and Chris, and, of course, the pilot. His name is Dixon."

Was this just an oversight! "Just the four of them, then?"

"Yes, Sir. Yes, Sir." Both women answered in unison, hoping that would be the last question before the man decided to leave.

"Then where is Sean Pfister? He must still be on the Island." He sensed a reaction from the ladies at this question, but they promptly recovered. Lobeth nervously responded.

"We were confused, Sir. Mr. Pfister left, also." *That is not quite a lie. He did leave.* She felt their visitor's eyes trying to penetrate her brain, trying to gauge the truth in her statements.

Charlie Reynolds was trying to get a read behind the words he was hearing…a truth. "Was he hurt when his lab was destroyed? Those must have been violent men from the looks of the room. If he is injured, I could possibly be of assistance. I have had adequate first aid training."

"No. No. He is gone. He is not here." Since this was closer to the truth, her voice had recovered some of its strength.

"Could I just see his room before I leave?" Charlie had already started for the stairway in the hall. "Would you show me which room Mr. Pfister used while he was here?"

Faced with the lack of an alternative, the women acceded with Mosa leading the way. In contrast to the laboratory, Sean's room was inordinately neat. After opening closet doors and drawers, it was obvious to Charlie that the man had not taken anything with him for this indeterminate trip. Even his bathroom was in order, with the toiletries lined up for daily use.

"Alright, ladies. I have seen enough. Let me make one phone call before I leave you to your duties." He quickly returned to the desk where he dialed Anderson on his cell phone. The usual procedure was for Charlie to leave his name for a return call. Mr. Anderson never answered the phone directly. Charlie could see the ladies moving about the rooms, trying to be as unobtrusive as possible as he waited.

Momentarily, his cell phone began to vibrate. "What does it look like, Charlie?"

"Before I go into detail, could you get some agents here? I think that their chemist, Pfister, has been murdered. There are several containers of his product untouched in the lab. I suspect that it could be the substance that has been causing death among addicts in the States as well as Europe. If you could get somebody here before I leave, we could make sure the housekeepers do not move anything else."

He could here Anderson's muffled voice in the distance. "Someone will be there shortly. We have a man in Beirut who can leave right away."

Charlie continued. "Mr. Riley has left and, from all evidence, for a lengthy absence. He has had some visitors since who tore up the place, especially the lab and Riley's safe. Pfister did not leave with them. I am bringing in samples of the powder from each container."

"When our people arrive, come on home, Charlie. They will do what has to be done and then call in Interpol or local jurisdiction as indicated. I will be here when you arrive."

Twenty minutes later, a U. S. Military helicopter landed with two passengers aboard. After a brief update, Charlie waved farewell to the two ladies huddled in the doorway and boarded his own transport for the mainland.

50

Jeff Lewis had mentioned to Riley that one of the first things they had to do on Roseau was find weapons since they had traveled on a public airline, leaving that equipment behind. Now, as Mandrake drove inland toward the mountains, they were looking for that same source...behind Corona's.

Corona's was simply a roadside stand, one of many on the road inland but located behind this particular landmark was the source referred to by Jeff.

When they arrived, Mandrake parked far to the side in the shade of a small grove of trees at one end of the lot. Leaving the motor running so that the air conditioning would keep his employer comfortable, Mandrake had been instructed to purchase two drinks for them while he looked around for the contact. As he was returning slowly with the drinks, he found the man. *That has to be the guy, tall, thin, wrinkled white suit.* The man's darting eyes had locked on to Mandrake's for just a second as he caught the signal motioning him to come over to the parked automobile.

Cautiously, the man glided behind the trees and came up beside the vehicle just as Mandrake reached the car. Since the windows were shaded against the hot tropical sun, he could not see Riley in the back seat as the huge man indicated that he should use the front passenger seat for their conversation. Not wishing to miss a business opportunity, the man hesitantly took the seat next to Mandrake. "My name is Miguel. How can I be of service?"

The voice from the rear seat startled him with its raspy tone as he had not taken his eyes off the driver not even for a second. "We need some laboratory equipment based on this list and we need a person qualified to set it up and operate it, preferably with some chemistry background."

Miguel eagerly took the list from the twisted fingers with his eyes partially diverted. He found that he would prefer to focus on the driver then his passenger. With a quick perusal, the swarthy entrepreneur responded. "I can certainly furnish this material but it will be quite expensive. Our resources on this tiny Island are limited. I, myself, have experience with systems similar to this diagram and could set it up for you." His greedy eyes attempted to project a smile.

"I need all this…and you…sometime this morning. I will pay you well if you are able to fulfill my requirements but only upon satisfactory completion."

"This material and equipment will cost three thousand American dollars and it may take some time to acquire all of it. I, on the other hand, would be willing to work at whatever you judge my services to be worth upon completion of the project."

"Miguel." Again the grating voice came from the rear seat. "Have I not made myself clear…*this morning.*" After emphasizing his point, he continued. "This lab must be up and running by noon. If you can achieve this, you will be reimbursed for your services. If it will enable you to acquire the material sooner, I am willing to pay five thousand dollars for the complete list of goods."

Miguel was forced to return his gaze to the crippled old man as he watched the man count fifty one hundred dollar bills from a thick stack. He nearly salivated on his white suit at the potential. Reaching across for the money, he decided that he could perform as required. "Yes, Sir. It will all be completed this morning. Give me directions to your place and I will deliver all the materials shortly in my van."

The directions were simple. Miguel knew of the estate.

"I have a man who is quite efficient at seeing that my agreements are followed through. He is already watching you. Please do not disappoint me. Now leave and get started on your part of the contract." Anthony put emphasis on the word 'contract' as the lanky man exited the vehicle.

"Let's go now, Mandrake." As the car sped away from the parking lot, the driver had his own thoughts. *He is talking about Dixon. I could have handled this guy. Why does he have to bring Dixon into this?* His eyes darted around as the vehicle made its way back to the road. *Is he already here somewhere? Mr. Riley did not tell me anything about that.*

Mandrake knew that his employer had been impressed by the pilot's innovative response to the almost disastrous encounter with the Iraqis. He had been impressed as well. None of them had realized how well Dixon could react to adverse conditions. Still, he could not reject the thoughts that his own capabilities were possibly being overlooked. Besides the damage to his ego, there could be a monetary effect as well.

Twenty minutes later, they were pulling into the property recently purchased by Mr. Riley. Mandrake had been able to justify the use of Dixon when his employer notified him of the drop to occur at Midnight tomorrow night. Mandrake would be the one to handle that operation.

Anthony Riley was again relaxing on his veranda, thinking and planning his future if this Akbar exchange did not go well. Suddenly, he sighted a dust cloud moving up the road in his direction. A chill reached his bones for just a second. *Have they found me? What will they do?* His voice choked out the word 'Jim' before he recognized the driver. Mandrake was standing close by at the moment and overheard. *There he goes again…calling for Dixon…has he lost confidence in me. Jim acted like a wild man in Kuwait but I can see why Riley was impressed. I guess if it were not for Jim we could have all been killed.*

Miguel drove his old Ford Excursion hard. The white paint had begun to rust on the lower panels but the powerful motor remained in excellent condition. The tinted windows and large cargo area enabled him to haul whatever merchandise necessary without being evident to prying eyes. He knew the purpose of this material in his current load and had preassembled some of the pieces, anticipating that it would be simpler to do so in his own shop rather than the large mansion.

Mandrake met him in the driveway and directed him to the garage area, which was to suffice for a laboratory, at least temporarily. Dressed in a yellow Caribbean slipover shirt with no collar, his hard body stretched the soft material, emphasizing every muscle in his upper body. Miguel was still dressed in his wrinkled white suit. He was just as tall as Mandrake but as he removed his jacket to unload and set up the equipment, his body seemed to shrink in comparison with the other man.

Miguel proved to be efficient. The lab was assembled exactly according to Anthony's diagram. This time there was sufficient water in a large tank to process the chemicals in the proper ratio before drying. A simple valve was installed to let in more water as needed. The plant was ready for startup.

Mr. Riley was summoned before starting the procedure in order for him to oversee the initial operation. This time there could be no glitches. As Miguel worked with the chemicals, he memorized the unusual combinations as well as the procedure. Anthony was following his original diagram to be certain nothing went wrong. Within two hours, fresh new product was ebbing through the final phase into the drying bin.

Anthony sifted the clean white powder through his fingers, satisfied that they had again produced a high grade product. This time, however, he had ordered cardboard boxes with plastic liners to seal in his product. Even the shape was radically different, deeper and longer instead of flat and almost square. The label had to be changed as well. *What shall I call this product?* Anthony's mind was churning out ideas as a rapid pace…*Compressed Phosphorous Fertilizer…CPF. I will add a few code numbers to complete the labeling. I will name the new company, Mid East Chemical Company.*

His thoughts drifted back to his approaching encounter with Saddam Akbar.

51

Impatient and fuming after ten unsuccessful attempts to contact Abdullah Amin on his cell phone, Saddam Akbar reluctantly decided to call the house where the man had set up his processing plant near Herat. After just two rings, a soft, female voice answered. "Hello." Sa-ina Kalemi's tone had been nervously cautious since the recent outbreak of violence in her home.

The Afghan Police had arrived the following day but she remained uncertain as to how they were notified. She suspected that the hated Amin had somehow bought them off for a day so he could wield his revenge against the American. There was also the possibility, however, that the Americans had discreetly notified the Afghan authorities. After a brief show of bravado, the officer in charge hauled off the two bodies. Badi and Arif had evidently recovered enough to flee the area before the Police arrived. With their leader dead, there was no future in being caught up in the investigation.

"Let me talk to Amin." It was more of a command than a request. Sa-ina had heard this voice before and the pure malevolence which the man projected made her shudder. She had to answer in just such a way to relate the fact that Amin was dead but also to keep the man from coming to see for himself the condition of the product about which he was calling.

"The Americans came and completely destroyed his work area almost two weeks ago. There is nothing left...no equipment...no raw materials. Amin is dead and his men have fled. There is nothing left here." She was trying to exaggerate the destruction without lying to the man.

"Amin is dead? He was supposed to be working up an order for me. What is the status of that? Are you certain that he is dead? Did you see his body?"

Saddam Akbar was almost shouting. Sa-ina tried her best to hold it together...she was shaking visibly. She quickly gained composure in her voice although her body belied her tone. "Sir, there is absolutely nothing left here. It all burned in the explosions and fire. I watched as Abdullah Amin attacked one of the Americans and I saw three bullets hit his body as he fell dead in the hallway. The police have already been here. They did what they had to do before removing the two dead bodies."

Saddam Akbar now was in a quandary. *I was counting on that shipment from Abdullah. I may have to change my plans for Riley, now, at least, until I can find another source. But that only means I will have to devise another plan for getting back the money he cost me.* His thoughts diverted his attention from the phone held loosely in his hand. Altering his tone of voice, he spoke aloud. "My dear lady, I am so sorry that you had to be put through such a terrible experience. Is there anything I can do for you...anything you need...please let me help you?"

Sa-ina Kalemi knew that the best thing he could do for her was to leave her alone. "Thank you, no. I have the bare necessities and a little money. I will get by. Thank you, Sir."

"Goodbye, then, my dear." Finally he was gone.

Both houses were decorated in very good taste as well as imbued with many expensive accessories. Little damage had been done...several bullet holes in the walls, a broken window and a busted door jam. She had a nephew who could make the necessary repairs and probably would not even charge her for them. He would know that she would find a way to repay him.

* * *

Saddam Akbar's attention had turned inward as he sorted his options. He decided that he would accept the delivery on Riley's guarantee, but only after it was tested on one of Riley's men.

52

Anthony Riley had found Miguel somewhat distasteful and swarthy but very resourceful. While preparing sufficient product for the initial deal with Saddam Akbar, Miguel had succeeded in transacting further business with Riley. Jim Dixon and Mandrake had visited the huge shop behind Corona's roadside stand to prepare themselves for a possible encounter with Akbar's men in Umm Qasr.

The building was about the distance of two city blocks away from the popular tourist attraction and was shielded by the cluster of trees in front and the mountain behind. Just inside the front door was an array of jewelry, ranging from very expensive to trinkets...then pottery, blankets, statuary. A very large area was filled with items to attract the fat wallets of tourists in search of a bargain. Miguel ran a legitimate business as well.

A panel on the back wall slid aside revealing a wide variety of weaponry displayed in an orderly fashion. Jim Dixon was interested in additional rounds for the automatic rifle which he had used in Kuwait and was able to purchase several hundred. While completing the transaction, he noticed a box of fragmentation grenades in their original packaging. He purchased a box of twenty, intending to have some with him at Midnight. With the touch of an electronic release, the panel slid back into place.

Mandrake had purchased additional rounds for his Glock as well. The two men carried their newly acquired goods to the car in nondescript brown shopping bags with a printed advertisement...'Visit Roseau, A Tropical Paradise.'

Anthony Riley watched intently as his two men loaded the cargo into Miguel's van for the trip to the local airport. Dixon had plotted his route in advance with Riley's direction. Mandrake and Riley drove separately and both vehicles arrived at the airport around noon. Little attention was paid to the four boxes from the Mid East Chemical Company being loaded into the cargo space of the private jet. Though Riley was apprehensive, he knew he needed to accompany his men to the drop as Akbar had demanded, but also to make certain that the man did not try to renege on the deal. They would possibly need direction at that point.

* * *

After a lengthy but otherwise uneventful flight, the plane landed on the airfield on Warbah Island. Fez was waiting with an Arab who was paid to attend to the airfield, running the heavy roller equipment daily to preserve the surface.

Darkness had engulfed the area and they could see the cruiser lights in the distance, Fez's pride and joy. It was not yet eleven in the evening and it would take about forty minutes to reach their destination in the cruiser. Mr. Riley had originally planned on Jim Dixon accompanying them to the meeting in case a confrontation should arise. However, it was decided that the safety of the aircraft was the most important element of the two. If something should happen to the aircraft, they would be stranded. They would have to return to Kuwait City with Fez.

Anthony found a way to compromise the two options. Fez had enlisted another boat which now lay docked next to the cruiser. If they did not return on schedule, Jim was to come to the meeting in the other boat and lay offshore until needed. At fifteen minutes past eleven, Riley, Mandrake and Fez set out for the exchange point. Unknown to Riley was the fact that there would have been a fire fight with the purpose of eliminating him and his consorts if Saddam Akbar had not had the phone conversation of that afternoon with Sa-ina Kalemi. Now, Akbar recognized the fact that he may need Riley until an alternative was found.

This time even Fez had been armed with a pistol, surprising Mr. Riley with the one he had kept on board the past few months. Mandrake and Fez were to unload the craft after which Fez would return to the boat to protect Anthony. Mandrake would make the exchange before returning. Reaching his hand in to touch the cold steel, Mandrake thought again of Jim Dixon's heroics and almost hoped for the opportunity to show what he himself could do in front of Mr. Riley.

Although the Arabs were heavily armed, the exchange proceeded smoothly until Akbar suddenly appeared from the shadows. "Mr. Riley, as you can see, I am willing to accept your product and that case in your man's hands holds the agreed upon amount of cash. However, I would hope that you would allow me, under the circumstances, to test the product before we part ways. I want this young gentleman to be the first to use it…and we will wait here for twenty four hours to see if he has any negative effect. You can hold the satchel while we test. Is this agreeable with you?" His men had shifted their automatic weapons from a casual position to alert, pointed in the general direction of the visitors.

Anthony did not have any consternation about the test. His only concern was that Dixon would most certainly arrive before the test was complete. Not certain as to how his man would respond when approaching the standoff, he feared the worst. "Mandrake, do as he says."

The big man strolled over to the cruiser and passed the satchel across to his employer. He stripped off his jacket as well as his weapon and left them on one of the seats before returning to confront his adversaries. Unknown to Riley, Chrisimminia had introduced Mandrake to the use of cocaine to enhance their sex life. One last questioning glance at Mr. Riley assured him that there was no alternative. He would be forced to go through with the test. Before leaving the boat, he tore a blank page from a notebook in his jacket pocket and unsheathed the knife from his belt.

When he reached the nearest of the containers, he smoothly cut the seal and pulled the cardboard box open. There was a three inch plastic fill cap in the lid. After snapping this open, he dipped his fingers into the opening and drew out sufficient product for a nice high. Mandrake then cut a one inch slice from the paper to fold into a makeshift straw. With his knife blade, he pushed the white powder into two separate lines and used the straw to travel down the first line, inhaling the substance as he did so. He then repeated the procedure using the other nostril.

He looked directly into Akbar's eyes before returning to the craft. Settling back on the pillows on the deck bench, he prepared to wait out the effects. It was not long before he appeared to be asleep. A lascivious grin appeared on his face. His body moved around gently as if in the grip of intense pleasure. This went on for about twenty minutes before the giant settled back into the pillows, apparently in a peaceful slumber.

"That should satisfy you, Akbar. This product is exactly like the original. It gives nothing but pleasure and relaxation. You can see that there are certainly no ill affects." Anthony was anxious to end the meeting before Dixon arrived. The arrangements had proceeded with no problems, even the unexpected test.

Saddam Akbar and two of his heavily armed men had moved closer to the boat to get a better look at the subject. "Just a little longer, Riley. Be patient. If all goes well, we may be able to build up a relationship profitable to both of us. You must realize that I cannot afford to again market a product which causes my customers to die. That cost me a great deal of money and I need to recoup it through the sale of your product or through that satchel that you are holding. Your brave man here will decide which."

His men were at full attention, now, with their weapons directed at the occupants of the boat. Fez was standing in the shadows at the bow but he knew his presence was discovered as one of the assault rifles was turned in his direction. All eyes were on the sleeping giant as he slept off the initial effects of the drug.

Two hours passed with everyone now seated, awaiting the outcome of the test. Akbar and his two men were seated on the cartons on the dock while Anthony was comfortably seated in his chair. Fez had settled against the railing, ready to drop behind the cabin at the slightest provocation. Silently, another boat approached in the distance. Two hours had passed since Mandrake had initiated the test and he was still smiling broadly in his sleep. The approaching vessel did not escape the attention of Saddam Akbar, who immediately rose to his feet. "Boat coming in."

Riley and Fez were immediately aware of at least ten more men appearing from behind crates on the dock. "Saddam, that is my man. He was instructed to come in case of trouble. With your permission, I will call him on his cell phone and stop his approach. Or we can simply end this unnecessary test and thereby end this meeting. Don't you agree that there is apparently nothing wrong with the product that we refer to as CPF?"

Not wishing to lose a renewed source of an effective and less expensive commodity, Akbar relented. "Go, now. I will be in touch."

53

Five weeks had passed since his return to the States and Harden was getting restless. He had been assigned again to recruitment, choosing and contacting candidates from basic training camps across the Country.

Sam had been stuck in Rosslyn, joining the staff as an instructor. Both had continued to hone their skills on the firing range as well as the exercise facility.

Through Anderson, they had received word that Jim Blalock and Andy Rasmussen had completed two more missions on similar targets in Afghanistan with unmitigated success. Now, that team, as well, was being reassigned out of that country.

With her husband due to return that evening, Samantha was enjoying a refreshing shower after an unusually stimulating day of hand to hand combat training in close quarters as well as simulated crowded public places. When Harden arrived home to the sound of the shower, he immediately stripped down to his boxers and entered the bathroom. Realizing the danger of entering unannounced, he gently flipped the edge of his towel over the shower curtain to get her attention. The gesture proved effective. Samantha immediately recognized the outline of her husband's body through the murky glass and pushed the glass aside to invite him in.

"Welcome home, stranger."

To accommodate his bulk, he had to duck his head as well as slide the glass open a little wider to enter the shower. He bowed down to meet the waiting lips and was instantly aroused by the touch of her breasts as they kissed, gently at first, then long and deep. Harden turned the knob to a cooler temperature and with a continued motion smothered his wife against him with his powerful arms. "I've missed you so much, Samantha."

She felt his arousal and spread her legs to accommodate him, only to feel the heat of his body intensify.

* * *

Later, as they lay exhausted side by side on the bed, they began to catch up on what news there was. "I talked to Ashley, yesterday. They really want us to come out there again. I would love to see both of them.

We never have really had a chance to talk about the adventure we involved them in. Anderson came up with the idea of having Conner represent you since he was so familiar with International Law as well as having experience in Military Law. But when they insisted on being included in the rescue mission, they actually risked their lives for us. I tried to stop them. It was foolish, I know, but there was no way of refusing them at the time. We need to thank them again for that."

"I know. What closer friend could you have then someone who would lay down his life for you? I know that is a cliché but there is some kind of bond between us whenever we are together. Conner feels it, too, I am certain. This class finishes up Friday. Do you want me to ask Anderson for a week off?"

"Oh, Harden. That would be great. I'll make reservations right away and also let them know we are coming."

"Whoa, Hon...let me get with Anderson first." Harden seemed to be deep in thought. "Maybe we could talk about finding Anthony Riley while we are together. That is an incomplete episode. It needs closure. Maybe it will not be pleasant but it still needs closure." Harden was drifting back to the old High School days when Conner and Anthony were his best friends. "I picked up Amin's cell phone off the floor. Maybe some of those names or numbers could help us find Riley. It is a long shot but there are only a few organizations controlling that entire market. There could be a connection that we are not aware of as yet."

"But first and foremost, it will be a vacation. I am sure there will be time for a little research as well…possibly while those two are working." Samantha was getting excited by the proximity of the opportunity to see her new friends again and was anxious to make a few phone calls. "Why don't you try to reach Anderson now? He does not seem to work on any schedule that I have been able to decipher."

"I'll do it, Sam." As soon as he reached the decision, he began to dial the number from memory. As always, Harden left his name on the answering machine.

Never failing to surprise the two of them with his intuitiveness, Anderson returned the call. "Harden, why don't the two of you take off for a week? That class finishes up on Friday and there is nothing pressing at the moment. When you return, give me a call. I may have something a little more challenging than the recruitment and instruction. Of course, what better course of action could we have then engaging our best agents to train our new agents?"

Harden did not even have to divulge the nature of his original call. "Thank you, Sir. We appreciate your offer. We both want to visit our friends in San Framcisco under more pleasant circumstances than our previous meeting. We have not properly thanked them yet. It will give us an opportunity to do that as well."

"Enjoy." Anderson was gone without even a query as to the nature of Harden's message.

The childlike joy that he saw in Samantha's face as he relayed the message only served to make him love her more. She jumped up and began to make notes and phone calls, a happy excitement radiating from all her pores. Harden watched her body's fluid motion through the thin folds of her sheer chiffon robe highlighted with satin sleeves and collar. *Man, how I love that woman, that girl, that lady…my lady!*

Her first contact was with their friends to be certain they would at least be in town next week. Ashley even confirmed that she and Conner would arrange to take some time off while they were visiting. Samantha was buoyed by the exuberance in her friend's voice at the prospect of their coming. Everything was falling in to place.

54

Charlie Richards had been monitoring motion activated reels of film from a camera atop the shed on Warbah Island. He had successfully identified several of the persons showing up on film. The American was difficult to trace. However, with the assistance of the FBI, the man was identified as the top aide to a New York crime boss named Anthony Rubella. Richards had passed on information about the activity on Warbah as well as copies of the film.

This morning he found a message on his computer to access the link for new clips. Long periods of inactivity occurred between hits. The activity started with another shot of the big Arab man docking his boat. This man was a local from Kuwait, never wore a shirt but sometimes a vest and never failed to be wearing a little round cap on his shaved head. *The man looks like every genie pictured in Arabic fairy tales.* Charlie had identified this man simply as Fez. He lived on his boat at the docks in Kuwait City.

The next motion was created by a private jet landing on the makeshift airfield. When the door opened, the pilot lowered the steps for his passengers. Another huge man in a dark suit emerged and went around to the cargo doors. *That man looks familiar.* Charlie hit the print button as he paused at that clip.

Fez had been picked up at the dock by the airfield attendant in a large black limousine. The Arab man had activated the camera on several occasions, primarily driving the equipment to maintain the field. After these infrequent activities, the man would seem to disappear. Fez helped the large man in the suit to unload four cardboard boxes and transfer them to the trunk of the car. They fit perfectly but protruded from the rear about two feet, holding the trunk lid open.

Charlie was sitting back in his chair casually reviewing the tape. As the men completed their freight handling, a wheelchair came rolling down the ramp. Reynolds jumped to his feet and bent his face to the screen. "That's Riley. My God. That's Riley." Not realizing that he had made that exclamation aloud, he was embarrassed to find that several curious faces had turned in his direction. "Sorry, guys." He raised his hands in supplication and sat again at his computer. *That is definitely Riley.* The limo sped away apparently to load the freight onto the boat. Several minutes later it returned with the man in the suit. *I knew I recognized that man. He is Riley's assistant…*a slight pause…*Mandrake, that's his name.*

After what appeared to be a heated discussion, the pilot disappeared back inside the aircraft as Mandrake loaded Riley and his chair into the limousine. The motion sensor shut down as the boat moved away from the Island with all its passengers safely aboard. Charlie checked the time on the clip…*twenty three fifteen hours.*

Shortly after one in the morning, the film was activated again as the pilot left the aircraft rather hurriedly and jogged down to the dock and into a second smaller boat. He was carrying an automatic rifle and had a satchel over his right shoulder.

When the picture returned, the boats were docking again. The limousine had remained at the dock. The driver now emerged and jumped aboard to help Fez support Mandrake, now without his coat and tie, as they made their way to the passenger seat of the car. Riley followed in his motorized chair. It was Fez, this time, who lifted Anthony Riley into the back seat and then stowed his chair in the trunk. With that completed, Fez loosed his moorings and sped away as if he was in a hurry to leave. The pilot emerged from the second boat and it, too, sped away with the impossible task of catching Fez.

Back at the airfield, the driver lifted Anthony back into his chair as the pilot came to assist. The pilot and driver then helped Mandrake up the stairs. On film, he appeared to be taking steps on his own as well. Riley had already driven up the ramp and the pilot hurriedly secured the doors and ran back to the front and into the aircraft. The stairs disappeared inside the plane and when the door was closed, there was a pause in the film until the jet taxied down the runway to take off again. *There seems to have been a big rush to leave and something was wrong with Mandrake. I did not see any blood. I wonder what that was all about.*

Charlie had called Anderson to report. An idea had surfaced and he was anxious to proceed but first he needed approval of the expenditures. When the call came in, he outlined what he had just viewed on the surveillance tape. "I would like to make one more trip to that Island. If I could secure a bug to that jet, we have the equipment to find it anywhere in the World. We have the software right here at Rosslyn."

Anderson was not yet convinced. "You may have to sit there for a month or more before they make another drop. It is very possible that they will not even use that site again. We can not afford to tie up your time for a fruitless endeavor."

"Give me just ten days. I have a feeling about this. They will be back. I am sure of it."

"Ten days, Charlie. No more. Good luck."

As the phone clicked off, Charlie Reynolds was already making the necessary arrangements. *I will go through Kuwait City and drive up to where that ferry boat is docked. If I rent his boat for ten days, it could give me a place to stay until the plane arrives. The presence of his boat will not arouse suspicion. That old Captain has been there often enough…he told me he makes the trip two or three times a week.*

55

Saddam Akbar was elated. Riley's new product was an immediate success. With just two days on the street, he was ready for a second shipment.

"Four more cartons, Riley…same place…Midnight, tomorrow. Looks like we can do business again after all."

Anthony was successful in bringing the price back up to what his TR7 had sold for in its original quality. "We will be there, Saddam." As he closed his cell phone, he smiled. *But not me, Akbar. That last trip was too tiring and much too risky.* Summoning his new chemist, Miguel, as well as the ever faithful, and now fully recovered, Mandrake, Mr. Riley informed them of their next assignment.

Miguel began work immediately, enthused by this wonderful opportunity for quick cash. His business had been experiencing a slowdown which he blamed on additional law enforcement in the area. He suspected that the stand in front of his business had alerted the officers. Miguel had always been generous with the assigned patrolmen thus avoiding problems to date. However, several new policemen had been showing up in the area. His budget had been limited. He was happy to find this work with Mr. Riley just at the right time.

Mandrake informed Jim Dixon of the next meeting. Both agreed to come fully armed and worked out situations to avoid being exposed to danger any longer then necessary. This time they would be ready.

* * *

"Akbar, where did you get this new stuff? It looks just like Riley's old TR7." Tony Rubella was feeling a mixture of anger and opportunity. If Riley had in fact discovered the problem with his formula and was again producing pure product, he wanted in.

"My dear friend, furnishing information of that kind could hurt my business. However, exchanging information is sometimes more beneficial to both parties. Do you know where Riley is?" Saddam Akbar was trying to gain better control of his supplier this time around. He had tried to locate Riley and failed.

"No, but we will find him. That means you are buying from him again. I thought so. Don't worry. We are not interested in Western Europe, yet."

"Alright, then, Mr. Rubella, I am doing business with Mr. Riley again and the product has proven to be of its original quality. He is calling it CPF, Compressed Phosphorous Fertilizer, and shipping it under the label of the Mid East Chemical Company. He has also altered the crates significantly. I hope that you will be able to return the favor someday soon. Good night."

Tony dialed the cell phone of his old supplier, hoping the man would not refuse to answer after seeing the calling number. Mandrake answered the phone in his deep, resonant voice. "How may I help you?" No longer did they dare answer the phone with their names. Too many people were attempting to learn their location.

"This is Rubella. I may be interested in doing business with Mr. Riley again. Could I speak with him, please?" Tony did not want to be shut out. TR7 had made him a great deal of money as well as prestige within his organization. He was using his most persuasive voice.

"Hold on." There was a period of silence until he heard the familiar croaking voice. "Mr. Rubella, it is good to hear from you again."

"You may as well know that I have been talking to Akbar. I am aware of the adjustments that you have made to your product. If the price is right, I am interested in another buy."

Not wishing to stretch his luck, Anthony agreed to the same price originally charged for TR7. Rubella, unknowingly, duplicated the order of Saddam Akbar. Thinking quickly as ever, Riley outlined the conditions.

"Tomorrow at eleven in the evening, we will meet you on Warbah at the same place. I want this exchange to go as quickly as possible as my men have additional assignments to fulfill. Is that agreeable with you, Mr. Rubella?"

"My man will be there. Don't try anything, Riley, and do not let me down on the quality of the product."

After informing Mandrake and Miguel of the additional load, Riley sat back in his chair and actually relaxed for the first time since his product had gone bad. He felt good. However, there was a gnawing ache in his upper shoulders which had been occurring with varying frequencies for the past several months. With a cold glass of water, he swallowed two of his ever present Propox tablets for the pain. His mind faintly registered that he had been doing this with increasing consistency lately. He soon fell into a deep slumber.

* * *

Charlie Reynolds hopped from the ferry boat as he heard the sound of the approaching aircraft and concealed himself behind the equipment shed near the airfield. If questioned, the old man agreed to claim he was just waiting around hoping for business.

As the door opened and the stairs were let down, he was surprised to see the striking young lady with the blouse tied around her slim waist and the very short skirt exposing her long tanned legs. She stood to the side as two men descended to the field. Charlie recognized the man in front almost immediately. *That is Al Molini. What is he doing here?* Joey Gondolfo followed him down the steps.

Before Charlie could decide whether to confront the gangsters, the sound of another approaching aircraft interrupted his thoughts. The jet settled to a stop, allowing a comfortable distance between crafts, yet close enough for a quick exchange of business.

When the door opened, he was immediately rewarded for his patience. After the pilot lowered the steps, Mandrake appeared in the doorway. There was no room for doubt as the man's bulk covered the entire shadow of the opening. The pilot followed him quickly to the rear of the jet and opened the cargo doors. Both men unloaded the four containers and placed them on the tarmac approximately centered between the two planes.

Cautiously, Mandrake approached Al Molini, who had begun to take several steps in his direction. Al shook the huge hand of the young man and handed him the briefcase. "Good to see you again. Take care." Al was sincere and it was not lost on Mandrake, making him feel a little more at ease. Molini motioned to Gondolfo to help him get the freight loaded on their aircraft just as the rear door opened and the pilot came out to help them. Alberto was always anxious to leave as soon as possible.

With orders not to leave the cash on the jet unattended, Mandrake carried the satchel to the waiting limousine while Dixon began to unload the balance of the merchandise. The Arab driver hastened to assist him in loading the four remaining boxes into the trunk.

Seeing two jets on the runway, Fez had pulled his powerful cruiser alongside the dock silently, not yet tying in. He idled the potent engine as the limousine approached. Recognizing the occupants, he tied down one rope only as he awaited their boarding.

The first jet had departed before Dixon had begun to unload the remaining boxes. Now, as Charlie Reynolds watched Fez leave with his passengers, the only person left to contend with was the Arab who drove the limousine and took care of the field. Through his field glasses, he saw the man's feet sling over the front sleep as he stretched out in the back for a nap during his long wait. Charlie silently raced to the aircraft with his small package. One of the products of the NASA investment was the production of a very powerful magnet with information gleaned from the Magnetar, a space fragment so dense that its magnetism would erase the strip off every credit card on Earth if it passed close enough to our planet.

Charlie inserted his locator bug under the wing next to the engine protrusion so as to protect it from the powerful wind at seven hundred miles per hour. He activated the switch and jogged back to the cover of the building. Riley was apparently not with them on this trip or he could have concluded his business with an arrest on site. He was now torn between leaving the Island or waiting for the return of Mandrake and his pilot. His Company had done research on Dixon as well and found him to be a well trained combatant having served in a similar position earlier in his career. The man could be dangerous if his skills had been maintained.

The old Captain was only too happy to remove himself from harm's way when Charlie returned. After returning to the mainland, Reynolds set in his car and started up the computer program to indicate the location of the targeted jet. The indicator light proved to be extremely accurate as he enlarged the map to show detail. The jet was still sitting on the Northern coast of Warbah Island.

* * *

The exchange at Umm Qasr went without incident. Akbar did not even show. Fez made an uneventful trip to and from the Iraqi Coast, anxious as ever to discharge his passengers and get paid.

56

The four friends were seated around a comfortable table over to the side of the room at Izzy's on Steiner Street in the Marina area of San Francisco. The ladies found the atmosphere to be delightful with soft music issuing from somewhere in the ceiling while the two men reveled in the masculine saloon-style motif. It was time to relax. Harden and Samantha has just arrived that afternoon and they had met Conner and Ashley for dinner.

When the drinks had been served, Conner carefully raised his overflowing martini glass and without spilling a drop of the precious liquid, he toasted his life long friend, Harden Kelly along with his wife, Samantha Chandler Kelly. Raising their glasses in unison, the warmth of their friendship encompassed the table. The arrival of the waiter interrupted their revelry momentarily.

"May I make a few recommendations for dinner or are you familiar with our menu?"

Conner Hayes and Ashley Jennings Hayes had dined several times before at Izzy's. "I know what I want but I defer to the ladies."

"I will have the New York sirloin au poivre with cracked pepper, please." Ashley began. "With au gratin potatoes. This is very good, Sam, if you have not yet decided."

Seeking lighter cuisine, Samantha was next to order. "I think the steak kebob with sautéed mushrooms."

"Now, Harden, if you want the best item on the menu, just follow my lead." Returning his attention to the waiter…"Young man, I will have the blackened filet with creamed spinach."

"Excellent choice, Sir and Madams."

"I guess I will try the filet as well." Harden was certainly not hard to please. His training had exposed him to survive off many food sources that would be repugnant to ordinary citizens.

The conversation returned to a more personal note as Harden was finally able to express his thanks in person to his best friends, who had risked their lives to save his in Afghanistan just a short time ago. "Conner, you have been there for me on numerous occasions, all the way back to our freshman year at St. Xavier. Although I do not possess the most adequate elocution to express my feelings, I want you to know that I will always be thankful for your friendship." Sensing the emotion in her husband's voice, Samantha squeezed his arm in support with one hand as she dabbed a Kleenex at her eyes with the other.

Conner had just reached for his friend's hand with a reassuring grip when a cell phone rang.

As Harden fished the small instrument from his pocket, he exclaimed his apology. "Sorry about that, Guys. I guess I was getting too sentimental anyway." He flipped the cover. "Kelly."

"Harden, we have located Anthony Riley and I think you and Samantha are the best team to go get him. When can you leave?" Anderson had decided that it was time to put this entire episode behind them. Charlie Reynolds' excellent instincts had proven correct and he had successfully traced the aircraft to Dominica, specifically the city of Roseau.

"Whenever you say, Sir." Harden stood and strolled over to a quiet corner of the entrance hall after whispering "Excuse me" to his dining partners. "We are with Conner Hayes right now. Is it alright if I tell him the news about Riley?"

"Harden, I would prefer to keep this assignment confidential. Hayes may insist on accompanying you if he knows we are going after Riley. I know I used him in Afghanistan but that was a case of International Law and Military Law conflicting and that choice gave us the best opportunity to avoid publicity since he is your friend as well as having trained at JAG."

"That will be awkward, Sir. Anthony Riley was a very close friend of both of us and it will not feel right to keep this information from Conner. I would like to at least inform him that we have located Anthony and that Sam and I are going after him."

Anderson paused momentarily. "Your mission, Harden...but do not tell him where until we are certain the information is accurate."

"Thank you, Sir. That will enable us to give them a satisfactory reason for our sudden departure."

"Can you be here at Rosslyn tomorrow afternoon? I will be here with Reynolds and we can give you all the detail that we have so far. There is a plane standing by. You will not have to depend on reservations or flight schedules."

"We will be there." As always, Harden was not sure if Anderson hung up before his last remark or not. This conversation had already exceeded the norm for the abrupt mannerisms of his superior.

Walking slowly back to the table, Harden was trying to devise the best way to word the sudden ending to what was to be a week of enjoying and strengthening the bonds of friendship which had begun so many years ago.

"I suppose you guessed that it was Anderson. Sam and I have to leave tomorrow on another assignment." As the other three were waiting for him to finish, the meals arrived, releasing delicious aromas as the covers were removed and the dishes set before them.

The impeccable service sustained the tension as the waiters busied themselves refilling water glasses and coffee cups. Samantha knew that she would receive a detailed briefing when they were alone but she was not able to hide her disappointment from the others. Ever inquisitive, Conner was the first to break the silence.

"What's going on, Hard? Do you have to leave so soon?"

Ashley chimed in. "We were so looking forward to spending some time together this week. I found myself missing you two already and it has only been a short while."

"Well, frankly, it has to do with our old friend, Anthony Riley. You remember Charlie Reynolds. Well, he came up with a method to track Riley down. We now know where he is living and Sam and I are going there to take him into custody for the Federal Government. I do not know what happens from there. Anderson thought it best that I handle the job since the three of us had been friends in the past. Hopefully, this will be a peaceful operation and not a confrontation."

It was time to change the subject. "This blackened steak is great…such a poignant taste…an excellent combination of the original steak flavor and pepper spices, without being dried out. Good choice, Conner."

"Wait a minute, Buddy. You are trying to change the subject. I can appreciate the fact that you like the steak, of course, but you have not told us enough about Anthony. Where is he, anyway?"

"Conner, I pressed Anderson to let me tell you what the call was about but I cannot divulge any other information, at least, not yet."

"I want to come along, Hard. Maybe I can help." Conner had tasted the excitement of his friend's occupation and found it tantalizing.

While picking at her food, Ashley was absorbing every word, also anticipating another adventure. The work of her new friends was certainly intriguing. Although she had always thought of her work as challenging and interesting and approached it with her natural enthusiasm, it now seemed dull by comparison.

"That is not possible, Conner. I couldn't keep the nature of the assignment from you because you have already been aggressively searching for Anthony but Anderson was persistent in limiting what I can tell you. I am sorry." He glanced at Samantha for support on this.

"Frankly, guys, I am surprised that Harden was allowed to divulge as much as he has. Anderson is prone to secrecy in his job as controller. He insists that the less information out the safer his agents will be." Harden looked directly at his wife as his eyes whispered 'Thanks'. She had found just the right thing to say.

"Enough about that, now. We are here to celebrate our friendship. Let's enjoy what time we have." Raising her water glass, Ashley proposed another toast. "Here is to safe missions for Sam and Hard and to a friendship that I hope will never end." As they clinked glasses, Harden was relieved at the change of venue. He wanted so much to tell his friends all that he knew about Anthony Riley, but could not.

Conner smiled broadly at his wife's ice water toast but Harden could still see the inquisitive gleam in his eyes.

As the evening ended, the four friends exchanged farewell hugs as Harden and Samantha had informed them of their early flight the next day.

Conner respected the confidentiality of Harden's position and did not press for further answers at this time.

57

Satisfied that things had finally turned around again, Anthony sat at his desk and reviewed his fortune. He now had a balance of five million four hundred thirty six thousand in his account at the Neubauer Bank in Switzerland and three million two hundred twenty one thousand in the Roseau International Bank here on the Island. The persistent pain again gathered in his shoulders as he tried to formulate plans for the future.

With a cold gulp of Dasani water, he swallowed two more of the Propox tablets to ease the pain. *This pain has been recurring too often...not only in my shoulders but down into my arms and chest. I will have to make arrangements with a new doctor soon.* The pills began to have their affect and he soon fell asleep in his chair.

* * *

"Mandrake, I don't give a damn if he is sleeping, I need to talk to him now." Jim Dixon was insistent and seemed worried, an unusual characteristic for the usually docile pilot.

"Well, if he gets upset, I am going to blame it all on you." Mandrake was still reluctant but he could sense some urgency in the tone of his co-worker.

As they entered Mr. Riley's office, the man's own acute senses awakened him. "What is going on, Mandrake?" The voice, blurred with sleep, was more difficult than usual to understand.

"Mr. Riley, Sir, Dixon insists on seeing you at once. He says it is urgent..." Dixon quickly moved around Mandrake with some small object in his hand. Mandrake grabbed the wrist of the hand holding the object, not certain whether the item was a weapon.

"It is just something that I have to show him, Mandrake." Jim Dixon did not attempt to use his early skills to disengage the grip of his new friend, though he felt that he could easily handle the larger man.

"It's alright, Mandrake." Then he turned his attention to his pilot. "What do you have there, Jim?"

"My old habits are coming back, Mr. Riley. I was going over the jet to make certain that it was ready for any emergency when I spotted this little baby stuck into a pocket between one of the engines and the wing. I have seen similar equipment before. I am certain that it is a locator device. Someone now knows exactly where that plane is berthed. I do not think that it is me that anyone is trying to find, Sir, so it must be you. I inspect the plane after every flight so that I am convinced that it is ready for the next use. What I am saying, Sir, is that this must have taken place on Warbah."

"Are you satisfied with the purpose of this piece, Jim?" It was not really a question. Anthony's thoughts had already started to wander, trying to piece together the most likely candidate for such a quest. *I do not believe either Rubella or Akbar would even have access or knowledge of such devices. Who else could it be? Is it possible...is it possible...*His ratcheting recall had reached Brantley Chemical and Jennings Pharmaceutical and his own use of renegade Government agents for that attempted takeover. Those two had been both dangerous and deadly. Several persons had died during that episode in his life. *Could the Federal Government be closing in on me? I do not see any other alternative for this kind of sophistication.* He was still turning the object over in his hand, oblivious of the two men standing nervously over his desk.

"We will have to make a prompt decision and response, Gentlemen. Leave me alone with my computer for about a half hour, no longer. Come back for another meeting and we will decide what action to take. Jim, thank you for being so thorough." Anthony started punching the keys as his assistants both glanced at their watches as they left the room.

One of the Government Agencies which Anthony Riley had been successful in penetrating when he first realized that he was going to leave the National Weather Service was a special operations unit of the CIA. His expertise was phenomenal as his delicate fingers flew over the keys. He was looking for the same opening which had delivered Jeff Lewis and Aubrey Long to him a few years ago. This time he could find no access. He knew that whoever was in charge of their unit would have to be the one responsible for this persistent manhunt. He located the locked door. The opening he found then no longer existed. Hitting the door from several more angles produced no new results…always *Access Denied.*

The process had taken longer than he realized as his two assistants were again approaching his desk for instructions. While engaged in the search process, his mind had been formulating alternative action. Reluctantly, he gave up on his computer search. "Gentlemen, here is what we must do."

58

At fourteen hundred hours the next afternoon, Harden Kelly, Samantha Chandler, Charlie Reynolds and Mr. Anderson were seated around a conference table in one of the safe rooms at the Rosslyn Base.

"It will just take a few hours for one of our jets to take you three to Roseau. Let's go over very carefully our plan for the confrontation that is certain to occur. Reynolds has done a little research so we know exactly which house Riley occupies there. We even have photographs of the place, including all the key rooms, which he had faxed from a local real estate broker on the Island. My initial thinking is for the three of you to fly together by Military transport. Harden and Sam will wait at the Hotel while Charlie does some reconnaissance. There is little chance that those people will recognize him if he probes around as a tourist. On the other hand, at least Riley and his assistant would recognize the two of you on sight."

"Sir, I suggest more immediate action. We do not know how long the element of surprise will be available to us. If we prearrange immediate transportation from the airport to the house, we could catch them off guard."

Harden was never patient enough for Anderson's careful precision planning. "Surprise can often produce the best results."

"Well, Harden, I have always preferred a good plan in advance of confrontation. Maybe the best idea would be a compromise of the two approaches. Charlie can make immediate contact with the house upon your arrival, possibly posing as a real estate agent. If Riley is there, he can contact you on your cell phone and the three of you can take him into custody."

"However, I want to caution you to be extremely careful. We already know that Mandrake appears to be a competent caretaker and we have done some research from the photographs on Riley's pilot. His name is James Warner Gibson. He was one of our agents in Vietnam, operated in the Mekong Delta region for three years. You can imagine what survival skills it takes to survive there, especially with the hazardous duty assigned to his unit. He separated from the Service about ten years ago...excessive drug use and liquor...he became impossible to control...no use to anyone, even himself. He started out as a fighter pilot, F14s and then Blackhawks. The man is well trained."

Anderson stood and the others followed suit. "Let's go, Gentlemen. Your plane is waiting."

* * *

"Mandrake, you and Dixon must find me a body, a cadaver. Before we leave the Island, I need to make whoever comes believe that I am dead.

Jim, you know how to handle it best. I want this entire facility destroyed by fire. We will put the cadaver in my wheel chair and he and it must be burned beyond any possible recognition. Just leave enough of the chair for them to get the desired effect. I want to leave within two hours. Whoever our nemesis is, they will not be long coming. It will be alright to leave part of the lab so that they will know that they have found the right place. However, it is imperative that the four of us be gone within two hours. I will pay off Miguel so he can return to his original endeavors. Now, go...make this happen. I will give you our destination as soon as we are airborne."

Dixon and Miguel left immediately for his shop to get adequate supplies. Mandrake ran to his quarters to tell Chrisimminia to pack everything necessary in order to leave momentarily. She was numbed by the news and he had to hold her tightly until she stopped trembling, assuring her that everything would turn out even better than here on the Island. Of course, he had no idea where that would be. "Chris, Chris, I love you and I will take care of you. Don't be afraid." His huge arms encircled her until the tremors ceased.

It was longer then he realized because he heard Miguel's vehicle coming back up the driveway as he was finally able to release his wife.

As she began to pack as he had requested, Mandrake ran to fulfill his part of the arrangements as Jim set up the explosives and timer. Miguel was busy settling up with Mr. Riley as he passed the office. "Miguel, I need your help. We need to find a male body for Mr. Riley as fast as we can. A new grave in the cemetery will do fine. We do not want this to be detected by the local authorities."

Miguel had many unusual requests so he only hesitated a moment at this one. "There was a funeral last week. One of the local business owners passed away. I have no idea what the cause of death was. Since the dirt is still loose, we could exhume the body without anyone knowing the difference." Miguel, of course, was very much aware of the cause of death. There had been a shooting over a disagreement involving territorial jurisdiction between two cocaine dealers on the Island. He told the story to Mandrake as they left for the cemetery. *Even better* thought Mandrake. *It will look as though Mr. Riley committed suicide before the fire consumed the place.* Their grisly task took place on a deserted portion of the Island and they were able to finish the exhumation of the body without detection. The large plastic garbage bag which they had brought to carry the remains worked perfectly.

When they returned to the house, Dixon helped Mandrake place the corpse on to Mr. Riley's chair behind his desk. Riley, himself, was waiting in an old chair which he kept for emergency in case his self-designed chair ever broke down. Chrisimminia had completed her task of packing luggage for Mandrake and herself as well as Mr. Riley. Dixon's small flight bag was waiting as well.

"It is set for one hour from now, Sir. There will not be much left of this place. I purposefully left part of the lab untouched as you suggested. We should go."

"Fine, my friends. Let us get airborne. I have arranged with Miguel to drop us at the plane. We should be off the ground within a half hour...about six."

* * *

The jet carrying Harden, Samantha and Charlie was crossing over the Florida Panhandle as the pilot called back to them. "We should be landing in Roseau about Eighteen Hundred. I have already secured clearance to land upon arrival."

Harden went over the final plan with his fellow agents. "It is agreed that we will take the rental van to the house together. Sam and I will remain concealed in the back seat with the tinted windows until you ascertain that Anthony is still in residence. When you hit the signal button, Sam will casually join you at the front door, posing as your wife. I will leave by the other door and circle behind the residence and enter from the rear. Remember, we definitely prefer to complete this mission without fatalities but use your discretion if confronted. We should be at the house by Six Thirty...just about dusk."

Their pilot circled the Roseau Airport one time. "There is another jet just about to take off. It will only be a minute." Even as he was speaking, they heard the roar of the jet engines as the other plane climbed and turned north. "We are cleared to land now."

59

Saddam Akbar was seated comfortably behind his desk smoking one of his favorite Cuban cigars and savoring his good fortune with the way the TR7 fiasco had worked out. Abdul Haddiq sat across from him nervously awaiting his dismissal from the meeting. Saddam had requested a personal update on the matters in Herat but had been too busy on the phone for the meeting to begin.

Smiling broadly, Saddam finally gave him his attention. "My good friend, now tell me the latest at the shop of our late friend, Amin."

"Ms. Kalemi had already contracted for the reconstruction of the garage complex which was totally demolished. The remains of the former structure have been hauled away and the construction has begun. The house has already been repaired...broken doors and windows and a few bullet holes. There has not been any further investigation by the Police from Towraghondi where they were holding the American. Not such good news from Zaranj. The entire complex and all of the raw material was completely burned out. We will be lucky to be able to start production for at least six more months. Then we will have to wait for another harvest for the farmers to make delivery of the raw material. There is nothing I can do to speed these people up. I have tried my best." Haddiq was becoming nervously defensive the more he relayed the unpleasant details to his benefactor. The job of Minister of Light Industry was quite prestigious in this poor country.

Saddam Akbar let him sweat, enjoying the verbal torture. Everything he needed was again being supplied by Riley at a significantly lower price then he could produce it himself through his incompetent underlings. It was almost one in the afternoon at Umm Qasr and Saddam had just finished reviewing the accounting statements supplied by his treasurer. Suddenly, he heard shots outside the building. His door burst open and his second in command, Shamu Famir, was pushed into the room followed by uniformed men.

"These men need to talk to you, Sir." Famir was too much at ease for the situation. Six armed men entered behind Shamu, two Interpol Detectives, one American Agent and three new Iraqi Police Detectives. The lead Iraqi Officer was first to speak to the now worried Saddam.

"Mr. Akbar, we are here to place you under arrest for twelve counts of murder as well as distribution of an illegal substance. Our men are outside with an International Court Order to seize any evidence found in their investigation of your facility. Will you come with us, Sir?"

The officer had rounded the desk with his weapon in his right hand as his left hand cupped Saddam's elbow to bring him to a standing position.

"What is going on, Famir? What have you told these men?" Saddam glared at his assistant who managed to keep two of the intruders between them at all times.

One of the Interpol Officers injected. "Mr. Famir has decided to cooperate with us in lieu of facing the death penalty. We have enough evidence to convict you on all counts. I suggest you accompany us peacefully. Your men are no longer of any use to you."

As he was being assisted from his chair, Saddam Akbar was enraged at his assistant. *How can things turn so badly so quickly. Famir will not get off that easily.* He had always known that it might end this way. He simply did not know when. Shoving the officer to the side, Saddam quickly withdrew his Sig Sauer P229 pistol from the bottom desk drawer and fired several shots at Famir before turning for the French doors. The officials in his office did not react quickly enough as Saddam disappeared through the broken glass.

Shamu Famir's hands grasped his bloody chest, his eyes wide with surprise. He knew it was over as he fell to the plush carpet, gasping his last breath before he hit the floor. He had not escaped the death penalty after all. One of the Interpol Officers who was partially shielding Famir was hit in the right arm, distracting the others from an immediate response.

The American spoke quickly over a communication device and his command was followed almost immediately by automatic gunfire at the back of the building. "They got him, Aldiz. If you have your men gather all the evidence from here, I believe this operation is closed." He left the way he had come in.

* * *

Saddam Akbar smiled as he broke through the glass doors to freedom. He knew he had hit the traitor, Famir. His car was waiting at the back drive with the key in it for just such an emergency. Suddenly, he was confronted from the side of the building by three armed men. As his weapon turned in their direction, acutely aware of the finality of the situation, Saddam did not even fire a shot as the automatic gunfire repeatedly hit him in the chest and abdomen. The evil in the man endured until the very end. *No regrets…it was a good life.*

In the confusion, Abdul Haddiq successfully backed out of the room and rushed to his waiting official vehicle. With Ministry markings on the side of the car, his driver was freed to drive away, which he did with as much speed as the limousine would muster. There was a long ride before him over poor roads all the way to Western Afghanistan and the small town of Herat. As much as he despised the man, Abdul was concerned both with his involvement being detected and the loss of funds provided by his benefactor, Saddam Akbar.

60

Tony Rubella had achieved second in command in his organization and immediately exercised that authority to bring his most reliable assistant, Al Molini, back from exile in Las Vegas. Joey Bono's uncle no longer entered in to the decision. Tony needed him.

Al was immediately put in charge of the new product and its distribution, as well as warehousing. Al Molini was exhilarated. His family and friends were still in The Big Apple…he knew this city. It was home.

Tony was relieved to have his friend in charge of such an integral part of his business. The new product, CPF, had been the reason for his position in the organization as well as putting him in a situation whereas Joey's uncle no longer had any effect on his decisions. Of course, in the natural flow of power, Al became another layer of insulation between himself and the Federal Bureau of Investigation. He hated to put his friend in jeopardy but there was no one as reliable or as loyal to him as Al Molini.

Al certainly understood the rules. He would accept full responsibility for the acquisition and distribution of CPF as well as TR7, if the need arose.

At exactly six in the evening, New York time, three FBI agents, accompanied by twenty local police officers, surrounded the small warehouse building. George Sullivan, the lead investigator, rang the bell at the front door. Thus alerted, Al and Joey Gondolfo jumped in to their Ford Taurus, which remained always ready just inside the overhead doors. When the door was high enough to see, the path was blocked by one of the New York Police cars with lights flashing. Without a shot being fired, Al was arrested and taken into custody along with eleven of his men who were also at the site. Joey Gondolfo had darted from the car and was now hidden under a barrel in the service area, where his new suit was ruined by the thin coating of oil remaining in the barrel. He waited, nervous and shivering in the completely defenseless hiding place.

George Sullivan had executed an unusually clean coup, arresting the top man and eleven of his cohorts. "I want you men to search this entire facility. Arrest anyone you find and bring any illegal substances as well as any paperwork in the office back to the Precinct. I will meet you there when you report in."

Joey overheard the orders and tried to shrink even smaller inside the barrel as he heard men moving about the warehouse.

Al Molini requested a cigarette. It helped him maintain his calm demeanor while being questioned.

Sullivan gently probed. "Al, you know we do not want you. We want your boss, Tony Rubella. We can probably make a deal right now. Just tell us how your organization operates and I am sure that the Prosecuting Attorney's office will cooperate with us…maybe you will serve a few years at most. What do you say?"

This was an accepted way of life to Al. If you get caught, you keep your mouth shut. "You busted up my business. What else can I tell you that you do not already know?" He took another puff, his eyes showing an extraordinary interest in the cigarette he was smoking. He did not look at the agent.

After two hours of relentless interrogation with no movement on the case whatsoever, Agent Sullivan was interrupted by the arrival of his two co-workers from the site. They had a jittery Joey Gondolfo in tow between them. Joey could not see Al in the enclosed room.

When the new prisoner was identified, Sullivan decided to try the same approach with him. Ushering him into the second of the interrogation rooms, he offered Joey a cigarette. Joey nervously shook his head.

"Joey Gondolfo, I see that you are an important man in this organization. Do you realize that we have you on five counts of murder as well as dealing in an illegal substance?" Joey continued to fidget, refusing to look at the interrogator. "However, Joey, we are willing to negotiate. We can forget the murder charges if you cooperate with us. How often does your boss, Tony Rubella, show up at the warehouse? How does he collect the money from you people?"

Joey's eyes darted around the room, looking for someone he recognized. "I work for Molini...that's all." It was not loyalty or an oath that kept Joey from talking...it was fear. He knew he was a dead man if word got out that he had talked.

"We have a witness protection program, Joey. You do not have to be afraid of those people. We will help you start a new life where they can never find you...new identification and new job. Just start talking. We have a recorder turned on so you will not even have to appear on the witness stand." That was, of course, an exaggeration but Sullivan was still searching for the thread that connected the man he wanted to Molini.

"I work for Molini. That's all. I don't even know any Rubella."

That was the first break. Joey certainly knew the name. Possibly with time, the man would break. George Sullivan felt certain that they could now contain the distribution of this artificial powder that had so engulfed the World.

Thanks to Anderson, we were able to coordinate our missions to avoid any contact between the interested parties. I hope Bill Patterson's operation in Iraq went as well as ours. Anderson said there was a third site that his people would handle. There were twenty three deaths total that we know about from this drug...sixteen in Western Europe and seven here in the States. Sullivan breathed a sigh of relief that the product was now off the market, at least the distribution points had been shut down.

After leaving the tiny room, Sullivan quietly spoke to his men. "Let him sweat a while. I think we have our witness."

61

Harden was becoming impatient as he and Samantha waited for Charlie to secure the rental car. Together they had agreed on a very simple plan. However, Jim Dixon was accustomed to violence and was probably the more potent of the problems that they would face due to his military training a while back. They were running late. The time coordinated for the raid was Eighteen Hundred Hours and it was already past that with no vehicle as yet.

"Do not take any chances with Dixon, Sam." His thoughts had become verbal. He knew it was not a necessary warning. Samantha winced at the words. Harden was letting their personal relationship interfere with his normally rational thinking. He saw the look in her eyes and immediately regretted voicing his concern. Sam Chandler could take care of herself and would never let herself be exposed unnecessarily to the risks of her occupation because this would also expose her fellow operatives. This was part of the unwritten code…and Harden was fully aware of it. He attempted to soften the warning by following through with information on the other occupants of the house.

"Mandrake will be fiercely protective of Anthony from what we have already seen of the man and I would hate to have to cause him any harm. He seems to have fallen in to this situation from a very rough beginning.

Anthony showed some propensity toward helping others when he took Mandrake as an assistant. Probably the only ones remaining are house servants…not many, I would guess. Anthony was a very private person."

Sam accepted the flow of words for what they were. The continuity was obviously to cover his blunder concerning her ability. She decided to move on. *At least, I know he said it out of concern for me as his wife.*

It was her turn. "There should be one more person. We know that his chemist died on Ramkin. I doubt that Riley would take it upon himself to complete the formula himself. Since the product is again appearing on the street, he must have hired another chemist. But, also, I would doubt if there is any real threat from that source." Another flaw in Harden's planning. *I cannot let his concern for me interfere with his realistic rationalization. Maybe we should not be on missions together. Maybe Anderson was right.*

"You are right, Sam. With Pfister dead, I did not think of a new man. But I agree that this person should pose no threat." Finally, Charlie returned dangling the keys from his finger.

"Nothing was ready…a lot of papers to sign. Also, they had to find us a van with tinted windows as we had originally requested. It is that third one in the front row." Sam and Harden jumped in to the back seats so as not to be seen from the house. Charlie squealed the tires as he left the lot. Unconcerned with local jurisdiction on the empty roads, he raced toward his destination at the other end of the Island.

Preparation was thorough. He knew exactly how to reach the house. When they saw the estate in the distance, Charlie Reynolds slowed the van to a normal rate of speed so they would not arouse unnecessary suspicions from the residents. It was almost six thirty in the evening…they were running late. They shared the same silent thought…*I hope there were no phone calls or other warning from Akbar or Rubella.*

Pulling in to the driveway near the front door, Charlie stepped out the driverside door. Coordinating perfectly, Harden and Sam slipped out the same side and stayed low to the side of the car. Charlie, on the other hand, strode confidently up the walk to the door. Harden Kelly did not like waiting in the van. They would be easy targets if someone had gotten suspicious.

Suddenly there was a loud explosion from inside the garage and flames poured through the gaps in the stone wall where pieces had been blown out. Caught completely by surprise, the three agents reacted quickly.

Drawing their weapons in unison, they fled for the cover of the trees on the front lot. A second explosion followed within seconds, blowing out the front doors and windows and part of the wall. There were flames everywhere as the explosions continued sequentially around the entire perimeter of the house.

Harden, Sam and Charlie looked on, each wondering if the explosions were meant for them or some other expected attack, possibly from Akbar or Rubella. "Someone set incendiary explosives…looks like the entire facility has been set to blow." Harden was almost shouting now to be heard over the continuing explosions. Debris was flying past them as they remained protected behind the ancient oak trees strewn generously throughout the front yard.

"Dixon could do this…he was somewhat of an explosive expert before leaving the Military." Sam was able to exhibit how thoroughly she had researched her adversaries. "We had better wait. There could be latent or motion activated traps. Since we do not yet know the purpose, we cannot be sure how their thought process was working."

Detonations continued around the complete circumference of the facility, each time followed by unrelenting flames. In less then one minute the entire facility was in flames as the bombs continued into the interior of the building after completing the exterior circle.

"We are not going to find anyone in there. This was obviously set up intentionally to destroy any evidence…some kind of timing device allowing the occupants to be long gone." Harden recognized the type of explosive, similar to the ones they had used in Afghanistan. The flames would die quickly but the chemicals burned at such high temperature that there would be nothing left in their wake. *Probably a good thing that we were late getting here. We could have been inside that building.*

With no new bursts for the last five minutes, the incendiary devices continued to do their work, reducing everything inside the building to ash.

The roof was almost entirely gone already and pieces of the stone walls were still overheating and falling onto the once beautifully landscaped perimeter of the mansion. "You are right, Sam. It must have been Dixon. Only an expertly trained and experienced demolition man could have handled a job as large as this place and so completely bring it down in a matter of minutes. We will just have to wait it out."

Harden pulled out his cell phone to update Anderson. After the preliminary message, Anderson returned the call immediately.

"Sir, we have run into a situation. Just as we arrived, the house was brought down completely by a series of pre-set explosive devices. None of us were near enough to be harmed but we are watching it from the trees in front...no sign of life before and definitely not after the devices were ignited...must have been on a timer. I would like to wait it out until it cools enough for us to see what is left and, particularly, if there are any casualties."

"Let me know what you find as soon as possible. Good luck."

62

"Where to, Boss?" Jim Dixon had just leveled off to head west as he had been directed. He had been alerted that there was another flight circling to land and made visual contact over to his right as Mr. Riley's jet rose from the tarmac.

"Jim, I had you file a flight plan for Paris, France, to delude anyone who may be interested in our whereabouts. However, I now want you to fly to our real destination, Guaymas, Mexico. It is circled on this map. Once you are satisfied with the directions, the map must be burned." Anthony passed the map to Mandrake who entered the pilot cabin to hand it to Dixon.

When Mandrake returned, Mr. Riley turned his attention back to his assistant. "Could you leave us alone for a few minutes, Chris? The galley has an assortment of food if you don't mind making sandwiches for all of us." Chrisimminia was delighted with her new position, having toiled all her life on the tiny Island of Ramkin. Mandrake's love was the best thing that had ever happened in her life. With her husband's help, she had no doubt that they could keep their employer's requirements assuaged. She busied herself slicing tomatoes and otherwise preparing lunch for the four of them.

"Mandrake, I have made arrangements to have this plane picked up in

Guaymas by some people from Mexico City. They will have a smaller plane waiting to take us into the United States." Anthony handed his assistant two black folders. "These are your passports. We cannot afford to use our given names as there most certainly would be an alarm sounded if we reenter the Country. You will be Terence James Owens and your wife, Becka Jean Owens. When we are in any public place, you will all have to get accustomed to using my new name, Richard Oliver Jameson, or just Mr. Jameson."

Mandrake absorbed all the information that was flooding his ears, with great anticipation. They were going to return home…Chrisimminia would get to see his great Country after all. "What about Jim?"

"I have already had a talk with our pilot. Unfortunately, he would be a dangerous asset to have around. He is going to leave us in Mexico to fend for himself. He has earned a great deal of money over these past few months so he will have an unlimited number of options. It will be much safer for both of us to separate now." Anthony let that information be absorbed before continuing, taking the brief respite to stretch and rub his shoulders. Again today, sharp pains cursed through his upper shoulders down through his lower back, as if the pains were a malediction of things to come. "We are going to retire, my friend. I have enough money now to pay you well and still retire comfortably. If you and Chris choose to remain with me, I will have an attorney make you my beneficiary upon my death. I have no relatives that I am even aware of so it would make me happy to see that any fortune left after I am gone would go to the person who helped the most to earn it." Again, he paused to rub his shoulders.

"Would you get me a glass of water, Mandrake? I need to take some of these pills." Mr. Riley had removed a prescription bottle from his side pocket.

"Yes, Sir…certainly." Mandrake was speechless. He could think of no better outcome of his relationship with Anthony Riley. *No killing…that has worried me ever since I started carrying this thing.* He softly ran his hand over the weapon under his jacket. *No more drugs…no more illegal activities. Chrisimminia will be overwhelmed.* Then the worried thoughts began their furtive movement to the forefront of his mind. He passed the glass of water into the bony grasp of his benefactor.

"But, Mr. Riley, what about the Police and Federal Authorities? They will still be looking for us. That will never stop...maybe even the New York mob and those Iraqis as well." They had made a number of enemies and this move could well eventuate even more if they stopped making the CPF available.

"Our new identities will shield us from all those people. When we reach our destination, all of that will be behind us. Since we are retiring, we will not need Dixon anymore...better that we should separate ourselves from him now. The man has been a good employee, but an incalculable risk. Trust me, Mandrake...just a little longer."

Jim Dixon was busily matching his coordinates toward the small town of Guaymas. Having just passed over Monterrey, the next sighting would be the little village of Delicias only a few air miles ahead. *Riley was more than generous with my separation, probably buying my discretion as well.*

Delicias...that may well be where I retire...sounds inviting. I would like to find a quaint little town where no one cares what I do or who I am. Delicias, Mexico...maybe. He spotted the tiny airstrip at Guaymas and started his descent.

"Buenas dios, Senor. Que pasa?" The air traffic controller was more attentive then Dixon had expected.

"Mr. Anthony Riley requests permission to land." Dixon had already aligned with the tarmac for maximum use of the length.

"Mr. Riley. Si, Senor. Gracias."

Dixon would be sad to lose this plane. He had nurtured it from his initial hiring and knew every scratch, every attitude, and every reaction to the controls. It had become his baby. *Riley says he has already sold it. Otherwise, I might want it for myself. But what would I do with it. I have made too many enemies...too many people would like to see me again. Delicias, here I come.* After a perfect landing, Dixon gathered his personal effects from the cockpit and grabbed the bag with his total earthly possessions from behind the Pilot's seat.

Mandrake had already opened the side panel and was carrying Mr. Riley down the stairs as Chris wheeled his chair through the cargo bay to meet them below. Three men were waiting to greet them.

"Mr. Riley, we were expecting you. Ramos, here, is your pilot. He will take you to the destination requested. Your passports must be in order, however. My friend and I will take care of your aircraft as agreed."

"Right there is my plane. Shall we go, now?" He pointed in the direction of a small but powerful looking plane. "I understand that there will be only three passengers." Ramos had stopped short when he counted the four persons who had disembarked. Greedily, he made a mental assessment of his chances of obtaining one third more for the additional passenger.

Jim Dixon paused briefly as he passed Anthony's chair. With a natural grin forming on his handsome face, he gave the threesome a quick salute of farewell before entering the tiny terminal building, never once a backward glance.

Ramos was somewhat relieved. He was experiencing doubt as to whether he should approach the two men, who had paid him for his services, to ask for more money. *A deal is a deal. I just want to get the hell out of here, anyway*

After placing Mr. Riley in one of the back seats, Mandrake then loaded his chair and the balance of their belongings. Helping Chrisimminia into the seat beside Anthony, Mandrake climbed in beside Ramos. They were prepared for takeoff but at this point only one of the passengers was knowledgeable of their destination…and he was not yet ready to make that revelation.

63

The highly combustible mixture dissipated quickly after disseminating its incendiary effects on the entire structure of what used to be Anthony Riley's home.

Harden, Sam and Charlie carefully sifted through the remains, being careful of secondary booby traps. The second floor either no longer existed or was not accessible. They split up in order to make a quicker analysis.

"Hey, guys, there is still part of a makeshift lab here in the back of the garage. This must be where they were producing all that powder being distributed around the World. I will see if I can find a sample somewhere in this mess."

Charlie Reynolds combed through the least damaged portion of the lab to see what he could find.

After circling to the rear of the house, Harden found what had been the main entrance to the gardens. French doors had once graced the large opening where now stood only the blackened remnants of the framework.

Entering Anthony's office from the garden, Harden was immediately drawn to the man's desk, or what was left of it.

"Circle around here to his office...Sam...Charlie. There appears to be a body here. The charred remains of a human corpse were melded to a once elaborate wheel chair behind the desk. As the other two appeared, Harden voiced his thoughts. "This looks like Anthony's chair. He had it made especially for his needs. There is no way to identify the body but it is seated in his chair and behind his desk. Is it Riley?"

"Let's see if we find additional bodies. This could have been some act of revenge or simply the end of a relationship. Maybe Anthony was backing out of his commitments and someone did not like that position. There were quite a few fatalities attributed to his TR7, which he produced at Brantley Chemical. Possibly those distributors were intent on revenge."

Samantha was trying to put the pieces together since the position of the body left little doubt as to its identity.

"Must be Riley. You can certainly make enemies in the drug business. One minute they love you then something goes wrong...you are discarded like so much waste. I have seen many violent deaths attributed to these people." Charlie had no doubt as well.

"Continue searching to see if there are any others. I want to get a few photos of this entire scene from different angles." Harden pulled a digital camera from his jacket pocket and begins clicking as he encircled the remains. He had just completed his circle when he spotted it...a miniscule red dot flashing from beneath Riley's chair.

"Booby trap...let's get out of here...NOW." With Harden's warning still ringing in their ears, they ran in three different directions, choosing the shortest route to clear the building.

Harden, being the closest, was blown to the ground by the impact of the ensuing explosion. He crawled rapidly to the safety of the trees before examining his back and shoulders. Sam was running in his direction between the trees. "Are you alright, Hon? I looked back when I heard the explosion and saw you fall." She quickly stepped behind her husband and examined his back for wounds. "Looks like just a few small cuts and scratches. How do you feel? Do you feel that the impact broke any bones or possibly caused a concussion?" She gently moved his arms up and down, then backward, to check the joints.

Sitting beside him in the grass, she then allowed herself to relax...and the tears came. Her self control squeezed them tightly and only remnants of the teardrops completed the journey that had begun deep in her heart.

Charlie sat beside them as they all watched the further incineration of the office. "Someone surely wanted to make certain that man was dead."

When no further explosions ensued, they carefully returned to their investigation. "We need to call Anderson. He will have to arrange for forensic experts to sift through this rubble. Look at what is left of Riley...even his teeth have disintegrated...the bones have burned to ash. That fire was as hot as a crematorium." Harden again flipped his cell phone open and hit the code button for Anderson. As they waited for the return call, Samantha had a puzzled expression on her face.

"That last explosion must have been triggered by a motion detector. We were lucky none of us was killed. I wonder what could have been the purpose of that." Her thoughts were interrupted by the vibrating ring of a cell phone.

"Sir, it looks like Anthony Riley is dead, killed in the explosion and fire. We could find no other bodies. That could be considered strange except for the fact that this fire was hot enough to turn Anthony into ash. It could have done the same for any others in the building. Do you want us to secure it until you can send some forensic people over here? It looks like this job is finished."

"Well, if there is nothing left to scavenge, there is no point in securing it. I do not think the Government there would appreciate our interference. Why don't you three get out of there before someone detains you? That would take a great deal of unnecessary explanation. Come on back to Rosslyn and we will see if any further investigation is necessary. Meanwhile, I should have some people there to do a quick search for any forensic evidence of the victims in a few hours. Better leave now. Someone surely heard the commotion...they could blame you."

Anderson was gone...so was poor Anthony Riley, on a more permanent basis, and probably his assistant, Mandrake...and possibly some servants as well.

This time Harden drove, obeying all posted speed limits as he hurriedly returned to the airport.

Samantha was still perusing the motion detector bomb. *Why would the perpetrator set a device to be activated by just anyone who arrived at the scene? It could have been a fireman, a scavenger, a kid, whatever. He could have set the explosives to do a complete job the first time around without taking a chance on leaving any evidence. Maybe they wanted Riley to be identified before the second detonation did its job. But, why? Possibly as a warning to any one else who caused trouble for their organizations. I would certainly like to know the real reason behind that. Chances are that the person who discovered the body and set off the secondary explosion would be killed in that blast and not be available to spread any warning. They could not have known that we were coming.*

64

"Say that again, Harden. Anthony is dead! I do not understand. What happened?" Conner Hayes could even now picture the shy young man in the wheelchair, his body twisted in intolerable shapes, his voice an inaudible croak until you became accustomed to the sounds, but always a soft smile on his face when the three of them were together.

Anthony Riley had a brilliant mind as far back as he could remember. It had always been difficult to vaunt his friend's accomplishments without giving the impression that he was touting himself as well. Conner had achieved Valedictorian over his classmate due to his incomparable ability to memorize material and then have that material stored in his mind for analyzing and evaluation.

"Please give me some details, Harden. That information surely is not classified."

"No, you are right there. Well, when we finally caught up with him, it was too late. Since the time that we lost track of him on Ramkin Island, we presume that he moved to the location where we found him…a little town called Roseau, Dominica. He had bought an estate there and had part of it converted into a laboratory where he continued to manufacture that same powder he produced at Brantley. Sam and I were just about to enter when the whole thing exploded, one blast after the other, sequentially, around the entire building." Training had restricted Harden…he made no mention of Charlie Reynolds.

"You two were not injured, were you?" Conner was concerned about his old friend and his wife.

"No. We waited in the trees until the activity subsided. Here is the most interesting part. We found what was left of Anthony in his custom-built chair behind his desk. It was impossible to tell if he was already dead when the explosions took place but whoever planted them was intent in destroying every shred of evidence that might be available to investigators. As I went around his desk to get a closer look, I accidentally tripped a motion detector. When I saw the red dot blinking, we got out of there just in time. Another incendiary device exploded right below his desk. When we were able to return to the scene, it was as if he had been cremated…nothing but ashes."

"We had timed two other joint operations at the same time. Both were successful and included Anthony's primary customers, possibly his only two customers. On first analysis, we agree that one of them was the perpetrator because of a problem with Riley's product. Several people had overdosed on the TR7, enough so the FBI was able to pinpoint the substance responsible. This not only resulted in a tremendous monetary loss to those two but the authorities were closing in on the distributors as well. Right now, we assume that was the reason Anthony Riley had to die."

"Could we bury him, Harden? We owe that much to our errant friend."

"Best we could do is a memorial service, Conner. There is nothing left. When the forensics people get finished with this scene, there may not even be ashes to bury."

"What about that young man who was always with Anthony, Mandrake? Did he die in the explosion as well? Was there any evidence of that in Anthony's office? He was evidently a personal assistant, always around." Conner's mental retention was opening the door to yet more questions.

"Conner, that is about all we know right now. If there are other bodies in what is left of the structure, the forensic people will have to sift through the ash to find them. I wish I could better describe the annihilation.

There is nothing of value…all melted or burned completely. There was nothing Sam or I could do there so Anderson had us return here to Rosslyn."

"Well, Hard, I would still like to have some kind of memorial tribute to the old Anthony Riley. Maybe we could have a Mass at our old Church, St. Bridgid. I feel like we should do something."

"Sounds good to me. Set it up and we will do our best to be there."

Harden's tone became a little more solemn. "This kind of makes me appreciate having an old friend like you, Conner. I will vow to keep in touch, in person as well as phone calls, if you will. I do not want to lose you, too."

"Thanks for saying that, Hard. I feel the same way."

The conversation had ended on that note and Conner Hayes sat pensively at his desk for a moment before punching the intercom.

"Janet, would you get me the phone number of the rectory at Saint Bridgid Catholic Church in Louisville, Kentucky, please?"

Printed in the United States
79626LV00004B/43-48